To John + Mary
With love and best w

Jan

A Victorian Rose

A Victorian Rose

A NOVEL BY

Jan Pollard

Eloquent Books
New York, New York

Eloquent Books
An imprint of AEG Publishing Group
845 Third Avenue, 6th Floor—6016
New York, NY 10022
www.eloquentbooks.com

ISBN 978-1-60860-287-2

Text Design by James Meetze
Production by Eloquent Books

CONTENTS

To my daughters.
Sallie and Kathryn
With love

PROLOGUE

The clipper ship, *The Fair Maid*, had made good time on this crossing from Liverpool to Australia, despite being momentarily becalmed in the Indian Ocean. Whilst waiting for a wind to fill her sails, a brief ceremony was taking place on deck. The intensity of the heat made it necessary to dispose of a corpse at the earliest opportunity. The Reverend Paul Briggs, a passenger on board, had offered to officiate in place of the captain, having made the acquaintance of the family concerned since embarking at Liverpool.

A merciless sun shone down upon the sad little company gathered at the gunwale. John Taylor, head bowed, stared down at the deck, listening to the sonorous tones of the Reverend Briggs.

"We therefore commit her body to the deep to be turned into corruption . . ."

John felt empty of all feeling. He had had such hopes for Julia in this new country to which they were travelling. The people at the manor where he had been an estate carpenter had done all they could to help once they had learned of Julia's condition, for John's family had worked at the manor for generations and were considered an integral part of the estate. The decision to leave had been the cause of much heart searching but Julia's constant racking cough had left them no choice but to find a warmer, dryer climate in which to live. The offer of a good job and a home in Australia had seemed like the answer to all their problems. Now it was over, and John wished with all his heart that he had never taken Julia away from the home she had loved so much.

Rosie stood very still holding her father's hand, looking towards the group of mourners. Amy Briggs, in her stiff black dress and bonnet, showed no emotion. She had attended too many funerals in the past to feel grief at the passing of a woman scarcely known to her. Slightly to one side stood Mr. and Mrs. Potts and the two Hopkins sisters. Alice Potts and Sarah Hopkins wept openly as they followed the service, but Lizzie's mind was elsewhere, and she remained quietly composed. Rosie wanted to run across the decking which separated her from Alice Potts and to feel the warmth of those comforting arms around her but she had promised Miss Briggs that she would behave well for poor Papa's sake, and she was too afraid of the consequences should she not keep her promise.

Reverend Briggs had stopped speaking. The short service was over. Rosie's small hand involuntarily tightened within her father's grip, and, as John raised his eyes to look at his eight-year-old daughter, Julia's last remains slid silently away beneath the waiting sea.

PART ONE

Birds of Passage

1860

CHAPTER I

From where she stood at the top of the field, Rosie could see the backs of the stone-built cottages nestling among the trees in the valley below. The last cottage in the row had been her home since her birth there eight years ago and was the centre of her small universe. Usually, she was cheered by the sight of the welcoming smoke as it wreathed upwards from the squat little chimney pot and would take to her heels down the meadow path and burst in through the kitchen door to surprise her mother.

Today, it would be different, and she felt no inclination to run and skip down the grassy slope where the fast growing lambs were gambolling in the late April sunshine. Her mother would be resting on the horsehair couch in the parlour, too weary from her constant coughing to take much notice of her return. And Papa would be there with her this afternoon, wearing the worried look on his face he so often wore since Mama's illness. An important visitor was expected to call, and she had been sent out to play for a while. Seeing the pale, yellow bells of the cowslips growing in the field beyond, she had picked a bunch to take home with her. Every spring for as long as she could remember, she had helped her mother gather cowslips to be made into wine, and sometimes she had been given a drop to sip during a restless night, and sleep had come easily afterwards. There would be no wine made this spring but the cowslips would bring some of their brightness into the dark parlour where her mother spent most of the day.

Rosie dawdled through the small back gate and along the stone path which divided the vegetable plot and softly lifted the latch to the back door. She could hear a voice she didn't recognise and her father's quiet reply.

The front door was opened with difficulty, and heavy footsteps crunched on the gravel path. The gate clicked shut and a horse's hooves scraped the ground restlessly as the rider mounted and quickly rode away.

The parlour door opened, and John Taylor came into the kitchen expecting to see his daughter there having heard the latch move.

"The doctor has just left, Rosie," he explained. "His Lordship arranged for him to see your mama as she hasn't been so well lately."

"Can he make her better soon, Papa?" asked Rosie, who had a child's faith in all superior beings.

"No one can make her better as long as we live here my little one, but there is something we can do which might help. We have been talking it over with the doctor and your mama is quite agreeable, although it will be difficult for her. Come into the parlour, and bring your flowers with you. They will please her."

Rosie followed her father into the front room where her mother lay on the couch, propped up by pillows. Her pale, oval face showed the strain of her illness and gave her the appearance of a woman much older than her twenty-eight years and nearer to that of her husband, ten years her senior.

"Cowslips," exclaimed Julia. "How lovely, my darling. Did you find them in the top field?" Holding the bunch up to her face, she smelled their sweet fragrance and then placed them on a small table beside her next to the spittoon—that hateful reminder of her illness. Rosie sat on the couch beside her.

"They were my surprise, Mama," she said lovingly.

Julia smiled and stroked her daughter's plump little hand. Rosie was the picture of health with her pink cheeks and her lively brown eyes, capped by a mop of unruly golden curls. Her very presence gave Julia the will to live, and she thanked God for sparing them this child, for Rosie was the only one she had carried without mishap.

"Has Papa told you we are going away?"

"No," exclaimed Rosie in great surprise, hardly believing her ears. It seemed a strange time to be moving when her mother was so ill. "Where are we going?"

John turned from placing another log on the fire. "A long way from here, Rosie—to another country on the other side of the world, called Australia. The climate is better there, and I have the prospect of work. It's too damp here in the valley and too cold in the winter for Mama's cough to improve. Lancashire can be a bleak place for an invalid."

Rosie felt too bewildered to take it all in. The tiny hamlet of estate cottages and the village in the next valley were the only places she knew intimately, and she had expected to live there all her life.

"Where shall we live, Papa?" she asked, apprehensively.

John smiled at her concern. "There is nothing to worry about, my dear—think of it as a great adventure. We are going to a place called Clay Cross on the Murray River where His Lordship's brother owns a sawmill, and I am going to work for him, building a wharf for the riverboats. But, in the meantime, you must do all that you can to help your mama to get stronger for the journey. We don't sail until September, and the summer days will soon be here to help her feel better, we hope."

A rasping sound from the couch drew John's attention to his wife's needs, and he lifted her gently forward to help her breathing.

"Fetch your mother some fresh water, Rosie—quickly now."

Rosie took the jug to the pump in the yard, feeling sad and dejected. To leave the estate where she knew everyone and to travel to the other side of the world was a frightening thought. She would miss the children she had grown up with, the rides on the haywain as it returned from the harvest field, and the picnics beside the beck, and most of all, the party, held every Christmas at the manor for the estate workers and their children, which was the highlight of the year. There could never be another place like this green valley in the whole world, and she hated the thought of leaving it.

She shuddered in horror when she recalled a picture which hung on the wall of one of the cottages, showing a storm at sea and men drowning. *Would it be like that,* she wondered?

The jug began to overflow like her tears, and picking it up with trembling hands she made her way indoors.

CHAPTER 2

Five months later, on a September afternoon, a smart carriage and pair drew up beside the clipper ship, *The Fair Maid*, as she lay at anchor in Liverpool's Salt Dock. The coat of arms emblazoned on the doors of the carriage and the smart livery of the coachmen created a buzz of interest among those gathered on the dockside to bid farewell to friends and relations. Some surprise was expressed when from the purple silk interior of the coach there emerged a poorly clad family whose only luggage consisted of a battered and much-used tin trunk and copious bundles.

John Taylor's generous employer had decided to lend his carriage to transport the family in as much comfort as possible to the point of their departure. As three generations of the Taylor family had worked on the manor estate as foresters and carpenters, and Julia Taylor had been lady's maid to his wife before her marriage to John, His Lordship had done everything in his power to help the family once it had become known that there was little hope of Julia's recovery unless she was transported to warmer climes. The loan of his carriage had been a last and most welcome gesture.

Rosie had sat on the edge of her seat for the entire journey, too excited to speak. The adventure ahead and the novelty of riding in a real carriage had dispersed her previous fears, and her brown eyes sparkled with anticipation of the things yet to come. She favoured her father in appearance and had the sturdy, red-cheeked appearance of a country child. Julia's features had sharpened since her illness had taken its toll, yet she still had the features of a beautiful woman. She had passed on her large brown, doe-like eyes to her daughter, but that was all, for Rosie had a mop of unruly golden curls and a complexion to match her name, whereas Julia was pale by comparison and had hair the colour of corn, which she wore in a low, heavy twist at the nape of her neck. She was quiet and gentle by nature and found her robust and energetic small daughter a handful to manage. Since her illness had weakened her, John had taken over the care of their daughter more than was usual in such a household, but it had worked well, and they were a happy, united family.

As the ship came into sight, Rosie was filled with wonder. She stood transfixed, gazing at the huge masts towering skywards as her father lifted her mother gently out of the carriage. There were people everywhere, for Salt Dock was a busy place, and she had a job to keep up with her father as he made his way towards the gangplank with her mother in his arms. Telling her to keep close behind him, they struggled among the other boarding passengers to get a foothold on the swaying gangway, which to Rosie seemed to go on forever. It was like climbing a steep hill in tight button boots, and she was glad to grasp every helping hand that came her way. When she was almost at the top, a pair of steely black eyes framed in a large, black bonnet stared down at her from what seemed a great height, making her lose her concentration for a second, and she stumbled. By some miracle, she found herself lifted up by her thick, woollen cloak and set down firmly on the deck beside a tall, thin, emaciated man wearing a clerical collar and a much-worn black suit whose hand had just pulled her to safety. It was over so quickly that Rosie had had no time to feel frightened, and her father, with his back to her, was totally unaware of the incident until a voice in his ear caused him to turn and face the speaker.

"This is your daughter, I presume, sir?"

John was surprised at the question. "Indeed it is," he replied shortly, being too burdened and bothered to engage in conversation with a complete stranger at that particular time.

"She narrowly escaped a ducking, sir—a fatal one, I fear, had it taken place. It was a blessing my daughter and I were standing here or her journey would have ended before it had begun." At this point, the speaker raised his tall hat. "Allow me to introduce myself. I am the Reverend Paul Briggs, and this is my daughter, Amy. We will be pleased to meet you later, once we are under way." Paul Briggs bowed stiffly and turned away before either John or Julia could utter one word of thanks, too shocked by what they had just heard to know what to reply.

"Hold onto my coat and stay close, Rosie." John spoke sharply causing tears to well up in Rosie's eyes. She had done nothing to make her kind and loving Papa speak so harshly and was too young to understand the fright her father had just experienced. It was all the fault of the lady in the black serge dress who had startled her so much. Her sallow, oval face with its thin lips and her impenetrable stare framed under the large black bonnet had given her the appearance of a witch. She had looked straight into Rosie's eyes, and, in that split second, she had felt a cold and inexplicable tremor of fear run through her veins. It was like a dreadful warning, and, as she followed her parents down the steps of the companionway leading to their cabin, she hoped she would never see Amy Briggs again.

Amy and her father walked away from the rail, over which they had been leaning while making their farewells to a small group of loyal parishioners gathered below, and discussed the Taylor family. Amy's attention had been drawn by the unusual sight of a sick woman being carried onto the ship, a ship that was to travel through unknown perils before it reached the other side of the world on a journey that would need all one's strength of mind and body to endure.

As the woman had passed close to her, she had noticed the high spots of colour on her cheekbones and her wax-like skin drawn like parchment across her finely modelled features, giving her a fragile, unearthly appearance. She had seen many cases of consumption on her parish visits and recognised the signs immediately. Behind the man there struggled a small girl in a thick, brown woollen cloak trying valiantly to keep up, who had almost reached the end of the gangway. Amy stared at her wondering if the child belonged to the ailing woman, when her father, on seeing the child stumble, had reached forward and snatched her to safety.

"Poor woman," remarked the rector as the Taylor family disappeared from view. "It seems a forlorn hope to expose someone so advanced in the disease to the rigours of such a long sea journey.

Indeed, I wonder at the captain taking a passenger on board in such a sad condition. We must visit them as soon as we set sail, Amy."

Amy nodded in reply. She could see her duties were to continue on board ship in the same way that they had for as long as she could remember. Her father had been the incumbent of the Church of St. Saviours in a poor area of Liverpool's dockland for the past thirty years, and Amy had been brought up in the crumbling brick rectory, a stone's throw away from the church. It was a poor living, and for thirty-six years she could remember no other life but one of varying shades of grey. Her early childhood had been spent in a different vicarage, no better and no worse than the one they had just left with its lack of heating and damp walls. She had almost given up all hope of ever knowing any other kind of life but one of duty, duty to the parish and its needs.

Being an only child and unmarried, she had been expected to nurse her mother until her death and had helped her father in his parish work, visiting the sick and needy who were scarcely any better off in life than she was herself. Her life had soured her, and she had grown mean by nature and had none of the warmth of spirit that a child can react to in a complete stranger. She had hated the children she was obliged to teach in her father's Sunday school and had been thoroughly detested by them in return. They played tricks on her when her back was turned, and, over the years, Amy had come to mistrust every child she met, however good mannered they might appear on the surface. Curates had come and gone without one of them hinting at marriage, and Amy had given up all hope of ever changing her single status until a quite extraordinary chain of events took place which was to alter her life.

One morning, *The Church Times* had been delivered to the rectory earlier than usual, and Amy had picked it up off the floor where it had fallen while on her way to prepare her father's meagre breakfast. The headlines caught her attention—"Sad conditions at the Ovens Gold Field." Amy read on, fascinated by the article, especially the last paragraph, which was to lead indirectly to a complete change in her circumstances.

"Men, unfit for hard physical labour, have died on the road to making their fortune, or met an untimely end in drunken brawls. Even worse, on making a find, murder between partners is often the result, and yet they still flock to the gold fields in their thousands.

There is a crying need for those dedicated to the mission field to serve in Australia where the lust for gold has driven Christ from men's minds."

Amy had folded up the paper and taken it into her father's study with his breakfast tray, her mind already made up—they would go to Australia. Recently, posters had appeared around Liverpool's dockland area offering assisted passage to healthy young women in their twenties, and a brief feeling of envy had passed through Amy's mind, but was soon dismissed. Apart from being too old to be considered, she was not the type of woman to look for a husband among rough, uncouth men, however much she longed to escape the grime and squalor of her surroundings.

Her father rapidly dismissed any hopes she might have of accompanying him to such a wild and terrible place, although he had been deeply affected by the article, which appealed to his missionary zeal. Disappointed by his reply, Amy had searched further until she found what she was looking for. In the personal column, she found an unusual advertisement—

> "Bishop's sister, residing in Melbourne, Australia, seeks a refined lady companion. Applications from the daughters of the clergy will be favourably considered."

Within a week, she had been granted an interview with the bishop's secretary, in England on private business, and had been accepted for the post. Her father, seeing her determination to emigrate, decided to accompany her and accepted a living in Ballarat; and so it was that Rosie met the woman, who unwittingly almost sent her to a watery grave and was to play an important part in her life, and Paul Briggs, whose intention it was to save souls, who had saved her in the nick of time.

Soon after John had found the small area that had been allotted to the Taylors, and their few belongings had been stowed away in every available place they could find, they ate the food they had brought with them, and, afterwards, before returning to the deck, Julia was made as comfortable as possible in the top bunk. Rosie's hand was held tightly in her father's strong grip as they climbed up to the top deck to watch the ship setting sail on the tide. Among the throng of people shouting and waving to those growing further and further away on the dockside, Rosie recognised the tall hat of the Reverend Briggs as he and his daughter watched the shores of England recede into the distance. The air of excitement began to die away, and small groups of passengers made their way below decks. The ship cast off the tug and a fresh wind filled the billowing sails. Rosie felt a wave of sadness. It was quiet on deck now and she became aware of a strange sensation as the ship scudded through the waves. This was to be her home for more weeks than she could imagine, and the thought of that as she looked up into the massive sails flapping above her made her shiver. It felt so different from walking on land, and she had difficulty keeping her balance.

"Time to get below, Rosie," said her father. "You look cold, my dear, and we must see if Mama is all right."

Rosie found herself tucked up early that night and slept, rocked in the cradle of the deep, tired out by the new experiences of the day. She was awakened after a few hours sleep as the motion of the ship threw her against the wide security plank, inserted along the outside of her bunk. The light, westerly wind, which had accompanied them out of port, had developed into a squall during the night and the ship began to roll heavily, giving the passengers a foretaste of what to expect in the weeks ahead. All hands were on deck, taking in the studding sails and the royals, as the crew balanced precariously on the ropes, tying down the heaving mass of wet canvas to the spars with the ship pitching and rolling through the darkness.

By the morning, the storm had abated and a watery sun shone through the remaining shreds of clouds. A few hardy souls appeared in the salon for breakfast but neither the Taylor family nor the Briggs was among them, for like most of the other passengers, they had suffered badly from seasickness.

Amy Briggs was confined to her bunk all that day in the tiny hole of a cabin she had found herself sharing with a Mrs. Alice Potts, a plump, middle-aged matron of cheerful disposition, and two sisters from Liverpool, Lizzie and Sarah Hopkins.

At the first sight of her travelling companions, Amy had decided to remain aloof; they were definitely not of her class, and she would not converse with them any more than was necessary. Mrs. Potts was travelling back to Melbourne with her husband, who was accommodated elsewhere in the ship, and the two Miss Hopkinses, both in their early twenties, had taken advantage of assisted passages to make a new life for themselves. The eldest sister, Lizzie, a beautiful creature of wanton disposition, hoped to do a little gold digging in the marriage market and had persuaded her sister Sarah, a quiet, amiable girl, to accompany her on her quest. Sarah had not needed much persuasion, for, whatever the outcome of their journey, it could never be worse than the cramped tenement in the back street of one of Liverpool's slum areas where they had lived, with the constant wailing of sickly children and the sharp tongue of their harassed, exhausted mother.

As the two girls had watched Amy unpack her precisely folded clothes and make room for her few garments among their overflowing frills and furbelows, they had found difficulty containing their mirth. She was so prim and proper and stiff-laced that their natural inclination had been to burst into fits of stifled giggles, until Alice Potts had thought it necessary to show some disapproval of their behaviour for the sake of their future relations with the fourth occupant of the cabin. However, after a storm-tossed night, nobody felt in the mood to poke fun; they were, after all, in the same boat and suffered similarly. Alice Potts dressed when she felt able and, seeing how distressed Amy was feeling, roused the two girls to search out Amy's father, who was travelling steerage, and to suggest that he found the ship's doctor to help her.

Rosie, who was taking a few tentative steps along the deck in the company of her father, recognised Paul Briggs as he hurried past, his face drawn with concern and his head lowered as he battled to keep his hat in place in the breeze.

"Look, Papa," she said, pointing him out to her father. "That's the gentleman who spoke to you yesterday."

John looked round as Paul Briggs disappeared down the steps to the companionway, followed closely by two attractive young women.

"Ah, yes," replied John. "I owe him a debt of gratitude, my dear, and one I shall never be able to repay. We must watch out for him and his daughter, but right now I doubt he will feel much like meeting us again. None of us feel too well at present."

Rosie was glad. She would like to prolong any meeting with the frightening Miss Briggs, indefinitely.

As the days passed, the sea became relatively calm and spirits revived generally. Julia felt well enough to sit on deck and Rosie, well wrapped up against the wind, was left in attendance while John took a brisk walk on his own. Being a countryman, he enjoyed fresh air and the fetid atmosphere in their poky cabin choked him. He was devoted to his wife, but as she was rarely fit enough to sit in the salon, he felt obliged to remain with her. Filling his lungs with pure sea air was a necessity, and he strode along briskly, cheerfully passing the time of day with those he met.

Rosie sat beside her mother playing at "cats cradle." She was more content now and had settled down to life on board. The passengers smiled at her, often from pity when they realised that Julia was her mother, but Rosie was too young to discern the difference or the reason for their kindly concern and shyly returned their smiles. Members of the crew stopped to talk to her as she watched them perform their routine tasks, and she began to feel more at home as each day passed.

Her mother touched her arm, gently. "Isn't that the Reverend Briggs and his daughter over there, dear?" she asked. "Papa so wanted to speak to them, and now he isn't here. What a nuisance. Still, I feel as if I should have a few words with them—just go over and ask them to come over here, will you Rosie? There's a good girl."

Rosie put her "cats cradle" to one side and stood up reluctantly. She wanted to defy her mother and pouted miserably.

"What's the matter?" asked Julia, surprised that such a simple request should make her daughter react in such an uncharacteristic way.

"I don't want to go, Mama."

"Why ever not, child?"

Rosie bit her lip. "I don't like Miss Briggs—she's a witch."

Julia laughed incredulously. "Oh, you silly goose!" she said, fondly. "You only think that because she was wearing black when you first saw her, but look at her now. She's changed her dress and looks quite different."

Rosie looked and saw that her mother was quite right. Miss Briggs didn't look as formidable as she had remembered her. She was wearing a grey woollen dress and a bonnet to match, and over her shoulders she wore a white, embroidered silk shawl. Alice Potts had been the moving force behind this transformation and had persuaded Amy to change from her heavy, black mourning clothes into something more becoming. Her husband Arthur owned the largest haberdashery in Melbourne, and Alice knew all about the current fashion and accessories having recently visited the fashion houses in London and Paris with a view to extending their business in Melbourne to include the manufacture of stylish clothing for women and children. As Amy's clothes were all severely practical, Alice had lent her the shawl to brighten up her plain woollen dress, and although Amy hadn't wanted to accept it, she felt it would be impolite to refuse.

Rosie swallowed hard and, taking her courage in both hands, approached the couple nervously. Standing away from Miss Briggs as far as possible, she pulled the Reverend Briggs's sleeve to attract his attention. Amy Briggs might look different, but Rosie wasn't taking any chances, and, when Amy turned to look at her, Rosie paled visibly. Miss Briggs's deep-set black eyes glittered as if they could read her very thoughts, and her lips were drawn into a tight thin line. She glared down at Rosie as if resenting the intrusion. Her father, however, recognised the child immediately and beamed at her.

"Why, if it isn't the little girl who wanted to join the mermaids," he remarked jokingly, chucking Rosie under the chin. "What brings you here, my dear?"

"If you please, sir," began Rosie, in a hoarse whisper, "my mother would like to see you. We are sitting over there while Papa has gone for his walk."

"Of course, my dear, of course—we shall be delighted to meet her. Indeed we have been looking out for your family—is that not so, Amy?"

Amy made no reply as she followed behind her father to where Julia was sitting. She had no obligation to this stranger and feared her father would be only too ready to offer her services to this sick woman. Amy's charity, cold at the best of times, had been left behind when she set out for other shores. She was no longer the rector's daughter, duty bound to help the sick and needy.

Rosie continued to play with her length of string, weaving intricate patterns between her fingers as Paul Briggs chatted to her mother. She sat some small distance away from the group and was soon forgotten by them, although her eyes and ears were alert to everything. Her father returned to join in the conversation, and Rosie noticed how Miss Briggs brightened up at his approach and smiled from time to time.

"I'm very used to taking care of an invalid," Rosie heard her say, agreeably, "so please don't hesitate to call upon me at any time—and if you should need someone to mind your daughter for an hour or two then I shall be only too pleased to help in anyway I can."

Rosie dropped the cat's cradle into her lap with horror. Her parents were smiling their thanks to Miss Briggs as if she was the kindest person in the world, and Rosie thought they must have taken leave of their senses. How blind they were, both of them, to trust her to someone like Miss Briggs, and anger swelled up inside her as she watched the Briggses prepare to take their leave. Just at that moment, a plump, jolly-looking lady whom Rosie hadn't seen before bustled past her and, on being recognised by Miss Briggs, was introduced to the Taylors. It appeared that she shared a cabin with Miss Briggs and was on her way to meet her husband. She smiled encouragingly at Rosie as Julia pointed out her daughter, and Rosie felt somewhat comforted. Alice Potts was childless, and the sight of a pretty child like Rosie warmed her heart.

"Why, there is Arthur," she exclaimed, catching sight of her erstwhile husband as he sauntered across the deck towards her with the two Miss Hopkins, one on each arm. "Arthur finds Lizzie and Sarah the most delightful company. Two such lovely girls, to be sure!"

Amy stiffened at this remark. The Miss Hopkinses lacked breeding, and Lizzie was up to no good—Amy was convinced of that. How Alice Potts could be so friendly towards them was beyond her understanding. Amy had come to appreciate Alice's kindness but considered her too ready to accept people at their face value, and, being a hard, bigoted person herself, she placed unselfishness and openheartedness in the same class as weakness of character and a mild case of softness in the head.

Everyone was introduced in turn and the meeting became quite lively with smiling exchanges and the mutual pleasure in making new friends. Sarah Hopkins walked across to Rosie and, taking a screwed up twist of paper out of her pocket, offered it to her.

"Have a humbug," said Sarah cheerfully, popping one in Rosie's mouth. "I expect you're a bit bored with no one to play with, aren't you? Lizzie and I left all our sisters behind—there were six of them, all much younger than us, so we are used to little girls. Do you like hearing stories, Rosie?"

Rosie nodded her head in the affirmative, too shy to speak to this friendly stranger.

"Well, I know lots of stories." Sarah's blue eyes twinkled under her blue bonnet, and she looked very young herself. Rosie fell in love with her immediately.

"Then we'll have to see what we can do about it, won't we?"

Rosie smiled shyly and waved as Sarah took her leave, hoping she would keep her promise and feeling as if she had made a friend.

The Fair Maid was travelling at a steady eight knots. The wind sighed in the rigging, and the afternoon sun shone on the brass fittings and the polished teak decking. All around, there was colour to delight the eye—bright silks and satins trimmed with heavy braid and sparkling jet beads, and ribbons fluttering in the breeze. The whole appearance of the ship was one of elegance from the graceful lines of her hull to the passengers promenading her decks.

Arthur Potts continued on his walk, accompanied by his two birds of paradise and his plump little wife, while Amy and her father found a seat on the poop deck in the sun. The Reverend Briggs soon became engrossed in a book of sermons, and Amy shut her eyes for a moment. Seeing John Taylor in the company of his wife, Amy had been deeply impressed. His quiet dignity placed him in a class above that of a common workman, and he spoke well when telling her father of his hopes for the future. His position had been obtained for him by a titled family who appeared to think much of him, and that meant more to Amy than his ruggedly handsome looks and his honest brown eyes. She could tell he was a hard-working man from his conversation, and he was a craftsman with a good trade. Such a man would not have appealed to her in England, but, in Australia, he would make a useful husband if he was free, and there was always that possibility. They had a long way to travel before they reached their destination and that gave her plenty of time to make herself indispensable to the family. The child, of course, was another matter, but she would cross that bridge when she came to it, providing things turned out as she hoped.

The sun made her sleepy, and, with her plans made to her satisfaction, she dozed off contentedly.

Rosie returned to sit by her mother, glad that the Briggs had moved on. She wanted to tell her mother about the new friend she had met so unexpectedly but her mother and father were talking, and Rosie had to wait her turn.

"Did you ever see such a dapper, pompous little man," laughed John, who was used to more down-to-earth people. "He looks as proud as a turkey cock!"

Julia had to agree with him. Arthur Potts had taken them all by surprise when he had appeared wearing a dove grey suit, a grey velour hat and matching kid gloves and sporting a large, diamond pin in his cravat. Had he been a younger man of slim build his apparel would have made him a prince among men, but Arthur did not fit that description, being short, middle aged and corpulent. Such vanity made him more of a figure of fun than one of envy.

"I would imagine the Potts are wealthy people, although his wife does not give one that impression," said Julia, quietly. "If I were her, I wouldn't make such a friend of that Miss Hopkins—Lizzie, I think her name was. She was the most beautiful girl I've ever seen, and Mr. Potts couldn't take his eyes off her."

"I hardly noticed her, my dear," said John, tactfully. "Mrs. Potts had so much to say it was difficult to get a word in edgeways."

Julia smiled weakly. She had noticed that too.

"I liked the other Miss Hopkins—the one called Sarah," said Rosie, as soon as she could speak without upsetting anyone. "She gave me a humbug and said she would tell me some stories. She's used to telling stories to her little sisters, and, now they're all left at home, I expect I'll do instead."

Her parents smiled indulgently at her, knowing how often adults forget their promises to children made on the spur of the moment.

"There are some very kind people amongst the passengers, Rosie, and we met some of them today, especially the lady whose father stopped you from falling into the sea." Julia looked hard at her daughter. "She was the kindest of all, and you were very silly Rosie to think such dreadful things of her. I hope you feel sorry for that now."

Rosie hung her head, and Julia took it to mean that her daughter felt contrite.

"We'll say no more about it, dear. Little girls are apt to let their imaginations run away with them sometimes."

"Yes, Mama," replied Rosie, having decided that sometimes it was best for little girls to keep their thoughts to themselves.

CHAPTER 3

The passage through the Bay of Biscay was an unpleasant experience for those on board. A pounding sea swept across the poop, and it needed two crew members to steer the sturdy clipper through the treacherous waves with both men lashed to the kicking wheel to hold her on course. By the end of the second day, the head wind had subsided, and soon *The Fair Maid* was sailing into the northeast trades.

Every morning, as soon as they had recovered from the buffeting, Rosie would accompany Lizzie and Sarah, dressed demurely in their white muslin dresses, onto the poop deck where they would enjoy the warm weather. Some of the more energetic gentlemen had devised various physical exercises among the rigging, much to Rosie's amusement, and as Lizzie passed by they made a great show of their strength and prowess for her benefit. Lizzie was always the centre of attraction, and, as Rosie was frequently in her company, she came in for some extra attention as well. Being an only child and from a small village where company was rare, Rosie found it a novelty to be among a crowd. Each day provided a new diversion for her; the two sisters were full of surprises—a new satin ribbon, a brooch or a carefully wrapped trinket which took her ages to unwrap while Sarah teased her about the contents. Sarah was quieter and gentle with her, but it was the vivacious Lizzie with her ready laugh and her sense of fun who fascinated her most, for Lizzie knew instinctively how to amuse children. Rosie's eyes would grow rounder and rounder as Lizzie, with a serious expression on her face, would relate an unbelievable story to her young listener, until she could keep up the pretence no longer and the tale telling dissolved into much laughter on both sides.

One morning, little flying fish were found on deck, their delicate fins shimmering in the sunlight. Sarah explained to Rosie how they flew on board during the night, attracted by the lights from the ship.

"They were too pretty to die," said Rosie, sadly. "Why do pretty things have to die, Sarah, when horrid things and horrid people go on living?"

The question alarmed Sarah, and she took Rosie's hand and led her away to look over the side, where a group of people were watching the antics of a school of porpoises playing round the bows. As she watched them leaping through the waves and returning to the ship to roll over in a gleaming display before disappearing into the distance, Rosie forgot all about the flying fish, and Sarah was saved from having to answer. Nevertheless, she wondered if Rosie was aware that her mother's condition had deteriorated over the last few weeks, and if she knew that was the reason for Lizzie and herself spending so much time with her.

Rosie knew that her mother was growing weaker; it was only too obvious when her mind began to wander and she became unaware of her surroundings. The nearer they came to the Equator the more suffocating the heat became and Julia's rasping cough gave her no peace in the brittle, dry atmosphere. Awnings were stretched across the poop deck to provide some shade for the wilting passengers, and most people slept on deck to avoid the suffocating heat below. The days and nights passed with scarcely a breath of air, and John rarely slept, keeping watch over his wife and seeing to her needs. In the daytime, Amy sat with her, supporting Amy's frail body as the coughing fits increased while John snatched a few hours sleep. Miss Briggs made it only too clear to Rosie that she was a nuisance hanging round her mother at such a time, and, although Rosie wanted to be near her mother, she was glad enough to escape with Lizzie and Sarah when Amy Briggs was around.

The great canvas sails flapped idly as the ship lay becalmed in the Doldrums and Rosie was thankful when it was her turn to use the improvised bucket shower which had been set up on the deck. This was such a strange contraption that Sarah had to take her inside the canvas tent the first time to show her how to work the pulley, and there was much hilarity when they both got a soaking. Such escapades helped Rosie to cope with the sadness she felt when she returned to her mother's sickbed. The sultry days and stifling nights seemed endless until one afternoon when a dark rim was sighted on the horizon moving rapidly toward the ship. The ensuing squalls and thunderstorms persisted for a few days, keeping everyone below decks and then, as suddenly as they had started, the wind changed direction and the vessel came to life again, making good speed towards the Equator.

Below decks, Rosie's ninth birthday had come and gone without celebrations of any kind, and when Sarah and Lizzie discovered this fact, they arranged to take her to watch the ceremony of crossing the Line as a special treat. Rosie was bursting with excitement when Lizzie and Sarah arrived to collect her. Lizzie wore a tiny sea-green hat tilted forward on her piled-up chestnut hair, which exactly matched her heavy silk dress with its pinched waist and large slit sleeves, showing a contrasting lining of cream silk, while Sarah wore a pale blue muslin to match her eyes. Lizzie resembled an exotic tiger lily, and was well aware of the dazzling effect her outfit had on everyone she passed, and Sarah looked just as delightful in her unassuming way. Rosie walked between them feeling like a princess on her way to the ball and gazed up at the sisters in awesome admiration.

"Such fashions, Arthur," exclaimed Alice Potts, catching sight of the girls as they made their way to the front of the crowd. "Did you ever see the like?"

Arthur Potts felt his heart miss a beat as he looked at Lizzie. With his wealth, he bought what he wanted from life, and maybe he could buy Lizzie Hopkins. He twirled his moustache in the happy anticipation of such a deal and considered how much he would need to invest in the lady before she came round to his way of thinking.

Rosie, in her white sailor suit, stood on her tiptoes to get a better view of the proceedings. Her cream straw hat with its navy ribbons bobbed up and down as she watched excitedly as the gun carriage carrying Father Neptune and his scrawny wife came into view. A huge, bearded sailor crowned with a tin circlet acted the part of King Neptune. He had one arm flung around the toothless hag at his side and in the other hand he held a long trident, which he waved in greeting towards the assembled company. Rosie laughed fearfully at the sight, and, had she not been with Sarah and Lizzie, she would have been terrified. A long procession of sailors followed behind, completing the cortege, with each man holding aloft a lighted torch.

The captain was summoned to the quarter deck and asked to call the new midshipmen forward. Three reluctant lads wearing long, striped trousers were dragged before King Neptune and his queen, who were now enthroned on the forecastle. A pair of swarthy sailors set to work to shave the unfortunate "middies" amid much laughter from the onlookers. Rosie shrieked with delight as buckets of water splashed in all directions in true slapstick fashion. She did not find it so amusing however when the smallest midshipman was forced to endure some vicious jabs from the end of the three-pronged trident, causing him to hop around the deck in pain, and, on stepping back slightly she found herself stepping on Mr. Potts's toes. Mr. Potts rapidly removed his arm from Lizzie's waist, where it had been lying for some time, and continued to look at the amusing scene on deck as if nothing had happened. Rosie looked up at Lizzie in surprise, but Lizzie appeared to be totally unconcerned. She found this very puzzling as she was sure Mr. Potts hadn't been there when the fun had started, and it was even more puzzling that Lizzie didn't seem to know either. Perhaps, with all her tight lacing she hadn't felt Mr. Potts squeeze her waist. Rosie turned her attention back to the ceremony and was just in time to see the bedraggled midshipmen disappear below decks and Father Neptune and his court take their leave. Everyone ran across to the rail to watch a large tub of flaming tar floating in the ship's wake, which represented Neptune's chariot returning to its briny home, after which Rosie looked for Lizzie and Sarah, but only Sarah could she find.

"Well," said Sarah, "did you enjoy the fun?"

Rosie nodded. "It was all right—I liked the funny parts, but I felt sorry for the man who was poked with the trident."

"So did I," agreed Sarah, "and he didn't have to be hurt, I feel sure. I think King Neptune was being cruel, don't you? Where has Lizzie got to I wonder? Can you see her anywhere?"

Eventually, they tracked Lizzie down and found her engaged in animated conversation with Mr. and Mrs. Potts. They all seemed very pleased about something as Sarah and Rosie joined them, and Mrs. Potts turned to Sarah with a wide smile.

"My dear Sarah," she enthused, "why didn't you tell me you could sew—Potts and I have been racking our brains wondering how you two girls could afford such clothes, and Lizzie tells us she designs them, and you make them up yourselves, apart from which, my dear Sarah, Lizzie tells me you are a milliner by trade. We would like you both to work for us in our new showroom in Melbourne—Lizzie to supervise the making of the garments and you, Sarah, to take charge of the fittings and accessories. There is accommodation above our new emporium with the workshops at the rear. Oh, we would be so delighted if you would accept—indeed we would."

Sarah stood rooted to the spot with astonishment, until Lizzie nudged her impatiently.

"Of course, Mrs. Potts," she blurted out, "and as long as Lizzie is happy about it—"

"Oh, yes, Lizzie is very satisfied with the arrangements," said Arthur Potts, bringing the matter to a hasty conclusion. "So we'll consider that settled then."

He smiled knowingly at Lizzie over his wife's shoulder, and Rosie thought she saw him wink, although she wasn't quite sure. She was beginning to find Mr. Potts a strange gentleman, and he certainly liked Lizzie a lot, but then that wasn't difficult to understand. Lizzie was lovely, and she liked her too, and so did all the other gentlemen, who smiled whenever she passed by. Whatever it was that had just been settled it seemed to have made Lizzie and Mr. Potts very happy and as long as Lizzie felt happy about it then everything must be all right.

The day ended with a quadrille party held on the poop, under a sky brilliant with the colours of a tropical sunset. The huge red ball of the sun sank slowly below the horizon in a blaze of orange and red, a fitting end to the day's activities.

Rosie had plagued her father to let her go and watch, just for a little while. She longed to see all the pretty gowns the ladies would be wearing and to listen to the music, and Mrs. Potts, who didn't dance because she got so puffed, had promised to look after her. It didn't take long to wear her father down with all her pleading, and he gave his permission for her to stay for an hour or two as long as she didn't bother Mrs. Potts. Rosie gave her fervent promise and rushed off to Mrs. Potts's cabin. John was glad the child was so happily occupied; it had been a bad day for him, and he was worried about his wife. At first, the sea air had suited her but the dry heat had made her worse, and she was coughing her life away. If it had not been for the kind attentions of Amy Briggs and the care of the Hopkins sisters and Alice Potts, who amused Rosie, he would have broken down long ago from the strain. To see Rosie so happy today had touched his heart, for the child would need all her courage to face the stark reality of bereavement before much longer.

As Rosie peeped inside the little cabin, voices from within begged her to sit on the steps and wait.

"No room, no room, not even for a little one," came Alice's cheerful voice.

Rosie waited patiently in a fever of excitement until Alice eventually emerged, her matronly figure encompassed in a deep burgundy silk.

"It's a good thing Miss Briggs isn't coming to the dance," puffed Alice, as they made their way up the companionway. "There isn't room for a midget to get dressed in that cabin, let alone three ladies, and me counting almost for two! My, oh my, Rosie dear, what a day it has been. Come along my love, and we'll find Potts and settle ourselves on a comfy seat."

Once seated to Alice's satisfaction, Rosie sat and watched the ladies appear in their ball gowns, as fascinating a sight as a cloud of tropical butterflies. Lizzie made her appearance in a white silk gown, the skirt trimmed with tulle and looped up with knots of blush pink roses. A similar bunch of roses was pinned to the front of her low-cut bodice and wreathed among the coronet of chestnut hair piled on top of her head. She looked magnificent, and Rosie gasped with admiration a she came into view, to lose sight of her almost immediately among the crowd. She had already caused quite a stir among the officers and crew, and below decks there had been some conjecture as to why she was travelling to Australia. She was frequently seen in the company of a small girl, and it was presumed that she was either a wealthy young widow or on her way to meet up with her husband. A wager had been made as to who would be the first to discover the truth, and one young officer after another approached her to request the first dance.

Arthur Potts, watching this parade of handsome young men vying for her favours, squirmed with annoyance as he kept his eyes firmly fixed on the object of his desire. His anxiety transmitted itself to Rosie, who found his fidgeting a perfect nuisance and moved closer to Mrs. Potts.

"Lizzie has a lot of admirers, my dear," observed Alice, unaware that her innocent remark only served to fan the flames of her husband's present state of agitation.

Arthur could bear the torment no longer and rising to his feet addressed himself to his wife. "Excuse me, my dear, but I really should, in all politeness, ask the Misses Hopkins for a dance. They are to become a part of our establishment, and it would appear churlish not to—I'm sure you would agree—"

"Why, of course, Arthur dear," replied Alice mildly. "But do take care, and don't over exert yourself."

Free at last, Arthur hurried across the deck, and Lizzie, noting the urgency of his approach, accepted his request to partner her in the first quadrille while explaining to the disappointed faces around her that, as Arthur was a very dear friend, he must have the honour of the first dance. Arthur swelled with pride, and, feeling like a conquering hero, he led his beloved away from her suitors and into the dance. Watching this little scene take place, Rosie was disgusted with Mr. Potts. He had behaved very badly, taking Lizzie away and not giving her a chance to choose a handsome young man to be her partner when so many of them wanted to dance with her. With his hat removed and the lamplight glistening on his bald head, Rosie thought he looked like an ugly little gnome, and her sympathies were all for Lizzie as she gazed with admiration at her beautiful heroine.

They certainly made an incongruous couple as they glided across the pools of light shed by the lamps swaying in the rigging. Lizzie, tall and as stately as a swan, stood head and shoulders above her portly partner, who, despite his rotund figure, proved to be an excellent dancer and light on his feet. Feeling the pressure of Arthur's hand round her waist, Lizzie smiled to herself. He needed no encouragement but she would have to be discreet and careful if she was to become his mistress in due course of time.

Sarah arrived late, looking resplendent in her cream silk gown with red roses in her hair, and she took Arthur's seat beside Rosie. She had had to wait until Lizzie had finished her elaborate coiffure before she could get to the mirror to brush out her ringlets, and now it seemed as if all the ladies had their cards filled and she would be left without any partners. She sighed resignedly and settled down to make the best of the evening. She had been used to playing second fiddle to her more dominant sister all her life and accepted her situation without complaint, although she did not always agree with Lizzie's flighty ways, being of a more sensitive disposition herself.

Rosie stroked the shimmering silk of Sarah's gown lovingly, letting the material slip through her fingers.

"How pretty you look, Sarah," she remarked shyly.

Sarah smiled gratefully at the compliment, wondering if it would be the only one she would receive that evening when she caught sight of her sister dancing with Arthur Potts, and her expression changed to one of concern.

The quadrille had finished, and the music had changed to that of a lively waltz. Arthur, anxious not to relinquish his prize so soon, held Lizzie tightly to him and waltzed her energetically round the deck, leaving her next partner waiting vainly for her return. The close proximity of her bosom, from which wafted the scent of Parma violets, intoxicated him, and he was consumed with desire for this voluptuous creature he held in his arms.

"Lizzie, my dearest —the love of my life—" Arthur began breathlessly, whirling his partner round until the perspiration trickled through his side whiskers and off the ends of his waxed moustache. The sentence remained unfinished as, with a sharp cry of pain, he hobbled away from the dancers. Alice ran to help him and, with his wife supporting him on one side and Lizzie on the other, they managed between them to get Arthur to a seat.

"How could you make such an exhibition of yourself, Arthur!" scolded Alice, her motherly face assuming a colour which closely resembled the burgundy silk of her gown. "You will have to rest your gouty leg for weeks now. Whatever were you thinking about?"

Arthur leaned back, closed his eyes and mopped his brow. The excruciating pain in his leg was worth his few moments of bliss, and Alice could scold as much as she liked. Sarah went to fetch assistance and returned with a young sailor who helped Arthur back to his cabin, with Alice in close attendance. Rosie knew she ought to feel sorry for poor Mr. Potts, but she was glad when he had been taken away in such an ignominious fashion. It was no more than he deserved, stopping poor Lizzie from enjoying herself, and she noticed that some of the gentlemen who had wanted to partner Lizzie when Mr. Potts had come along and swept her away, seemed to feel the same as she did.

Lizzie came and sat beside them for a few minutes to rest her tired feet—her new satin dancing boots were beginning to pinch uncomfortably. Sarah decided there and then to take her sister to task.

"Lizzie, do take care, I beg of you," she whispered urgently, hoping Rosie would not hear what she had to say. "I know flirting is just fun to you but he fancies you—you know he does—and Alice has been good to us both. We've got a decent job to go to when we get there and somewhere to live into the bargain. Don't go and spoil our chances—he isn't worth it. Women are two a penny to him."

Lizzie finished lacing up her boots. "I can cope with his kind, Sarah, so stop fretting and enjoy yourself. I intend to." And, without further ado, Lizzie was claimed by the first mate and swept back into the dance.

"What were you whispering about?" asked Rosie, who felt left out of the conversation. "Was it about Mr. Potts?"

"Never you mind," said Sarah, "and I'm sure we've got better things to talk about than that particular gentleman."

"I didn't like him dancing with Lizzie," commented Rosie. "They looked just like Beauty and the Beast in that story you were telling me yesterday."

Sarah smiled. Rosie was a bit too observant sometimes. "Don't you think it's time you went to bed now, Rosie. Your papa will be wondering where you are, I should imagine, and I don't think Mrs. Potts will be coming back anymore this evening."

Rosie was about to protest that she didn't feel at all tired when the sailor who had helped Arthur Potts to his cabin returned to ask Sarah to dance. Sarah blushed with pleasure as she accepted his invitation, and Rosie, seeing that she was going to be left alone, decided to say good night.

As she made her way back to the companionway, she stood for a few minutes and watched Sarah and her partner making a terrible mess of the complicated movements of the quadrille, but they were both laughing and somehow, to Rosie, it seemed to be much more fun than when Mr. Potts and Lizzie had danced together, although they had made no mistakes at all.

CHAPTER 4

Blown by the southeast trade winds *The Fair Maid* sailed through the Tropics towards the Cape of Good Hope. The passengers became lethargic in the heat and lazed the days away, doing as little as possible. Even food lost its appeal to those with the heartiest of appetites, and sea pie, boiled mutton and salt beef were viewed with equal distaste. The sighting of whales surfacing and spouting huge fountains of water through their blow holes was the only happening to stir any real interest among the bored and exhausted passengers.

In the cooler evenings, the ship came to life again and the passengers would gather in the salon with its handsome mahogany panelling and its red plush furnishings, to play cards and listen to the old songs thumped out on the piano by one of their company. Lizzie was a popular visitor; she had a good voice and was as entertaining as any of the music hall artistes of that era. In fact, the moment she appeared, the game of squaills was discontinued, hands of cards were turned face down on the tables, and chess and solitaire were forgotten as those present clamoured for a song. In the early evening, before the men became too rowdy, Rosie was allowed to visit the salon with Mrs. Potts while Mr. Potts enjoyed a game of cribbage, and this she loved. To hear Lizzie sing was like being in heaven to Rosie with Lizzie playing the part of an angel.

One evening, as the applause died away after a noisy chorus of, "In the Strand," Lizzie began to sing "Oft in the Stilly Night" very softly, without any accompaniment. Not a sound could be heard but her clear voice as it wafted through the open skylight and into the soft night air. Rosie wondered why it had gone so quiet. They had all heard Lizzie sing before and usually made a great deal of noise about it, banging their glasses on the tables and thumping their feet, but now, as she looked around, some of the men were unashamedly wiping tears from their eyes as the pure, clear voice conjured up visions of the homes they had left behind and the people they would never see again. Mr. Potts looked as if he had been transported to heaven, and Rosie wanted to laugh at the silly expression on his face, but she just smiled instead because everyone else was so serious. During the tumultuous applause that broke out as Lizzie's voice died away, Sarah took Rosie's hand and led her out of the salon. She could see how her sister was working on the men's emotions and knew there would be a great deal of drinking that night. Soon, it would be no place for a child or a young woman either.

Sarah walked with her to the forecastle, where the sailors congregated on warm evenings to spin yarns and to smoke. As Sarah had hoped, Midshipman Brown was among them, and he left the group to walk with them. Rosie recognised him as the sailor who had tried to dance with Sarah and was surprised that Sarah seemed to know him quite well. Perhaps they had danced together some more after she had left them to go to bed.

"This is Ben," said Sarah, introducing him. "He was one of the sailors we saw when we crossed the Line. Do you remember, Rosie? We felt very sorry for him, didn't we?" Rosie remembered then and looked up into Ben's face.

"Did it hurt when you got poked?" she asked out of interest.

"I should say so," remarked Ben, pulling a wry face for her benefit.

"And is it better now?" asked Rosie with a worried look on her face.

Sarah laughed at her. "That's enough of your questions, Rosie. Ben and I have a lot to say to one another so you go and play over there for a while."

Rosie was put out. She didn't want to go and play, as Sarah had put it, and, anyway, there was nothing to play with, so, after a while, she left them to return to her own cabin. She passed Mr. and Mrs. Potts standing close to the entrance down to the salon. Mr. Potts was complaining that it hurt his leg to walk any further, and Mrs. Potts was grumbling at him. Rosie could hear Lizzie still singing and thought that

Mr. Potts looked as if he wanted to go back to the salon and listen to her as he became extremely cross when Mrs. Potts pulled him along to continue their evening stroll.

After this, it became the general thing for Sarah to take her with her when she went to meet Ben. Rosie could never understand why Sarah needed her there because as soon as Sarah and Ben got deep into conversation they forgot all about her, and she drifted back to her cabin without them even knowing she had gone. There were stars in the sky these nights, huge stars, and one of them she was told was called the Southern Cross. Sarah told her that Ben was teaching her all about the stars—well, perhaps he was, because Sarah was so starstruck these days she hardly seemed to know if she was there or not, and Rosie didn't know what to make of it all.

And then, one evening, on returning to the cabin she shared with her parents, Rosie had the shock of her life. Instead of her mother lying coughing in her bunk and her father reading quietly beside her, there was Miss Briggs waiting for her. She was so terrified that she stepped out of the cabin in her fright and began to run back to Sarah and Ben, until Miss Brigg's sharp retort stopped her in her tracks.

"Come back this instance, Rosie," she called out. "Where on earth do you think you're off to?"

Rosie turned round slowly and began to retrace her steps. "Where's Papa gone?" she managed to ask as she gathered her wits. "Why isn't he here? And where's Mama? Is she worse?" She felt very close to tears, and suddenly, very alone.

"Come in, Rosie, and your questions will be answered. I don't intend standing here and talking to you. Come along—be sensible now." Amy Briggs turned on her heel and re-entered the cabin, and Rosie, seeing she had no alternative, followed nervously.

"Come in and shut the door behind you," said Amy in as reasonable a tone as she could muster with this troublesome girl. "Come along, child—I shan't eat you."

Rosie half closed the door and sat herself down on the edge of her bunk, ready to make a quick get away.

"I have some sad news to tell you, Rosie, so you must be a brave girl now. Your Mama went to heaven an hour ago and is now with the angels. Your Papa is busy seeing to things, and he was afraid you might come back before he finished, so he asked me to see you to bed and to stay with you until he returns." Amy paused for a moment to give Rosie time to take in her words and then continued as she felt was fitting under the circumstances. "Put your hands together Rosie, and we will say a prayer together for the repose of your Mama's soul."

To Amy, this was a routine procedure, and, without any consideration of the shock her words had been to the child, whom she imagined had been prepared for such an eventuality, she knelt down between the bunks and began to pray. Rosie, dazed and shocked by the terrible news this frightening woman had just told her, put her hands together and automatically closed her eyes. Miss Briggs's voice came and went as numbness crept through her small frame, and, gradually, the realisation of what she had just heard began to take shape in her mind. All the time they had been on this ship her mother had got worse and not better, as Papa had told her she would. Mama had gone forever, and she would never see her again. Papa had told her a lie. Why hadn't he told her that Mama was going to die? She would have stayed by her side for as long as possible. She loved Papa, but now it seemed as if he didn't love her anymore.

As these wretched thoughts passed through her mind she felt Miss Briggs shake her, and, on opening her eyes, she screamed in fright at the sight of those impenetrable black eyes, so close to her own. Amy, who had got to her feet and found Rosie in a trance-like state was taken aback at this reaction, and thinking the child was hysterical, slapped her sharply across her cheek. The shock stopped the screaming instantly, and Rosie sat unnaturally still and silent.

"I think you need to get to bed, Rosie," said Amy, somewhat alarmed at the child's staring eyes and deathly white face. "You'll feel warmer there. Lift up your arms and I will undress you."

Rosie lifted up her arms like a lifeless puppet as Amy pulled her clothes over her head and dressed her in her nightgown. Hearing that she was to get into her bed, she clumsily clambered into her bunk and lay down. Amy drew the bedclothes over her and sat down to await John's return. Rosie lay like a statue with the occasional tear rolling down her cheeks. Nothing mattered anymore—nothing at all now that Mama had gone.

When John returned and Amy left, she cried in her father's arms and felt his tears mingle with her own. John brushed them away; he felt cheated and angry with those who had held out hope when there was none, leaving him to bring up a child in an unknown land where their future was uncertain.

"Stop crying now, Rosie," he said gruffly, wiping away her tears. "Your Mama has found peace at last, and we must be glad that her sufferings are over. I am very tired, my dear, and need some rest, and you must try to sleep as well."

Rosie nodded dumbly, and, on closing her eyes, she fell into a deep and dreamless sleep.

CHAPTER 5

"Come along, Rosie, its high time you stopped moping," Amy said sharply as she pulled her young charge along during a brisk walk on deck. "A good walk is what you need to take you out of yourself."

Rosie bit her lip and struggled to go faster. Her father had designated Miss Briggs to be her keeper since Mama had died and her life had turned into a long misery. She viewed her father in a different light these days, although he continued to be kind to her when they were alone together, but such moments were rare. Miss Briggs was always there, smiling at Papa and offering to wash her clothes or seeing to her general well-being. She was so agreeable to Papa, but, once he had gone away, Rosie found her most disagreeable. She had begged her father to let her spend her time with Sarah and Lizzie, or Mrs. Potts, but her father had been quite adamant about it—the Misses Hopkinses had been very kind in the past, and so had Mrs. Potts, but now Miss Briggs was free of her nursing duties and had offered to take care of her, and she was a much more suitable person to look after her. Rosie had got nowhere with him, and her life had become a living nightmare. When she cried out in her sleep, her father had tried to comfort her, but she couldn't be comforted. There was nobody to talk to about the depth of sadness she suffered, and she felt lost and bewildered, becoming more and more withdrawn as the weeks passed.

A gust of wind dislodged Miss Briggs's hat, and she decided, to Rosie's relief, to retire to the comfort of the salon where her father, the

Reverend Briggs, would doubtless be in conversation with John Taylor, and she could join them. Amy's father had proved to be a source of comfort to John since the loss of his wife, and Amy was delighted by their friendship, hoping that it would bring John closer to her.

Sure enough, the two men were sitting at a corner table, engrossed in a book of sketches by the "artist of the goldfields," S.T. Gill, whose recent and popular publication had been lent to Paul Briggs by a returning colonial who had heard of his intended ministry in Ballarat.

As they moved between the tables, Rosie caught sight of Sarah and Alice Potts chatting pleasantly together. Sarah smiled and waved and Rosie escaped from Miss Briggs's restraining hand to join them. Amy let her go without comment, glad to see the back of her for an hour or two.

Snuggled into the crook of Sarah's arm, Rosie listened contentedly to Alice Potts's description of the strange animals and birds that lived on the other side of the world, although she had often wondered if she would ever get there; the sea just went on and on.

"Do you think this ship will ever get to Australia, Mrs. Potts?" she asked.

"Lor' bless us," replied Alice. "I should certainly hope so and before much longer too. I've had more than enough of this journey I can tell you."

Rosie laughed, her cheerful self again for a moment. Sometimes, Mrs. Potts could be so funny. "Tell me something else about Australia, Mrs. Potts, please," she begged, wanting to stay longer in the warmth of her company and the security of Sarah's protective arm.

Alice thought for a moment. "Well, my love, how about the day Potts and I went on the maiden run of the Iron Horse? That was a day to remember, to be sure."

Rosie looked puzzled. "An Iron Horse, Mrs. Potts? What's that?"

"Well," continued Alice, "that was the name the people gave to the first train in Melbourne, and Potts and I were invited to travel in one of the carriages. We were very excited, as you can imagine, and when the great day arrived we dressed in our best clothes because we were to be presented to the lieutenant governor at the banquet afterwards. There were three handsome carriages, and we sat in the last one."

"I wish I could have been there," said Rosie wistfully. "Did the train go fast?"

"Not exactly! Oh, dearie me." Alice chuckled to herself as she thought back to that day of days. "The flags were flying, the brass band was playing, and all the people in Flinders Street were waving and cheering. Then the whistle blew, and the train didn't budge! You never saw so many red faces in all your life! The crowd began to laugh, and we felt such fools sitting there. My, oh my!"

Alice rocked backwards and forwards with mirth, her hand over her laughing mouth.

Rosie began to smile, for the laughter was infectious, and she giggled as she snuggled into the folds of Sarah's dress, her eyes bright with anticipation.

"And then, Mrs. Potts? What happened then?"

"Why, bless you, my love, everyone began to push," continued Alice, delighted to have such a captive audience. "The porters pushed and the policemen pushed—even the directors of the railway company pushed. Then, some of the gentlemen in their top hats and dress suits got out of the carriages to help."

"Did Mr. Potts push too?" asked Rosie.

"But of course, my love. After a while, the train began to move, and, as it gathered speed, poor Arthur had to run to catch up with it, and he only just got back on board before it reached the bridge across the River Yarra."

The picture this conjured up encouraged everyone around them to join in with the laughter. Arthur Potts looked up from his game of backgammon and wondered what all the merriment was about. In his opinion, Alice talked far too much.

Rosie laughed until she cried and then found she couldn't stop. The laughter in the salon died away, and the passengers quietly returned to their previous occupations.

John hastily pushed back his chair and hurried across to his daughter. Lifting her swiftly up into his arms, he carried Rosie to their cabin and let her sob her heart out, hoping a good cry would help her to come to terms with the sorrow she was bottling up inside after losing her mother.

Sarah was near to tears herself, and Alice took out her lace-edged handkerchief and blew her nose vigorously. "It's a blessing she has us here to comfort her," she told Sarah. "I've really taken to the poor child, and that's a fact. How her father can leave her with Amy Briggs I just don't know. Amy couldn't give warmth to any child—she hasn't got it in her, poor thing."

Sarah was sure Alice was right, and, getting up, she made her way to the Taylor's cabin to tell John that she would stay with Rosie for a while. On seeing his daughter look at him with such sad, beseeching eyes, John left the cabin and allowed Sarah to stay with her until the storm of weeping had passed and Rosie had fallen asleep at last.

A few days later, Rosie had to endure a storm of a different kind, for, as the ship rounded the Cape, she was caught in the aftermath of a whirlwind, and, for a few hours that seemed like a lifetime, *The Fair Maid* was lashed by tremendous waves, whipped up by the frenzy of the wind. She had been running under double-reefed topsails, but the force of the gale was so great it carried away her foretopsail and the royals, leaving the deck a mass of broken spars and tangled ropes.

Below decks, Rosie and her father thought that their last hours had come as they lay huddled together on the floor of the swaying cabin. The noise above them was terrifying, added to which, the knowledge that all the skylights and hatch covers had been doubly secured left John with a fear of no escape should the ship founder. They could hear the screams from the terrified passengers and the smashing of crockery and other utensils in the galley as the ship lurched from one side to the other, and Rosie whimpered with fear as she cowered in her father's arms.

Hanging on for dear life, the crew clung to the lifelines rigged along the deck as they struggled to the pumps to relieve their mates, working like madmen to keep the ship afloat. The vessel laboured through the mountainous seas with her stern and bowsprit alternately pointing skyward as she pitched and tossed and was thrown over onto her side with her lee rail under water and then miraculously righted herself.

The wind dropped as the whirlwind lost its impetus and moved away, leaving the ship a battered wreck of broken masts and shredded sails. The spanker sheet was lost, and the mizzen topsail hung forlornly from a spar like a tattered battle flag, but the ship was upright and, after a thorough examination, was proved to be seaworthy.

Below decks, it was awash, for the sea had broken through the weatherboards and flooded the cabins. The Reverend Briggs took off his shoes and stockings and waded through the passageways to bring what comfort he could to the shocked passengers. Rosie clung to him when he appeared, thankful to see a face she recognised after such a terrible experience.

By the next morning, the crew were up aloft, rigging up a temporary main topgallant and royal, and the passengers were able to recover their shattered nerves. A great feeling of comradeship born of shared experience enveloped the ship as people searched out their friends and relatives to find them bruised and battered, but safe.

As soon as it was possible, a service of thanksgiving for their deliverance was held, and Rosie looked around to see if Sarah's friend Ben was standing among the ranks of sailors as rumour had it that some members of the crew had been swept overboard at the height of the storm, and she felt anxious for Sarah's sake; however, her fears were unfounded and she happily pointed Ben out to her father. John gave her leave to tell Sarah the good news after the service, Sarah and Lizzie not being present, as both had sprains and bruises to nurse, and a happy reunion took place between them all.

Now that they had rounded the Cape, the remainder of the long journey proved to be uneventful, and the ship raced through the Roaring Forties with scarcely any sail set, and all spirits were raised at the prospect of new beginnings and getting one's feet back on terra firma. Spyglasses were passed from hand to hand to view the horizon long before a coastline could be distinguished, so anxious were those on board to leave their self-inflicted purgatory. It was at this time, just before they reached land, that John decided to speak to his daughter about his plans for the future and broke the news to her that he had asked Amy Briggs to become his wife.

"She will never be my dearest Mama—never, never," Rosie had raged, stamping her foot with anger and frustration, shocked and appalled at her father's decision.

"No," said John, looking steadfastly out to sea, and angry with her reaction to the news. "No one will ever take the place of your dear Mama, and Miss Briggs understands that, but you are very young still, Rosie, and you need a mother as well as a father."

"I don't! I don't!" insisted Rosie. "I'm big enough now to look after myself and you too, Papa. We don't need anyone else, and anyway I—." She was about to say that she hated Miss Briggs but the look of stern disapproval on her father's face at her distraught outburst made her think better of it, and she dissolved into a flood of tears.

"Whatever has come over you, Rosie," said John, angrily. "Miss Briggs was kindness itself to your poor Mama and has been very good to you. You should feel grateful to her for taking your mother's place, as indeed I am." His mind was in a turmoil, and a niggling doubt worried him as to the wisdom of making such a rapid decision to remarry, although he had chosen a woman of impeccable character to take Julia's place in his life and should have nothing to fear. Amy was much older than Julia had been and in no way could she match her serene beauty or her gentle, loving temperament, but he wasn't marrying for love; he was marrying Amy so his child would have a better start in a new country, and he would have a companion in the long haul ahead. A man of his type was a lonely one without a wife. He had been happily married once, and he didn't doubt that he could make another woman happy, even if he was marrying her for quite different reasons. In time, it was possible that love would come from their relationship, and he, being a patient man, would wait until it happened. Rosie was still suffering from the shock of losing her mother and would come round to it in time. Being an only child, Julia had made such a lot of her, and they had become very close—too close for Rosie to adjust easily. John turned to her and looked down at her tear-stained face.

"Trust me child," he said, kindly. "Papa knows best; believe me. It'll be all right, you'll find."

Rosie was certain without the slightest doubt that her father was quite wrong in his assumption that all would be well, and, seeing Alice Potts in the distance, she ran across the deck to her to weep inconsolably into the depths of her comforting skirts.

Outside the Rip, the pilot had been taken on board, and the passengers congregated on deck to watch the ship's progress through the Heads and into the great bay itself, with its dangerous sandbanks and desolate shores.

Rosie stood at the rail watching the scenery unfold before her with Sarah at her side. The sandy shoreline was broken by low sand dunes dotted with scrub, and, in the far distance, the shape of the misty blue Dandenongs was etched against the cloudless blue sky in the clear bright light. It was very hot, and she found it hard to believe when Sarah told her that tomorrow it would be Christmas Day. Christmas Day never came in the middle of the summer in England, but she had to remember that this wasn't England. This was Australia where she was going to live, and things would be very different from now on—very different if Papa was going to marry Miss Briggs, and she feared that he meant to, although Miss Briggs wasn't coming with them straight away. Papa had told her that Miss Briggs was going to the home of a Mrs. Armstrong first of all, as arranged, but later, when he had a home of his own for them to live in, he would go and fetch Miss Briggs, and then they would be married, and she would come to live with them. Rosie hoped that time would never come and told Sarah so as they watched *The Fair Maid* edge her way cautiously round the bay.

Sarah placed an arm around her. "You worry about today and let tomorrow take care of itself," she said wisely. "I'm going to tell you a secret, Rosie, that no one else knows about yet. How about that! That should cheer you up."

"Haven't you told Lizzie?"

"No, not even Lizzie—you'll be the first to know."

Rosie shivered excitedly. "What is it then?"

"You won't tell anyone, will you Rosie, if I tell you now—not until we land. I shall tell Lizzie in a minute before we get off the boat, but I want to tell you first." Rosie promised faithfully. "Well then—I'm engaged to be married. Can you guess who to? Yes, to Ben! He asked me last night, and I've just said 'yes' to him. I'm so happy Rosie, and sad too, because he will be sailing back to England soon, and I might not see him again for years and years, but he says he will be an officer when he comes back to Australia, and then we will get married, and he will take me back to England with him. Just imagine, one day he might even be the captain of his own ship. Isn't that wonderful—and tomorrow, when he's on leave, he's going to buy me a beautiful ring so everyone will know I'm going to be his wife." Sarah was radiant with happiness as she finished speaking, her thoughts on the future and not on the long wait in between.

"I like Ben," said Rosie, somewhat despondently, "and I hope you'll be very happy with him, and I'm sure Ben will be happy with you too, but I wish that Papa had asked you to marry him first."

Sarah burst into gales of laughter to Rosie's amazement. What was funny about that? Rosie considered she had made a serious statement and certainly not one to be treated with such hilarity.

"Your Papa!" spluttered Sarah, in between her laughter. "You dear funny little thing—what a suggestion!"

"My Papa asked Miss Briggs to marry him, so I can't see why he couldn't have asked you first, Sarah," said Rosie, feeling hurt that Sarah shouldn't consider her father as a suitable candidate for marriage. "I would have liked you for my new Mama—really I would."

Sarah wiped the tears of laughter from her eyes and hugged her. "Dear Rosie," she said, kissing her, "it isn't that I don't like your Papa, it's just that I don't love him, and he certainly doesn't love me. I hardly know him, do I? I know you much better."

"I don't think he loves Miss Briggs," said Rosie, sadly.

Sarah was sure he didn't either, but she could hardly agree with the child. "Well, there are other reasons for people getting married, Rosie—it's something you'll understand when you grow up. Come on, let's find the others. Shall we?"

Most of the passengers were by now gathered in the bows of the ship watching the approach to the harbour. Sarah's happy news soon spread among them and, after the congratulations, to Rosie's delight, she heard that the Potts had generously invited their travelling companions to share Christmas with them before going on their separate ways. She was to stay overnight with Lizzie, Sarah, and Miss Briggs whilst her father and the Reverend Briggs slept at the mission, coming to join them the following day, and, now that Sarah was officially engaged to Midshipman Benjamin Brown, he was invited to come later, once his duties on board were over.

At Williams Town pier, the ship cast anchor and a fleet of small boats rowed out to *The Fair Maid*, crowded with welcoming friends and those seeking business among the passengers. Rosie found herself engulfed in a mass of good-humoured, noisy people, who spoke kindly to her as if they had known her all her life, and the warmth of their welcome made her feel as if she too had returned home to the place where she belonged.

And, once on dry land, as she travelled on the train from the pier to the town in the company of her father and the Reverend Briggs, whilst Mr. Potts and the ladies travelled in an open carriage towards Potts Famous Haberdashery, Rosie felt as if she really had arrived at last.

CHAPTER 6

A cloudless blue sky heralded Christmas morning. Rosie woke early and finding no one else awake, crept downstairs, lured by the tantalising smell of bread baking and the soft voices of the servants as they prepared breakfast. The staff had expected their master and mistress to return about this time and had made considerable preparations for their homecoming but had not expected extra company for Christmas and had no time to stop and talk, so Rosie, with nobody to say she shouldn't, decided to look around for herself.

She opened doors and peeped inside to find large airy rooms opening off the long corridor, which ran the length of the house. French windows in every room led to a continuous veranda where birds sang and fluttered among the hibiscus. At the far end of the corridor was a door with a small pane of glass at the top, and, seeing nobody around, she pushed it open and found she was standing in Potts Famous Haberdashery. It might have been Aladdin's Cave as far as Rosie was concerned, for she had seen nothing like it before in her life. Around the walls were shelves stacked high with cardboard boxes and bolts of brightly patterned cloth, below which stood large mahogany counters, their glass display units gleaming in the bright morning light. On closer inspection, she made out their contents: kid gloves, collars and cuffs, laces and ribbons, and cards of buttons, sparkling like jewels. Upon the counters stood elegant brass stands holding large hats covered with flowers and ribbons and feathers—so pretty she was sorely tempted to try them on. She had almost succumbed to the temptation when she had a feeling that she was being watched, and, on turning round, she saw two small faces pressed to the glass outside, looking in. Rosie felt guilty standing in such a grand place in full view of the street, wearing her nightdress, and made a rapid exit. She had been trespassing, and it was time she got back upstairs before she was missed. She skipped along the corridor to the foot of the stairs and stopped in astonishment as a long line of maids ascended and descended carrying cans of hot water to the bedrooms above.

Arthur Potts's strong tenor could be heard as he serenaded the morning from the warm soapiness of his hip bath, and a voice from one of the bedrooms was enquiring as to her whereabouts. Rosie stayed no longer and fled upstairs before Miss Briggs came looking for her.

A late breakfast was partaken of such gargantuan proportions that Rosie wondered how she would find room for anything else that day. The Potts seemed to think that a breakfast of chops, steaks, eggs and rissoles eaten with hot rolls and butter and washed down with tea and coffee was a perfectly normal way to start the day and nothing out of the ordinary, so she was glad to hear that Christmas dinner was not being served until early evening, to give the guests time for a sightseeing tour of Melbourne.

Before the company set out, Alice Potts took Rosie to see the latest litter of puppies born to her favourite bitch. Alice's dogs were allowed the freedom of the house, and litters of puppies were a common occurrence in the Potts household, as Alice believed in letting nature take its course, which it did all too frequently. Rosie was asked to choose a puppy for herself and joyfully chose a sturdy black dog with large brown eyes. She felt a fellow feeling for him standing all alone while the rest of the litter romped around their mother, and she picked him up immediately.

"May I have this one please, Mrs. Potts?" she asked as the puppy squirmed in her arms, struggling to get free.

"Yes, of course, my dear. As long as your papa agrees," said Alice cheerfully.

John agreed at once, pleased that his daughter had chosen a fine, strong dog which would be useful out in the bush. They had left their own dog behind in England, and John was glad to have another one.

"He looks like the best in the litter," remarked Arthur, who had joined them. "A real little prince isn't he?"

"Our other dog was called Prince," said Rosie as the puppy wriggled free. "Perhaps that could be his name too. What do you think, Papa?" John thought it as good a name as any, and so the matter was settled.

The chaise was at the door, the two horses standing patiently in the heat, flicking their tails to rid themselves of the persistent flies. Sunshades at the ready, the party members took up their seats and set off up the dusty street, past the sapling trees tied by the shopkeepers to their veranda posts to give the street a festive air, and on to the cooler shades by the riverside, leaving Alice behind to supervise the preparations for the evening meal.

On their return, Benjamin joined the party, and the assembled company sat down together to enjoy Christmas dinner in the large, airy dining room. Rosie thought it looked beautiful with the table festooned with garlands of flowers and greenery and loaded down with good things to eat, the sight of which soon brought back her appetite. Arthur Potts sat at the head of the table with an enormous roast turkey in front of him, and, at the opposite end, a roast goose was set before the Reverend Briggs. Glasses were filled with a sparkling wine and toasts were drunk after which the soup was served. On hearing Alice Potts say that it was kangaroo tail soup, Rosie had some doubts about eating it, but, seeing that the plates around her were soon emptied, she finished hers too. Some time elapsed before the meat course was cleared away and replaced by sweets and custards to please all tastes. Applause greeted the pudding as it was brought flaming to the table, born aloft by the cook, to be served with a rich brandy sauce. Rosie tried a little of everything, until she could eat no more—for all Alice's efforts to tempt her—and she sat sleepily in her seat while Arthur toasted one and all with a growing enthusiasm for his task, until Alice decided to call a halt to the proceedings and the ladies, with Rosie in tow, withdrew to the drawing room, leaving the men to their brandy and cigars.

Rosie sat very still beside a small, covered table upon which a wax bouquet of flowers languished beneath a glass dome and gazed around her. A magnificent rosewood grand piano partly covered by a tasselled silk cloth stood in one corner of the room, over which hung a gold-framed portrait of Arthur Potts facing a similar picture of his wife in a less conspicuous position on the opposite wall. Glass-fronted cupboards full of china and knickknacks scattered over every available surface, for Alice was a great collector of things that took her fancy. Rosie would have loved the opportunity to pick up some of the things and examine them more closely, but she felt too overwhelmed to ask.

Having finished the brandy, the gentlemen entered in a good-humoured group, and Arthur, disengaging himself, walked purposefully across the Brussels carpet towards the piano, where he sat down and opened the lid with a flourish. The jolly company gathered around the piano to sing carols together, John's deep bass harmonising with Paul Brigg's thin tenor, whilst Lizzie's pure soprano soared above them all. Rosie found a comfortable settee and curled up on it and was soon asleep, lulled by the music, the warmth and an overfull stomach.

She awoke as the singing died away, and an embarrassing silence had filled the room. Mr. Potts was kissing Lizzie's hand with great fervour, and, looking as if he intended to kiss her too as he put his arm around her waist and began to pull her towards him. Alice Potts called his name sharply, and he came to his senses all of a sudden and excusing himself, left the room with as much dignity as he could muster. Her father and Paul Briggs decided of one accord that it was high time they left for the mission, and Benjamin felt he should be returning to the ship too and would walk back with them. Sarah and Alice Potts went to see them off, and Miss Briggs came to put her to bed and hustled her off upstairs. In her bemused state, Rosie wondered why there was so much activity all of a sudden, but it seemed to have had something to do with Mr. Potts and his liking for Lizzie which had upset everybody.

Once in bed, sleep soon overtook her and with the remaining company deciding to retire early too the only sounds to be heard over Potts Famous Haberdashery were the creaking of bedsprings and the loud snores of Arthur Potts as he slept off the effects of having wined and dined too liberally.

Rosie awoke late the following morning to find she was alone. Miss Briggs, who had shared her bedroom, was gone, and, in Sarah's and Lizzie's room, the beds had already been stripped of their sheets. She quickly splashed her hands and face with cold water from the jug on the washstand and pulled on her clothes. Voices from below wafted up to her, and she could just make out Alice Potts's voice as she issued instructions in a brisk, business-like way.

"There's no time to lose, Arthur," Rosie heard her say. "We have been away too long, and there's work to be done. Today, we must interview the girls for the workroom and start cutting out the patterns. The silk bales are being unloaded today and by tomorrow we must have the cutting tables set out ready for work to begin. After all our work in the past to make this into a thriving business, we must take care that we keep up our output."

There was a long pause, and then Mr. Potts spoke. "Have the Miss Hopkins moved out yet, my dear?'" he asked, in an offhand way, as if he had no real interest in their whereabouts.

"Yes, they have," replied Alice, sharply, "and right now, Arthur, I would be glad if you would turn your mind to more important matters."

Mr. Potts cleared his throat nervously. "Just as you say, my dear," he replied, meekly chastened by his wife's reproving manner.

Rosie ran downstairs to meet Alice coming along the corridor with a list in her hand. "Ah, there you are, my dear," she said, cheerfully. "You'll find your breakfast in the kitchen this morning, Rosie. Miss Briggs has just left to see her father off on the Ballarat coach and will be coming back here with your Papa to collect you, so don't you be long now."

"Where are Lizzie and Sarah?" asked Rosie, wondering what had become of them.

"They've been gone a long time, my love. You've overslept, but no matter; the Miss Hopkins are settling into their new accommodation right now but intend to see you before you leave with your Papa—and now I must go too—I have a lot to see to today."

Alice bustled off as Rosie made her way to the kitchen. She had been up betimes that morning making sure that all was prepared for Lizzie and Sarah to move out before Arthur was awake. She was well aware of his fondness for the ladies and normally turned a blind eye to his little indiscretions, but this was a different matter. She needed Lizzie's help in building up the new side to their business. The girl had a natural flair for fashion and between them the two sisters were an invaluable asset. She simply couldn't afford to lose Lizzie and would need to keep a sharp eye on Arthur from now on to see he had no opportunities for anything more than a harmless flirtation. Once work started in earnest, there would be no time for anything else, and a good thing too.

Later that morning, John and Amy arrived in a hired gig to collect Rosie on their way to Heidelberg. Rosie would have preferred to remain where she was and to play with the puppies but her father had other ideas. He had the task of persuading Mrs. Armstrong, Amy's employer, to release her from her position of companion as soon as possible now they were to be married, and he hoped that Rosie's presence would lend weight to his request. Rosie sat uncomfortably between them both and longed for the interview to be over and for Miss Briggs to be gone for good. She longed to get started on the last lap of her journey and to see the new home Papa was taking her to at a place called Clay Cross. Going to Heidelberg with Miss Briggs was another journey, and Rosie was tired of journeys.

At Heidelberg, they met with a cool reception. The bishop's sister had not expected her new companion to be accompanied by a future husband and his child and left them in no doubt as to her feelings on the matter. Amy Briggs was certainly a plain spinster in her middle years and no doubt she was everything that Mrs. Armstrong had requested her brother's secretary to look out for but she had enough about her to attract a marriageable man; quite a good looking decently spoken man too, for one of the working classes. Rosie watched keenly as Mrs. Armstrong lifted up her lorgnette to peer closely at her and her father. The lorgnette magnified her eye and was quite the strangest thing that Rosie had ever seen. There was something about Mrs. Armstrong that reminded her of Miss Briggs—perhaps it was her stern unyielding look—Rosie knew instinctively that she didn't like Mrs. Armstrong, who appeared to feel the same way about her and her father. John Taylor, looking acutely uncomfortable, asked Mrs. Armstrong if Miss Briggs could leave her employ in six month's time when she would have paid off her passage money, but Mrs. Armstrong had argued about that and wanted Miss Briggs to stay with her for a whole year. Rosie was glad to hear that, but her father became very angry at such a suggestion.

"I have a young daughter, ma'am, who needs a mother. A year is too long to wait," he said with feeling, and Rosie had drawn closer to him, a little afraid to hear the hostility in her father's voice as he argued with this formidable stranger.

"That is your business, sir, and none of mine," was the haughty reply. "You should have thought of that before you proposed marriage to Miss Briggs."

John Taylor flushed a deep red, too angry and too proud to continue to converse with such an insufferable woman. If he had possessed sufficient money to pay off Amy's passage he would have done so on the spot to release her from her bondage, but he needed all he had to set them up for the future, and Amy would have to serve her time with Mrs. Armstrong.

Rosie could see her father's dilemma and Miss Brigg's dismay once her situation became apparent and felt a twinge of sympathy. She would have hated to have had to live with Mrs. Armstrong herself, and Miss Briggs looked upset at the thought of having to do so, and that made her seem a little more human for once. It appeared that they were dismissed as Mrs. Armstrong rang for a servant to take Miss Briggs's bags to her room and then turned towards the door.

"She may leave on the first day of July, and has no salary in the meantime," announced Mrs. Armstrong in an icy tone of voice, as she conceded to John's original request. "I have no wish to have a person in my employ who bears a grudge—that would be most unpleasant." And, with a rustle of her black silk taffeta skirts, she was gone.

Rosie breathed a sigh of relief and made for the door, anxious to be on her way. Her father bade a brief farewell to his future wife, promising to return for her on the appointed day, and they gladly left the premises to return to the Potts establishment.

"What a woman!" remarked John bitterly as the gig made its way from the outskirts to the city centre. "Your stepmother will have a hard time of it there. Poor Amy—her life won't be worth living in that household."

This was the first time that Rosie had thought of Miss Briggs as her stepmother, and the word sent shivers down her spine. She made no reply to her father and for the rest of the journey she sat, hoping against hope that no such thing would ever happen.

When the gig drew up outside the store, the whole company was waiting to say good-bye. Alice had a travelling basket in one hand, from which Prince could be heard objecting to his confined quarters, and provisions for their journey in the other. John collected their baggage as Rosie went round to everybody in turn to be kissed and hugged, with promises from them all to see her again in six months time when her father returned to marry Miss Briggs.

Lizzie and Sarah accompanied them to the depot to see them off, and once on board one of Cobb and Co.'s coaches, Rosie leaned out of the window and waved until she could see them no longer, then with Prince on her lap she settled down for the long dusty journey to Clay Cross.

PART TWO

Clay Cross

1861–1868

CHAPTER 7

Great clouds of red dust infiltrated the closed windows of the coach, choking the occupants and parching their throats as they were lurched and jolted from side to side when the coach swerved to avoid the obstacles and potholes along the iron hard surface of the road. The stuffy, cramped interior made Rosie's head ache, and she felt uncomfortably sick until, just as she had given up hope of ever arriving at their destination, Cobb's coach clattered to a standstill in the town square. Rosie shakily emerged to feel the relief of a slight breeze pass across her hot, sticky face and took stock of the place that was to be her new home.

The exhausted horses stood with bowed heads and shivering flanks as the sweat poured off them, waiting for the passengers to retrieve their baggage before being driven away to the stables. Standing beside her father in this large empty place, she felt as lost as she might have done had they landed on the moon. Three of the widest roads she had ever seen radiated from the square, along which straggled a few sleepy weather-boarded houses and stores with raised wooden walkways roofed over to give some protection from the sun. A little further down the main street stood a brick-fronted hotel to which most of their fellow travellers had made their way. The town seemed dead and deserted apart from a woman leaning against the door frame of a small store, watching the coach and its passengers. She smiled in their direction, hoping they might need provisions, for trade had been slack since the drought. Seeing the woman standing there, and her being the only living thing in sight, John picked up their few belongings, and, with Rosie dragging her feet behind him, they made their way across the square to ask for directions.

"The saw mill is some way from here," said the woman, her Scots accent quite unmistakeable. "Andrew, my youngest boy is somewhere around. I'll get him to find Mr. Hammond while you take a rest—why, the poor bairn is near to dropping. Sit you both down while I give him a call."

Rosie sank thankfully onto one of the chairs placed in the shade of the doorway and blinked sleepily in the bright sunlight. She had almost fallen asleep when the woman returned with two large cups of tea and a plate of scones.

"You'll be needing these, I'm thinking," she said, pleasantly. "Now you rest while Andrew's gone. He'll be a wee while yet."

As they drank the welcome cups of tea, she told them her name was Beth Macdonald and that she ran the store with the help of her three sons, when they were around. John told her about the new wharf that was to be built and the job he had been promised at the saw mill. Beth listened to him intently when he mentioned the wharf, her bright blue eyes alight with interest.

"Och, I hope you're right, for this summer has been the worst I can remember. Years ago, this was a good place to live. It was a crossing place for the mobs of cattle and people began to settle here. Trade was good then, but now it's bad—really bad." She picked up some crotchet work as she spoke, and Rosie watched her busy fingers deftly twisting the cotton through the tiny loops, in the same way she had watched her mother work with her thread after the day's work was done.

"On the squatting stations," continued Beth, "great numbers of sheep and cattle have died of the drought and that has meant less money for everyone. If a bigger wharf is to be built here it will bring in the river trade and be the saving of us all. We have heard vague rumours, but not until today have I met anyone who could speak with any certainty about it."

John smiled wistfully. "Aye, and to think I've come from the other side of the world to tell you. It's a strange world we live in, to be sure."

He turned away and looked through the open door of the store, and from where he sat he could see that Mrs. Macdonald stocked everything from ironmongery to groceries. He had certainly come to the right place.

"While we are waiting for your son to return perhaps I could look around. I shall be needing some tools and provisions to start with, and you appear to stock most things."

His words were music to Beth's ears, and she hurried inside to see to her new customers' requirements while Rosie cuddled Prince on her lap, feeding him alternatively with tea from her saucer and pieces of scone. Delighted by the amount of money John had spent in her store, Beth insisted that her three sons should carry all their purchases to their new home in return for their custom, for it was unheard of for a customer in these hard times not to ask for credit.

When Andrew returned, he was joined by his two brothers, Malcolm and Rory, and the party set off along the river path to find the workman's cottage that had been allotted to John and his family. About a mile upstream, they came to the edge of the forest where a rough slab building stood amid the scrub. Rosie stared at it in disbelief. Surely this tumbled down ruin wasn't going to be their home! Some of the horizontal slabs which had formed the walls had come adrift from their fixings in the vertical posts, and the corrugated iron roof had rusted into holes. Compared to this derelict shack their estate cottage had been a palace, and for the first time since his wife's death, John was glad she was not with him. It would have broken her heart to have seen it.

Malcolm, the eldest boy, emerged from the broken doorway. "It's not too bad," he remarked cheerfully. "This was old man Parker's place—went out of his mind before he died and shot off his gun at anything that moved. Folks just kept away. No one saw him around for a couple of months until a timber cutter found him, stone cold dead in the undergrowth. Reckon he stumbled and shot himself, poor ol' digger."

Rosie and her father listened to this narrative, becoming more apprehensive every second until John decided to look around for himself. The shack provided no protection from the heat or the flies, although he could see that the framework was still sound. A slab table with two long seats on either side, built onto stakes driven into the ground, furnished the first room. In the adjoining room, a roughly constructed bed leaned drunkenly against one wall, covered by leaves and dust blown in from the half open door. Packing cases were strewn over the floor, their unsavoury contents spilling out into the yard beyond. Kicking the litter to one side, John strode outside. A lean-to shed containing a rusty range had been joined roughly onto the back of the building, and above it all there rose a solid, red mud brick chimney, tall enough to be seen for miles around.

"At least that won't fall down," muttered John to himself, feeling a little more hopeful about making the place habitable.

"Much better than a bush humpie," remarked Malcolm, who had noted his reactions. "I don't mind giving you a hand with it. There's many a worse place than this in the forest with whole families living in them. We'll soon have it shipshape."

Somewhat humbled by this remark, John turned to the boy. "Thank you, lad, I'd appreciate your help. Would you bring something suitable to mend the roof with when you come? I'll pay for whatever's necessary, of course."

"Mr. Hammond said you can take any wood you need from the forest," chipped in Andrew, anxious to be a part of this new venture despite his young age. "There are some felled trees not far from here. I'll show you where to find them tomorrow." John shook each boy by the hand, a politeness which caused them much amusement as they left. Rosie watched them as they ran laughing through the scrub, three red-haired urchins whom she would be meeting again soon.

Her father called to her to collect some of the brushwood which littered the scrub as he made his way towards the small creek behind the homestead where he filled his newly acquired billycan. Then, as the billy boiled on the old range he tacked some of the loose slabs roughly back into place and propped the broken door up against its frame. Rosie unpacked the new china cups and laid the table as her father swept out the worst of the rubbish and placed one of the mattresses which Beth Macdonald had advised him to buy onto the dirt floor. Rosie was to sleep on the other one on the wooden base which had once served as a bed—she would be safer from creeping things on a raised surface.

They ate a simple supper by the light of a candle, around which a cloud of moths fluttered and danced, floating down like petals from the holes in the roof. The meal over, Rosie took off her tight, button boots and her stockings and, apart from her dress, she kept the rest of her clothes on. Prince jumped up and snuggled down beside her, and, within a few minutes, they were both asleep. Her father sat for some time, his head in his hands, watching the moths dropping helplessly onto the table in front of him. He was scarcely aware of them as he thought of his promise to Amy only a few days ago. He could never expect her to live here in such primitive surroundings in this wilderness. He was a man of his word and intended to keep his promise to return for her in six months time, but it would be difficult. Maybe he could earn enough money at the saw mill to buy a block of land and build his own house—he would have to think about that possibility. In the meantime, he would need to make this shack habitable and construct some decent pieces of furniture for their use.

Lifting up his head, John stretched his weary limbs. Tomorrow was another day, and things might look different then, but right now he needed some rest. Blowing out the flickering candle he lay down on his straw mattress and fell into a deep and dreamless sleep.

As the days grew into weeks, the strange sounds emanating from the forest ceased to worry Rosie, and she became unaware of them, accepting them as part of this strange new country. Each morning, she was awakened by the bubbling call of the magpies and ran down to the fast disappearing creek to wash her face before beginning her household tasks. These were soon dispensed with, and then the rest of the day was hers to enjoy as she wished. Left to her own devices after her father's early departure for the sawmill, she had become careless of her appearance. Her curls had grown long and straggly and were tied back with a grubby, faded ribbon, and her petticoat trailed untidily below the hem of her dress. The only people she saw were the Macdonalds, and the boys never noticed what she looked like, although their mother took note but said nothing. Her father had ceased to worry about her; she was happy playing with Prince out in the bush or fishing with the Macdonald boys, and he was too busy to bother anyway. After a long day at the mill, he worked late into the night at his carpentry and had little time for anything else. He had warned Rosie not to wander too far into the forest, through which the creek meandered, and expected her to be sensible enough not to do so— she was old enough to look after herself now.

Country born and bred, Rosie felt no fear of wild places, and, full of childish curiosity, she had often followed the trickle of water in the creek over the sun-baked mud to find pools deep within the green, silvery coolness of the gum trees where the ibis nested and the marsh wattle grew in all its honeyed sweetness. The heat was bearable here, and Prince found plenty to amuse himself with, sniffing out the basking lizards and disturbing a sleepy wombat from its daytime rest. She was always careful to avoid any snake that crossed her path and kept to the muddy creek where she was less likely to step on the large bull ants and spiders that inhabited the leafy undergrowth.

One day, she decided to follow a small branch of the creek which she had not as yet explored. Here, the blossoms hung down in profusion close enough for her to pick, and she gathered armfuls of them to decorate the homestead on her return. A painted honeyeater flew ahead of her, darting from branch to branch, luring her on with his clear, shrill song. As the sun rose higher in the heavens, so Rosie ventured deeper and deeper into the forest until the creek dried up altogether, and she found herself standing on the edge of what had been a small waterfall. A deep pool lay before her surrounded by eucalypts, and, in its stagnant water, she could see the twisted reflections of their branches and the birds among the foliage. The tinkling sound of the unseen bell birds high in the trees and the fluttering of tiny finches at the water's edge made her feel less alone.

As she stood watching, a pair of black swans finished their preening and stepped delicately into the water, gliding gently across its dark surface. Rosie made no sound as if she too could sense the secret stillness of this long forgotten place. Beyond the pool, the trees thinned out, and, between their peeling trunks, she glimpsed a shimmer of water in the distance. Perhaps she had arrived at the next bend in the river; she would just go that far and then turn back, or Papa would miss her on his return home. She picked Prince up in her arms so as not to disturb the peaceful swans and pushed her way through the tangled undergrowth and into a clearing. An old ruined chimney stack stood starkly among the weeds with little else to show where the original building had stood. Rosie put Prince down and traced the outline of the building with her feet. Prince scratched among the stones, whimpering and whining as he followed her. Rosie caught his feeling of unease and turned her steps towards the protection of the trees. It was then that she realised she was not alone.

Two naked aborigines in a dugout canoe were watching her silently from the river. Fear gripped Rosie, and she froze in her tracks. She had seen plenty of blacks before in Clay Cross but they had appeared harmless enough hanging around the main street dressed in cast-off clothing, hoping to sell an opossum rug or a string of fish. They lived on the opposite bank and never bothered the inhabitants by their presence, but these men were different. Their painted faces and bodies and the sinister silence as they looked at her terrified her. Suddenly, both men began to paddle upstream, and the canoe disappeared from sight. Rosie dropped her flowers and, with Prince at her heels, fled through the trees, startling the birds in her flight. Struggling up the dry path of the waterfall, she reached the dead creek above and ran like a crazed creature, her breath coming in great sobbing gasps as she painfully retraced her steps towards home and safety.

The next morning, she awoke late and set off in haste to the store to collect the bread she had forgotten the day before. She had been too frightened and too exhausted on her return home to tell her father what she had seen, as he had been most displeased to find the bread crock empty on his return from work. Her own efforts at baking had been disastrous despite Beth's kindly advice—the ancient stove became too hot and burnt the bread black, or the fire refused to draw satisfactorily and the soggy lumps of dough had to be thrown into the yard to feed the ever-hungry magpies. She hated the rusty monster and only used it out of necessity. Beth had taken pity on her and now baked the Taylor's weekly supply of bread when she baked her own, much to Rosie's relief.

At the back of the store, Beth was busy ironing before the heat became too intense for such an activity. Seeing Rosie, she called to her to come through into the kitchen and pointed to the loaves wrapped up on the table.

"There you are, lass, all ready for you. They've been sitting there waiting for you to collect them since yesterday."

Rosie stood beside the table twisting her fingers together, nervously. There was something she wanted to ask Mrs. Macdonald if she had time to listen. Rosie found her a comfortable person to be with, although Mrs. Macdonald was always busy doing something. She was a small person with bright blue eyes and auburn hair which was turning grey at the temples—a chirpy little bird of a woman with a dour sense of humour and a fund of common sense. She could see that Rosie had something on her mind and waited for her to speak in her own good time. Poor wee thing, living in the middle of nowhere with no mother to care for her, she was only too pleased to help when asked.

"Mrs. Macdonald," began Rosie hesitantly, "who used to live in the homestead on the other side of the forest? You know, the one that's fallen down near the bend in the river."

Beth stood stock still with the flat iron poised in midair. "Dear God, lassie, you've ne'er been to that awful place? Why, it's almost ten miles from here up river. How did you get there, for goodness sake?"

"I walked there with Prince," replied Rosie. "We found it at the end of the creek when we were exploring."

"Did you indeed," said Beth, replacing the iron on the range to reheat, and sitting down in her rocking chair for a few moments. "And what did you see when you got there, may I ask?"

"Well, nothing really—just an old chimney. It was just that it was such a lonely place, and two blacks in a canoe frightened me. They had spears and painted patterns on their bodies. They went away when they saw me, and Prince and I ran home as fast as we could."

"My dear child, you went to a place where nobody ever goes," said Beth, drawing Rosie towards her. "Not even the bravest timber cutter will go there. They say it is haunted by the ghosts of the family who once lived there, for a dreadful thing happened to the people in that homestead."

Rosie shivered, reliving her fear. "What happened there, Mrs. Macdonald? Please tell me."

"Well, I don't want to tell you," began Beth, speaking slowly and giving the matter some thought, "but I will because it might stop you from wandering so far away. A long time ago, when I was a young woman, a family of squatters lived there. They had a number of young calves they wanted to keep nearer the homestead where the pasture was better and had just begun to clear part of the land on the edge of the forest to make more room for their stock without realising that by doing so they were leaving their homestead and their cattle in full view of the river. One evening as they were at supper, a large party of natives crept up from the river to steal their calves. The owner took up his gun when he heard a noise in the yard but he was killed in the doorway and the rest of the family was speared to death, a young girl amongst them. It was some time before the news of the tragedy reached Clay Cross, and by then the natives responsible for the murder of those poor people had travelled on, taking their cattle with them. They have never been found, but it made the people who lived out in the bush more careful."

"Would those blacks have killed me too?" asked Rosie, paling at the thought.

"No, lass," replied Beth. "They were hunters I would imagine, no doubt searching for grey kangaroos upstream. Malcolm told me he saw a large group of them browsing near the river recently—the drought brings them out of the forest. The dangers there are more likely to be unseen ones. You could be bitten or stung and nobody around to help you. Does your Papa know you wander alone in the forest?"

"Oh, no—please don't tell Papa, Mrs. Macdonald, he will be so angry with me."

"Very well," sighed Beth, resuming her work, "but I shall suggest to your Papa when he comes in to pay his bill at the end of the week that it's high time you started school. On Monday, I will send Rory to collect you if your father agrees, so you be ready for him. And, in the meantime I'll wash and starch that pinafore you're wearing and Rory can bring it with him when he comes to fetch you. Off with you now—I'm busy today—and no more exploring mind."

Rosie walked home sadly, the bread wrapped in a clean white cloth tucked safely under her arm. It was all her own fault. Papa had been right to warn her about the dangers of wandering too far in the forest, and she should have listened to him. He had mentioned school before but he had been too busy to do anything about enrolling her. She could read and write well enough and hated the thought of being shut inside a stuffy schoolroom when she could be playing with Prince down by the river. She idly picked up a stick and threw it for Prince to fetch and then chased along the path after him. Monday was almost a week away, and her father might not agree with Mrs. Macdonald, although she feared that he would.

Rosie was to be disappointed, for her father considered Beth's suggestion to be a sensible one and something he should have seen to weeks ago. School would certainly keep her out of mischief and would give her the opportunity to meet other children of her own age. Beth had been a great help to him in many ways, always cheerful, whatever her own difficulties, and there had been plenty from what she had told him.

She had been married to a good, hard-working Scot like herself, who had opened a general store for prospectors en route to the goldfields. As trade slackened off, they had moved to Clay Cross where a small community was developing close to the river crossing. The years of consistent drought had almost put an end to that venture, so her man had become a prospector himself. For seven years, she had heard nothing of his whereabouts and had given up all hope of his return. The store provided a small living for herself and her boys and was more than most women had who had lost the breadwinner in the family. Her eldest son, Malcolm, was sixteen and helped to load the outrigger barges, and with him in regular employment she had found it easier to keep her family going. John admired her grit and determination, and above all, her kindness to his daughter.

That evening, he wrote to Amy, feeling it only fair to warn her of the difficulties that faced a woman in the outback, and, as he wrote, his thoughts kept turning to Beth. She could cope, but would Amy?

> "*My dear Amy,*" he wrote. "*Before I bring you here as my wife I feel I should tell you something about Clay Cross, as compared to your lifestyle in Melbourne there is very little to offer you and should you wish to change your mind I shall not hold you to your promise.*
>
> "*The town consists of a wide main street and two other roads, one of which borders the river and leads to the sawmill. A general store, an ironmongers and a small drapery provide for our essential needs. There is an imposing brick-fronted hotel in the main street and various hostelries and drinking houses to cater for the travellers passing through and the local populace. Regrettably, there is much drunkenness in the town, which is not only confined to the residents but includes the blacks who live across the river when they can get hold of strong liquor, and for this reason I hope eventually to purchase a block of land away from the town. Most of the homesteads are poorly constructed shacks built along the riverfront and scattered among the bush.*

> *"The town has a large square with the prospect of further development once the wharf is constructed. There is a small school which Rosie is to attend, and this is also used for the occasional service and as a meeting place for the townspeople.*
>
> *"You need not feel the slightest concern about my deep regard for you, but I must beg you Amy to give our forthcoming marriage your deepest consideration before our total commitment to each other—"*

And so John ended his letter, feeling he had been both truthful and considerate towards his intended wife, without realising that his growing attachment to Beth Macdonald might have had something to do with the somewhat pessimistic tone of his letter.

Rosie watched him seal down the envelope and guessed correctly that her father had been writing to Amy Briggs. She had almost managed to forget that one day Miss Briggs would be marrying her father and coming to live in Clay Cross. It didn't bear thinking about.

A month later, John received Amy's reply. She had no wish to stay in her present position, and, without a reference from Mrs. Armstrong, she had no hope of obtaining another. She had heard that the bush could be beautiful, especially after the rain, and as John was already making plans to build them a good home away from any unpleasantness, she could see no reason to change anything. She was expecting John to return to Melbourne as arranged and looked forward to their life together in Clay Cross.

John folded up her letter thoughtfully and turned to Rosie.

"Your stepmother is looking forward to coming to live here," he said shortly.

Rosie looked miserable at the news. She was not looking forward to that day herself, and her father looked none too happy about it either.

CHAPTER 8

A pair of galahs perching on the yard fence tilted their heads to one side and watched Rosie through their heavy grey eyelids as she made her preparations for school. Suddenly, they took off, their pink and grey plumage flashing across the bright blue sky. Rory was calling her from the river path.

"Rose-ee. Rose –ee. Hurry up—we shall be late."

Rosie sighed and gathered up her belongings. She hated these school mornings, but Papa had insisted on her attendance, and his wishes had to be obeyed. Catching hold of Prince, she tied him to the doorpost where he could lie in the shade until her return and ran to meet Rory.

Of all the Macdonald boys, she liked him the best. Unknown to Rosie, her discovery of the haunted homestead had won her his undying admiration. His mother had told him that Rosie had been in great danger, and, had the natives not thought her a spirit, anything could have happened to her. She had made no fuss about the incident, which to Rory's way of thinking placed her in a different category from the other girls he knew. He paid her the greatest compliment by treating her as if she was a boy, and Rosie was happy to live up to his expectations of her as a friend.

"How about a swim in the lagoon after school?" he asked as she reached him.

"Can't swim yet," replied Rosie cheerfully.

"Can't swim!" retorted Rory derisively. "About time you could then."

"I'll come if you teach me," laughed Rosie as she chased off with Rory in close pursuit.

They arrived at school in the best of spirits to be met with a stern rebuke from the sallow-faced schoolmaster for their lateness. Suitably chastened, they slid into their seats, and the morning lesson began.

Sitting on the bench behind Rosie, Mary Ann Pendle smirked with self-satisfaction on hearing her archenemy chastised. The smirk rapidly changed into one of cloying sweetness as she caught Rory's eye. Before this girl had joined the class, Mary Ann had considered Rory as her chosen mate. Being the only child of the owner of the Clay Cross Hotel, she was used to having her own way and did not take kindly to the presence of a contender for Rory's affections. Rosie's appearance on the scene had resulted in a spate of spiteful outbursts from the spoilt Miss Pendle and her group of adoring friends. To make matters worse, she found herself far below Rosie's academic standard, and this was an added thorn in her side. In fact, Mary Ann's nose had been firmly put out of joint, and she made sure that Rosie suffered for it.

Today, Rosie longed for the end of school to arrive more than usual and the prospect of the cool water of the lagoon helped to lessen her annoyance as her hair was pulled roughly from behind by Mary Ann.

Free at last, she and Rory whooped and shouted along the river path until the lagoon was reached. Here, Rory stripped naked and stood with his arms outstretched and his wiry young body poised on the edge, ready to dive into the red-brown depths below. Rosie watched him, fascinated by the sight of his nakedness, and then he was gone, only to appear a few seconds later, laughing as he surfaced in the middle of the pool.

"Come on, Rosie. What are you waiting for? Get your clothes off and come on in."

As she watched him swim to the far bank, turning and twisting like an eel, Rosie felt a great urge to join him and began to remove her clothing. Stripped to her chemise and bloomers she stepped tentatively into the muddy water.

"Are there any snakes here, Rory?" she called out, nervously.

Rory swam across to her. "Of course not. I wouldn't swim here if there were, now would I? The tigers get swept downstream when the river floods but there aren't any at this time of the year—and, anyway, you can always see them because they swim with their heads sticking out of the water—like this—see!"

Rosie laughed at his antics, but she looked round apprehensively just the same. She certainly couldn't see any tigers or anything resembling a wild animal and supposed he was just teasing her. Feeling a little more confident, she waded out until the water came up to her waist and allowed Rory to support her, kicking out her legs on his instructions. A wonderful feeling of freedom swept over her. Her hair drifted round her face like strands of water weed, and she felt refreshed, and, for the first time for weeks, really clean.

The swimming lesson over, the two children clambered out onto the bank and lay in the sun to dry.

"What did you have to wear those silly girl's clothes for?" asked Rory. "You can't swim properly with them on." Rosie smiled as she stared up into the great upturned bowl of the sky. "It's different for me," she said, lazily. "I'm a girl. Boys can do what they like but girls can't. I don't think it's fair."

"Of course it's fair," argued Rory, pulling on his strides. "Boys are—well—superior to girls."

Rosie flushed with indignation. She couldn't let that pass.

"Witchu, witchu, will little breeches fit you," she teased, as she had heard the children call out in the schoolyard when they wanted to poke fun at someone.

"You're daft sometimes, Rosie," said Rory hotly. "If you say stupid things like that I shan't teach you to swim anymore, so there!"

Picking up his shirt, he stalked off towards home without a backward glance in her direction. Girls were all the same when you got to know them, he thought bitterly.

Hastily collecting her shoes and stockings, Rosie tore after him.

"See you tomorrow then, Rory—please," she begged.

Rory walked on, his pride somewhat soothed as she tagged along miserably behind him. "I'll think about it," he answered vaguely.

Reaching the river path where they parted company, he called out cheekily, "Put your shoes on or you might tread on something as nasty as yourself."

Rosie threw a shoe at his retreating back and missed. His cheerful grin and parting salute left her in no doubt as to his forgiveness, and she continued on her way, happily whistling through her teeth the way Rory did. She would be more careful in future, for she wouldn't lose his friendship for anything in the world. He wasn't called "Hothead" at school for nothing, his flaming red hair matched his quick temper as many a boy with a bloody nose had discovered. That she had now seen Rory naked must make a difference to their relationship. He would never have allowed that if she hadn't been someone special. Mary Ann could do and say what she liked, for Rosie felt sure she had never been honoured in that particular way. For a few moments, a cloud blotted out the sun and its shadow crossed the path in front of her. A few stray drops of rain began to fall, rippling the smooth surface of the lagoon, and Rosie quickened her steps towards home.

With the coming of the rain, the old homestead rapidly became uninhabitable. John had mended the roof but had not taken into account the force of such a tropical deluge. For weeks, the rain continued, beating an ear-splitting tattoo on the iron roof and trickling down the inside walls in a steady stream. There was no time for school now; Rosie had scarcely a minute's peace emptying the buckets, bowls, and jugs placed beneath the countless leaks. With no dry kindling for the range, they were unable to cook or boil the billy, and John soon realised they would have to move elsewhere. Struggling along the rapidly flooding path, they carried as many of their belongings as they could manage to Beth's homestead, and she found room for them, partitioning off a corner of the storeroom until the rain lessened. In return for her shelter, John made new shelves for the shop and cupboards for the dried fruit and sugar, for the store was plagued by mice and the occasional rat. Rosie spent sleepless nights listening to the scratching and squeaking around her and longed for the rain to stop. When at last it eased off, they returned to their home to sweep away the remains of the water and to dry out the new furniture. As soon as he could, John made arrangements to purchase a block of land on the outskirts of the town and set to work to construct a decent dwelling. His timber-framed cottage was much admired for its workmanship and design by those who came to give a helping hand or as was more often the case, their advice.

On the riverside of his new home, he placed a covered veranda and carved a rocking chair to stand under the eaves. From here, Amy would see the silver green river gums on the opposite bank of the Murray and could watch the paddle steamers as they plied their way upstream. No one in Clay Cross had such a view, and he could hardly wait to show her. Inside, there were two bedrooms and a parlour which boasted the most delicately carved furniture for miles around. The kitchen was built onto the back with plenty of room for the family's everyday use and had fitted wooden cupboards on either side of the heavy black range. Outside in the yard stood a separate brick-built wash house with the bread oven set into the wall. No longer would Beth have the added burden of baking their daily bread once Amy arrived. The final luxury was a small, brick-built dunny situated close to the river and some distance from their living quarters. John viewed it all with considerable pride and, on its completion, wrote to Amy describing her new home in glowing terms and giving her the date of his expected arrival in Melbourne. She would need to make the arrangements for their wedding as he intended to spend as little time as possible in the city.

Mr. Hammond had promised him a better job on his return from Melbourne with his bride. No longer would he be working in the dust of the sawmill, but with a mate he would fell the red gums in the forest during the hot season and then pole them out by pontoon after the floods, ready for the outrigger barges to carry them downstream to the mill. Once the great wharf was under construction, he hoped to find employment there as a carpenter; he much preferred working outside, and now he had the opportunity to do so. His prospects were good, and, with Amy at his side to care for all the domestic matters, they would soon be one happy family, or so he must hope.

John tried to show a cheerful countenance as he and Rosie boarded Cobb's coach for the return journey to Melbourne. The last six months had flown past, and he had found it difficult to complete the homestead in time despite the simplicity of its design and would not have done so without the cooperation of his work mates, who gave so willingly of their time, it being the custom in small communities to help one's neighbour if he needed it as an insurance against one's own needs in times of hardship.

As a result, he had had little time to spare for corresponding with Amy, but the few letters which had passed between them had left him in no doubt as to her wish to marry him. In fact, she had entreated him to return for her as promised, and John had wondered whether her need to leave her employer was of greater importance than her desire to live with him in Clay Cross. Whatever the reason, he felt honour bound to return and make her his wife. His feelings for Beth Macdonald had begun to bother him, but once he was married he hoped things would fall into perspective. He had been lonely, and so had Beth, and that had been the reason for him to lose sight of his promise to Amy on a few occasions. Living so close together during the flood had meant a change in their relationship, and, on some occasions, when the children were asleep they had shared the same bed for a brief time, making his return to Melbourne even more difficult. Beth had known all along that he intended to keep his promise to Amy and made no fuss about it, although it broke her heart to see him so saddened.

Rosie dreaded the journey back herself and only the fact that she was to see Sarah and Lizzie again could bring a wan smile to her face. Her father had told her that she would not be seeing dear Mrs. Potts again because Mrs. Potts was no longer there. Miss Briggs had written to tell him that she had gone to heaven to be with Mama a few months after they had left. She had had a growth that neither the doctors in England or Melbourne could cure. Rosie had wanted to know why God left the worst people behind but her father had been unable to give her a satisfactory answer, and she had to accept that as far as God was concerned people like Miss Briggs still had work to do on earth, which Rosie considered unfortunate for herself. Miss Briggs had been to visit Mrs. Potts before she died, and, apart from wanting to see her, she had also wanted to return the shawl which Mrs. Potts had lent her on the boat. Mrs. Potts had insisted that she keep it for herself and had even told Miss Briggs that she and Mr. Potts wanted her to be married at their home, as she had no home of her own. They were giving Miss Briggs a dress to be married in, and Lizzie had designed a special dress for her as she was to be a bridesmaid. Rosie was not looking forward to being a bridesmaid, but if that was what Mrs. Potts had wanted then she would go through with it.

Beth and Rory watched them set off with mixed feelings, Rory with envy, for he had never been to the big city, and Beth with sadness. With John's departure, she had lost the second man in her life to mean anything to her. They had become more than good friends to one another, and he had always been willing to lend her a helping hand about the place. She had looked forward to his visits to the store when he came to buy his weekly provisions and his tobacco, bringing Rosie with him. He had the same open trusting look that her Jock had always had, the look of a countryman born and bred, and she knew in her heart that he had grown as fond of her as she was of him. Having him stay had proved to be too much of a temptation to them both, and it made his going all the harder for her to bear. He would be back in a few days with a wife—a woman he hardly knew, and she would be alone again.

CHAPTER 9

Potts Famous Haberdashery was a different place without the comfortable presence of Alice Potts, and Rosie found the atmosphere strained despite the joyous welcome she and her father had received on their arrival. Although she had never troubled about her appearance at Clay Cross, she suddenly became uncomfortably aware that Lizzie and Sarah were showing discreet signs of disapproval as they viewed the rents and dark stains on her best dress and the torn hem which showed beneath her white pinafore. As soon as they had finished their meal and her father had set off to find a good barber, Sarah had whisked her off upstairs to the bathroom. The sight of Rosie in such a dishevelled state had filled Sarah with misgivings as to how the exacting Miss Briggs would take to her stepdaughter, and Rosie found herself being vigorously scrubbed from head to foot by the normally gentle Sarah. As Lizzie and Sarah sorted out clean clothes for her to wear from the store she was left to soak in the bath. Her underclothes were put to one side to be disposed of and her frock was sent to be cleaned and mended. A trim and scrupulously clean Rosie was then escorted to the store to have new button boots fitted, and a second pair was put by to be packed away among her belongings before she left.

What had her father been thinking about? thought Sarah, as she carried away the worn-out shoes with some of the buttons missing. It was just as well Amy Briggs was taking over the Taylor household, although how she would cope with Rosie Sarah dreaded to think. It was only too obvious that John Taylor had left his daughter to run wild.

"Come on now, cheer up," exhorted Sarah, seeing Rosie's downcast expression. "Most young ladies would be only too pleased to be given a new wardrobe."

"It's very kind of you and Lizzie, I know," said Rosie, who was anxious not to offend her dear friends, "but I was more comfortable in my old clothes."

"I'm sure you were, dear, but by the look of the others these will soon become just as comfortable. A right little tomboy you've turned into." Sarah was smiling at her as she spoke, but Rosie shrugged her shoulders, her old clothes had gone so she would have to make the best of it.

"How about coming to meet everyone else," suggested Sarah. "They're longing to see you. It was a great surprise to the staff when you came here to stay last Christmas, I can tell you. The Potts had never had so many unexpected guests before."

Sarah led the way to the kitchen quarters where the cook could be seen beating the eggs with such fury it was a miracle they remained in the basin.

"Mark my words," she was saying grimly, giving voice to her bitter feelings about Lizzie. "It won't last—he'll soon get tired of her and then—out—she'll—go!" Thumping the basin down on the table, she turned slightly and caught sight of Sarah and Rosie walking across the yard.

"Why," she exclaimed, her good humour completely restored, "if it isn't little Rosie! My word, how she's grown—hasn't she girls?"

The cook, now full of smiles, welcomed her warmly, and the maids gathered round, pleased for a few minutes break from their preparations for the wedding breakfast. The cook hastily came to Rosie's rescue, giving her a large tin of brownies she had baked especially for her. Sarah left her in the kitchen and returned to the workrooms to tidy up as the store was being closed for a whole day in honour of the wedding. Arthur Potts was determined to carry out his late wife's wishes in every respect. In life, Alice had organised everything, and Arthur was so used to obeying her wishes that it had never occurred to him to ask the opinion of the bride or groom, who would have much preferred to have had no fuss at all.

Rosie was taken to see the wedding cake and gazed in wonder at that monument of confectionery, finding it difficult to believe that such a wonderful cake had been made to celebrate her father's union with Amy Briggs.

"The late mistress wanted your Papa and Miss Briggs to have their reception here, and I have done my very best to see it done as she would have expected," explained the cook, as Rosie stood in silence before the cake.

"I wish Mrs. Potts was still here," said Rosie, as they made their way back to the kitchen. "It doesn't seem the same without her."

The cook gave a snort of disgust. "No more it is, my dear, God rest her. She's sadly missed by us all. We didn't always see eye to eye, but we respected her. She was fair with us, and we knew where we were with her. With Miss Lizzie, no one knows where they are from one minute to the next. Meals at all times, with no warning, and such meals as you've never heard of—why, the poor dear mistress would turn in her grave if she knew the half of it."

"But Lizzie isn't the mistress here now—is she?" asked Rosie in surprise.

The cook burst out in gales of laughter at the innocence of the remark.

"Did you hear that, girls?" she chortled, addressing the giggling maids. "Out of the mouths of babes and sucklings, as the Good Book tells us.'" Her double chins shook with laughter, and she lifted the corner of her apron to wipe away the tears.

"Oh no, my dear. Miss Hopkins is the housekeeper now—God help us!"

"Oh," said Rosie, amazed that they should laugh at Lizzie being a housekeeper. It must be a very dull position for poor Lizzie, and Rosie began to feel uneasy. "And what does Sarah do then? Does she help Lizzie with the housekeeping?" she asked, seriously.

The cook could see the necessity to choose her words more carefully or they would all be in trouble. Picking up the basin, she began to fold the beaten egg whites into the mixture in the bowl before her as she answered Rosie's question.

"Miss Sarah's in charge of the workrooms now," replied the cook, "and very good at her job, so it seems. A nice, quiet young woman is your Miss Sarah—not that we see much of her these days. She keeps to herself and lives quietly on her own over the workrooms—seems happy enough, though—she's waiting for her young man to return from the sea, so we understand."

"That's Ben," remarked Rosie. "I know, Ben. He's very nice."

"So I should imagine," commented the cook.

Rosie had been surprised to hear that the two sisters were no longer living together—it seemed strange, almost as strange as Lizzie's being a housekeeper.

"Where does Lizzie live then?" she asked, puzzled.

The cook sighed. "You are a persistent young lady with all your questions, that you are," she complained good-naturedly. "Why, she lives here of course. She is Mr. Potts' housekeeper. I told you that, didn't I? Housekeepers have to live on the premises so they can see to the needs of the people who employ them." The hidden meaning of the cook's words was not lost on the maids, and they smiled knowingly at one another as they worked. Rosie began to feel like a pawn in a game she didn't understand and was glad when Lizzie called her from the doorway to come and have a fitting of her bridesmaids dress. The cheerful faces surrounding her changed like magic into expressions of dumb insolence at Lizzie's brief appearance, and Rosie was glad to escape. Something was wrong somewhere, and whatever that something was it seemed to concern Lizzie.

Later, in the fitting rooms, Rosie saw reflected in the long mirror a person she hardly recognised. Layers of pink satin flounces made up the skirt of the bridesmaids dress; a wide white sash was tied around her waist, and white stockings and pink satin shoes completed the picture.

"You look a treat, Rosie dear," said Sarah admiringly as she finished tying a huge pink bow around her unruly curls.

"I look just like Mary Ann," said Rosie in disgust.

"Well, I don't know who she might be," laughed Sarah, watching the faces Rosie was pulling in the mirror, "but if she looks as pretty as you do then she must be a very sweet girl."

"No she's not!" replied Rosie with feeling. "She's horrid!"

Sarah put her arms around her. "You are a funny girl. Your new mama will be very pleased with her pretty daughter tomorrow. Just you wait and see."

Rosie put down the basket of artificial flowers she was holding and turned to face Sarah. "I shall wear this dress tomorrow because you and Lizzie made it for me, but I don't care if Miss Briggs likes it or not. I don't like Miss Briggs, and she will never, never be my mama!"

Sarah was taken aback by the defiance in the child's tone of voice and made no further comment as she carefully removed the outfit. Things boded ill for the future if Rosie continued to feel so bitter about her father's remarriage, but there was little or nothing that she or Lizzie could do to change her attitude. She only wished there was, for she loved the child. Hopefully, Amy would win her round with affection but Sarah feared that would not be, for Amy appeared to have no love for children, and Rosie must have felt that in the past. Clay Cross was too far away for Rosie to come and visit them on her own, and, anyway, they had enough troubles of their own to contend with at the moment. Perhaps, one day in the future—who could tell—for their own future hung in the balance right now, and that was worry enough.

The next morning Rosie was dressed with care and left Lizzie's bedroom where she had slept the night to go downstairs to the parlour where the wedding was to take place. She felt as trussed up as a prize chicken and was most uncomfortable. Rory wasn't there to laugh at her looking like this, for which she was thankful, and, with any luck, she might never have to wear this dress again.

The wedding was taking place early in the morning so that the wedding party could catch the midday coach back to Clay Cross. Arthur Potts had already sent his carriage and pair to fetch the bride, and John Taylor hovered about nervously awaiting her arrival. He had called to see Amy the previous afternoon and had been shocked at how ill she looked. Grey streaked her hair, and her face was lined and drawn. Her sufferings at the hands of her intractable employer were only too plain to see, and he felt an immediate wave of pity for her, but that had been all, for he had scarcely recognised the woman he was about to make his wife. He had wondered if her father was coming from Ballarat to marry them, but that was not to be, for the Reverend Briggs had become ill with the strain of his ministry in that desolate place and was unable to make such a long journey. Nursed back to health by a poor widow, he had decided to make her his wife when the bishop had called on his yearly visit, and Amy realised she was unlikely to see her father again. All her hopes were centred on her marriage to John Taylor, as John could see only too clearly, and as his daughter watched him pacing up and down on his wedding morning, she too could sense that her father was uneasy about his marriage to Amy Briggs.

At last, the bride arrived looking pale and wan in a black faille silk gown with a white chiffon front. Black satin ruching on the bodice and skirt and a high lace collar made it into an elegant gown despite the sombre colour. Amy had only wanted a simple, practical dress of which she could make good use and felt that black was the most serviceable colour, much to Lizzie's dismay. However, she had designed Amy a gown she would be proud to wear on her wedding day, and Amy had been astonished when it had been delivered. With it had come a tiny black hat which Sarah had trimmed with a curled ostrich feather clipped to one side with a diamante brooch. A black jet trimmed mantle had been included for travelling on the coach after the ceremony. In her hand, Amy held an ivory prayer book which Augusta Armstrong had presented her with that morning—the only token she had received for her six months labour as companion to her disagreeable employer.

Arthur Potts took her arm and escorted her into the parlour where John was waiting, the unwilling bridesmaid following behind. Her stepmother had not spoken one word to Rosie since her arrival, and Rosie wondered if perhaps she had failed to recognise her, looking so different from her usual self.

A curate from St. Paul's church officiated at the wedding with Arthur Potts standing as John's best man after giving the bride away and Sarah and Lizzie acting as witnesses. Lizzie looked as beautiful as ever now that she had discarded her grey housekeeper's attire. Her eyes shone with happiness, which Rosie put down to the wedding, although it did seem odd that Lizzie should be so happy at her father's wedding to Miss Briggs when she herself could feel nothing but sadness.

The ceremony over the small party repaired to the dining room where the wedding breakfast awaited them. As John led his bride through the door, the household staff, the shop assistants, and the girls from the workrooms all lifted their glasses and drank to the health of the happy couple. John and Amy were speechless at the reception they received while Rosie gazed in awe at the table laden down with cold meats, creams, trifles, jellies, and in the centre the wonderful cake she had seen before, taking pride of place. The cook had excelled herself as a tribute to her late mistress.

The toasts were drunk and justice was done to the feast. The cake was cut and a happy future wished to the Taylors, when, just as the proceedings were coming to an end, Arthur raised his glass and called for silence.

"One last toast, ladies and gentlemen—to my future bride—Miss Lizzie Hopkins."

A strained silence fell upon the assembled company at this unexpected announcement and a few awkward moments elapsed before John raised his glass in salute and the others followed suit, for there were those among them who felt the announcement premature so soon after his wife's death, and there were others who guessed the reason for it, and guessed correctly.

That morning, Lizzie had told Arthur that she thought she was pregnant, and he had decided, there and then, to make his decision to marry her public knowledge. His staff would all be gathered together and a wedding was as good a place as any to announce another happy occasion. He would hopefully have an heir to his empire after all these barren years and a passionate, sensuous young woman for his wife, who would give him more children if they were fortunate. What more could any man with his advancing years hope for, and his round face shone with the pride of his achievement as he presented his beautiful Lizzie to the guests.

Rosie watched this charade in utter bewilderment. Surely Lizzie didn't really want to marry fat, ugly Mr. Potts, but one look at Lizzie's face, radiant with happiness at the thought of a lifetime of security was enough to show Rosie that she was happy to become his wife. In Lizzie's eyes there shone a gleam of triumph; she had won him at last and everything that went with him, which was of even greater importance. She had held him at arm's length while Alice had been alive, just waiting for the right time to pounce. To have been his mistress then would have meant being deserted once he tired of her if the stories of his unfaithfulness were to be believed. Yet, after his wife's death, he had mourned visibly and had taken no interest in life. Alice had been the mainstay of the business and without her constant nagging he felt lost and motiveless. The necessity for deceit had gone and with it the fun of the chase. Lizzie had been alarmed at his sudden lack of interest in her, and it fell to her to play the part of the seductress before Arthur's old passion was awakened. She soon installed herself as his housekeeper and comforted him in bed at night until Arthur could hardly bear her out of his sight, and their capers by day and by night became a source of scandal among the staff, who considered her as no better than a common trollop.

A great weight was taken off Sarah's mind at Arthur's announcement. Bearing Arthur's child had tipped the scales firmly in her sister's favour, and there would be no going back now. She had feared that the amoral Arthur would have soon tired of Lizzie and then what would have come of them both? Her sister had played a dangerous game which fortunately had succeeded.

"Did you know Mr. Potts was going to marry Lizzie?" whispered Rosie to her when she could reach her side.

"No, but I hoped he would," replied Sarah softly.

"But Lizzie is so pretty, and Mr. Potts is so—" began Rosie, until Sarah cut her short.

"Quiet now, Rosie. You really mustn't make personal remarks. Lizzie is very happy, and I'm happy for her. It doesn't matter at all what people look like. They can't help their looks."

"I know that—but he hasn't got any hair."

"Shh," retorted Sarah sternly. "He might not have much hair but he does have a great deal of money, and Lizzie will be very rich. That counts for a lot where we come from. You just don't understand, my dear."

"Oh, yes I do," Rosie spoke with the conviction of one beyond her years. "I'm going to marry Rory one day, and he hasn't got any money. Money isn't important."

Sarah looked down at her serious little face and smiled. As far as she knew, Ben would never have much. It was a subject they had never discussed—loving one another was enough for them.

"A little money helps to butter the parsnips," smiled Sarah. Rosie shook her head in despair. Grown-ups never took her seriously, and now Sarah was poking fun at her. She picked up her basket of flowers and wandered off to see if there was anything left to eat. Sarah watched her go with wry amusement and looked across to where her sister was holding court. The need for pretence was over at last and Lizzie could now take his arm in public and parade in all her finery round the block in Collins Street with the rest of Melbourne society. Lizzie had what she wanted, but Sarah didn't envy her—the thought of marrying Arthur Potts revolted her.

The time passed quickly, and the Taylors prepared to leave. Rosie, to her great relief, changed back into her old frock, now cleaned and mended, and went to make her farewells. She had enjoyed seeing Lizzie and Sarah again but she didn't want to stay any longer. Things were so different without Mrs. Potts, and she couldn't imagine Lizzie in her place. It didn't seem right somehow.

As Cobb's coach carried them back to Clay Cross, her father turned to his new wife.

"Didn't you think Rosie made a charming bridesmaid, my dear?" he remarked, by way of conversation.

Amy stared across at her sitting in the opposite seat.

"Charming," she replied, without a glimmer of feeling.

Rosie looked down at her feet. It was the first sign of recognition her stepmother had shown her that day. It was cold outside the coach but the atmosphere inside was noticeably colder.

CHAPTER 10

Life with Amy as her stepmother was a time of utter wretchedness for Rosie and proved to be even worse than she had feared. Her freedom had been severely curtailed from the start, and she found that she was expected to perform all the menial tasks in the household. Amy and her father had been as poor as church mice when they had lived in the old rectory but by scrimping and saving they had managed to keep a young girl on starvation wages to help with the chores. A rector's daughter had a position to maintain, however poorly situated, and old habits die hard. Amy had never wanted John Taylor's daughter but while she had to suffer his child under her roof she made good use of her. Being a child of some spirit, Rosie had stood up for herself at first only to discover that to argue was to court disaster. Her stepmother was a cold woman of stern discipline who believed that the only way to bring her wilful, wayward stepdaughter to obey was to beat her into submission. A few sessions of this brutal treatment, and Rosie argued no more.

Amy was clever enough to leave the child alone when her father was about, and John, who was rarely at home, was unaware that his daughter was being ill-treated. School became a haven of peace for her despite the unkind jibes from Mary Ann and her followers, for Rory was always there, and with him she could be her old self again until home time. She had changed beyond recognition, for her stepmother believed in a godly appearance. Her hair had been cut short like a boy's, unlike the other girls of that period, whose luxuriant tresses were considered their crowning glory even if their heads were infested with lice. Rosie made no objection when Amy chopped off her curls. She looked more like a boy and felt closer to Rory as a result.

If her father was around the place at weekends, she was allowed to spend a little time visiting Beth or taking Prince along the paths they knew so well. She saw less of Rory at weekends and holidays now that he was getting older, as he worked part time at Pendle's Hotel, and she dreaded the time when he left school to work there permanently. There was little time nowadays for fishing or swimming in the lagoon for either of them.

One day, as Beth was chatting to her, Rosie could bear her situation no longer and broke down and wept. She was tired and weak and unable to face returning home to the tasks that awaited her. Beth placed her arm around her to comfort her only to feel her flinch away in pain. Having had her suspicions for some time that Rosie was being ill-treated, Beth decided there and then to speak to John of her fears, which she did that evening. John strode home angrily and demanded the truth from his wife. At the sight of the wheals on his daughter's bruised and reddened back and legs he had pushed Amy out of his way as he left the room, threatening to give her the same treatment if she ever struck Rosie again. Later that night, he returned home the worse for drink and bent on revenge. Amy locked herself in the closet for safety, and Rosie, who had never seen her father in such a state before, cried herself to sleep with fright. The next morning, an uneasy peace settled over the household, after which Rosie was never beaten again by her stepmother; Amy slept alone in the big feather bed, and John spent more time at the store in Beth's quiet company.

Amy found comfort in good works and started a Sunday meeting in the town as, much to her disapproval, a service was not held there every week. Eventually, she extended this to weekly sewing meetings for the women, and many attended as she was an expert needlewoman, although they disliked her overbearing attitude towards them. Completely unaware of their feelings towards her, she consoled herself by thinking that her coming to Clay Cross had been of benefit to the ungodly inhabitants, some of whom she considered almost beyond redemption. She was tolerated by the townspeople because she was John's wife, and for that reason alone. He was one of them, and they felt sympathy for the poor bastard, married as he was to such a hard woman.

Beth continued to take a kindly interest in Rosie's welfare, and she saw that she never went hungry again, sending packets of food with her to school each day, and when her school days were over, Beth took her on to help in the store despite the fact that she could only afford to pay her in kind. Rory came back to see them whenever he could, although nowadays he lived and worked at Pendle's Hotel as a boot boy and general help, sharing a small room over the stables with the groom.

Amy was more content with Rosie away all day, but, as soon as she returned, the old resentment at her presence would flare up again, taking hold of her like a kind of madness. She railed at her stepdaughter for not earning her keep, although Rosie always brought back something to help fill the larder for Beth never sent her home empty-handed. There was something so wild and uncontrolled about these frequent outbursts that Rosie began to fear for her stepmother's sanity. She had long realised that it was her presence that triggered off Amy's blackest moods and her violent attacks of criticism and that she would have to look for some kind of work away from Clay Cross. Her father expected her to earn enough to keep herself as she grew older, and she feared to remain any longer under the same roof as her stepmother. There was only one place where she would be safe until she could find a situation elsewhere and that was with Beth, although where she would go eventually she had no idea. She was still little more than a child and employment was scarce enough in Clay Cross for her superiors as the township was a poor place and the majority of its inhabitants were poor people.

Beth took pity on her and moved Rory's small bed into her own room for Rosie. It made more room for Andrew and Malcolm, although Malcolm was rarely home these days. More often than not he was off on one of the boats working his way down river and taking what work came his way.

For a year, Rosie lived at the store working hard for her keep. She spoke to her father to see if he had any ideas about her future, and John promised to see what he could do. He was grateful to Beth for taking in his daughter as for some time previously he had begun to worry about her safety at home, for his wife's attitude towards her was unnatural and much as he hated to admit it, he knew he was responsible for bringing so much suffering upon his only child. Beth had assured him that Rosie earned her keep and it was no hardship to her having her to live there; nevertheless, John made it a habit to add a little extra to his weekly account to help Beth to keep her. Nothing was said between them both on the matter; Beth knew why it was given and accepted it gratefully.

Mulling over the problem of employment for Rosie, John decided to contact Arthur Potts. There was a slight possibility that the Pottses might take her on as a junior in the haberdashery or the workrooms, and feeling sure that his daughter would be well cared for with Lizzie and Sarah on the premises, he felt confident in making an enquiry on her behalf. In due course, he received a reply from Lizzie to say she had been looking for a young nursemaid to help their present nurse, as she was expecting their third child shortly, and who better to fill the post than dear Rosie, of whom they were all so fond. They now lived in a new house on Port Phillip Bay and would be happy to receive Rosie whenever she was ready to come. Rosie was delighted at the news, and John was thankful, knowing that she would have a comfortable position among people who cared about her.

As the time grew nearer for her departure, Rosie's thoughts were of the people she would be leaving behind and whom she might never see again. Her holidays would be spent with the Potts family caring for their children, and she would not have time to return to Clay Cross. Family employees were never expected to have lives of their own apart from the occasional afternoon off. She was going to miss the bush country and the lagoon where she had spent so many happy hours with Rory, and worst of all, she had to leave Prince behind. Beth had offered to keep him, as Prince had lived in the store for the past year, and her father had promised to take him for a run each evening after work so Rosie had to be content with this arrangement. Rory also assured her that he would see the dog came to no harm as they took Prince for a last run along the river path together.

"You won't forget me Rory, will you?" begged Rosie miserably, "and promise you'll take good care of Prince while I'm away."

"You know I will—and, anyway, you'll be back soon I expect. I can't see you pushing a pram and bathing babies for long—you aren't the type."

"I don't think I am either," agreed Rosie. "I don't know one end of a baby from the other, but I expect I'll soon learn."

"Reckon so," said Rory, throwing a stick for Prince.

"I don't really want to go but there's nothing for me to do around here and I've got to work somewhere. I shall be all right with Lizzie. I know I shall, but it will feel strange at first, won't it?" Now that the time for leaving was upon her, Rosie was beginning to worry and who better to confide in than Rory, who understood her better than anyone.

"Aw, stone the crows, Rosie, cheer up for Christ's sake," entreated Rory. "You're damn lucky when you think about it—why, you even like the family, don't you? Do you think I want to work at Pendle's? No way! Being a boot boy means running all the errands for the guests and that's no joke I can tell you. I wanted to work on the barges like Malcolm—that's proper man's work—but Ma won't hear of it. Andrew's still too small to lift the flour sacks and the sides of bacon, so she can't spare me yet."

"Mary Anne's at the hotel and you know how sweet she is on you," remarked Rosie, thoughtfully, giving voice to her worst fears.

"Mary Anne!" Rory was indignant. "Fair dinkum, Rosie, she's nothing like you, you know that. Put her out of your mind—she isn't worth a thought. I don't even pass the time of day with her. Her nose is that high in the air she'd find it hard to see me if she wanted to."

Rosie laughed. Rory knew just what to say to make her feel better. Of course she would come back one day and he would still be here—she was worrying about nothing.

The next morning, as she left on the early coach, there was no one to see her off but Beth. John had taken leave of his daughter the previous evening, and Rory couldn't be spared from his duties at such an hour. Rosie had called round at the homestead to see her stepmother, who had showed no emotion at the parting, for when she had gone to live with Beth it was as if Rosie had ceased to exist as far as Amy was concerned.

"Don't fret now, lassie," said Beth as she kissed her, "write when you can, and I'll do my best to keep in touch. Take care of yourself, mind."

Rosie had clung to her for a few moments before getting into the coach, too upset at this parting to speak. Beth was the nearest person to a mother that she could remember, and suddenly she felt very alone. A final wave and a new chapter in her life was about to begin.

It had been more than four years since Rosie had travelled across the hard empty road that stretched for miles across the barren countryside before it met up with the hilly tracks to the north of Melbourne. It was still as she remembered it; a dull, desolate landscape dotted with tall gums, their dead bark hanging in tattered strips, and, here and there beside the road, the black scavenging crows with their hard beaks and crafty eyes, looking out for the next meal. She was glad when the coach left this harsh place behind and the outskirts of the city came into view.

Arthur Potts had sent his groom with the chaise to meet the coach, and she continued her journey in comfort. The chaise made its way along the Nepean Highway to where Arthur had built his new house, situated within easy travelling distance from the haberdashery but far enough out of the city for his children to have all the advantages of a country upbringing. Rosie could hardly believe her eyes as the chaise turned into a wide driveway flanked by large, decorative iron gates. A long, two-storied house stood at the end of the drive surrounded by beautiful grounds. Buffalo grass edged with aromatic tea scrub stretched almost to the shoreline and a large fig tree on the front lawn spread its shade over an artificial lake where black swans and water fowl swam. The chaise stopped in front of the grand portico, and she was helped down the steps to wait as the groom unloaded her small portmanteau. Large plaster urns filled with arum lilies and brilliant geraniums stood on either side of the entrance, and a long verandah covered in flowering creepers stretched the length of the house. It was the loveliest place Rosie had ever seen, and she could hardly believe this was to be her home.

The door opened, and there was Lizzie come to meet her—a plumper Lizzie but still as beautiful as ever. In her pale pink cotton crinoline with collar and cuffs of pure white lawn, she resembled a full blown rose, blooming with good health. She was heavy with her third child and as usual had suffered no ill effects from her pregnancy, which had only served to heighten her beauty.

"Dear Rosie," said Lizzie happily, "how kind of your papa to write to us. I hope you will be happy here—I've had such trouble finding the right staff for the nursery, and it was Arthur's idea that you came here rather than to the haberdashery. You would have found the hours very long in the workrooms, and the work can be tedious for a beginner, especially one so young. This will suit you much better, you will find, and Jane, the children's nurse, will teach you all you need to know—she is such a nice girl. I feel sure you will get along well together. Did you have a good journey, dear? And how are your papa and mama? Are they both well?"

Rosie hardly knew how to answer as Lizzie chatted on, walking the length of the front corridor to where the back stairs led to the nursery wing.

"Come along, Rosie dear. This is the way to your room. You have a dear little room all to yourself next to Jane, so she will be company for you. The children sleep here, and this is the day nursery. You must come and meet them, and then we'll have tea."

Lizzie opened the door of the nursery, and Rosie followed her into a large airy room. On a rocking horse sat Master Percy, Lizzie's pride and joy, whipping his horse and shouting at the top of his voice. Jane was feeding little Arty, who sat solemnly in his high chair and lifted up his sticky hands as soon as he caught sight of his mother. Lizzie patted him on his head keeping well away from his outstretched fingers and spoke to Jane, who bobbed a slight curtsy in her direction.

"Good afternoon, Jane, this is Rosie, who has come to help you. I'm sure you will get along well together. Master Percy can get used to her before the new baby arrives, and then she can take him entirely off your hands."

Jane smiled. "Pleased to meet you, miss, I'm sure," she said, pleasantly.

Jane was a practical, homely girl of eighteen, and Rosie took to her immediately, which was more than she did to the vociferous Percy.

"Oh, do stop making that terrible noise, Percy darling—let Mama lift you down. This is Rosie who's come to look after you—come and say 'hello' to Rosie—there's a good boy."

"No, won't," said Percy firmly, pushing Lizzie's hand away. "Don't want to!"

"Never mind, then," said Lizzie resignedly and turned to Rosie. "You'll find him rather a handful, I'm afraid. He's just too much for Jane with Arty to look after as well, and now another baby arriving soon—Percy needs someone all to himself, don't you, my darling, and that's where you come in, Rosie. I'm sure you'll manage him perfectly."

Rosie looked at her new charge with some apprehension. Both children had tow-coloured hair and fat, freckled faces and resembled their father, having none of their mother's fine features apart from their fair colouring. Little Arty had a sweet, toothy smile and was obviously the better tempered of the two boys. Percy's lips were pulled tight in an attitude of defiance as he climbed back on his rocking horse, and Rosie began to wonder how they would get on together. She would need a firm hand with Master Percy by the look of things.

"Oh, before we leave the nursery," added Lizzie, "I must tell you, Rosie, that Mr. Potts and I do not believe in punishment. The children are to be kept happy at all times—and now, dear, we will have tea. I'm sure you must be feeling tired and hungry."

Rosie and Lizzie left the nursery to sit on the cool terrace under the vines, and afternoon tea was served.

"One more thing dear," said Lizzie, as she poured the tea from an ornate silver teapot, "I think it best if the children call you Rosie—and you must always remember to address me as 'Mrs. Potts.'"

Rosie blushed as she took her cup from Lizzie. It would seem strange to call Lizzie by that name; the old familiarity would have to be forgotten now that Lizzie was such a grand lady, and she was little better than a servant in this large house.

"I won't forget," said Rosie humbly, learning her first lesson.

After tea, she was allowed to rest in her pretty room and to tidy herself up, ready for dinner, which on this one occasion she was to take with Mr. and Mrs. Potts.

Sitting on the window seat and looking out over the vast expanse of Port Phillip Bay, she felt a gentle breeze touch her cheek, bringing with it the scent of the tea trees and the tang of the sea. How different it was from Clay Cross, where the northerly winds carried the desert sands across the sky, burnishing it a deep red and colouring the sunsets. She had left behind the raw white heat of summer, which beat down mercilessly on the dusty roads leading to the crossing place over the river, draining one's energy and setting fire to the surrounding forest and bush. She had come to live in this pleasant place, and, at that moment, she was glad of it.

CHAPTER 11

Jane and Rosie leaned out of the nursery window to watch the guests arrive. It was a warm evening, and the sun had already set leaving a luminous glow in the sky. Venus rose in all her glory soon to be joined by other less brilliant constellations, reflecting their light in the calm dark waters of the bay.

The Potts were throwing a party to welcome the arrival of their third son, Henry, now two months old and soundly asleep in his cradle. Their wealthy friends and neighbours had been arriving for the past hour, and the two girls had been watching the cavalcade of carriages rolling up the circular drive to the front door where the fashionable guests were greeted by their hosts.

"After the dinner is over and the dancing begins, we'll creep downstairs and have a look," whispered Jane.

Rosie was only too anxious to see the magnificence below. "How can we do that?" she asked her companion.

Jane knew everything there was to know about the household and kept the new nursemaid well informed.

"When the double doors of the salon are opened for the servants to go in and out we can see from the back stairs," explained Jane, who had seen it all before. "If the children are asleep, it won't hurt to leave them for a few minutes, and we can take turns to sit on the stairs and watch."

Rosie nodded. She had seen all over the house now and had been into the white and gold salon with its richly ornamented ceiling and hanging candelabra. The gilt-framed mirrors and large pier glasses which decorated the walls to give the room an added spaciousness had made her feel very small and insignificant.

The salon was only used for grand occasions such as this and normally the family used the drawing room where a portrait of Lizzie with Arty on her lap and Percy at her knee took pride of place over the marble fireplace. It was to this room that Jane and Rosie took the children after nursery tea to spend an hour with their parents. Arthur was inordinately proud of his sons and returned home promptly every evening so as not to miss this happy time with his children. Occasionally, Rosie was allowed to stay with them and enjoyed being treated as one of the family.

Since Henry's birth, she had looked after Master Percy on her own. At first, she had found him an impossible child, spoilt and demanding, and she had difficulty controlling his temper tantrums. Gradually, she had won his confidence, and now he related to her more than to his mother, who soon tired of her children once they were weaned and was only too pleased to pass them on to somebody else. Rosie's presence in the drawing room was a blessing as far as Lizzie was concerned. Arthur kept them amused and never tired of their company—they were the fruit of his old age, and he spoilt them accordingly.

Once dinner was over and the music began, Jane and Rosie crept down the back stairs to watch and wonder. The big mahogany doors of the salon were left open to draw in more air as the night was warm and humid, enabling the watchers on the stairs to get an excellent view of the dazzling company below. Halfway through the evening, Lizzie stood beside the grand piano, and to her husband's accompaniment, she sang the popular ballads of the day. Her beautiful soprano voice filled the large room, and as each song ended she received rapturous applause. Standing on the dais in her wide-skirted cream dress of the finest Lyons silk, embroidered with pearls, she commanded the admiration of everyone. A pearl-studded Spanish comb held her curls in place, allowing a few stray ringlets to frame her beautiful face, and as she bowed her head in graceful acknowledgement, jewels sparkled round her throat and flashed in the light with the slightest movement of her hands.

It took Rosie's breath away, and she sat on and on, forgetting to relieve Jane who had long since returned to her duties. Had the children cried or stirred in their sleep, Rosie was far too engrossed in the glittering scene below to have heard them.

The applause over the guests returned to the dance floor until the first signs of the dawn tinged the horizon and it was time to leave. Their departure woke Rosie, who had fallen asleep with her head resting on the banisters, and she crept upstairs to her bed. Jane was already asleep, for the baby woke early and she was often tired having spent many sleepless nights caring for him.

Lizzie stood at her bedroom window watching the dawn rise over the water and stretched luxuriously. It had been a very successful party, and her popularity with the male guests had pleased her, especially the open admiration of one guest in particular, a handsome, well-dressed man of about thirty who had come alone. She had longed to dance with him and find out where he came from, but Arthur had made it impossible. How possessive he was becoming and how it bored her. He had never been far from her side all evening and had shown his obvious disapproval every time she had been partnered by another man, however well known to him. He was beginning to behave like an old man and how it displeased her—oh, how she wished he had been thirty years younger.

"Did you see the stars last night, Arthur?" she called lazily. "I can't remember them looking brighter or nearer to the earth—perhaps it was the champagne going to my head."

Arthur came out of his dressing room and, putting his arms around her, cupped her swollen breasts in his hands. "You are my Venus, my darling—my incomparable Venus," he murmured, kissing her bare shoulders.

Lizzie moved away from his embrace. She didn't want Arthur's attentions at the moment. "I'm tired Arthur," she said, shortly, "and I ought to feed the baby before I go to bed. He will be awake soon, and I don't want my sleep to be disturbed."

"Of course not," said Arthur, understandingly, "but when he has been fed—then, my love? It's been so long, Lizzie and I desire you with all my heart. Can't you see how I suffer without you, dearest?"

"You must be patient a little longer, Arthur," said Lizzie, as she made her way to the door to fetch Henry. "I suffered too, bearing your three sons, and if I become pregnant again so soon I might not be able to wean the baby properly. I haven't felt as well since Henry was born, and I need a rest from child bearing. If you truly cared for me Arthur, you would be more sympathetic."

As Arthur prepared to sleep in the single bed in his dressing room, he could see Lizzie contentedly suckling her son. She had weaned all her children successfully and had borne them without undue difficulty, and there was no reason for her refusal to sleep with him now. Arthur felt anger well up inside him—a righteous anger. His head should be resting where his son's was so sweetly cradled. He must tempt her back into his arms where she rightly belonged. To force his attentions upon her would spoil the passion they had previously enjoyed and that was what he craved, the wanton lustfulness of her young body, given to him so willingly, until now. In return, he had given her everything she had desired, a home fit for a queen, servants to wait on her, and more jewels and clothes than she could ever wear. He would have to think of a new diversion to give her pleasure and one that would place him back in her affections.

That same evening, one of his neighbours had offered him a fine chestnut mare, thinking it would suit his wife, but as Lizzie didn't ride he had refused it. Reconsidering the offer, Arthur thought it might be the very thing. It would be good for her to ride rather than to be taken everywhere. He would buy it for her tomorrow and then maybe she would relent towards him.

A few days later, Arthur presented his wife with the chestnut mare, which had cost him a small fortune. Lizzie was pleasantly surprised by this unusual gift.

"But I can't ride, Arthur dear. Why did you buy it for me?"

"I felt the exercise would be good for you, my love, and riding is a great pleasure, you will find. Our groom will give you lessons until you are competent and then we will ride together." Lizzie stroked the horse's muzzle—it was a well-bred animal—even she could see that.

"I shall need some riding clothes, Arthur dear," she said, smiling at him.

"Of course, my angel—they have already been ordered and will be here in a few days." Arthur smiled happily; he had done the right thing as he discovered that night when Lizzie invited him back into their marital bed.

Lizzie began to ride every morning, taking lessons from the groom. She looked forward to this new activity and soon gained sufficient confidence and expertise to ride alone. Each morning, her horse splashed through the surf along the bay and cantered along the firm sand of the beach. She looked radiant with good health as she rode the chestnut back to the stables to be rubbed down after the morning's exercise, and Arthur was delighted to see her so happy in her new found freedom.

Before long, a fat little pony was acquired for Master Percy, and Rosie found herself walking round the paddock, leading her small charge along as he sat sedately on his new plaything. Once he was off the leading rein, she was able to sit on the grass and watch him enjoying himself for hours on end as he trotted his staid little pony through the buttercups, and when Lizzie felt her son could ride well enough, he was allowed to accompany her, trotting alongside his mother as her horse walked gently beside the rippling waves.

It was on one such afternoon that Percy called her attention to a string of horses being ridden at a fast gallop along the sands. Lizzie dismounted quickly and led Percy's pony to a safe distance. She had never seen anyone on that quiet stretch of beach before and wondered where so many riders had come from. After the horses had passed, the leading horseman turned sharply and rode back to where they were standing. Lizzie recognised the handsome stranger whose presence had intrigued her at the dinner party some months previously.

"Mrs. Potts, I believe," he said, smiling broadly, "and Master Potts, I presume. I trust my horses did not disturb your ride. Normally, we exercise them early in the morning, but that was impossible today as we have only just returned from yesterday's race meeting."

"I see—they are race horses. I have never seen them along this stretch of the beach before, and I usually ride in the morning myself."

"I don't think you would," laughed the stranger, "unless you ride at the crack of dawn, and that I somehow doubt."

"Forgive me," said Lizzie, "I recognise you from our dinner party, and you obviously know who I am, but I'm afraid we were never introduced, and I don't know your name or where you are from."

"My apologies, dear lady. I thought you knew of me. Harry Trevern, at your service, from the Trevern Stables."

"Pleased to meet you, Mr. Trevern," said Lizzie, offering him her hand. "And Mrs. Trevern—she is well, I hope? I noticed you came alone to our house."

Harry burst out laughing. "There is no Mrs. Trevern, I can assure you. I am only interested in thoroughbreds, and I've never found one to come up to my expectations, until I set eyes on you."

Lizzie blushed scarlet. "Really, Mr. Trevern! That is not a proper thing to say, as you well know. Why you have only just this minute introduced yourself to me."

"And so I have. Forgive me. My manners belong to the stable, I fear, and I'm used to saying what I feel. The truth is I've had you on my mind since that evening. I came expecting to be bored and left with the sight and sound of you to disturb many a night's sleep. If that offends you, dear lady, then please forget we ever met."

Lizzie was taken aback by his speech. She had no wish to send him away for good; he had attracted her from the first time she had seen him, and meeting him again so unexpectedly had secretly delighted her.

"I'm not offended," she said softly, "just the opposite. I am flattered by your kind remarks, which I do not deserve."

"That's more like it," said Harry, as he dismounted. "And now, Mrs. Potts, my men are waiting for me, so, before I take my leave, allow me to help you mount your horse; a real beaut she is too—just like her owner."

Before Lizzie had time to say anything, she had been lifted up like a puff of thistledown and placed in the saddle. A cheeky smile and a brief wave, and Harry Trevern had joined his string of racehorses to return the way he had come, leaving Lizzie with a wildly beating heart, wondering if they would meet again.

At tea time, Percy related the incident to Rosie at great length, getting very excited about it. He loved horses now that he had a pony all to himself, and he had never seen so many before in his short life.

"Lots of horses, Wosie, lots and lots of horses."

"Yes, I'm sure there were, dear, but eat your tea up first and tell me all about it afterwards." Percy obediently stuffed his mouth full only to continue with his narrative. It was much too exciting to keep until tea was over.

"And a big man came to talk to Mama, and he lifted her up and put her back on her horse, and Mama was pleased."

Rosie was puzzled. "Why did he do that? Did she have a fall?"

"Oh, no—he wanted to because she got off her horse," explained Percy. "He liked Mama, like I do."

"Of course," said Rosie. "Everyone likes your mama—she's a lovely lady."

"Oh, that's just what the man said," continued Percy, spluttering crumbs everywhere. "I forgot about that bit."

That evening, when Rosie took the children downstairs to spend an hour with their parents, Percy told his story again, but this time to his papa.

"Whatever is the child talking about?" asked Arthur. "What happened on the beach this afternoon, my dear?"

"Oh, nothing of any importance, Arthur, but you know how Percy loves horses and seeing so many of them at one time made a great impression on him. We went for a ride along the strand and were surprised to see a line of race horses out exercising—that was all. I dismounted to lead Percy's pony to a safer place and one of the riders helped me to remount—nothing more than that."

Lizzie shrugged off the incident, but Percy hadn't finished his story.

"And then, Papa, when the man got back on his horse he told Mama—"

"That's quite enough Percy, darling—you really are getting too worked up after all that excitement." Lizzie swept across the room towards her son and kissed him. "Rosie, would you take the children upstairs now, please. If Percy goes on like this he won't settle down at bedtime. You know how highly strung he is."

Rosie gathered the children together and took them back to the nursery as instructed with the reluctant Percy raising his voice in protest. The child had been silenced, but for what reason, she could only guess.

"Harry Trevern keeps racehorses. They were probably from his stables," said Arthur, thinking it over. "He is very successful, so I hear. I invited him to our dinner party, but I don't think you met him, my dear. As he lives out of the district, I didn't realise he was unmarried, and I wouldn't have asked him if I'd known; a lone male without a partner at family functions isn't a good idea—nevertheless, I would have thought he could have found a partner to bring with him." Arthur poured himself another glass of port and returned to his seat. "His place is out in the wilds—about twelve miles from here I believe. Bit of a character, so I've heard."

Lizzie was silent. Twelve miles across a trackless waste was too far for her to ride alone so paying a visit was out of the question. If what he had said was true then she had made something of an impression on him and the more she thought of their encounter the more anxious she was to meet him again.

"I think it would be best my love, if Percy rode in the paddock and you rode on the beach later in the mornings, don't you?" Arthur sipped his port, thoughtfully. "The very idea of you having an accident or meeting undesirable people is a worry to me my angel. You will do as I suggest, Lizzie?"

"Yes, of course Arthur, if it will please you," answered Lizzie sweetly, knowing full well that Harry Trevern exercised his horses early in the mornings.

So, Lizzie began to take her rides along the foreshore earlier than she had done previously, and Harry Trevern exercised his horses a little later each morning. His stable boys returned without him and, whenever it was possible, and he didn't have a race meeting to attend, he accompanied Lizzie on her morning rides. He taught her to handle her horse better, and they would race each other along the beach and through the surf. When Lizzie was tired, they dismounted, and Harry would place his arm around her shoulders as they walked along the sand. At first, he kissed her gently as they parted, as if she was made of porcelain and would break in his arms, but as time went on their longing for each other increased, and their partings became more passionate and prolonged.

One morning, he asked her to return with him to his homestead, and she went willingly, knowing she would be missed but not caring if she was. If Harry needed her, then nothing else mattered, and she would make some excuse on her return. They rode for miles through the bush until the wilderness gave way to lines of vines as far as the eye could see. This was Harry's land and the main part of his income. Lizzie could just make out a long low building in the distance, and, as they came closer, she could see stables round a large courtyard.

An aboriginal woman served them cool lemon under a vine heavy with peaches, and then Harry took her to see his horses, talking to each of them in turn and stroking them gently. Lizzie could see they meant everything to him and took his arm to draw him away. Harry laughed at her. "If you think I love them more than you then you are mistaken, my lovely," he said as he gathered her into his arms and carried her into the house.

Some hours later, as they rode back towards the Bay, Harry leaned across and pulled Lizzie's horse to a standstill. Lizzie sat silently with downcast eyes, afraid to look at him. In Harry's bedroom, she had unleashed the pent-up feelings that had burnt within her since their first meeting on the strand, and he had taken full advantage of her until the ferocity of their passion had passed its peak, and they had been content to lie in one another's arms. Realising how much he meant to her, Lizzie was fearful of the future. If he was to treat her like any other wanton woman and turn her away when he had tired of her, she would die. The thought of being without him was intolerable. He had awoken her real self, and she loved him for it. No longer did she have to pretend to love a man for the sake of position and security; she had already had the things that money could buy, and she found them worthless set against what she already possessed—*but for how long?* she wondered.

"Look at me, my love," Harry's voice was full of concern. "You haven't uttered a word since we left the homestead—why? I made you happy, didn't I? Come now, Lizzie—what is it?"

Slowly, Lizzie raised her head and looked at him. "I love you so much Harry that it frightens me," she replied, her voice scarcely audible.

Harry took her hand in his and pressed it to his lips. "I know that, my sweet, and there will be no other woman for me after this—I swear it, Lizzie. Does knowing that make you feel any better?"

"Oh yes, Harry—oh yes.'" Joyously, she took hold of the reins and set off at a gallop across the scrub with Harry in hot pursuit.

Where the scrub met the shoreline, Harry left her to make her way back home alone. Lizzie galloped wildly along the sand, glad to feel the sea spray on her burning cheeks. Her hair was loose and streamed behind her like an unfurled banner as she sped along the Bay feeling at one with the earth, the sea and the sky above her.

Rosie was watching for her from the nursery window. It was growing late, and Percy was inconsolable because his mama hadn't come to kiss him good night. Arthur, who had begun to wonder where his wife could be was about to send out a search party to look for her when the chestnut came clattering into the stable yard, and Lizzie ran into the house.

"I won't be a minute, Arthur," she called out. "I just have to see the children for a moment and then I'll change for dinner. The mare went lame, and I had to walk for miles."

As she burst through the door to the night nursery to throw her arms around her children, happiness shone from her glowing face, filling the room with radiance. Rosie watched as she kissed each of the children, showing an unusual tenderness towards them. It seemed strange she should be so happy and carefree after walking for miles along a wind-swept beach. Just by looking at her, Rosie could see she was a woman in love, and slowly the happenings of the past few weeks began to make sense to her.

CHAPTER 12

At weekends, Sarah joined the Potts family at The Great House, where a room was kept solely for her use. She worked hard all the week, as, since Alice's death, she had virtually taken over the mail order side of the business and enjoyed the summer picnics with her nephews and the games of croquet on the lawn with Lizzie and Arthur and their guests.

She lived comfortably enough during the week in the old house behind the haberdashery with some of the domestic staff who had remained behind to look after the property. Where the workrooms had been situated, Arthur had built a small clothing factory which employed forty workers and included a busy packing department. Four supervisors dealt with the manufacture of the clothing, with the assistance of a fitter and an alteration hand, who also worked in the haberdashery and the showroom. Sarah saw to the smooth running of the business and continued to work as Alice had done, creating a happy atmosphere in which good relationships flourished. Every morning, Arthur arrived to deal with the financial side of his thriving business with the help of an elderly, hard-working clerk who had been an employee since the early days of the haberdashery.

Sarah had no wish to live in the lavish style enjoyed by her sister and dreamed of a time when she could return to England as Benjamin's wife, where they would live in a modest house in a coastal town, and she could bring up a family of sons to follow in their father's footsteps. Ben had acquired his Masters Ticket and had written to tell her he would be coming to marry her as soon as he was offered a suitable sailing to Australia as ship's captain. Sarah's happiness at this news was tinged with sadness. She had become an integral part of the haberdashery over the past few years and would sadly miss the organisation and the loyalty of the staff to whom she had become so attached. Her memories of Ben were still as clear as the day she had first seen him, suffering the sadistic jabs of the bo'sun's trident as they crossed the Line. She loved her gentle Benjamin all the more for that hateful incident and would be a good and faithful wife to him for the rest of her days.

Rosie was sad to think that Sarah would be leaving them. When she was there, the children behaved better, and the days passed serenely in her company. The little boys loved their aunt dearly and would run to the window as soon as they heard the wheels of the chaise on the driveway and tear down the stairs to greet her. Their mother was rarely at home these days, out riding most mornings and often returning late in the afternoons. When the children visited the drawing room, Lizzie sat in moody silence, not wanting to join in their games or listen to their chatter. She had no patience with them and sent them back to the nursery earlier each evening.

Rosie often wondered what was wrong with Lizzie these days, and Arthur worried too. It was like living with a totally different person from the one he had married. She took no interest in the running of the house or the care of the children—not even Percy, who had been her favourite. She lay beside him at night like a dead thing, lacking any response to his attempts at lovemaking, and nothing he did could arouse the passionate side of her nature, which he had enjoyed so fully in the past. She showed no enthusiasm for anything he suggested to change her mood and only wanted to be out riding the chestnut mare he had given her, which seemed to be the one and only interest in her life.

"My dear," said Arthur cautiously one evening. "I think maybe you are riding too much and exhausting yourself. You are so remote these evenings and too tired even to have a conversation. Too much physical exertion is obviously not good for you."

Lizzie opened her eyes. "I am not ill, Arthur," she said dully, "just a little weary. I rode a long way today."

"Then be sensible, my angel, and ride less, or I shall feel inclined to sell the beast. You seem obsessed with the animal."

"I hope you will never do that, Arthur," said Lizzie, sitting upright in her chair. "The chestnut is the most precious thing you have given me and has provided me with the happiest hours of my life."

"That's as may be, it has certainly taken you away from your duties at home and changed your feelings towards your family."

Lizzie knew he spoke the truth. Her love for Harry was driving her to the point of madness, and there were times when she longed to be free of his hold over her and to feel at peace again. There was something of the devil in his black eyes as he pressed his mouth down onto hers and took possession of her body. He filled her every waking thought, leaving no room for anyone else, not even her children. Arthur's vain attempts to awaken her feelings sickened her—Harry loved her with an all-consuming passion that left her drained physically and mentally.

For some weeks, Lizzie had known she was expecting another child. She had told Harry and had begged him to let her stay with him but Harry had refused.

"Is it mine?" he had asked, but Lizzie had to admit that she didn't know. Her answer angered him so much that he had thrown her from him.

"God dammit, Lizzie! I'll have none of your little draper's brood in my stable. How could you sleep with him after being with me?"

Lizzie had wept bitterly. "You are all I want, Harry—please believe me—Arthur is my husband, and I can't refuse him every time. I don't want to go back to him. Let me stay, Harry—I beg you—don't send me away."

"When your baby is born, then I'll come for you. You shall bear my sons, Lizzie—I promise you that."

Lizzie had been distraught at their parting. It would be months before she saw her lover again and in the meantime she would remain a prisoner in her own home, unable to ride to a rendezvous with him and carrying a child she did not want.

"I shall not be riding again for some time, Arthur," she said, wearily. "I am expecting a child in May of next year."

"Oh, my love," exclaimed Arthur, with relief, "that accounts for everything. We have all been so worried about you, my angel. Now, you must take great care of yourself— another child! That is marvellous news—ah, yes indeed."

Tears rolled down Lizzie's cheeks. If only Arthur would leave her alone. She didn't want his sympathy or his kind concern for her well-being. She didn't want Arthur at all for her love lay elsewhere.

On the warm sunny afternoons of the summer of 1866, Jane and Rosie took the children onto the beach. Rosie loved these idyllic days, searching for tiny blue crabs in the soft sand with the boys and collecting shells and pebbles to amuse the baby. The children were happy too, paddling at the edge of the surf and building castles in the sand. Mama was at home most of the time, and they felt more content as a result.

Lizzie had persuaded Arthur to take her to the races sometimes, and he was happy to oblige, glad to find her taking an interest in something at last. Once there, she had looked for Harry among the crowd of race goers and had slipped away for a few moments to speak to him. He was as anxious to see her as she was to see him, and they arranged for him to visit the house on the lazy afternoons when the family would be absent.

On one such afternoon, Percy had been in an aggressive, quarrelsome mood and had swung his metal spade at his brother, cutting him on the side of his head. Rosie had run up the beach to help Jane staunch the flow of blood and had then run into the house to fetch Lizzie, but Lizzie was nowhere to be found. Running up the main staircase to the front bedroom where she presumed Lizzie would be resting, Rosie knocked urgently on the door.

"Go away," came Lizzie's voice from inside. "I don't want to be disturbed."

"Please, Mrs. Potts—you must come," urged Rosie, continuing to bang on the door. "It's Arty—he's had an accident, and we need a doctor."

After a few minutes, Lizzie appeared with her hair dishevelled and her robe pulled round to cover her nakedness.

"Oh, it's you, Rosie. Whatever is all the fuss about? What has Arty done?"

"He's cut his head—it's bleeding badly, and he looks very white. Jane is bringing him in now."

"Tell the groom to go for the doctor—I'll come once I'm dressed."

As she shut the bedroom door, a whiff of cigar smoke hung in the air of the landing. Something was not as it should be; the master was never home at this time in the afternoon. Rosie had no time to ponder over such irregularities as she ran to give the message to the groom and then to help Jane with the children.

When Arty had been bandaged and the doctor had left, Rosie returned to the beach to collect the children's scattered belongings. A big black stallion and its rider passed her, galloping away from the house. There was a wild arrogance about the stranger as he spurred his horse onto the strand and galloped rapidly along the beach and into the far distance. Rosie watched them go until horse and rider merged into the sweeping landscape of the bay and she could see them no more. Some instinct told her that this man was the cause of Lizzie's unrest and that she must keep the knowledge of his visit to herself. Not even Jane must be told. She had been happy living here until now, but today's discovery made her fear for the future.

Percy's screams greeted her as she returned, and she hurried up the back stairs as fast as her legs would carry her to find Lizzie with her eldest child over her knee, beating him soundly. Rosie watched in silence, shocked and dismayed at the change in Lizzie, who had once forbidden her to chastise the children.

Unknown to Rosie, Harry had just told Lizzie that he would not be visiting her again as the risk of discovery was too great, and Lizzie was taking her frustration out on the unfortunate culprit.

One morning, a few weeks later, Arthur arrived at the haberdashery to find Sarah absent. After making some enquiries, he discovered that she had received a letter by the last post the previous day and had not been seen since. Sarah was found in her sitting room, unable to face anyone after a night of weeping. Her letter had come from Benjamin's mother, telling how his ship had foundered rounding the Horn with the loss of all hands. He had been on his way to marry her and take her back to his parents' home until they found one of their own. All these months, she had been thinking of him and yet she had no inkling of his death when it had come. She had always imagined that people who were close to one another knew the moment when disaster overtook a loved one and that had upset her more than anything else. Surely she should have felt something as he had struggled for life in the cruel sea? For Sarah, it was almost as if she hadn't loved him enough, and she was inconsolable.

Arthur returned in the chaise to fetch Lizzie, feeling she would know better how to comfort her sister. Lizzie did her best, but could not stop poor Sarah's tears, so she packed up some of her sister's clothes and took her back to The Great House, hoping that a quiet time with the children around her would help her to come to terms with Benjamin's untimely death.

It took Sarah a long time to recover and Arthur decided she should make her home with them and go to the business when she felt like it but an idle life held no appeal to Sarah; a working girl she had always been and a working girl she would remain. Her friends were the women whose working lives she shared, and she needed to be back among them. As soon as she felt more composed, she travelled to the store on the three busiest days of the week, accompanying Arthur in the chaise and returning with him at the end of the day. She was content to live with the Potts as part of the family and found comfort in the company of her little nephews, joining in their games and reading them stories.

Rosie loved having her there all the time. Sarah had a calming influence on everybody, and even Lizzie was more at ease with her in the house. Sharing her monthly letters from Beth had helped Rosie to feel less homesick, for she had begun to yearn for the simple life and the easygoing people of Clay Cross. She had glimpsed something rotten in this beautiful place, and it had disturbed her. Perfect though Lizzie appeared on the surface, Rosie knew she was flawed in some way. Sometimes, a worm lay at the centre of a peach, spoiling the fruit. Lizzie was like that, and she was the only person in the house who knew it. Sarah's presence took away the fear she had felt as the black stallion and its rider had galloped past her, but Rosie felt it was still there somewhere in the background, just waiting to make its presence felt.

CHAPTER 13

Certain changes had taken place in the nursery wing in anticipation of the new arrival. One of the bedrooms overlooking the bay had been turned into a schoolroom for five-year-old Percy and a governess was already in residence. She had taken care of Percy's daily welfare, leaving Rosie to care for the two younger boys with the assistance of a new nursery maid. Jane, being the most experienced was to take sole responsibility for the new baby.

During the last weeks of her pregnancy, Lizzie had little rest. The child had kicked and turned in the womb as if it shared her own anxiety to be free of this troublesome confinement and live. When her time came, she had a lengthy and difficult delivery, giving the doctor attending her some anxious moments.

Arthur paced the floor of his dressing room until he could bear the sound of her suffering no longer and retired to his study to find comfort in a glass or two of port. His other children had been born without all this trouble, and Lizzie had carried them with ease. He felt guilty; this was his fault. She had warned him after Henry's birth and he had given her no rest. If she survived the birth of this child, he would take his pleasures elsewhere until she had fully recovered, for life without his angel was unthinkable. Feeling deeply worried, Arthur drank a few more glasses of port and then, to steady his nerves, started on the whisky. After a while, he slumped in his chair and fell into a heavy sleep.

He was awakened with some difficulty some hours later by Sarah who had come to tell him that Lizzie had given birth to a daughter. Arthur stood up unsteadily and kissed Sarah enthusiastically.

"A daughter!" said Arthur, happily. "I can hardly believe it—they have always been boys, and I expected another—but what about my poor wife?"

"Lizzie is asleep, but you can come and see the baby." Sarah smiled at his boyish enthusiasm. "She really is the most delightful little thing."

Holding onto the stair rail, Arthur made his way up to Lizzie's bedroom and peered into the cradle beside the bed. Sarah picked up the sleeping child to show him.

"Why, she has black hair," exclaimed Arthur. "The boys were almost bald when they were born. She is a pretty child—yes, indeed." He attempted to touch the baby's tiny fingers but found it too difficult. The child seemed to be swaying about, and he was glad when Sarah put her back.

"This calls for a celebration," said Arthur, cheerfully waving his hand in the direction of the doctor and the nurse at the bedside.

"Any more celebrations, Mr. Potts, would be unwise in my opinion. You have only just recovered from your last attack of gout, and I would suggest, sir, now the worry is over you take a long rest and allow your wife to do the same."

"Just as you say—just as you say," mumbled Arthur, crossly, as he made his way unsteadily into his dressing room and eventually onto his bed.

Visiting Lizzie's bedroom late the next morning, Arthur found it in a state of confusion. The baby was crying pitifully and thrusting its tiny fists into its mouth while Sarah and Jane were trying to persuade Lizzie to take the child in her arms.

"What's wrong here?" asked Arthur, in amazement.

Sarah looked distressed. "Lizzie won't feed the baby," she answered.

"What!" shouted Arthur angrily. Going over to the bed, he took Lizzie by the shoulder and turned her towards him. "Pull yourself together, Lizzie—you have a duty to the child. Come now—take her and all will be well."

"No Arthur," replied his wife wearily. "I can't."

"I've never heard such nonsense. You've had no difficulty before. I simply don't understand it."

As Lizzie made no reply, Arthur left the room to send a message to the doctor. He badly needed some advice about his wife's strange behaviour but the doctor was not particularly helpful and suggested a wet nurse to feed the baby. In his wisdom, he considered Lizzie was still suffering from the emotional shock of a difficult birth and was too weak to feed her child. Arthur was left with no option—the child had to be fed and a wet nurse was found to satisfy her hunger.

When she was strong enough to sit under the shade of the verandah or stroll in the garden, Lizzie never once asked to see her daughter. Arthur failed to understand this total rejection of the baby. She spoke occasionally to her sons and sometimes dandled Henry on her lap but never once held the baby in her arms. It was as if the child had never existed, and she had blotted out all memory of her.

One evening, Arthur broached the subject of a name for his daughter.

"I have decided to call her Elizabeth, my dear, after you, if you have no objection. She is six weeks old now and needs a name. I wish you would see her, my love, now you are so much better. She is quite the sweetest little thing and resembles you in so many ways."

"I can't love her Arthur," said Lizzie in a toneless voice. "You don't understand."

She couldn't tell him how afraid she was to look at this last and most precious baby or how she had steeled herself against it. As soon as she had seen the child she had known that Harry was the father, but Harry would never accept the child as his flesh and blood. Once she had taken the baby into her arms and placed her to her breast, the ties of motherhood would bind her forever to this house, and she would never find the strength to leave when the time came. Her need for Harry was like a physical illness and nothing was going to prevent her from spending the rest of her life with him. She would sacrifice her child for his love, although it tore her apart to do so, but before she left she would give the baby her rightful father's name. That was all she could do for the poor little unwanted thing.

"I'd like her name to be Harriet," said Lizzie, without feeling. "And if you wish it Arthur then her second name can be Elizabeth."

"As you like, my dear," sighed Arthur, "but why Harriet?"

"It was my mother's name."

Sarah looked up from her embroidery, surprised to hear this. "I never knew that was mother's name? She was always called Annie."

"Yes, I know," replied her sister, "but Harriet was her real name, and she didn't like it so father called her Annie."

"Oh, I see," said Sarah, doubting the truth of this statement, "and to think that I never knew that before." She continued sewing her tapestry with a worried look on her face. Something was seriously wrong with her sister these days, and she began to wonder just exactly was the cause of her strange behaviour.

One morning, a few weeks later, a basket of fruit was delivered for Lizzie with Mr. Trevern's compliments. Lizzie searched through it frantically until she found a small note from Harry. It was brief and to the point.

"I am waiting. Come within the hour. Harry."

Lizzie sent word to the stables to have her horse saddled and then hastily dressed in her warmest riding habit. She ran down the main staircase and out through the front door, passing Rosie and Percy without a glance as they walked along the front drive.

A cold wind was blowing off the sea, and the stable lads were surprised to see their mistress riding for the first time in such weather, but Lizzie was in no mood to argue. The ride would do her good, she explained as they helped her to mount. Rosie and Percy watched her canter away from the stables and gallop onto the windswept sand as if she had no time to lose, and Rosie knew she must get help. Lizzie must be mad going out today in such weather, and there had been an urgency about her as if she was bent on some life or death mission. Taking hold of Percy's hand, Rosie hurried indoors to find Sarah.

Sarah's suspicions were immediately aroused. A fire had just been lit in the drawing room on her sister's orders, and she expected her to be sitting there as usual, taking little or no interest in anything. She remembered the fruit that had been delivered that morning and ran upstairs to Lizzie's bedroom where she found the note from Harry lying where Lizzie had left it.

The pieces were falling into place. Sarah shivered with fear and sat on the edge of the bed to think. Lizzie had wanted the baby to be named Harriet, so perhaps this Harry was the real father of her child. It scarcely bore thinking about. How could she do such a thing? What was to happen to her children and the poor innocent baby—the baby she had never wanted? Sarah felt disgust well up inside her for she loved the children dearly and would never have any of her own now her Benjamin was lost to her. Lizzie had left her four without a backward glance. It was a terrible thing to have done, and she would never forgive her sister for that—and what about Arthur? However was she going to break the news to him of his wife's desertion? Sarah groaned and hid her face in her hands.

It so happened that there was no need for her to tell Arthur anything, for when he returned from Melbourne that evening he went first to his dressing room and found a letter from his wife.

> *"Forgive me, Arthur,"* she had written. *"I have left you to live with Harry Trevern and will not return. Take care of the children. I pray they will forgive me one day for leaving them—and Sarah too. She will be a far better mother to them than I could ever be— .*
>
> *Your wretched wife, Lizzie"*

Arthur trembled violently as he screwed the paper into a ball. So that was the reason for her withdrawal from her family and from him, her infidelity. Angrily, Arthur threw open the connecting door to her room and went inside. All the beautiful clothes he had given her still hung on their hangers; nothing had been taken. A thought struck him, and he took out her jewel box. She had left them all behind, even the large opal pendant he had given her on the birth of their daughter. Her jewels and clothes had been of such importance to her that to have left them behind could only mean one thing. She had not just amused herself with Harry Trevern; she had fallen in love with him. Well, he could do without her; there had been no pleasure in her company of late, and he had shown great patience—far more than she deserved. Thankfully, she had shown an unnatural disregard for her children, and he still had his precious family around him. He would deny her any right to them. They would be taught never to mention their mother in the future, and he would make quite sure that she never saw them again.

Downstairs, Sarah was awaiting Arthur's return in a fever of anxiety. He seemed remarkably self-possessed as he greeted her.

"So, your sister has left us, I see," he remarked as he poured himself a drink.

Sarah was astonished. She knew her brother-in-law well and expected a display of grief and outrage. "But how did you know, Arthur?" she asked. "I expected I would have to tell you, and I didn't know where to start."

"Did you know of your sister's affair with Harry Trevern?" asked Arthur coldly.

"Most certainly not," replied Sarah, angrily. "If I had I would have done everything possible to dissuade her from such foolishness. Lizzie was always wilful but never stupid and would have listened to my advice."

"It's quite obvious, Sarah, that she fell in love with this rogue and had no wish for anyone to stop what she intended to do, and that's why you were never told, in case you interfered with her plans."

Sarah burst into tears. It was the first time that Lizzie hadn't shared a confidence with her.

"It's all so terrible," sobbed poor Sarah. "I don't understand how Lizzie could have left without saying good-bye to any of us, especially the children. I shall never, never forgive her for that."

"Come, come, my dear," said Arthur kindly, leading her to a chair. "Your sister has gone, and we must accept it. There are the children to consider now. You are their aunt, and they care for you. Think of them and love them as if they were your own. Lizzie's going will be eased for them that way."

"Thank you, Arthur," said Sarah, gaining control of her feelings. "That won't be difficult for I have always cared about them."

"Which is more than their mother did," remarked Arthur dryly.

That evening after dinner, in which Sarah didn't partake, having lost her appetite, Arthur sat by the fire in the drawing room and enjoyed a cigar. He had been a fool to marry Lizzie; he had been besotted with her at the time, and it had been the only way to get her into his bed. She was more clever than most, but he doubted she had been so clever this time. Her heart had ruled her head, which is not how it had been when she set her cap at him, and he knew it. For months, he had led a bachelor existence, which could now come to an end. He had enjoyed the flesh pots of Melbourne during his marriage to Alice, and, being a wealthy man, he could now afford the best and most select brothels that Melbourne had to offer. Lizzie's going was a blessing, the more he thought about it. His one regret was the humiliating situation in which he found himself—her desertion had wounded his pride. Melbourne society would laugh behind his back for a while, but not to his face, for he was too rich for that. He would get over it, but Lizzie never would. She would be shunned by the influential people she had known in his company, and she would find that a worse humiliation.

Arthur puffed away contentedly on his cigar and poured himself another drink. He must remember to tell Sarah in the morning that he would not be returning home with her from the haberdashery as he intended dining out in the future.

The next evening, on her return from the haberdashery, Sarah gathered the staff together to tell them their mistress would not be returning. No reason was given, and they were left to decide among themselves as to why she had left. The following morning, she spoke to the nursemaids, requesting them not to mention their mother to the children and to be discreet and turn the conversation away from her if her name was mentioned.

"I shall speak to Percy and Arty myself and tell them their mother no longer wished to live here. That is the truth of the matter, and they need to know no more than that. Mr. Potts does not wish her name to be mentioned again, and the children will forget her in time. They still have you, Jane, and you, Rosie, and I shall do more for them in the future. The baby and little Henry will never remember a mother and soon the older children will get used to her absence. I hope you understand what I am saying. It's important that the children are shielded from this shock as much as possible."

The nursery maids and the two older girls shook their heads, dumbly. They were all bemused by the turn of events except for Rosie who had seen it coming for a long time and showed less surprise than the others.

Percy was deeply shaken on hearing of his mother's desertion and despite Sarah's patient explanation refused to accept that she had gone forever.

"But I saw Mama," he kept insisting. "She only went for a ride along the sand, and she always rides there, Aunt Sarah—nearly every day."

"But this time she decided she didn't want to come back, Percy. You have to believe me, dear."

"But why?" insisted Percy. "Doesn't she love me anymore?" Tears welled up in his eyes at such a dreadful thought.

"Of course she does, and she always will," comforted Sarah, putting her arm around him. "She asked me 'specially to take care of you all for her and that's just what I shall do."

"But why didn't she take me with her if she wasn't coming back?" implored Percy, who could make no sense out of this situation despite his aunt's explanations.

"I expect she thought you would be happier here with your brothers and your new baby sister, and everybody who loves you," said Sarah, desperately.

"But Mama loves me—you said so, Aunt Sarah, and I want to be with her."

"I understand that Percy, but I'm afraid it's just not possible. You must be big and grown up and sensible now, and you will soon forget all about it."

Percy sulked and ran off to the stable to bury his head in his pony's long mane. His Aunt Sarah didn't know what she was talking about. He knew for certain that his mama loved him better than anyone else in the world; she always used to tell him that, and he knew she would never go away and leave him for ever like Aunt Sarah had told him. Mama had gone along the strand the same as usual, and he would go and find her and bring her back this minute. He looked for a stable boy to saddle up his pony, but there were none to be seen so he stood on a box to reach the saddle and bridle and put them on as he had seen the stable boys do many times. The leather was stiff for his small fingers, and he buckled the saddle with difficulty as the pony moved restlessly in his stall. He led the pony quietly out of the stable and down the path towards the beach. There was a low wall there, and he stood on it to mount, and, once in the saddle, he set off at an easy trot along the sand in the same direction he had seen his mother ride. It was cold and blustery along the shore and the sea looked rough and unfriendly, but Percy soldiered on bravely, convinced that sooner or later his mother would materialise before him.

"Mama—Mama!" he shouted into the wind, which whistled around him.

The little pony thought he was urging him on and began to gallop faster. Percy hung onto his mane as he felt the loose girth slacken and the saddle begin to slide beneath him. The reins flew from his hands, and he lost his balance and fell. The pony galloped on, dragging his rider through the stones and boulders that littered the shore.

Percy was trapped with one foot caught in the stirrup, unable to save himself from the death that awaited him. His small frame caught on a boulder, slowing up the pony's headlong flight and bringing it to a standstill. The pony, not knowing what to do next, turned for home and slowly walked back the way he had come, pulling Percy's limp and lifeless body behind him.

When it was realised that Percy was missing, the first place that came to Rosie's mind was the stable. His little pony meant more to him than any of his other possessions, and when he was upset, he would go to the stable to stroke and fondle his dumb friend. It was to the stable that she ran first and finding the pony gone, alerted the groom while she searched the paddock and the garden. The groom set off along the beach, not thinking for one moment that the child would have ventured along it in such conditions. He soon came upon Percy's pony, and to his horror, found the boy caught in the stirrup. Releasing him and realising the child was dead, he picked him up gently in his arms and carried him home, leading the pony behind him. Sarah was waiting with the other searchers at the open doorway as Percy's body was brought in to the shock and dismay of all who witnessed it, and to Rosie in particular, who could not control her grief.

"It was Lizzie's fault—Lizzie's fault," she sobbed as she was led away by kind hands. "He was looking for her—I'm sure of it."

Arthur returned that night to a grieving house to find he had not only lost a wife but his eldest son as well, and the elation he had felt in his newfound freedom was suddenly turned into bitterness and gall.

CHAPTER 14

Rosie could only think of returning home to Beth after Percy's death and begged Sarah to allow her to do so, but Sarah in her wisdom felt it would help her to recover from the shock and distress if she was given another child to love in Percy's place. She spoke to Jane about it, and Jane agreed that Rosie could take sole charge of the baby if that would help. She still had plenty to keep her busy with Arty and small Henry to look after, and she would always be at hand to help if necessary. If they changed over bedrooms, Rosie could have the baby in a cot beside her until Hetty, as the baby was now called, was old enough to sleep in the night nursery.

At first, Rosie was apprehensive when Sarah suggested it but with Jane's encouragement she began to bathe the baby and care for her until she loved the poor unwanted child almost as much as she had loved Percy, and became so jealously possessive over her that she longed for the time when the child would be weaned and the wet nurse dismissed.

As the months passed, Sarah ceased to worry about Rosie; she seemed happy enough in her new role and things had almost returned to normal at The Great House on the bay. It was Arthur she had to be concerned with now and the undermining of her discipline at the store. His free and easy behaviour with the assistants at the haberdashery and his advances towards the women staff at the house were a worry to her. By lunch, he was usually the worse for drink and became a nuisance to the customers and assistants alike, and the business, of which she felt justly proud, was suffering badly, and they were losing some good custom. He was hardly ever home during the week, and his children could have been orphans for the amount of time he spent with them, and, to make matters worse, she had to dismiss two of the maids, both of whom he had made pregnant. When she implored him for the sake of his children, if for no other reason, to change his ways, he simply laughed at her and told her to live elsewhere if she disapproved of his lifestyle, knowing full well that she would never leave the children. He drank to forget the past and enjoyed what he could of the present when he was sober, and who could blame him for that—certainly not his sister-in-law, and he took no notice of her whatsoever.

However, on one occasion when he appeared more reasonable and less drunk than usual, Sarah managed to make him understand that his children missed him.

"I cannot play the part of both mother and father in their lives, Arthur, try as I will. They need you and love you. Surely you wouldn't want them to forget you as they have forgotten their mother," she implored.

Suitably flattered by Sarah's description of him as a much-loved father missed by his children, Arthur promised to forego the pleasures of the town for one evening and returned home with Sarah. His heart warmed towards his family as he fondly imagined their joyful greeting after so long an absence, and he would not disappoint them.

On arriving home, Arthur went straight upstairs to the nursery, where Rosie was bending over the cot, rocking the baby to sleep. The noises coming from the bathroom told their own story as Jane and the nursemaid bathed the two boys. Arthur closed the door gently behind him and stood quietly beside Rosie, who was unaware of his presence.

"Is my little daughter keeping well?" he asked.

"Oh sir," exclaimed Rosie. "You made me jump! I didn't hear you come in."

Arthur smiled at her surprise. "I can see you are looking after her well, my dear," he said, looking down at the contented baby.

"Thank you, Mr. Potts. She is very good, and no trouble at all." Rosie was pleased with his praise. "Would you like me to ask Jane to bring in the boys? They will be so pleased to see you."

"No—no, that won't be necessary, Rosie. I'll surprise them, eh?"

Arthur crept into the bathroom, where all the fun was going on, to see Jane bending over the bathtub, busily scrubbing Arty while the nursemaid was drying little Henry. Jane had her back to him, and, for a while, Arthur stood fascinated by the sight of her generous proportions. He hadn't realised what a comely young woman she had become since entering their service, and that must have been all of six years ago. Arty caught sight of him and began to shout his name with great enthusiasm. Jane turned round in surprise.

"Oh, sir," she said, all a fluster. "If only we'd known you were coming, I'd have bathed them earlier."

"No matter—no matter at all," said Arthur genially. "I'd rather see the children in the nursery—saves you bringing them downstairs."

He stood watching Jane as she fussed around getting the boys ready for bed and then went into the night nursery to bid them good night. The very idea of having the children brought to the drawing room was horribly reminiscent of the past, and he had successfully put all that behind him. Watching Jane was a most pleasant activity, and he didn't see why it should end there. He hated having to sleep alone and avoided it as much as possible. Plump arms around him took away the nightmares, like the drink, and tonight the comely Jane could comfort him. Refusal was out of the question, since refusal meant dismissal, and he could see that Jane was dedicated to her work. A little present was all that was needed, and he would have to purloin Lizzie's jewel box yet again.

That night, when the house was still and quiet, Arthur made his way to what he thought was Jane's bedroom. Rosie heard footsteps on the landing outside and thinking it was Jane, she turned over and closed her eyes. The door was pushed open, and Arthur stood by her bed, looking down at her, not realising this was Rosie and not Jane. Rosie turned over and in the brief moment before Arthur blew out his candle, she recognised her visitor as Mr. Potts—Mr. Potts in his nightshirt and smelling strongly of drink. Rosie, who had heard all the stories about him and his amours realised why he was there, but terror struck her dumb—she wanted to scream, but no sound came and her limbs refused to move.

"Don't be frightened now," said Arthur. "I won't hurt you—look, I've brought you a present." He swung the opal pendant on its silver chain drunkenly in front of her, and as the moonlight from the open casement caught the unusual colours in the huge opal, Rosie watched helplessly, hypnotised by the movement.

"If you please me tonight, this will be yours," continued Arthur, his eyes glinting in anticipation of things yet to come. "Remove that enveloping garment, so I can see you my dear. Come now—don't keep me waiting."

With trembling fingers, Rosie undid the buttons at the top of her nightdress as she had been told while Arthur put a match to the candle. He needed to see her plump, young body more clearly before he took his pleasure of her, for Jane was a virgin, he was sure of it, and a virgin would make quite a change for him. Rosie turned away, sobbing with fear. He was standing too close to the door for her to escape, even if her legs would carry her that far, and she had no idea what he intended to do to her—she knew it was supposed to hurt the first time, but exactly what went on to make it hurt she was still to discover.

"Take it off!" commanded Arthur, who was becoming impatient.

Slowly and shakily, Rosie pulled the nightdress over her head and the higher she raised her arms the higher Arthur held his candle to illuminate the scene. He watched in amazement for the body that revealed itself before him was not the one he had expected, and worse still, he could see a face floating above him reflected in the candlelight, a face he knew only too well. Alice's eyes glittering in the candle's flame were staring straight at him and her mouth was drawn in a tight line of disapproval. He lowered the candle in horror at the sight and the light fell upon Rosie's terrified face. Arthur caught his breath and felt his heart miss a beat as the candle fell from his grasp. It was Rosie and not Jane. He had come to the wrong room and Alice had come back to punish him for the sin he was about to commit upon this child. His legs had turned to rubber and felt as if they no longer belonged to him, and he felt a pain, a terrible searing pain in his chest. With a crash, he fell to the floor, his eyes rolling and his mouth twisted to one side as he gasped for breath.

Rosie struggled out of bed on the other side clutching her nightgown to her. A terrible choking sound was coming from the floor near to the door. Perhaps he had fallen down in a drunken stupor, and she could get away. She edged nervously towards the door, and then she saw him—a moaning, twitching mass on the floor—his mouth a hideous grimace and his eyes staring out of their sockets. Rosie could take no more. She opened her mouth and let out an ear-piercing scream of terror.

Jane never slept very deeply, always aware that if the children cried out in the night she must see to their needs. Rosie's screams woke her instantly, and she ran across the landing thinking some catastrophe had occurred in the night nursery. She could hear the children murmuring in half wakefulness, and a strange sobbing sound coming from Rosie's room. Jane tried to push open the door, but there was some obstruction blocking the way. Needing light, she ran to fetch one of the children's night-lights from the nursery, and, holding it through the small opening, she managed with some effort to squeeze into the room. Once inside, she discovered Arthur, his crumpled body huddled against the door, throwing a grotesque shadow onto the far wall in the candlelight. Easing her way round him, she went up to Rosie and put her arm round her.

"Whatever has happened, Rosie?" she whispered, shocked by the situation she had discovered.

Rosie seemed to have turned into stone, unable to move or speak, and Jane realised she would have to take charge of things. She forced Rosie's stiff arms into the sleeves of her nightgown and began to move her round the bed and towards the door.

"Don't look, Rosie dear," she said kindly. "Just follow me. I will find Miss Sarah, and you must stay in my room until I get back. You will be quite safe there. If the children wake, just leave them. I promise I will be as quick as I can."

Once Rosie was settled under the warm sheets, Jane fled along the shadowy landing to the far wing where Sarah slept. She roused Sarah and led her back to the nursery wing, explaining on the way that Arthur had been taken ill. Sarah was puzzled as to the direction they were taking until she arrived at the door of Rosie's room. One look at Arthur on the floor, and she had no need to ask any questions. The reason for his visit was only too apparent. Opening the connecting door into the day nursery where the baby now slept, she asked Jane to help her move him.

"Jane dear, try to help me to lift him—it's not far. I will hold his head and you take his feet. It will look better if he is found in the nursery."

Jane nodded—she understood Sarah's reasoning—and between them Arthur was pulled and pushed into the nursery where Sarah made him as comfortable as possible. Jane wheeled the cradle out and into Rosie's room and then went to fetch help. Sarah remained with her brother-in-law until the doctor arrived and explained to him that Arthur must have wandered in to see his youngest child and then had been taken ill. The doctor, who knew that Arthur drank too much for his own good, decided that he must have been drunk when he wandered into the nursery. He had given him plenty of warnings in the past, and now it was too late. Arthur Potts had suffered a seizure and a bad one at that, leaving him partially paralysed. It was possible that he might recover some use of his limbs, but he would never be the same again.

Eventually, with the help of some of the menservants, Arthur was carried to his bed, and the house settled down again. Rosie had fallen into an exhausted sleep in Jane's bed, so Jane crept between the sheets in her old bedroom so as not to disturb her. Over the mantelshelf hung a sepia-coloured photograph of Alice's likeness, which Lizzie had kept for sentimental reasons. Jane lay and looked at the grim-faced Alice before she fell asleep thinking how much the old portrait looked like an avenging angel, without realising how much of a guardian angel Alice had been to Rosie that night.

When she awoke the next morning, Jane found the opal pendant on the bedside table where Arthur had left it and picked it up and looked at it as it lay in the palm of her hand. So, the master had tried to buy Rosie's services with this had he—the despicable old man. Better that Miss Sarah knew nothing about it. She knew it had belonged to the mistress, so by right it should belong to little Hetty when she grew up. Jane dressed early and slipped into Lizzie's old room, replacing the pendant in the jewel box on the dressing table, and no one was any the wiser.

At first, when she awoke, Rosie wondered why she was back in her old room and then the events of the previous night came flooding back to her. She would have to go and as soon as possible. Much as she loved little Hetty, she would have to leave her in someone else's care, and the tears began to roll down her cheeks. If only she had never come to The Great House on the bay. She had known much happiness there, but the horror of last night and Percy's death had wiped out her happy memories. All she wanted now was to return to Clay Cross and start her life again. What if Mr. Potts got better and tried to come near her again. She could never risk such a thing and shuddered at the thought. She would have to leave and would tell Sarah as soon as she was dressed.

Sarah understood her anxiety and felt partly responsible, having encouraged Arthur to spend the night at home, but she had done so in the best interests of the children and had never expected him to behave badly with the nursery staff, and with Rosie in particular, who had always been considered as one of the family. She explained to Rosie that there would never be any opportunities for a repeat of the previous night's disgraceful episode. Arthur would be nursed by the male members of the household and, once recovered, he would find walking difficult and would probably need a bath chair. Rosie must remain with them until arrangements could be made for her future, and, until then, she would sleep in Sarah's room and a lock would be placed on the door. She couldn't just run away. Where would she go and who would keep her now that she was a young woman?

Rosie saw the sense in Sarah's arguments and agreed to stay until she found another situation and then she would leave. Sarah accepted her decision with deep regret, feeling she had failed her in some way and knowing that she would miss her company. She had felt a great love for Rosie since she had met her as a child and their relationship had been more one of an older sister to a younger one than anything else, and she felt genuinely sad to see her leave.

But Rosie was adamant and wrote immediately to her father and Beth, telling them of her intention to return home and asking them to make some enquiries on her behalf regarding a live- in position somewhere in the district. She was old enough now to take a responsible position, and Sarah would give her an excellent reference. She knew where she stood with the people of Clay Cross. They were forthright country folk, and she belonged to them and their ways. Right now, she longed to see Rory again and wished she could turn the clock back to the carefree times they had spent together.

Her feelings when she had first arrived in this beautiful place had changed over the years, and she had grown to realise that all was not as it had first appeared. Under the glittering surface lay a web of deceit woven by Lizzie, and, for all his importance, Arthur Potts was a wicked man. The happy days had long since gone when the house had hummed with the activity of a forthcoming event and the sound of laughter mingled with the click of mallets against wooden balls had floated up to the nursery windows from the croquet lawn.

It was time to leave, and leave she must.

PART THREE

Red Gum River

1868–1871

CHAPTER 15

Leaning out of one of the Anchor's upstairs windows, Rosie watched the commotion going on in the street below. A teamster was urging his lead bullocks in no uncertain manner, his oaths filling the air as he desperately attempted to prevent them from sinking onto their knees in the soft mud and pulling the wagon to a stop. Once this happened, it was a devil of a business to make the weary beasts rise to their feet again, and, with the wharf in sight, they only had a few hundred yards to drag their load to its destination.

Fanny appeared at the door to the bar, her huge bulk filling the entrance, and took stock of the situation. "You've overloaded the poor beasts," she shouted indignantly as she viewed the wagon laden high with grain sacks. "No wonder they can't get any further."

Turning her head, she called inside to the barman. "Joe! Get the men out of the bar to help. We don't want this load on the doorstep—it's bad for trade."

A few minutes elapsed, and some of the men trooped outside to push and pull until the team got moving again. The excitement over, Rosie pulled down the casement to shut out the stench and the flies and continued to change the bed sheets. She had lived at the Anchor since her return to Clay Cross and enjoyed the easygoing atmosphere of the place. She had taken to Fanny at first sight—they got on well together and now she considered the Anchor as home.

John had persuaded Fanny to take his daughter on once he had heard her mention that she was looking for a good, hardworking girl to help now that trade was picking up, and John had been at his wit's end trying to find a place for Rosie on her return. Since the birth of their baby, Amy was in no fit state mentally to receive anybody, and he had left her in the care of an aboriginal girl, calling in daily to see her while he had returned to live with Beth. Rosie knew nothing of his present circumstances and her decision to leave the Potts's household had come at a bad time for him, but, thankfully, things had turned out well. Fanny kept a clean, decent place where a working man could find respectable lodgings at a price he could afford. There were no red plush hangings or gilt furnishings as you would find at Pendle's Hotel in the High Street, but good sturdy brass beds with clean mattresses and bedding. Rosie was employed as a chamber maid and waitress and helped in the kitchen when needed, but not in the bar—that was no place for a woman. Fanny had made it clear from the start that roughnecks were not welcome in her establishment, although most of her customers were heavy drinkers. Rosie was a cheerful, good-looking young woman who knew how to behave with the patrons of the Anchor—she worked with a will, and that was enough for Fanny. Rosie could stay as long as she liked.

With the development of the wharf had come the river traffic and the expansion of the town. Rosie had hardly recognised the place when she had alighted from the coach in the great square. In the space of four years, a post and telegraph office had been built on one side of the main street, and next to it there was a police station and a lockup. Beth's store was a tumbledown wooden shack compared to the new buildings stretching along the street, and the waterfront hummed with activity. A short distance away, her father was waiting to greet her, and she was startled to see how much he had aged since she had last seen him. She flung her arms round him and kissed him, and John's face lit up with the warmth of her embrace. How like Julia she was, and how charming she looked in her travelling clothes. She had acquired a certain sophistication living with a grand family, he could see that, but her open, loving nature was the same, and it gladdened his heart. It pleased him to have her back—his little wild rose.

He bent to pick up her baggage, and it was then that Rosie noticed his twisted left foot.

"Oh, Papa," she exclaimed, distressed at the sight. "What happened to your foot?"

John smiled wryly. "I'm quite used to it, my dear, and manage well enough. A year or more ago I slipped on the wet surface of the pontoon when we were poling the red gum out of the forest and my foot became caught in the crab winch. It broke my ankle and crushed part of my leg, which never healed properly."

"But why didn't you tell me?" asked Rosie as they made their way slowly to the Anchor Inn, where Fanny awaited them.

"What good would that have done, Rosie? It would only have worried you, and it healed in time. I still have a job supervising the work on the wharf, and that's what I came out here to do in the first place." John stopped and looked back towards the river. "Well, what do you think of it then? It's changed a lot, hasn't it?"

Rosie stared at the paddle steamers lined up at the wharf, waiting their turn to unload the wool clip from the sheep stations upstream. The scene fascinated her.

"What are those men doing over there, Papa?" she asked, pointing to a sweating gang of workmen laying girders close to the waterfront.

"Why, they're finishing off the line. We're to have a railway here soon—hadn't you heard? Clay Cross is an important place these days."

Rosie turned away. She had liked it better as she remembered it—a sleepy little town where kindly folk like Beth lived.

"How is Mrs. Macdonald, Papa, and Mama, of course? I've not heard any news for some time—I'm longing to see Rory and Prince again. Do you think he will remember me after all this time?"

John was silent for a while. Rosie had to be told. As he had been standing, waiting for the coach to arrive, he had been wondering how to break the news to her. Now that he had seen her, he realised his daughter had grown into a self-possessed young woman, and he hoped she would understand what he had to tell her.

"Things have changed in other ways since you were last here, Rosie. There's a lot I have to tell you, but it can wait until we get to Fanny's."

Rosie's curiosity was aroused by her father's words, and she kept quiet for the remainder of their walk. A warm welcome awaited them at the inn where Fanny had prepared a light meal for Rosie in the empty dining room. Once they were settled, she left father and daughter together, realising they would have much to discuss after so long apart.

For a while, John sat drinking his beer until Rosie had finished her meal and then set down his glass.

"It's not easy, Rosie, and I hope you'll understand what I have to tell you. I don't want you to hear it from anyone else."

"What is it, Papa, that worries you so?" asked Rosie, puzzled by her father's reticence to divulge some knowledge of which she had been kept in ignorance.

"Your mama has had a child."

"A child! But surely she was too—" Her voice died away as she watched her father nervously fingering his glass.

"Yes—we never expected her to become pregnant at her age. It was a shock to us both. The baby—a little boy—was born prematurely and only lived a few hours, a tiny scrap of humanity without a chance of life." The memory of the little wooden box he had made for his son buried in the graveyard was still painful to him.

"I'm sorry, Papa." Rosie wondered what exactly was troubling her father. Babies often died at birth—it was a fact of life and almost inevitable if a child was born before its full time. Her own mother had lost two children before she was conceived, so her father had been through this experience before. Perhaps he was feeling guilty about giving Amy a baby so late in the change of life. She could hardly ask him that, or if they had lived as man and wife again after she had left home.

"How is Mama, now?"

"That's the trouble, Rosie. It turned her mind. She lives in a world of her own and hardly recognises anyone. She thinks the baby is still alive, and it's kindest to let her continue to think so. Before this happened, she nursed me back to health. I was at home for months with my leg strapped to a splint, and Amy changed the dressing every day. Without her medical knowledge, I could easily have lost my leg. She was never a kind mother to you, Rosie; it wasn't her nature to be so, but she nursed your mother and took care of me when I was in great pain and unable to move. We grew a little closer to one another at that time, although we had never been happy together as I had been with your mother."

Rosie felt a wave of disgust sweep over her, to think that her father's gratitude had led him to give her stepmother a child when there had never been anything but bitterness between them. She sat on in silence, unable to find any word of comfort to give him.

"There is more you should know, Rosie. I no longer live at the homestead. I left some time ago."

Rosie looked up. "Then how does Mama manage if she is unable to look after herself?"

"I call in every day and do what I can for her, but she rarely notices me. An aboriginal girl lives in and looks after her, and they do well enough together."

Rosie recalled her father's pride in the homestead he had built for his new wife and felt some pity for him. He had lost so much in his life—his home in the old country and the wife he had loved, and now he no longer lived in the home he had built in this new country or lived with the woman he had married with such high hopes for the future. He had asked for Rosie's understanding and needed her kindness, for she was all he had left. "Where do you live now, Papa?" Her enquiry was tinged with sympathy.

"With Beth, at the store—when we heard of your intention to return we wondered how you would feel about it. It has worried Beth ever since. She tried to write and tell you, but every time she put pen to paper the words refused to take shape. She loves you, Rosie, like a daughter and felt she might lose your affection for her if you knew the truth."

Rosie smiled and placed her hand over her father's. "Dear Papa, that is good news at least. I'm glad you are together—it's high time you had some happiness. Tell Beth I'm pleased for you both, and I will come and visit her soon, if I may."

"My dear, you will always be welcome. Come whenever you wish. Beth wants you to feel a part of the family—in fact, she insists upon it."

Rosie laughed. That sounded like the Beth she remembered and she looked forward to picking up the old ties of friendship with the Macdonalds again.

John rose to leave, and Rosie accompanied him slowly to the door. Life in Clay Cross had certainly changed in more ways than she could have imagined possible.

The following Sunday afternoon, Rosie donned her smartest outfit and set off to take tea with the Macdonalds. Sunday was to be her day off, and once breakfast had been served and cleared away the rest of the day was her own. Beth had sent her an open invitation to spend Sunday with them whenever she pleased, but today was to be a special occasion—a welcome-home party. Sarah had altered some of Lizzie's less flamboyant gowns to fit her before she had left the Pottses household, and now she had a very respectable wardrobe for a girl in her position.

It was only a step from the Anchor Inn to Beth's store in the square, but as she walked along under her pink parasol, Rosie caused quite a stir among those citizens abroad at the time. Her long, flaxen hair tied back with a pink satin ribbon to match her pink and white gingham dress and her merry smile reflected in the laughing brown eyes all contributed to her youthful charm. Happiness bubbled out of her, infecting those around her. Today, she would see Rory again, and she could hardly wait. The frilly pink parasol bobbed along the wooden walkway as if it shared its owner's enthusiasm for the outing.

At the door to the store, Rory was already waiting—a smartly turned out Rory wearing his best embroidered waistcoat and high polished boots. As soon as she caught sight of him standing there, Rosie ran across the square towards him, losing her parasol in the process. Having retrieved it, Rory returned it to the owner, scarcely recognising in this laughing young woman the scruffy little companion of his youth.

"Oh, Rory," exclaimed Rosie. "Just look at you—how handsome you are these days."

"Stone the crows, Rosie," breathed Rory, in amazement. "What's happened to you, for Christ's sake? Turn around—my word—you're really something. I'd never have guessed you would have turned out like this!"

Rosie blushed with pleasure. From what she remembered of him, Rory was never overly generous with his compliments.

"It's real good to see you again, Rosie. Come on in—Ma's waiting for you in the parlour. I've never known her to use it before unless it's for something special."

Inside the kitchen, Prince lay on the mat. He lifted his head and thumped his tail slowly in greeting. Rosie went over to him and spoke quietly as she stroked him under the chin. The tail thumping increased as Prince rose to his feet, whining with pleasure.

"He remembers me—he still remembers me," she said happily as the dog licked her face affectionately.

"Of course he does. You'd never forget our Rosie would you, old boy, any more than I would."

Rosie looked up. Rory's remark had placed them back on the old footing again. Nothing had changed between them, she felt certain of it.

In the parlour, Beth had a grand tea waiting and welcomed her with open arms. Her father sat comfortably in the old armchair as if he owned the place, and Andrew ran in from minding the store, which never closed until dusk, whatever the day of the week. Rosie talked her head off to everyone's amusement, for there was so much to tell them, and then, when it was almost time to return to his duties at the Pendle's Hotel, Rory and Rosie took Prince for his evening walk beside the river. It seemed natural for her to take his arm as they strolled along the well-worn pathway to the lagoon, talking of times remembered.

As Rory left her at the door of the Anchor Inn, Rosie realised he had told her nothing about himself, or his work at the hotel. She supposed she hadn't given him a chance, having had so much to say herself.

"You'll come again next Sunday will you, Rosie?" asked Rory as he turned to leave.

"Of course, if you'd like me too."

"If I'd what?" retorted Rory. "You're still as daft as ever Rosie—know that!"

Rosie laughed as the door closed behind her and began to walk towards the stairs. A drunk lurched out of the bar and seeing her there put his arm round her waist.

"Take your filthy hands off her, Tom Price," came Fanny's bellow from the bar. "She's not the sort you're looking for."

The man stepped back a pace as if he had been struck and stumbled through the door into the street. Rosie was shocked at the encounter and hurried up to her room. Working in the dining room, she had not come across his type before and would take more care in future.

There was a brief lull in the bar and some heads were turned in her direction.

"Who's the good looking Sheila?" asked one of the men.

"Reckon our Fan has a daughter she don't want us to know about," said another.

"Oh no, I haven't," said Fanny, sweeping away the empties off the counter. "I wish I had—that's John Taylor's daughter—that's who she is."

A few eyebrows were raised and then the men got back to their drinking. They knew why John's daughter was unable to live in her own home. It was a bad business for the poor kid.

Fanny made her way into the back room behind the bar where she washed the glasses and found Rosie already there, occupied on the same task. There was no need for her to be doing that on her day off, but it was just like her to help without being asked, thought Fanny. A right good girl she was to be sure.

"You should come through the back way next time, Rosie," said Fanny, as she bustled about. "You won't meet the drunks then. Did you enjoy your afternoon off?"

"Oh, yes—I had tea with the Macdonalds, all except for Malcolm—he's married and lives at Swan Hill."

"So, you saw young Rory, I suppose. Full of his own importance now old George has made him part of the management. Never had a son did old George, and he and his missus have all but adopted young Rory. Make a rare fuss of him they do, taking him out with them as if he was already a member of the family."

"How's that?" asked Rosie, surprised that Rory had made no mention of the Pendle's to her. Fanny must have got it wrong.

"Didn't he tell you then? The Pendles expect him to marry their daughter."

A glass slipped out of Rosie's hand and smashed on the floor. "Not Mary Ann! You can't mean Mary Ann?" she said in a horrified tone of voice.

Fanny looked at her curiously. "Who else my dear—she is their only child and will inherit the hotel when old George has gone. I get the feeling that you don't care over much for the idea. Well, they're both a bit too young to settle down as yet but it's as good as arranged."

"He didn't say anything to me about it," said Rosie in a small voice.

"No, my lovely, I can see he didn't, and if I'd known he meant anything to you I wouldn't have mentioned it. Will you be seeing him again?"

"Yes—next Sunday," answered Rosie, miserably.

"That's a good thing," said Fanny cheerfully. "It'll give you a chance to sort things out with him and know where you stand. You get him to tell you fair and square and then forget all about him. You're a pretty girl, and you'll soon find someone else. There are plenty of good fish left in the sea and better ones than Rory Macdonald at that."

Rosie looked down sadly at the broken glass at her feet. She didn't want Fanny to see how upset her words had made her feel.

"I don't know, Fanny," she said quietly as she bent down to pick up the pieces. "It's just that I don't want anyone else—ever."

Fanny chuckled. "They all say that at your age, my love. You'll get over it in no time, you'll find."

But Rosie made no reply. She knew that wasn't true.

CHAPTER 16

During a short break in the almost continuous drizzle the following week, Rosie had ventured out to buy a few necessities she was lacking and had caught her first sight of Mary Ann. She was stepping delicately across one of the planks in the High Street, holding up her wide crinoline skirt out of the mud while Rory helped her to keep her balance. Rosie had stood and watched them from the privacy of the drapery where she had slipped inside to avoid being seen. She had no desire to meet Mary Ann face-to-face; it was quite gruelling enough to witness Rory being so courteous and gentlemanly to her. Once across the street, Mary Ann had smiled her prim, conceited little smile, acknowledging those she passed as she minced along on Rory's arm, her tipped up nose and self-satisfied smirk announcing to everyone that Rory Macdonald belonged to her.

Like a cat with the cream, thought Rosie as she watched the pair disappear down one of the alleys leading to the wharf. *She hasn't altered one bit except that her clothes are much grander.*

Fanny was right about getting things fair and square, and that was exactly what she intended to do when she had him to herself next Sunday. Rosie seethed inside with anger; there had been plenty of time when they had been alone together for him to have mentioned his intentions. She had worn her heart on her sleeve for the world to see, and Rory wasn't blind.

She worked fitfully that week. It was unlike her to be moody but a black depression hung over her and wouldn't shift until Sunday had come and gone. Fanny could see her eating her heart out and hoped the matter would soon be resolved; it was affecting the whole atmosphere of the place, and she was glad to get behind the bar counter and share a few jokes with her customers.

When Sunday eventually arrived, the frivolous pink outfit was left in the cupboard, and Rosie set off wearing a plain brown gown; there was no need to dress up and make an impression today. Fanny called after her as she was leaving. "Make sure you bring back some better weather with you this time."

Rosie grinned as she turned to wave. Fanny might be rough and ready but her heart was in the right place.

When she arrived, Beth was serving in the store. "We'll be eating a wee bit late today, lass. Your pa has taken Andrew fishing, and Rory's nae here yet."

"I'll take Prince along the river then—it will do us both good to get a breath of air." She had no intention of sitting around and waiting for Rory.

"Aye, lassie. He'll enjoy that," replied Beth as she tipped the sugar from the brass shovel into the bag and folded the top over firmly. "Anything else, noo?" she asked her customer, hopefully.

Rosie called Prince and set off downstream. She would give the old homestead a look, although she would not call in to see her stepmother. The lazy flow of the Murray helped to ease her tension as she dawdled along the path. A paddle steamer chugged slowly past, disturbing a long-legged heron fishing among the reeds. A bright blue flash of wings and a pair of jewelled kingfishers darted from a hole in the bank and disappeared upstream. Rosie leaned up against the smooth trunk of a river gum to watch a group of water wagtails dipping their tails and weaving in and out of the shallows. She loved the old river in all its moods and would never have been happy living inland. In the distance, she could see the squat chimney of the homestead and a thin line of smoke rising upwards. Nothing moved; time seemed to have stood still in that tranquil place. Drawing closer, she could see a hunched figure seated in the rocking chair on the verandah. Long black hair streaked with grey hung untidily around the sunken cheeks, and in her arms the woman held a dirty white shawl which she was bending over, mouthing words, although no sound came from her lips. Rosie turned away in distress—to think that her proud stepmother could be reduced to this. It was small wonder that her father found it impossible to remain there. She wondered why she had felt a need to walk in this direction instead of taking her usual path upstream: perhaps she had wanted to lay the ghosts of the past.

As she retraced her steps towards the town, a figure came striding towards her, and, when she realised it was Rory, her heart leapt within her despite all her good intentions to keep her feelings in check. Showing every appearance of being delighted at having found her at last, Rory walked along beside her.

"Been looking everywhere for you, Rosie. Ma said you'd gone along the river, but I didn't expect to find you down here."

Rosie shrugged. "I just thought I'd walk as far as the homestead, that's all."

"Did you see your stepmother?"

"Only from a distance—I didn't really want to."

Rory understood her reluctance. "Reckon she's best left to herself—there's nothing you can do for her, so your pa says."

They walked along without speaking, until Rory had enough of her silence. He knew Rosie well enough to know that something was wrong. "Come on Rosie—don't take it so hard. You never cared for her, so why the long face?"

"It's not about Mama—it was something I was told ...," Rosie began miserably.

"'Bout me, I suppose. Well —let's see. I drink quite a bit—gamble when I've got some money, which ain't often, and kiss all the pretty girls I can lay me hands on. Don't amount to much, to my way of thinking."

"Oh, Rory, be sensible. I saw you with Mary Ann last week and Fanny says—"

"It's what Fanny says, is it?" Rory began to get angry. "I'm surprised at you, Rosie. There's always plenty of gossip in a town like Clay Cross; you should know that."

"But I saw you myself," insisted Rosie, determined that he should hear her out. "You were helping Mary Ann to cross the road and walking arm in arm with her as if the two of you were already married. And what's more, I saw the look on her face—there's no denying what she was thinking."

Rory sat down on an old, fallen tree whose branches stuck grotesquely into the mud of the river bed and began to throw sticks into the water. After a while, Rosie sat on the opposite end with her hands in her lap and waited for him to say something. For some time, the only sound to be heard was the soft plop as a stick hit the surface, to sail away down stream. Tiring of this activity, Rory stretched lazily and turned towards her.

"I work for the Pendles, Rosie—you know that." Rosie nodded, looking away. "Well then—sometimes I have to do things that I don't enjoy."

"Like taking Mary Ann out, I suppose," said Rosie huffily.

"Yeah—like taking Mary Ann out and seeing she don't get her fancy clothes muddied or gets spoken to by undesirable people."

"Huh! Well you didn't seem too unhappy about it when I saw you, and she certainly thinks she's the one for you."

"I know that without you going on about it, but she ain't the one for me, and that's for certain. You're the only girl for me, Rosie—always have been and always will be."

But Rosie doubted he was telling the truth. "Don't say things like that Rory when you don't mean them—it's cruel."

Rory moved along until he was sitting close beside her and placed his arm around her shoulders.

"I mean it, Rosie—honest to God—how was I to know you would be coming back here again. You might have fallen for someone in that grand house where you worked. It's not my fault that old George and Mary Ann's ma want me to marry her because it's what *she* wants. They've even promised me a share in the hotel when I marry her. It makes it bloody impossible for me, especially now that Mary Ann knows you're back in town. She's plaguing me to name the day, and I keep putting her off. I want you Rosie—just you."

Rory held her close and kissed her gently. Rosie sighed and rested her head on his shoulder, and so they remained for some time, in perfect harmony with one another and their surroundings.

"What will you do? You can't go on working at the hotel if you don't marry Mary Ann; so where will you go?"

"I'm thinking about that." Rory had been bothered for some time ever since he had discovered that Rosie had returned to Clay Cross.

Perhaps if he told old George that he didn't love his daughter and a marriage between them would never work he might show some sympathy, but he doubted it. What Mary Ann wanted she usually got. If he left to try his luck in the town or on the goldfields, his prospects were pretty poor. He had been spoilt living at the hotel with everything found and more besides, and apart from that he had gambled heavily and never saved a penny, leaving him nothing to invest in a future for himself and Rosie. He had spoken the truth when he had told her he only wanted her but he could see no way out of his present situation.

Rosie moved in his embrace. "Will you come every Sunday, Rory?" she asked, sleepily.

"Sure—every Sunday, sweetheart," replied Rory, kissing the tip of her nose.

A much brighter and calmer Rosie returned to the Anchor Inn that evening, leaving a worried and troubled Rory to make his way back to the hotel to be met in the carpeted foyer by his intended, wearing a gown of such a bright yellow it put the billy buttons to shame. As soon as she saw him, Mary Ann linked her arm in his, to Rory's annoyance.

"Not just now, Mary Ann, if you don't mind. I'm going to the bar to get a drink. I need one rather badly."

Mary Ann pouted and flounced off to have a word with her mama. Rory must be told that was not the way to treat her. It was all the fault of that Rosie Taylor coming back, she was sure of it. The sooner they were married the better, then Rory would have to treat her properly or her papa would not make him a partner in the hotel.

For the next few months, Rory saw Rosie every Sunday. It was his day off, and it was presumed that he went home to see his family, but his main purpose was to continue his friendship with Rosie. When he was approached by the Pendles about his forthcoming engagement to their daughter, he made excuses rather than tell them of his true intentions. Mary Ann's attentions became more persistent, and, wherever he went in the hotel, there she was waiting for him round the next corner. He began to feel like a hunted animal and started to drink more than was good for him to blot out her whining voice and beseeching eyes.

Rosie, on the other hand, was content to leave things as they were for the time being. Fanny had told her she would employ Rory at the Anchor and they could help to run the place together once she realised how dead set Rosie was on having him, but Rory was not interested in her offer. He would need to work in a different place altogether once he had left the hotel, for Clay Cross wasn't large enough to avoid meeting Mary Ann or her family at some time or another, and he would have to make a fresh start somewhere else. Rosie sympathised with his point of view and hoped he would take her with him—to the ends of the earth if necessary.

A few weeks later, word reached the Pendle household of Rory's courtship. He had been seen on Sunday afternoons walking with Rosie Taylor beside the lagoon with his arm around her waist, deep in conversation. The Pendles insisted on the truth but Rory, not wanting to lose his job until he found another one, refused to admit to an association with Rosie apart from saying that he thought of her as a sister now that their parents lived together. Mary Ann fumed inwardly and decided there and then to bring Rory to the altar before things went any further.

That night, when Rory had stumbled upstairs to his bed, Mary Ann gave him time to lapse into a state of unconsciousness and then slid under the sheets beside him. Rory was too heavily asleep to be aware of her presence beside him and was stunned to find her head on his pillow when he awoke the next morning.

"What are you doin' here, Mary Ann?" he asked thickly, nursing his aching head. "Get out, or I'll throw you out."

"That's a way to talk, I must say, Rory, when you invited me here yourself."

"I did what?" exclaimed Rory in total disbelief. "Never on your life."

"Told me you couldn't wait until we were wed," continued Mary Ann sweetly, "and now Rory I can't wait either—my mama and papa will understand when I tell them, 'cause Mama was having me before they were married. Comes of being too much in love, don't it, Rory?"

Rory groaned. He had no recollection of inviting Mary Ann into his bed. He must have been too drunk to care or taken leave of his senses.

Mary Ann eased her way from under the sheets and waved coyly as she left the room. As soon as she was dressed, she spoke to her parents and begged them to forgive Rory for his conduct, in the hopes that they would grant permission for him to marry her.

Later that morning, Rory had the call he was dreading and made his way to George Pendle's private room.

"My dear boy," beamed old George, giving him a hearty slap on his back. "I know how you must be feeling right now—got your tail between your legs, eh? Mary Ann's a wily little baggage and no mistake. Best to marry her within the month, don't you think, in case she has a baby. The missus and I are mighty pleased about it—always wanted you as a son, right from the time Mary Ann took a shine to you." George gave a chuckle and handed Rory a glass of whisky. "Drink to it, my boy—to your future happiness." Rory said nothing in reply for he had nothing to say—his future had been decided for him. He had been caught like a rat in a trap and how he would tell Rosie he had no idea; she was lost to him forever and the thought of that plunged him into the depths of despair.

The afternoon was hot and humid and trade was slack at the Anchor Inn. Rosie missed the cool breezes of Port Phillip Bay and longed for a swim. She asked Fanny if she could spare her for a while and as Fanny raised no objections she had taken a towel and gone to the lagoon to swim in the secluded part she remembered from her childhood. On her way, she collected Prince to guard her clothes and to warn her of any passing stranger; then she could swim without the encumbrance of any clothes under the watchful protection of her faithful old dog.

Rory called in at the Anchor, expecting to find her there. He needed to get the matter off his conscience and the sooner the better, for Mary Ann would spread the news of their engagement far and wide, and it would be the talk of the town soon enough.

"She's gone for a swim, but she'll be back soon if you care to wait," said Fanny, moving her perspiring bulk towards the back room where it was a bit cooler.

"No thanks, all the same, Fanny. I think I know where she'll be, and I need to see her right away."

"Please yourself," shrugged Fanny, wondering what all the haste could be in this heat. If people had any sense at all, they stayed in the cool when the sun was as hot as this and not get themselves all worked up about things.

Rory walked to the end of the lagoon where the river had carved out a small basin, making a natural swimming pool. He had often swum there with Rosie in the past and that was where he expected to find her. As he rounded a clump of marsh wattles, he saw Prince lying in the grass beside her folded clothes and sat down beside him in the shade of the bushes. Prince made no move except to open one eye to acknowledge his master. It was far too hot for tail wagging.

Rosie floated on her back in the blissfully cool water, pushing away the fronds of water weed as they drifted round her. Rory sat watching—entranced by the sight of her lissom young body. The green weed clinging to her hair turned her into a water nymph, and his longing for her increased. After a while, she stood up, waist high in the water, and began to wade to the bank. Rory got to his feet, holding her towel in his hand; he had no wish for her to think he had come to spy on her nakedness.

"Rory! You have no right to see me like this—turn round this minute!" She took the towel from his outstretched hand and covered herself as Rory obediently turned his back.

"Why are you here? Has something happened?"

Rory turned towards her and took her in his arms. Seeing her in all her innocence was more than he could bear, and he was fast losing control of his feelings.

"Rosie, sweet Rosie—I love you more than life itself—don't push me away my dearest—I want you so much. Let me make love to you—"

The towel dropped onto the grass at their feet as Rosie struggled to get free. He wanted her in the same way as Mr. Potts had wanted her and, much as she loved him, the spectre of that lecherous old man stood between them. She wanted Rory to love her, but she felt terrified of what was going to happen to her—the scars of that frightening experience were still there, and physical contact became repugnant. During the struggle, they fell to the ground and Rosie was pinned under Rory's weight, unable to move. Rory continued to kiss and fondle her until her struggles ceased and she lay quietly beneath him, feeling his hardness pressing against her.

"I love you, Rosie, that's why I want you like this—it's not that you're a woman I fancy, but because you're Rosie—my Rosie—who loves me. You do love me, don't you Rosie—you want me too?"

"Yes, yes, I do, but I'm afraid—I can't explain—and I do love you Rory, I really do." She shook a little in his arms, although she was calmer now.

Rory slipped off his strides, and she saw his need for her and gradually relaxed as he moved between her thighs. He was gentle and loving, trying not to cause her any further distress until she too felt the joy of possession, and all her fears were swept away. They lay in each others arms under the shade of the wattles, the yellow puff balls of blossom screening them from the outside world and watched only by the inquisitive finches peeping through the branches above.

"Will you marry me soon?" she asked sleepily, as she lay contentedly in his arms.

Rory felt badly and moved away from her embrace. He had made matters worse for them both by his impetuous behaviour and hid his face in his arms.

"That's what I came to tell you, Rosie—dear God, how can I tell you now?"

Rosie sat up quickly at the change in his mood, frightened to hear what he couldn't tell her. "What is it—tell me—whatever is it?"

"I came to tell you my love that I have to leave the district now—right now—I can't stay for another day."

"It's Mary Ann, isn't it?" Rosie saw by look on his face that she was right. "Tell me, Rory, you've got to tell me—you can't just go and leave me without knowing why."

"Mary Ann got into my bed last night when I was dead drunk. I didn't ask her, and I didn't even know she was there until I woke up late this morning. Then she went running to her pa and ma to tell them the good news so she could force me to marry her. She plotted it Rosie—it was nothing to do with me—but I'm getting out of here as fast as I can get going. No way am I marrying that little horror, and leaving is the only thing I can do. I can't take you with me because I'm going with a travelling group of drovers, and I don't know where I shall end up. I shouldn't have made love to you just now, but I couldn't help myself—you're the love of my life, and I've wanted you that way ever since you came back. I promise I'll marry you, Rosie, one of these days after I've saved up and found a place where we can be together."

Rosie couldn't believe her ears. After all the loving things Rory had said to her and what he had just done to her, it couldn't be true, could it? But one look at his face and she knew it *was* true, and anger soon replaced her love for him. She lifted up her hand and struck him hard across his face. Rory's eyes filled with sadness; he deserved her hatred and her wrath and loathed himself for causing her such unhappiness.

"How dare you treat me like a common woman, Rory Macdonald—how dare you—you knew I loved you, and yet you took advantage of me." Rosie began to sob as if her heart was breaking, and Rory took hold of her hand, but she pulled it away.

"What could I do, Rosie? I loathe Mary Ann—she set me up to catch me, and I fell for it—she knew I had to marry her or leave, and she didn't think I would do that. Her pa even promised me a half of the hotel if I'd marry her, but I'd rather have nothing than be tied to that scheming little bitch. I love you, Rosie, and I always will—I should have left long ago, then this would never have happened. Oh, don't cry like that my darling—I can't bear it. One day I'll come for you—I promise on my life—."

"I don't want to hear anymore, Rory. Go away. I never want to see you again—leave me alone—I'll go home on my own. Just go away—please go away."

Rosie got dressed with the tears coursing down her cheeks, sobbing uncontrollably. Rory got up feeling angry with himself, and, seeing she would have nothing else to do with him, he turned away in utter wretchedness. He had tasted the sweetness of Rosie, and he would love her for the rest of his life. Even if he begged her to wait, he doubted she would have anything to do with him, and he couldn't blame her for that, but before he left he would write her a letter and hoped she would read it.

As soon as she walked through the door, Fanny knew by her tear-stained face what Rory had wanted to tell her so badly that it couldn't be put off.

"What did he tell you, my love?" asked Fanny, as she held her close to her commodious bosom.

"He's leaving or else he will have to marry Mary Ann," wept Rosie, in despair.

"I thought as much," commented Fanny, sadly, wishing that Rosie had listened to her in the first place. "It's what everyone expected."

Rory wasn't one for writing letters, and a love letter would be a difficult thing to write, but he decided he must tell Rosie that he truly loved her, and he had made love to her because she was the only girl in the world for him, and he wanted only her for his wife as soon as he had sorted out his life. He had nothing to offer her but his love and an uncertain future until he had made something of himself.

"My dearest Rosie,

When I've made enough for a home for us both I'll come and find you, Rosie, wherever you are, but this isn't the time or place. Mary Ann would have made our lives hell if we had lived in Clay Cross as man and wife. I kept hoping that once she saw I had no interest in her she would have found someone else to marry but she had made up her mind about me, and nothing ever changes that. My money will be hard earned working the sheep stations, but I will save it for our future if you will have me when I return. But should someone else come your way who you want to marry, then he will have the dearest girl that ever lived, and I will have loved and lost.

Dearest, dearest Rosie, my love is yours and only yours and will remain yours for the rest of my life. Rory."

John brought her the letter after Rory had called into the store to tell his mother he was leaving with a group of drovers who were in town and the reason he was leaving, and John promised to give Rosie the letter and to see that she read it.

Rosie wept, wishing she had spoken to him before he had left and wishing she could feel his arms around her again and his kisses on her lips. She would forgive him everything now that she had read his letter, but it was too late, and he had already gone. She read and reread his words until she had memorised them, and, folding the letter carefully, she placed it in the bosom of her dress, keeping him there forever, close to her heart.

Beth and John found Rory's leaving a great sadness as they had fostered the hope that their children would marry one day. They seemed made for each other, and Beth was sure they had fallen in love since Rosie's return to Clay Cross, but parents never really knew their own children and were usually the last people to learn of their plans. All Beth could hope for was that Rory would make something of his life and not suffer the same fate as his father and would return home one day once he had made something of his life. She was thankful to have John to share her life, for without him she would have found Rory's going very hard to bear.

That evening, Rory could not be found anywhere when he was needed at the hotel. He had taken all his belongings from his room and had left two notes—one to old George, whom he thanked for employing him, and one to Mary Ann.

His note to Mary Ann was short and to the point. He could never marry anyone he did not love, he had written, and so he was leaving—never to return.

Mary Ann had set up a loud wailing on reading the note as her father had already let it be known that she was to be married to Rory. She had been jilted and was unlikely to find anyone else who would want her now the word had got around. People would laugh behind her back and that was insufferable—she would never live it down.

"I will never be wed, Mama—the shame is too great—no one will have me," she had sobbed.

"I sincerely hope you are not with child, Mary Ann," her mother had remarked, thinking of more practical matters.

"Oh no, Mama—there was no chance of that—no chance whatsoever," she had assured her worried parent in between her sobs.

Her mother had given her a searching look. She had caught Mary Ann's father under similar circumstances and had a shrewd idea that things had not been quite the way her daughter had explained them.

"That's quite enough of all that noise, Mary Ann—come to your senses for once. He's gone, and that's an end to it."

The sharp tone of her mother's voice had caused Mary Ann to open her eyes in astonishment and to cease her weeping. She took the note and tore it into a hundred pieces and threw them angrily into the air, scattering them like confetti. Sweeping upstairs to her room, she slammed the door behind her, leaving no one in any doubt as to how she felt about Rory Macdonald.

CHAPTER 17

After Rory had left, John made a habit of calling in at the Anchor each evening to have a few words with his daughter before returning home, and Rosie appreciated these visits. She rarely went to the store these days apart from calling in to take Prince for a run, as the place reminded her too much of Rory. Since he had gone, she had come to the conclusion that he had really loved her, and if she had only listened patiently to the dilemma he had found himself in through Mary Ann's behaviour, she might not have lost him. If only he would come back she would beg him to forgive her lack of understanding, and she blamed herself for her lack of trust in him. She longed for the day when he would return, but month after month went by without any news of Rory, and she grieved for her lost love. To those who knew her best, she had changed a great deal; outwardly, she appeared to be her calm sweet self, but the laughter had gone from her sad brown eyes, and the happy smile rarely came back to her lips.

Her father's concern touched her because she knew he had enough worries of his own to cope with. Every evening, he visited Amy before calling in to the Anchor, for Amy had become a liability, living in a world of her own where the days and nights had become one long eternity in the deep dark recesses of her mind. Rosie had heard how she spent her time rocking backwards and forwards in her chair, nursing the empty shawl in her arms, lost to the world. She felt pity now for the woman she had once hated and pity for her father who had given

Amy a child in a moment of weakness and despair and still had to carry the burden of that responsibility. She had seen Nellie, the aboriginal girl whom her father employed, leading Amy along the river path and had been shocked to see Amy's total dependence on her companion. Nellie was protective of her mistress, as if they were two of a kind, poor wild things, neither of whom could communicate with the world in which they found themselves. As Rosie watched from the opposite bank, Nellie, dressed in a peculiar assortment of Amy's petticoats and hats, had wandered off to collect some wild berries, and Amy had stood, confused and unhappy, until she had returned to lead her mistress back home. The sight had moved Rosie deeply, and her sympathy for her father's situation had increased as a result, drawing them closer together. At first, tongues had wagged in Clay Cross about her father's two wives, but Rosie knew no harm was meant by the remarks, as it was well known that never a day passed by without her father visiting his poor crazed wife, and no man envied him that. Judgements were rarely passed when one's own needs might be at stake, for anyone might need the help of his neighbour at some time or another in a pioneer community, and a man had a right to live his life however he chose to live it.

Each evening, when John pushed open the door to the bar, the regulars would acknowledge him briefly and nod in his direction. They knew his reason for coming, and not one of them would have made an improper suggestion to his daughter; they respected him too much for that, rough men though most of them were.

One evening when John arrived as usual, he noticed a stranger sitting among the locals, a muscular man of heavy build with black bushy eyebrows and a thick black beard, who looked as if he could fell an ox with one blow. Strangers were not unusual in the bar now that the wharf was in operation, but this stranger, who was a man about fifty, was taking more than a passing interest in Rosie, following her progress among the tables in the dining area with his piercing blue eyes. John felt some slight annoyance at the man's obvious interest in his daughter and tried to place him. His clothes were practical, and he had the face of one who thought before he acted. Maybe he was a squatter en route for Melbourne now he had money to spend. John had no wish to see Rosie captivated by a prospector, rich for the moment and then ready to pass on once his money was spent.

Rosie smiled across at him, seeing her father sitting in his usual seat, and the man averted his gaze and turned to look at John.

"My daughter," commented John briefly.

The man took his pipe out of his mouth and smiled. "Pretty girl," he remarked. "She does you credit, sir, if I may say so."

John nodded and turned away. He would stay in the bar tonight until Rosie had finished her work and gone to her room. This man was too old to be taking an interest in his daughter, apart from which she had suffered enough heartbreak of late in his opinion and needed breathing space before any new involvement.

Rosie knew the man had been watching her and was quite unconcerned. She had shown him to his room, and he had behaved like a gentleman. He was only staying one night while he saw to business at the wharf and would be gone the next morning, and, anyway, he looked as old as her father. Perhaps she reminded him of someone he knew who was far away or whom he would never see again. Many travellers who passed through Clay Cross had come from far off places to rest a while and then travelled on to the next settlement where they might find work, but this man looked as if he had real business in the town.

"Come far, skipper?" asked a voice.

One of the new steamboat skippers to be sure, thought John, looking at the man's bronzed face. They rarely came this far into town, preferring to stay on board or at one of the cheap hotels springing up along the waterside where there was some kind of entertainment offered, if you could call it that.

The man took his pipe out of his mouth and refilled it.

"Some way," he answered, looking at the speaker, "further than I expected in the time. There's been a big rise up river—been a tidy bit of rain recently—reckon you're in for a flood in these parts in a couple of days' time if it moves at the rate it's going at present."

There was a general discussion among the men in the bar after this news. The last time the river had flooded it had come almost to the top of the wharf, and they were concerned. The river trade had increased to such an extent since then that the wharf was now crowded with boats, some tied together due to a lack of moorings, and these would be swept away in a flood.

Fanny appeared from behind the bar, easing her large frame deftly round the counter as she approached her new customer to direct him to his table where his meal awaited. John never ceased to be amazed at the agility with which she moved or her constant good humour to all and sundry. The sudden roar of laughter, which welled up from the depths of her ample bosom, shaking the many necklaces she always wore, made all the men glad to hear and uplifted many a downhearted soul. She was fair to her customers and to those who worked for her and was kindness itself to Rosie. John thought her a fine woman and was glad his daughter lived under her care and protection.

Once the skipper had left the bar, the men finished their drinks and drifted off in twos and threes down to the waterfront to view the situation. John changed his plans to wait until Rosie had finished her work and had a few words with her before leaving. She was amused to think that her father should be worried about Captain Steven's interest in her and soon put his mind to rest.

"He's a real gentleman, Papa," she assured him, "and, anyway, I have Fanny here if anyone should get out of hand. You should see her sometimes—she's been known to knock a man out cold when he started a fight in her bar. Mind you he was pretty unsteady on his feet at the time." Rosie laughed, and John left her in a cheerful mood to walk home by way of the wharf to sum up the situation himself.

The night was pitch black, and as he made his way across the square the rain began to fall, a few spots to begin with, which rapidly turned into a deluge. John hurried back to the store, for if this kept up all night they could be in real trouble. There was a loft high up in the roof which could be used in an emergency, and the sooner they began to move some of the foodstuffs the better.

Before they went to bed that night, John, Beth, and Andrew managed to heave the heavy sacks of sugar and flour and the boxes of foodstuffs into the roof space. Beth had never known the square to be flooded and thought John was being overly cautious, but as the night wore on, she began to wonder. Frightening noises could be heard from the direction of the wharf as if the boats were being smashed to pieces by a gigantic force and the water began to seep through the planking of the store. By the morning, the river had burst its banks, and the whole town was flooded. The remaining items left in Beth's store were awash, bobbing about in the tide which swept through the broken front door and out through the back. Beth surveyed the chaos from the safety of the loft, where they had taken refuge during the height of the storm and sighed deeply. She had coped with many disasters during her lifetime, but this looked like the end of the general store. The floorboards had been ripped up, leaving jagged ends of wood sticking out of the muddy water, and it was a miracle that the posts of red gum which had held the framework of the store had held firm. The loft, viewed from below was like a raft held up on poles and had certainly saved their lives.

At first light the men of Clay Cross waded through the flooded streets to rescue what they could after a night of destruction. John struggled through the water, dragging his left leg, to join the men already grouped around *The Lively Lady*, which had been lifted by the force of the water driving down from the upper reaches and swept across the wharf into the town square. Her battered hull was a splintered mess and her starboard side, with water still pouring from it, lay open to the sky. Among the men, John recognised the skipper from the Anchor and presumed from the conversation that the boat belonged to him.

"A bad job, Sam," remarked one of the men, shaking his head. "Never known it to flood as badly as this before—we always thought we were safe on this side of the river but we've been proved wrong this time—that's for sure."

"I'm luckier than most," replied Sam stoically as he took stock of the damage.

"At least she wasn't smashed to pieces against the wharf like so many others or swept away to sink down river. I have much to be grateful for—she can be put to rights, but it will take some time."

Around them floated the debris of wrecked boats, and further away, in midstream, the cargoes of wool bales from the outback stations drifted in the current. The storm had blown itself out, and the day dawned calm and still, giving those who were fortunate enough to possess a boat that would still float a chance to embark on a salvage operation and to search along the banks for people who might need their help.

From one such boat, loud voices were raised in an attempt to gain John's attention.

"John Taylor! Ahoy there! Your homestead's been swept away—nothing left standing."

The men around *The Lively Lady* turned to John in consternation.

"Your wife, John—was she there last night?"

John covered his face in his hands. "My God, yes—if only I'd known the river could rise like this—I thought they were safe—poor Amy. And the black girl who cared for her, she was there too! Oh, my God—I must look for them!"

He hadn't given them a thought. The homestead was built high up, away from the bank, higher than any flood could possibly have reached in his estimation, but then no person in Clay Cross had ever witnessed such a flood before, and he could not have known that they had been in danger.

"We must get a boat, if possible, and make a search immediately," said Sam Stevens. "We might still find them alive."

Hailing the men who had made the discovery, John shouted across the water.

"There were two women there last night. Can you take us on board? We need to search the banks."

Willing hands assisted John into the boat, and, with the skipper and those already there, they set off downstream to search both sides of the river.

Unknown to the searchers, before the storm broke, Nellie had a premonition of danger and had tried to pull Amy out of the rocking chair where she was dozing and persuade her to leave the homestead. Despite all her frantic efforts Amy refused to budge; she was tired, and the darkness outside when Nellie opened the door frightened her. Nellie could wait no longer; her senses told her she must take flight and like a terrified animal she ran like lightening towards the safety of the bush, never to be seen again by the inhabitants of Clay Cross.

The noise of rushing water awoke memories of the sea crossing in Amy's muddled mind, and she got up from her chair and leaned over the verandah rail, as if she was still on board ship. The dead branch of a tree rushing past in the torrent caught her a blow across the head, and she fell into the raging water below. For a few moments, her old black dress held her up as she was whirled along by the current before it sucked her beneath the surface. Amy knew nothing; the blow had knocked her unconscious, and death claimed her without a struggle.

The searchers found her shawl hanging in shreds from a partly submerged tree and pointing like a marker to where her body lay, facedown in the mud. As they carried her back to Clay Cross, past the pepper trees and the red brick wash house, which was all that remained to show where the homestead had stood, John was filled with remorse. Poor Amy—to have survived the journey to the promised land only to lose her mind, and now to end in such a way as this—he should never have married her or even thought of marrying her. She would still have been alive and probably still in her right mind if he had left her in Melbourne. It had been a tragedy for them all, and he had been the one to blame. The tears rolled down his cheeks, and the men looked at one another in surprised embarrassment, wondering why John Taylor should mourn the loss of a woman who was better off dead than alive.

On waking in the morning, Rosie had waded through the water to the store to see if she could help Beth and had been horrified to find the place a shambles. She had fallen asleep in the early hours after the storm had begun to abate and had no idea of the devastation until she found Fanny sweeping the water out of the bar. The Anchor was on the outskirts of the town and had not suffered any damage being a brick built building, but it was obvious that the dwellings closer to the river would have been damaged considerably, so she set off through the water towards the square. Fanny did not detain her, knowing how anxious she was to find out how her father and Beth had fared. Rosie watched as her father lifted the dripping body of Amy from the boat and carried her to the mortuary, feeling as if a great weight had been lifted from their lives. She had felt pity for the poor woman she had seen being led along the river path, but she felt no sorrow at her passing, just an overwhelming sense of relief. Her father was free at last to begin a new life with Beth, and she was glad for them both.

With Amy gone, John felt no compulsion to remain in Clay Cross. Beth had no heart to build up her business again, and the best way to recover from their losses seemed to be to start again, working together on something different. John, who had always wanted to be his own master, decided to apply for a block of one hundred acres of agricultural land. Beth had been a prudent saver during their period of comparative prosperity, and he had earned a good wage as an overseer when the wharf was being built, so between them they could manage the deposit and hoped to pay the balance to the state over the next eight years as arranged. Ten of the acres had to be cultivated by law and the rest enclosed. John expected it to be difficult; he was no longer the healthy man he had been when he first came to Clay Cross, but with determination and Beth's help, he hoped to succeed. The land at Seven Creeks was good for raising sheep and cattle, and he intended to invest in a few Merino sheep for a start. Hopefully, with a lot of hard work and a fair amount of good luck they would make a go of things.

Beth put by the most useful commodities from the store to take with them and sold off the surplus cheaply to her customers. With the proceeds, they bought a small cart and a sturdy little cob to pull it, and once the sale of the land was completed they bade farewell to their friends and family and set off to begin a new life together at Seven Creeks. Andrew and Rosie elected to remain at Clay Cross, although both of them would have been welcome to accompany them on their new venture. Andrew had been helping Captain Stevens rebuild *The Lively Lady*, and as the work had progressed, Sam, who had grown to like the cheerful willingness of the lad, suggested he might like to crew for him once he set sail again. This solved a problem for Beth; it meant one less mouth to feed and gave her son a worthwhile trade in the bargain, and, as working on the boats was what Andrew had always wanted to do, the arrangement suited everybody. Rosie was afraid to leave in case Rory returned one day for her and found her gone. Whatever anyone else thought, she kept faith in his promise and intended to stay with Fanny until that happy day arrived.

It was a sad moment for her as she stood in the square beside Andrew, seeing their parents set off, and she wondered when they would all meet again.

CHAPTER 18

Rosie felt lost for a while after her father had gone. The residents of Clay Cross had little time for visiting the Anchor when so much needed to be put to rights after the flood. The red-brown soil dragged up from the river bed covered a large part of the town and had infiltrated the shipping agencies and ship chandlers which had sprung up along the waterfront. With the long hot months of summer soon to follow, it was imperative that the foul-smelling mud should be scraped up and washed away as soon as possible. There were boats to mend and the wharf decking to repair before the season began again, otherwise the town would lose its present prosperity and commerce would move elsewhere. News of the flood had spread, and few travellers stopped over at Clay Cross. As a result, Fanny had almost no custom to speak of except for Captain Stevens and Andrew, who had remained at the Anchor while putting *The Lively Lady* to rights.

Rosie wrote a long letter to Sarah to help pass the time. She had a lot to tell her, starting with an account of her stepmother's death and ending with her own dashed hopes for the future. Before the month was out, she had a reply. Sarah had news for her too.

Arthur had died recently, leaving her as the sole guardian to his children with a large annuity for the remainder of her life to recompense her for this grave responsibility. He had also left her a half share in the business, to revert to his sons on her death. His last years had been spent quietly with his family often sitting in the garden watching them at play. Harriet was by far his favourite, and he had never tired of her prattle or devising ways to amuse her.

> "*She is an enchanting child,*" wrote Sarah, "*with a growing resemblance to her mother, which Arthur frequently remarked upon. On hearing of Arthur's death, Lizzie had returned unexpectedly one day to visit the children. She came laden with gifts for them and found to her sorrow that they hardly remembered her. She made an uncommon fuss of little Harriet and asked me to release her into her custody, but I refused. The children are happy together, and the boys adore their little sister. A parting between them was quite out of the question. Lizzie forfeited all claim to them when she deserted them—she only has to read Arthur's will to know that, and I would not agree to it either. Lizzie is still beautiful although much plumper and tells me she is happy with Harry Trevern, whom she has recently married. They have a son of their own but she wanted to claim Harriet back as she told me the child was her husband's natural child, but this I chose to disbelieve. Harriet stays here where she belongs, and I will never part with her.*
>
> "*When she asked about Percy, I had to tell her the wretched story of his death, and she went away in great distress. I doubt she will visit us again.*"

Rosie folded up the letter thoughtfully. It was almost as if Sarah was punishing her sister for the past. She sounded possessive over the children but then Sarah would never have any of her own and had all the responsibility of bringing them up while Lizzie had always had the fun and had never cared much for responsibility.

During the hot months of that summer, while the river trade was at a standstill, Sam Stevens and Andrew laboured to finish the repairs to the boat. Sam was determined to have her ready by the time the first rise of the season came along in order to steam away to catch the cargoes of wool clip ready to be carted from the outback sheep stations along the Murrumbidgee River. It was a matter of first come, first served, and he intended to be one of the first to arrive. It had cost him dearly to put his boat to rights, and he badly needed to replace his capital outlay. After John and Beth had left town, Andrew had moved into the Anchor Inn and his board and keep were paid for by the skipper in return for his help in rebuilding *The Lively Lady*. It all added to the cost, and the sooner they got her afloat and lived on board the better. Living at the Anchor Inn had its compensations, however, for apart from Fanny's company and her excellent food, Rosie also lived there, and Sam Stevens had taken an instant liking to her, which had blossomed into a deep attachment as the weeks went by. Whatever the subject might be to begin with, Sam's conversations with Fanny usually turned into a discussion about Rosie before they ended, and Fanny was only too pleased to tell him all he wanted to know. She felt the skipper would make Rosie a good husband, and if she could help things along in that direction then she was only too happy to do so. To her way of thinking, at forty-five, he was still an eligible bachelor.

Rosie was sent up to his room every morning with his hot water, and Rosie was the one who served him his meals. She was always the same, gentle and polite as she went about her duties smiling in his direction, yet never giving him any encouragement. Sam longed to bring a smile to her sweet sad face and to give her the happiness she deserved, yet, for all his years, he felt as bashful in her company as if he was still a lad. Fanny was good to her—Sam could see that, but the Anchor Inn, with its ever present smell of drink and stale 'baccy smoke was no place for a girl like her.

"What do you think of the skipper, Rosie?" asked Fanny one day, anxious to see how things were going. "He's a good man to my way o' thinking."

"Yes—he's very kind," replied Rosie, politely.

"Taken a likin' to you Rosie—he'd make someone a good husband one of these days if that someone would show a bit of interest," continued Fanny, pointedly.

"Do you mean me?" asked Rosie, in a surprised voice.

Fanny made a gesture of despair. "Of course I mean you, you silly goose. Men like the captain don't grow on trees!"

"I don't expect they do, but I'm sure you're wrong, Fanny—he's much too old to consider me for a wife. Why he must be as old as Papa!"

"That doesn't matter one little bit, my girl. It's the way a man treats you that matters—not his age. The skipper's a gentleman, and he'd treat you a lot better than some I could mention."

"That's as may be Fanny," said Rosie, hurt by the reference to her past love, "but I loved Rory, and I don't love Sam Stevens, however nice he might be."

"I wish I could put some sense into your head that I do. I lost my late husband when he was buried alive. The shoring in the mine he was digging collapsed and fell on top of him, leaving me a widow with enough money to buy the Anchor—but what good was that without him to help me to run it. I was a slip of a girl in those days and look at me now—you'd never believe it, would you?" Fanny laughed at the memory. "I ate everything I could lay my hands on—nibbled night and day—stupid of me I know—just to stop myself thinking of how things might have been—enjoy the here and now, my girl, and stop hoping for something that might never happen."

Rosie was stunned by this confidence. To think that Fanny's jollity was a cover-up for the tragedy in her life and her huge size a monument to her lost love. Fanny's double chins began to shake with emotion, and Rosie felt the tears fill her eyes.

"Dear Fanny—I'm sorry it went so badly for you, and I know Rory might never come back, but I can't stop loving him, however hard I try."

"Love comes in a marriage, Rosie—a different kind of love; deeper, and often more lasting. You'll find it so, my dear."

Rosie took her hand in hers. "I'll not forget what you've told me Fanny, and I'll think about it—but the skipper hasn't asked me to marry him yet."

"He will," replied Fanny, with conviction. "He will."

Sam hired a team of horses to haul his boat to the slipway once the major part of the reconstruction had been completed, and with the water level high enough to refloat her, she was slipped back successfully. This only left the wheelhouse to be repainted and her name on the side, and Sam had a mind to change that.

The week after the boat had been launched, Sam was ready to sail up river, but before he left there was something he wanted to ask Rosie. He realised the time wasn't ripe to ask her to marry him just yet, but he hoped that if she agreed to come with him on this first journey up the Murrumbidgee, they might grow a little closer. He was a river man and felt more at home on his boat than anywhere else. When Rosie got to know him as he really was and grew to love the creeks and the rivers as he did, they would have more in common to talk about and in that way he could continue his gentle courtship. Once on board his boat, he would feel more confident and more at ease with her. There was quite a celebration on his last night at the Anchor Inn with free drinks provided by Fanny to celebrate the launching of the boat and to wish him a good season. During the evening, Sam asked Rosie to go with him.

"Just a little holiday, Rosie—it will do you good to get on the river for a while, and I will take good care of you. Andrew will be there as well, so you will have other company beside myself."

Rosie, who had never had a holiday before, was pleasantly surprised by the offer. "It sounds lovely, Sam, thank you, but I will have to see what Fanny thinks about it first. How long would it take?"

"Only about three weeks there and back, and less if we don't hit any snags in the river, and have a good journey coming back. And Fanny won't mind because I've already mentioned it to her, and she's of the same opinion as me, that it would bring back a bit of colour to your cheeks and a sparkle in your eyes."

Rosie smiled. Fanny would agree to anything the skipper suggested if it brought them nearer to getting married. Well, she could see no harm in it; he was an honourable man with honest intentions towards herself, and it would give her a chance to get to know him better before she made up her mind whether to marry him or not. The invitation left her in no doubt as to his true feelings for her. She had become fond of Sam, but she could never grow to love him; nevertheless, a few weeks in his company might change that. It would give her a chance to find out.

"Then I will come, Sam, as you and Fanny seem to think I should, but I'll not come as a passenger. You will need someone to cook for you both, and I'll do that and wash the clothes too. I shall make myself useful, you'll see."

Sam took his pipe out of his mouth and chuckled. "I see I shall have a young woman with a mind of her own on board. We'll have to watch our step—eh Andrew—or she'll have us both in irons!"

Rosie blushed. It was obvious that the skipper was delighted she would be coming with them.

The next morning, Rosie collected her few belongings together, said her good-byes to a smiling Fanny and set off with Andrew and the skipper for the waterfront. Sam's boat was by far the most handsome craft on the river that day, with her new paint glistening in the sunlight.

"What do you think of her now she's finished?" asked Sam, as they drew nearer. "Bright as a new button, eh?"

Rosie didn't answer—she was too busy reading the letters painted on the side.

"*The Murray Rose*—Oh, Sam!—I didn't know you'd changed her name."

Rosie was covered in confusion and hardly knew what to say. Sam had named his boat after her. "It makes me feel sort of special."

"And so you are, my dear," said Sam gruffly as he handed her aboard, "and now you can see why we had to have you on board for her maiden voyage. You'll bring us luck—eh, Andrew?"

"Aye, skipper," agreed Andrew, somewhat put out with the skipper's insistence on bringing him into it all the time. It hadn't been his idea to take Rosie with them; he would rather she had stayed behind. Everyone knew old Sam was sweet on Rosie once he had named his boat after her, and there was no fool like an old fool in his opinion. Andrew hoped Sam would soon get her out of his system and put his mind on teaching him how to work the boat instead of mooning over Rosie Taylor. What with his brother Rory and now Sam Stevens, Andrew began to wonder what it was about her that turned men into such moonstruck idiots. He would never be so daft over a girl—that's for sure.

With the engine started, Sam disappeared into the wheelhouse and Andrew got ready to cast off the ropes. Rosie stood in the bows, her pink and white gingham dress fluttering in the breeze, looking for all the world as if she was a figurehead on her namesake. As *The Murray Rose* steamed past the wharf, the men raised a cheer for the skipper, and to Rosie's embarrassment, she heard shouts of "good on ya, Rosie" from those who recognised her. Sam blew the whistle in recognition of their applause, and this was taken up by the other river boats, making such a cacophony of sound that Mary Ann was drawn to the upstairs balcony to see what all the fuss was about.

From her grandstand view of the river, she watched Sam's boat steam past until it reached the bend in the river and disappeared from sight. Her lip curled in disdain for she had heard of the skippers liking for Rosie and wondered if they had been married that morning before setting off. If that was the case, then Rosie Taylor would never have Rory Macdonald, wherever he was hiding, and that gave Mary Ann considerable satisfaction.

CHAPTER 19

Rosie seated herself on a pile of ropes in the bows and settled down to watch the passing scenery. Distance lent enchantment to the view, and the familiar landmarks took on a new dimension. Old Parker's place appeared almost habitable nestling in the shelter of the forest's edge, and further downstream the deserted lonely ruin where the massacre had taken place many years ago looked less bleak and foreboding than it had on the day she had stumbled upon it unawares. Rosie shuddered involuntarily as they chugged slowly past, reliving the panic she had experienced there. What a wild child she must have been in those far-off days of innocence when she had wandered fearlessly where others had feared to tread. Rory had admired her bravery when all it had been was the thoughtlessness of youth. She must stop thinking about Rory and put her mind on other things. Fanny was right about the past being the past—it was the future that mattered.

Sam tapped on the glass front of the wheelhouse with his pipe to draw her attention to the flood damage, and she nodded and smiled up at him. The banks on either side of the Murray had been badly eroded and half uprooted trees lay partially submerged across the course of the river, their spreading branches a danger to the unwary. Andrew watched out for these unexpected snags and warned the skipper in advance. Fortunately, *The Murray Rose* was a light draught boat, and, being empty, they were able to negotiate the obstructions without any mishaps.

As they rounded each bend in the twisting turning river, Rosie expected to see a change in the scenery, but she was to be disappointed. The river gums stretched along each bank for mile after mile, sometimes forming magnificent groups of leafy shade at the water's edge which petered out to become scrubby forestland. The sounds of carolling magpies and the screech of parrots came from within their secret depths, and occasionally there was a flash of brightly coloured wings as a group of crimson rosellas flew through the trees. Sometimes, a paddle steamer travelling upstream passed slowly by, leaving a wake of brown and green ripples to wash against the sides of the boat and follow one another to the river bank. Herons and egrets stood at the water's edge, watching for fish beneath the surface and coots and moorhens swam back to the safety of the reed beds as the boat chugged slowly past.

By the end of the afternoon, Sam moored in the shelter of a creek and Rosie prepared a simple meal using the primitive facilities the boat had to offer. Sitting later in the peaceful stillness of the creek and watching the sunset paint the sky in shades of red, green, and orange behind the silhouettes of distant trees, Rosie felt the quietness of the forest steal over her. There seemed no reason to speak and disturb the silence around them, and she sat for a while in perfect contentment as Sam puffed away on his pipe. When the sun sank beyond the horizon, she gathered up the dishes and cleared away the meal. Andrew took a lamp and hung it over the stern where he sat hopefully fishing for yellow belly. He had no wish to play gooseberry on the other two or to join in their conversation. People who were courting needed to be left alone, and he felt in the way—he'd rather keep the mosquitoes company.

Returning to talk to Sam before turning in for the night, Rosie marvelled at the luminous glow in the sky as the sunset faded, giving place to the velvet night, lit by the first stars.

"The blacks have strange beliefs about the universe," said Sam, noting the wonderment in her gaze. "You see the evening star hanging there in all her glory?" Rosie nodded. "She's held there by the hand of the spirits in the place of the mist; and sitting here I could almost believe it myself. It's a mystical notion, like their idea of creation. To the aboriginal people, it's the dreaming place and creation they know as the dream time. That's what this country is to me, Rosie—a place of dreams, and I can't imagine living anywhere else but here now."

"Nor can I Sam," agreed Rosie. "I've loved it since I was small—the beauty and the vastness of the forests and the bush, as if nothing had changed for thousands of years. I used to discover new parts of the forest every time I played in it. It was strange to me then like everything else, but now I feel as if I had been born here."

"We're all born anew in this country," said Sam, "saint and sinner alike; and there's plenty of reformed characters to tell you a tale or two about how they came to be here in the first place—that's for sure."

Rosie laughed. "And what about you, Captain Stevens?" she asked. "Are you one of those reformed characters?"

"Huh, that I'm not! I came of my own free will—jumped ship when I was a cabin boy and took any amount of jobs 'til I could buy my first boat. I've had a few boats since then, and *The Murray Rose* is the best of 'em—took me a long time to be my own master, but I've never regretted it—except perhaps for one thing."

"And what was that, Sam?" asked Rosie.

"I never stayed long enough anywhere to meet the right woman, so I have no family to call my own. It's time I settled down before it's too late."

Rosie was silent. She didn't want to get onto that subject just yet. There was time enough for that later on when she'd had time to get to know him better.

"I think I'd like to turn in for the night, Sam, as long as you don't mind. Where am I to sleep?"

"Got the cabin all shipshape for you m'dear," said Sam, cheerfully. "If there's anything you need you must let me know. Andrew and I are bedding down on deck. We have plenty of blankets, and the nights are warm. You may find the sounds of the forest strange at first, but you'll soon get used to them, and we shan't be far away."

"Thank you, Sam," said Rosie as she got up to go to her cabin, "you're very good to me. I've always slept well, and I'm sure I shall be comfortable." On a sudden impulse, she kissed him as she would have done had it been her father.

"Good night, Sam. Sleep well."

"Good night, m'dear," said Sam, his voice gruff with emotion.

Inside the tiny cabin, there were two bunks, and Rosie felt a pang of guilt at taking up all the space—if she hadn't come along at Sam's invitation, the men would have shared the cabin. No wonder Andrew had looked put out having to sleep on deck while she occupied his bunk. Sam had gone to a lot of trouble to make it homely for her. There was an old oil lamp, a wash basin and jug and a mirror nailed onto the wall above the empty bunk. She had to share the other facilities with the men but this had caused no embarrassment to her. Riverboats were male preserves, and she had expected the living accommodation to be of the simplest. It was a good life on the river when the weather was fine, and she had enjoyed her first day. Sam's tobacco smoke lingered in the night air, and she found the smell of it as comforting as the man himself. For a long time, she lay awake, listening to the croaking of the frogs and wondering about her own feelings. If only she knew for certain she would never see Rory again she would feel happier about marrying Sam. When he asked her, what was she going to say? It was a problem she was still turning over in her mind when the gentle rocking of the boat lulled her to sleep before she had come to any conclusion on the matter.

The next day passed in a similar fashion as they made their way slowly and leisurely downstream towards Swan Hill. There was always something to watch along the river, the ungainly pelicans taking off into a graceful flight as the boat's engine disturbed them or a goanna climbing up the nearest tree. As they passed a group of grey kangaroos browsing on the grass in a forest clearing, two males stood up and engaged in a sparring match, cuffing each other with their forelimbs and kicking with their hind feet. Sam slowed down to give Rosie and Andrew a chance to enjoy the fun. When the boat had passed, Rosie thought of the fight for dominance in the family group she had just witnessed. She had felt sorry for the old kangaroo, but he'd had his day, and it was time he gave in to a younger male. She thought of Sam afterwards and about his kindness to her—rather as a father figure—but she had already been awakened by the passions of youth, and it wouldn't be the same with Sam, fond as she was of him. She needed the love of a younger man and now that she'd had time to think about it she knew the answer she would give him when he got around to asking her to be his wife.

Once they arrived at Swan Hill, Sam moored the boat and took Rosie into town to buy some fresh provisions for the rest of the journey. While they had gone, Andrew made some enquiries about the whereabouts of his brother Malcolm and discovered he was working on a boat travelling to Adelaide. He left a message for him, hoping to see him the next time *The Murray Rose* came that way to give him the news of Beth and John's move to Seven Creeks. They soon left Swan Hill, as Sam was anxious to get to the Murrumbidgee turn, where the going would be slower. One more night was spent in a sheltered spot on the Murray, and then they started upstream to where the loading point was situated for the outback sheep stations. On the last evening before their arrival, Sam decided the time had come for his proposal and cleared his throat in preparation for his ordeal. Rosie, sitting on the deck beside him, knew what to expect and felt as nervous as he did, especially as she had made up her mind to refuse him.

"Rosie, my dear, would you do me the honour of becoming my wife—that is, if you're willing to take on an old man like me? I've asked for the position of wharf master at Clay Cross so you would have a home of your own. A boat, however good she may be, is no place for a wife and family, and a house goes with the job. I would see to it that you would want for nothing, Rosie, and I would be a good husband to you. Will you take me for your husband? It would make me such a proud and happy man if you said yes, my dear."

Sam took her hand in his and looked at her with such love in his eyes that Rosie wished with all her heart that she didn't have to disappoint him.

"Dear Sam," she said, looking away for fear of seeing the hurt she was causing, "I care for you very much, but I loved someone else who went away, and, however hard I try, I can't forget him. If only I could, for you are the best of men, but it would be wrong of me to marry you and to love someone else in my heart. Please forgive me—I hoped that while I was here on the boat with you I could put the past behind me, but my feelings haven't changed—I am so sorry, Sam, truly sorry." Refusing his offer of marriage distressed her kind nature, and she burst into tears, tears for Rory whom she wanted so much and tears for Sam who loved her so dearly.

"There, there, my dear," said Sam, putting his arm around her comfortingly. "I'm nothing but an old fool to have thought you would take me in the first place. Don't cry my love—I understand how it is with you, and I won't ask again, but if in the years to come you change your mind then I'll still be waiting. A bachelor I've always been, and a bachelor I shall remain."

"You won't sell *The Murray Rose*, will you, Sam? You'll go on being the skipper of your own boat?"

"Aye, reckon I will—I love the old boat and would only have parted with her if I'd had to—no need for that now."

Rosie felt a little happier on hearing that, knowing how much *The Murray Rose* meant to him, and she felt humbled to think he had considered taking a position on the wharf to enable her to live in comfortable surroundings.

The next day brought them to the loading station, and Sam was too busy seeing to the business in hand to give a thought to anything else. Rosie watched the cargo being unloaded from the camel train and stacked into the hold. It was the first time she had seen camels, and she was fascinated by the haughty aloofness of the great beasts as they waited patiently to have the bales of wool clip unloaded from their backs.

The Murray Rose wasn't the only steamboat there that day, and the landing dock was a hive of activity with plenty to see. To one side of the camels stood a bullock team hitched to a long cart laden with heavy sacks. Rosie stood idly by watching the men on the cart heaving the sacks down for others to load into the boats. There was something familiar about one of the men on the cart, a strong wiry man with a red beard. If he hadn't looked so rough and sun burnt it could almost have been—was it Rory? Rosie wasn't absolutely sure. She kept her eyes riveted on the figure in the distance until one of the men noticed her persistent stare and pointed her out to his neighbour.

"There's a Sheila on that boat who can't take her eyes off you mate—look—over there."

Rory straightened his back to look. There was no mistaking her; she was wearing the same pink and white dress he remembered her wearing the first time he had seen her when she had come back to Clay Cross, the day her parasol had blown away.

Rory took off his hat and waved it wildly. "Rosie!" he shouted, joyfully.

Leaping off the cart in one bound he sprinted across the dock and onto the boat to gather her up in his arms and twirl her round in his excitement.

"Oh, Rosie, my darling—it's a miracle! How do you come to be in this godforsaken place? And whose boat is this you're on?"

Rosie, who was laughing and crying at the same time with the joy of feeling his arms around her and his kisses on her lips, was incapable of speech.

"Rory—oh, Rory," she managed to say at last, her arms clasped tightly round his waist as if she would never let him go again. "This is Sam Steven's boat. He's been staying at the Anchor until he got her patched up after the storm, and he asked me to come with him on this trip up the river. That's why I'm here."

"Took a fancy to you, did he Rosie? And what about you? Do you care for him?"

"Oh no," said Rosie hurriedly, "it's nothing like that. I came for my health. Fanny thought it would do me good, and, anyway, Andrew is on board too—he's working for the skipper now."

"Ah," said Rory, feeling relieved. For one dreadful moment, he had thought that his precious Rosie had got herself married, and he was making an idiot of himself. Looking towards the hold, he could see his brother and a much older man helping to load up. Nothing to worry about there; the skipper was fully occupied and had his back turned on them. A typical old river boat captain from what he could see of him.

"Rory, you won't leave me again, will you?" begged Rosie. "I love you so much; I just want to be with you wherever you go."

"Do you forgive me Rosie for the way I treated you? I couldn't stay in Clay Cross after what happened, and I thought I had lost you forever."

"It was my fault too," said Rosie, anxious to make amends. "I was so angry. If only we had talked sensibly I might have found a way to come with you. Not knowing where you were has broken my heart."

"Dear little Rosie, how faithful you have been to me. I don't deserve your love, sweetheart, but I'll make it up to you if it takes the rest of my life to do it. I'll be finished here when the unloading is done and you can ride back to the sheep station in the cart. Tomorrow, we'll set off together. Get your things—I'll be back here for you before long."

Rory left her to return to his work, and Rosie, her heart singing with joy, went to collect her few belongings. Sam had turned his back on the reunion; it had been too much for him seeing her uplifted face transformed with happiness. If only she had looked at him like that.

He stacked up the hold with grim determination as if his life depended on having each bale neatly arranged and snapped at Andrew, who was taking a brief rest. Rosie would be leaving the boat and walking out of his life forever in an hour or so. It was no good hoping anymore; he had been a fool to fall in love at his age. That kind of nonsense was for the young. The sooner he got steam up and started off back to Clay Cross the better. The old familiar routine of river life was the best antidote he knew of for putting his troubles behind him.

Rosie stood looking down into the hold. "Sam," she called softly, "I'm getting off here. I shall never forget you or the happiness you brought me in finding Rory. Please tell Fanny what happened so she knows why I won't be coming back—take care of yourself, won't you."

Sam nodded. "Be happy, my dear," he said gruffly, turning back to the hold.

Rory came to escort her to the now empty bullock cart and to have a few words with his younger brother before they left. Rosie waved farewell as *The Murray Rose* set off down river, and Andrew returned her wave, but the skipper, busy in the wheelhouse, had eyes only for the river straight ahead.

CHAPTER 20

That night, Rosie slept on a makeshift bed at the sheep station homestead, worn out by the day's events and the long bumpy journey in the bullock cart. In the morning, the farmer's wife found her an old pair of breeches and a wide-brimmed hat to wear on the long trek across country on horseback. Rory used some of his pay to purchase a quiet old horse for her to ride and the necessary tack she would need. Then, with their belongings stowed away in their saddle bags, the pair of them set off in the direction of Deniliquin.

They were making for the homestead at Seven Creeks and had a long journey ahead of them. Once Rory had heard that John and Beth had bought a block of grazing ground, he was anxious to help John build up the farm into a thriving sheep station. Rosie had explained to him how their parents had left the store and put their money together to pay the deposit on the land and Rory, remembering John's crook leg, had wondered how on earth John would ever find the money to pay off his debt to the state. He would need a stronger man than he was to help him raise the rest of the hundred pounds before the eight years time limit elapsed and Rory intended to be that man.

Since leaving Clay Cross, Rory had been among other things a contract drover, driving the sheep overland. He had watched them die in their hundreds on the road, smothered in the wool of their companions when they panicked or bogged down in swampy land unable to move and left to die. Sometimes, they starved or ate the poisonous native fuchsia to allay their hunger. Sheep were foolish creatures, and he had learned how to doctor the sick and ailing animals, becoming more resourceful and patient himself as a result. His character had hardened into that of a strong and resolute man, one who knew how to put his hot-headed impulsiveness to good use and to keep his temper under control.

Of late, he had travelled round the sheep stations, rounding up the animals for shearing and working in the shearing sheds. There wasn't much he didn't know about sheep these days, and, if John Taylor had decided to keep some Merino stock, he could be of great help to him. Once they arrived at Seven Creeks, he intended to offer John his savings and become a partner in the land, so Rosie would always have a roof over her head. Beth loved her as if she was her own daughter and as soon as they reached Deniliquin, Rory wanted to make her just that. Hopefully, there would be a parson somewhere around the township to marry them for more than anything he wanted to ride into Seven Creeks with his wife by his side.

Rosie had never ridden a horse before, and the going was slow. Rory held onto her bridle and kept his own horse in check until she had gained enough confidence to ride alone. The first night she was stiff and weary, and every bone in her body ached, but she didn't complain for to be with Rory was all she desired of life.

They unsaddled their horses beside a billabong and left them to graze as they collected wood for a campfire under the trees. They cooked damper in the glowing embers of the fire and boiled the billy for tea, sitting in the gathering darkness to eat their simple meal, to which they added a few provisions the farmer's wife had insisted they took with them. Then, using a saddle for a pillow, they slept in each others arms under the stars. Rory made love to her tenderly, and this time Rosie's ecstasy of surrender was followed by complete contentment. She had her love by her side at last, held safely in his embrace, and nothing would part them again.

It took them many weeks to reach Deniliquin, fording the creeks and rivers as they went, following the long dusty route taken by Cobb and Co.'s coach as it travelled between Hay and Deniliquin. The first thing Rory did was to find a parson to marry them and then to book a room at a hotel for their wedding night. They wouldn't eat damper or sleep under the stars tonight, for he wanted this night to be one Rosie would always remember.

Rosie wore her pink and white gingham dress for the simple ceremony in the parsonage. It was a bit grubby by now and rather crumpled, but she had little choice having only brought her most practical clothes with her on the boat, and, anyway, Rory had recognised her wearing it, which made it seem special to her. It hardly mattered what she wore, for she looked radiantly happy as she held out her hand for her mother's wedding ring to be transferred from her right hand, where she had worn it since she had grown into womanhood, and placed onto the third finger of her left hand to make her Rory's wife.

That evening, after a quiet meal at the hotel, they slept in a large brass bedstead with a feather mattress, and Rosie, unused to such blissful comfort, couldn't keep her eyes open and soon fell into a deep sleep. Rory smiled down at his little bride and kissed the tip of her nose; he wouldn't disturb her slumbers, even if it was their wedding night. She belonged to him at long last and they had the rest of their lives to enjoy the days and nights together. He put his arms around her and held her close to him, and Rosie sighed contentedly in her sleep.

The next day, she donned her breeches and tucked her hair under the dusty felt hat so no one at the hotel recognised the bride of the night before, and, with fresh provisions and full water bags, they continued in leisurely fashion on their journey towards Euroa, where they were directed to the Taylor homestead.

Looking around him, Rory could see that John had chosen a good place to rear stock—there was plenty of water in the creeks and grazing as far as the eye could see, so it came as a bit of a shock when they rode up to the homestead to see the dilapidated appearance of the place.

"Your pa sure needs help by the look of things," said Rory, as he helped Rosie to dismount. "I reckon it's as well we came."

They recognised Prince, an old dog now, lying in the shade of the verandah and could hear Beth calling to the hens in the yard. She took scant notice of the two strangers hitching their horses to the rail fence. It was no good coming to look for work on their land. They couldn't afford to take on casual labour much as they needed help.

"Chooks laying well, Ma?" called out Rory, cheerfully.

At the sound of his voice, Beth looked up and, seeing who it was, dropped the bowl of corn among the squawking fowls in her astonishment. She had scarcely gathered her wits before she found herself all but smothered by the two young people so dear to her whom she had feared she might never see again.

"John!" she called excitedly, as soon as she could free herself. "John, come quickly. We've got visitors. Just look who's here!"

Sitting on the verandah together that evening, the four of them talked until long after the sun had set. There was so much to talk about and the future to discuss, a future that would concern them all. Unable to keep up their payments on the land, the future had seemed bleak indeed for John and Beth, but now that was a thing of the past. Rory had promised to pay off their debt and to buy more grazing land and increase their flocks. The potential was there if the land was grazed properly, and a fortune could be earned from sheep. He had seen the huge sheep stations in the outback and intended to have one of his own, given time and careful planning.

They would all live together, and, while he and John ran the station, Rosie would be company for Beth, and when the children began to arrive, Beth would be a help to Rosie. Youngsters needed a family to grow up amongst, and, at the Taylor homestead, that is just what they would have. Rory had it all planned, down to the last detail, and Beth smiled at his enthusiasm for the task ahead. Rosie listened, full of admiration for her husband as he expounded his theories on sheep farming and the gradual expansion of stock and considered herself to be the luckiest girl in the world to be Rory Macdonald's wife.

PART FOUR

The Melbourne Cup

1890

CHAPTER 21

Lizzie found her life different in every way from the years she had spent as the cosseted wife of Arthur Potts. Living out in the bush for so long, Harry had no use for the usual conventions. He lived a carefree existence, and Lizzie was obliged to take him as she found him.

Harry had been packed off to Australia when he was seventeen after shooting dead a poacher on his father's estate. Fearful of reprisals, and rather than see his son hang or bring further discredit to his family, his father had dispatched him on the next boat to Victoria with sufficient money to start him off in his new life. Once there, Harry had started by gambling away some of his fortune until he had come to his senses. Hearing of land for the taking in the outback, he had set off and staked his claim, settling on a large area of bush where he intended to breed horses. As the years passed, he encouraged the aborigines who walked across his land to settle nearby, giving them a weekly ration of grog and flour as a payment for their help. They came and went, never settling for long, although the grog encouraged many of them to return.

He had built his homestead and stables for the horses over the years and had cleared the land for a vineyard to supplement his income. He had no time for society and avoided it as much as possible, unless he was selling one of his thoroughbreds to a wealthy buyer. That was a different matter, for then he played the part of a gentleman. He had been amazed to receive an invitation to The Great House, addressed to

Mr. Trevern and wife, after being introduced to Arthur at a race meeting. Harry had tossed the invitation to one side, wondering at the time which of his women he would have taken to shock the prim matrons and their stuffy husbands. At a race meeting later that week, he had heard talk of the beautiful Mrs. Potts, who sang like a canary and had the face and figure of a Venus. Harry threw caution to the winds and decided to take a look at this fascinating creature for himself. Although the evening had bored him stiff, he came away burning with desire for his hostess, never expecting to meet her again.

Lizzie found the homestead bare and comfortless, but the passion for her lover left little time for her to bother about her surroundings, however bleak. Harry spent as much time with her as he could manage, riding together round his land and through the beautiful wild bush which bordered his property. They made love wherever they happened to be—on the empty seashore beside the rippling waves or lying in the soft hay of a stable loft. Lizzie had never been so happy or felt so free to be herself. She discarded her tight corsets as she had discarded her restrictive life with Arthur and took to wearing billowing skirts and loose blouses, giving her a freedom she had never before experienced. To Harry, she was perfect, a woman with no inhibitions who was willing to satisfy his every desire. He thought of her as his goddess and adored her. When she became pregnant, he fussed over her, as if this was to be his first child, but Lizzie knew he had many children apart from the daughter she had left behind. The half caste children she saw playing in the bush were Harry's progeny she felt sure, although Harry had been evasive when she had asked him. These children had not been allowed into the homestead since her arrival.

The old aboriginal housekeeper had two daughters, Minna and Leah, and both of these women had half caste children. *Were they both Harry's women?* she had wondered. It no longer seemed to matter, as they were a part of his past life, and he took no interest in them or their children. They lived in a shack with their mother some way from the homestead, and Lizzie rarely saw them.

When her time came, she gave birth to a strong baby, a fine son whom they named Adam. This time, it was an easy birth, the baby being delivered by the housekeeper who had delivered all Harry's children. She had made an infusion of herbs and leaves for Lizzie to drink, to ease the pain of her labour, which Lizzie had dreaded after her last experience. Harry found an aboriginal girl to be the child's nurse. Lizzie had some reservations, but the girl showed great kindness to the baby, having lost one of her own recently.

When Adam was three years old, Harry read an account of Arthur's funeral in a Melbourne newspaper. Legalising their union meant little to either of them, but Lizzie secretly hoped that by becoming Harry's wife, she would be able to gain custody of his daughter. She longed to see Harry's children growing up together. To please her, Harry married her on their next trip into the city and then Lizzie made plans to return to The Great House to claim Harriet, but Sarah, as the children's legal guardian had been adamant and would not release the child into Lizzie's custody.

Lizzie returned home, moody and upset, but Harry wanted nothing to do with her past life; they had their lives before them, and if Lizzie wanted more children, he was only too happy to oblige her. Their lovemaking became more passionate as a result, with Lizzie becoming more and more obsessed about having a baby girl to replace the one she had lost and might never see again.

A deep burning hatred for Lizzie smouldered in Minna's breast. Both she and her sister Leah had been Harry's women before Lizzie had come on the scene and had borne him many children whom he now rejected. Leah cared nothing for her master. His rough lovemaking had bruised her young body, and she was glad to be left alone, but with Minna it was different. She had truly cared for Harry, nursing him back to health when he had suffered the fever and helping to mend his broken leg when he had been thrown from his horse. He had treated her with more kindness than her sister, perhaps because her children looked more like a white man's children than Leah's. He only slept with Leah when Minna was heavily pregnant or had her time upon her each month. Minna had considered Harry as her man, and she and her children had lived in the homestead with him until Lizzie had arrived to take her place. Now, she had been cast out after all those years of devoted service to her master, and Harry never visited her anymore. She had expected him to tire of his new love, but Harry seemed to care for his white woman even more now that she had given him a boy child. There seemed no hope left for her.

One day, jealousy had led her to watch them as they made love, and Harry had caught her spying on him. He had taken his belt to her, and

Minna remembered that beating with hatred in her heart. She would find a way to punish Harry for all the hurt he had caused her and then go walkabout so nobody would ever see her again. Her opportunity came when Harry and Lizzie had gone to a race meeting and would not be returning until late. Minna crept into the homestead, bent on causing mischief. Everything looked different now that Lizzie lived there. Minna handled the heavy velvet curtains which Lizzie had looped across the windows and then turned her attention to the thick chenille cover draped over the table. Rugs covered most of the dirt floor, feeling strangely soft to her bare feet. She opened the cupboard where Harry kept the spills to light his cheroots and lit one as she had seen Harry do on many an occasion. With this in her hand, she went on an orgy of destruction, setting light to the curtains, cushions and covers until she came to the door of the bedroom. It was here she had witnessed Lizzie making love in wild abandon to the man she considered as her own. There were white muslin hangings round the bed, and, once these were ignited, they rapidly went up in flames. She wanted to see the bed burn, but there was no time for that. Minna opened the door onto the verandah and quickly made her escape before anyone saw her.

Adam had been taken for a picnic into the bush by his nurse, who, on seeing the flames coming from the homestead, took fright and pulled the child along as fast as his small legs would carry him until they came to the creek, which supplied all the water to the stables. Picking him up in her arms, she waded into the deepest part and held him close to her with his head just above the surface. When the scrub and bush around them caught fire as it doubtless would, her instincts told her that this was the safest place to be.

By the time Lizzie and Harry were returning home, a dark glow showed on the horizon. The homestead had been destroyed, and the fire had reached the stable block. Galloping closer, they could see the stable hands silhouetted against the flames, setting the horses free.

"Make for the strand, Lizzie," shouted Harry urgently. "Ride your horse into the sea and stay there until it is safe."

Lizzie hesitated. "Do as I tell you woman!" shouted Harry angrily. "Get moving, will you!" The land was tinder dry at this time of the year and he had to do what he could to help but she must make her escape while there was still time.

Lizzie was frightened. "What about Adam? I want to come with you. I must find him—please Harry."

Harry grew angry and gave her horse a thump on the rear so it galloped away. There was no time to be lost in arguing, for the situation was dangerous.

Eventually, Lizzie managed to control the headlong flight of her horse and pull it to a standstill. She could see the bush burning all round the homestead, but there was no sign of Harry. Flames began to leap across the tops of the trees, small creatures ran and slithered through the undergrowth, and the sky was thick with birds. She knew she should go in their direction towards the sea but, without Harry and Adam, what did she have to live for if she was saved and they died? She must go back to those she loved.

The northerly winds drove the flames before it as Lizzie turned her horse in the direction of the homestead. She intended to circle the flames from a safe distance but she had never experienced a bush fire before and knew nothing of the speed and ferocity of the flames once they took hold. A ball of burning debris rolled towards her, and her horse reared up in terror and began to gallop out of control. She held on tightly to the reins but soon found she was surrounded by a circle of flames. There was nothing for it—she would have to force her mount to leap through them or they would both perish. The horse snorted wildly as she urged it on, whipping it cruelly in her panic. It pawed the ground in terror and, rearing up, threw Lizzie violently off its back before plunging through a gap in the flames.

The wind changed direction as the night wore on, setting the scrub alight to the south of Harry's property. Harry and the stable lads were exhausted by their efforts to quench the flames. The homestead was a smoking ruin, and all around them the land was a black, stinking mess.

At first light, the aboriginal women and their families came down from the creek where they had been sheltering as the fire passed over them. There was no sign of Minna, but Adam's nurse was among them, holding the frightened child in her arms. Harry muttered a prayer of thanks as they came into sight. There was a sound of hooves as Lizzie's horse galloped into the yard, sweating with fear. Harry called the men together to search for his wife along the strand, fearing she might have been thrown, while he remained to put out the last lingering embers.

The men searched diligently but, on finding no sign of Lizzie, they returned to the stables. Harry set off on his own, and, after wandering through the burnt out bush for hours, he came across the silver top of her whip lying beside her charred remains. He was grief stricken at the sight, and some hours passed before he was capable of returning home. All around him, his life's work lay in ruins but he cared nothing for that. He could rebuild the homestead and the stables, but, without Lizzie, the light had gone out of his life.

That night, Sarah saw a faint glow on the horizon as she looked out her window and wondered where the fire had been, without ever realizing she had been looking at her sister's funeral pyre.

CHAPTER 22

When she half closed her eyes, the lights shining from every window in The Great House seemed to Harriet to glow as brightly as the huge stars reflected in the calm black waters of Port Phillip Bay. She had run into the garden to view the scene before the guests arrived and was standing in the middle of the lawn, holding her breath with wonder at such an unusual sight. The house and garden were still as if they too were waiting for the party to begin and the night sky to explode in a burst of coloured stars, for Arty had arranged to end the evening's entertainment with a Chinese firework display. There had been nothing like it in her lifetime, and she felt as delighted as a child given a special treat. She shivered with excitement at the thought of what was to come, determined not to miss one moment of this wonderful evening.

Today was her twenty-first birthday, and it had been Arty's idea to throw a party. Shut up in this house under the strict supervision of their Aunt Sarah, his sister Harriet had little chance of meeting members of the opposite sex. Arty was now the head of the Potts household and wanted to see his sister married and off his hands. It was bad enough to have one spinster under his roof to care for in her old age, complaining about his boisterous behaviour until he had felt a need to move into the stable block. The horses never complained; horses had more sense than women in his opinion.

"It's time this place looked less like a morgue," had been his comment when Aunt Sarah had shown her disapproval at such an immense amount of money being totally wasted on nothing more than an evening of frivolity.

A long guest list had been drawn up, and new staff had been recruited for this occasion, and preparations had been going on for weeks. The house fairly hummed with activity and looked as it had in the old days when Arthur and Lizzie had lived there.

To Harriet, it was a daily wonder seeing the old house gradually come to life again. For the very first time, she had seen the furniture in the salon uncovered and the portrait of her mother hung in its original place over the mantelpiece in the drawing room. How beautiful she had been. Harriet wished she knew more about her but Aunt Sarah had refused to be drawn into the subject, and Harriet had been left to imagine all kinds of reasons for her disappearance and her early death. Tonight, she had pinned up her jet black hair and placed a dark red rose on one side to match the colour of her dress, which she had copied from the dress her mother had worn in the portrait which she so much admired. She had inherited her mother's jewels this very day and had found among them the same choker of diamonds Lizzie had worn in her portrait. They fitted her perfectly, complementing her dark brown eyes and her lightly sunburnt skin. Harriet had never looked lovelier than she did this night.

Hearing the sound of distant horses' hooves, she ran through the pillared portico and into the marble hallway where her brothers were waiting.

"Where have you been, Hetty?" asked Arty as she took her place between them. "It's your party, you know. A fine state of affairs if the guests arrived and you had been missing."

Harriet shrugged. "No one was here when I came downstairs, so I took a turn in the garden, that's all. Where's Aunt Sarah? Isn't she coming?"

Arty pulled a long face. "I expect she'll put in an appearance later on—you know how she dislikes my parties."

"I sincerely hope it won't turn into one of your parties, Arty," said Henry, fearing the worst. "This is just for Hetty, and I don't want it spoilt. There will be ladies present this time."

"No worries," exclaimed Arty, soothingly. "With so many pretty faces to look at, the lads will have other things on their minds—they'll be on their best behaviour, you'll see."

The first of the carriages swept up the driveway and the Potts family was soon engulfed among a crowd of excited party guests.

Sarah had decided not to come downstairs until the cake was cut. Over the years, she had become used to living simply and quietly in two rooms at the back of the house while the children had been away at school, and the noise now that they were young adults bothered her. Hetty and Henry were no trouble, but Arty and his hangers-on made up for all of them put together. She had sent Arty to a boy's boarding school in Melbourne, hoping to knock some sense into him but he had been a hopeless pupil and only learned how to cheat at cards and gamble on the horses there. Henry had attended a small private school with few boys that had suited his nervous, sensitive nature, and Harriet had been educated at home until she was of an age to travel to Sydney to a finishing school for girls with her governess as a chaperone. Sarah doted upon her niece and hoped that one day the wealth she would now inherit would attract a suitable husband, although the thought of her beloved Hetty leaving home for good filled her with sorrow. They were children no longer, and she had no right to dictate what they did with their lives, although she had found it necessary to remonstrate with Arty of late. Arthur Potts had left her the right to live at The Great House for the rest of her life, and she refused to be driven out by Arty and his drunken revelries with his wild companions.

Henry had decided to live at the business during the week and only came here to relax at the weekends. To Sarah's surprise and gratification, Henry had taken to all forms of mathematics. As a child, he had loved to sit and puzzle out the logic of numbers and stuff his head full of equations and logarithms. His wizardry in such matters made him indispensable to the firm, and Sarah relied on him to help to run the haberdashery. As for Arty, he was happy to let Henry get on with it, and he left him strictly alone to deal with the accounts, sitting in his stuffy little office all day. Henry was happy making money, and Arty was never happier than when he had it to spend. Sarah had insisted on Arty visiting the store from time to time to show some interest in the family business, but Arty only made the girls giggle with his silly remarks, and Sarah had given up with him.

Maudie Muldoon was expected to come to the party tonight. Sarah wondered how such a shy and retiring young woman would cope among so many strangers. She was the daughter of Arty's bookmaker and seemed a strange choice of girl for Arty to choose as his intended bride. They appeared to have nothing in common—not even racing, although her father was a bookmaker. The poor girl had survived a bout of smallpox during the epidemic of 1884 which had left her motherless and destroyed her looks. She rarely mixed in society, feeling too embarrassed about her pocked complexion, which had made her shy in company. To overcome this problem, Maudie dressed well in a quiet fashion and wore large hats with veils to cover her wispy, mousey-coloured hair and to hide her face. People who knew Maudie liked her. She was both kind and generous and had a loving nature. Sarah had taken to her immediately, although how she had come to love the irresponsible Arty, Sarah could not imagine. Maudie had been a frequent visitor to The Great House since the announcement of her engagement to Arty and was liked by them all. Arty was rarely present during these visits, but Henry made a point of being there. He shared an interest in books with Maudie and would often read to her, sitting under the vines on the verandah. At these times, they enjoyed quiet strolls along the strand beside the tea trees, neither of them speaking much; silent companionship was sufficient for them both. Henry knew she belonged to Arty, but he often wished he had met Maudie first.

He made up his mind to always be there for her as her friend. Sarah had watched their friendship grow and was glad. She had little time for Arty and hoped the marriage might work if Maudie had Henry to turn to as a friend when she needed one.

Hearing the sound of guests arriving, Sarah came out of her room and looked down upon the assembled company below. There was Henry fussing round Maudie, who had just arrived, while Arty was surrounded by his racing friends, quite unaware of Maudie's presence. And then Sarah saw Harriet, laughing and smiling as she passed between her guests. Catching sight of her aunt leaning over the top banister, Harriet waved gaily in her direction. Sarah took a step back into the shadows and gave a muffled cry. It could have been Lizzie standing there with her hair piled up into a coronet and the diamonds sparkling at her throat.

"Dear God," prayed Sarah, as she regained her composure, "give her more sense than her mother ever had." She returned to her small room and sat down on the low, straight-backed chair she preferred to any others. Time had sweetened some of Sarah's memories, and she could think of her sister without enmity; Lizzie's sexual promiscuity not quite forgotten but certainly forgiven. After nursing Arthur and enduring his coarse oaths and fractious behaviour, she had come to see her brother-in-law in a different light. The suave, dapper little man, full of ingratiating ways, was a monster of self-indulgence when one really got to know him, and a more frustrated, querulous old invalid it would be hard to find. Lizzie must have longed to be free of him, and Sarah felt some sympathy for her. Lizzie had left Harriet behind for her to love and for that Sarah was willing to forgive and forget. A close and loving relationship had grown between them over the years, and Sarah thought of Harriet as if she had been her own child. She had protected Harriet from all hurt, and the child had grown into a beautiful woman, ready for life to unfold before her.

A burst of laughter and cheering rose up from the dining room, and Sarah could hear Arty's loud voice making a speech. They must be cutting the birthday cake. She hoped that Arty wasn't too drunk at this point in the proceedings—there had been too much of that lately.

The orchestra struck up a lively tune and the guests, replete with food and drink, wandered back into the salon. Sarah decided not to go down and join them and went into her bedroom. It was quieter in there, and she would read until the last carriage had rolled up the drive, and the house settled down again.

Henry stood protectively behind Maudie's chair and watched his brother Arty with ill-concealed contempt. Arty was drinking too much as usual and encouraging his friends to do likewise. A race had been suggested, amid much laughter, with the ladies taking the part of the jockeys mounted on the men's backs. Henry considered this was going a bit too far, although some of the ladies appeared to be rather keen on the idea. He spoke gently to Maudie, suggesting she might like to leave early now that things were getting a bit out of hand. Maudie got up thankfully and took Henry's proffered arm. She had realised from the start that Arty didn't love her and that the arranged marriage had something to do with the money that Arty owed to her father. He had hardly spoken to her all evening, and, if it hadn't been for Henry, she would have died of shame. Her father was deaf to all her pleas and had threatened to turn her out if she refused to marry Arty. For a woman with a pock-marked face to make such a good match and then to throw away such an opportunity was something her father would never understand. She would never get another husband with her looks, and Arty Potts had no interest in women, only horses, so her future would be secure. He had cancelled Arty's enormous debt in return for the young man's marriage to his daughter.

"Perhaps we could walk along the shore—it's such a lovely warm evening, and I wouldn't like to upset your dear sister by leaving early. I'll leave after the fireworks, Henry, if that suits you?"

"Of course—of course," said Henry, hoping he hadn't been too presumptuous making such a suggestion. "I was only thinking of you, Maudie."

Maudie smiled at him. "You always are, Henry. You are the most thoughtful person I know."

Henry blushed, and they wandered across the grass to the edge of the sea where they stood and watched the waves in silence. After a while, Henry plucked up the courage to ask her if she was looking forward to becoming the new mistress of The Great House. He could hardly ask her if she was looking forward to marrying Arty, as he felt sure she was not.

"The house is lovely Henry, but it's rather grand. If it wasn't for your aunt and Hetty, I think I would be very lonely living here. I'm used to something much smaller, and I find it rather overwhelming."

"You'll get used to it in time and then it will feel more like home," said Henry kindly. "And I expect Arty will take you to the races from time to time, and then you'll make new friends."

There was a long silence until Maudie broke it, speaking in a low, sad voice.

"I don't want to marry Arty, Henry, and I'm sure he has no interest in me—it's an arranged marriage. I'm surprised you haven't realised that before. It must be obvious to everyone that we have nothing to do with each other, although I do think that Arty could make more of an effort to acknowledge my existence when there's company about."

Henry was appalled, although he said nothing for a long time—he stood there thinking about it—there must be something he could do to help the poor girl, but he couldn't imagine what that could be. If he tackled Arty about it, he would come off badly and would probably make the situation worse. He had never got the better of Arty over anything as long as he could remember.

"How did this arrangement come about, Maudie? There's no need for you to tell me if you'd rather not, but I might be able to do something about it." Henry was amazed to hear himself make such a statement. It wasn't like him at all. He always kept clear of any involvement where a difficult situation might develop, and this could be very difficult.

"It was my father's idea—no one else—and certainly not mine," said Maudie bitterly. "Your brother owed my father a large sum of money—he places his bets with him you see—and he couldn't repay them. My father cancelled all his debts on condition that he makes me his wife. He agreed, and that's why I'm here."

"That's disgusting!" exclaimed Henry angrily. "How could your father sell you like that—he should be horse whipped! He's a monster—I've never heard of such a thing in all my life!"

Maudie placed her hand on Henry's arm to calm him. "He was thinking of me too, Henry. He thought he would never see me married with my looks, and Arty was a good match."

"Arty a good match? What nonsense! He'll end up a pauper the way he's going on, and anyone would be proud to have you as his wife. I'll not hear another word of this, Maudie. Not another word."

Henry's face had turned a dark red, and he began to shake with anger. Maudie, who had never seen him in such a rage, suggested that they should walk back. She felt responsible for his outburst and wished she had never told him. There was nothing he could do even if he wanted to—her fate was sealed.

Screams of laughter greeted them as Henry and Maudie made their way back across the lawn; the jockey race was drawing to an end. The men were galloping as fast as they could to the finishing line, carrying their partners in a piggyback fashion. The girl's wide-skirted dresses covered the men's eyes in many cases, causing much hilarity as they lost their way around the course and landed in a heap on the grass. Harriet, catching sight of Henry, left her partner and ran across to him.

"Would you find Arty, please, Henry. I think he's indoors somewhere, and it's time we had the fireworks. Come with me, Maudie, and we'll find a good seat."

The two young women strolled off together, and Henry made his way indoors. His anger at what had happened to Maudie filled him with a courage he didn't know he possessed.

He found Arty in the billiard room, holding forth among a group of his racing cronies, a glass in one hand and a cigar in the other. He was popular and told racy stories, keeping those around him in good spirits. Henry went straight up to him, his eyes blazing with anger and called his name. Arty stopped speaking and looked round. He had never seen Henry look like this before and could hardly believe what he was seeing. Obviously, something was seriously wrong. He motioned to his friends to leave them and put his glass down on the green baize top of the table.

"Are you ill, Henry? Whatever's the matter?" Henry's face was twitching uncontrollably.

"I'll tell you w-what's the matter," stammered Henry angrily. "You bought Maudie to settle your account with her f-father—that's what's the matter. How could you do such a despicable thing, Arty? Maudie's a decent woman, and you've treated her rottenly. Give the poor girl her freedom for God's sake—you c-can't carry this thing through."

Henry looked as if he was about to suffer an attack of apoplexy, and Arty pushed a chair towards him with his foot. So this is what Henry's outburst was all about. Just like Henry to get all worked up for nothing.

"It's all settled, Henry—a fait accompli, as the saying goes—I couldn't meet my obligations, and I have Maudie in exchange. A fair exchange, if you look at it from my point of view."

"But she doesn't want you, Arty. Can't you see that?"

"I don't expect she does, and I don't want her either for that matter. She's free to do what she wants once we're married. I won't bother her. Her father was becoming a damn nuisance, worrying me for money, and now I've got him off my back. It's as simple as that."

"No, it's not as simple as that, Arty. You haven't given one thought to Maudie or how she feels about it. You never think about anything but that bloody race course."

Henry paused, and Arty hoped he'd come to the end of his tirade. He had no wish to be made to feel guilty by his brother.

"How much do you owe Maudie's father?" asked Henry, eventually.

"A lot," replied Arty, vaguely.

"How much, Arty?" reiterated Henry.

"Henry, will you just shut up about it—it's no business of yours." Arty was beginning to get annoyed.

"How much?" shouted Henry.

Arty sighed. He wanted to get this over with. "Two thousand pounds, if you must know—now, will you leave me alone. I must see to the firework display or the natives will be getting restless."

"It's no laughing matter. Maudie's happiness is at stake."

Arty had begun to move towards the door. "Ah—so that's it, is it, Henry? You want her for yourself—now I can see what this is all about. Well—I'll make a bargain with you. You pay off my debt, and Maudie is all yours. I'll give her to you as a wedding present."

Arty roared with laughter at what he considered to be a good joke and went off to light the fireworks, leaving Henry slumped in his chair. All the bravado he had felt initially had faded away. Two thousand pounds was a small fortune, and he was wondering where he could find such a sum. His legs felt weak at the thought, but he was determined to see this thing out to the end having come this far. Henry had made a few investments of his own with the capital that had come to him from the business at his father's death. He had bought some blocks of land on the edge of the rapidly expanding city and had also acquired some shares in the Melbourne and Williamstone Railway Company. All of these would now have to be sold and added to his own savings. Then he would need to raise some further capital to meet Arty's enormous debt, but it could be done with some careful thinking, and Henry was good at that. It might take him years to get straight again but Maudie was worth every penny if she felt as much for him as he did for her.

The door opened and there stood Maudie coming to look for him now the fireworks had started. Henry got up—he was glad she had come as he had a lot to tell her. To Maudie's surprise, he put his arm round her and led her to the window where rockets were shooting up over the bay and cloud bursts of silver and gold stars were falling towards the delighted crowd below.

"Isn't it beautiful, Henry," breathed Maudie in wonderment at the sight. "Have you ever seen anything like it?"

Henry smiled at her childish enjoyment. With Maudie here beside him he felt calm and content, and he hoped she felt the same.

"Maudie," said Henry quietly, "you don't have to marry Arty now—I've spoken to him, and he's agreed to break off the engagement. You're free to marry whom you choose."

Maudie stepped back a pace in astonishment at this announcement. "Oh, Henry—I can't believe—but how did you—?"

"That doesn't matter. What matters is that you are free to make your own decisions, whatever they might be. I shall see your father tomorrow so that he understands and will leave you alone in the future to marry whom you please."

"Oh, Henry, you are the dearest friend. I'll always remember what you've done for me, but I'll never get married—nobody would ever want me with a face like mine. I accepted that fact years ago."

Henry was filled with pity for her, although Maudie felt no pity for herself. She accepted her disfigurement. Other people had suffered the same fate as her—she had been fortunate to survive, for many had not.

"It's not what you look like; it's the real person that matters," said Henry with some feeling, "and to me you are the most beautiful person in the world."

Maudie's eyes filled with tears. She had never expected to hear such words addressed to her with such sincerity.

"Do you think you could love me, Maudie?" asked Henry nervously. "If you felt you could then I would be honoured to have you as my wife. We could be quite comfortable in the old rooms over the business, if you would be happy living there?"

Maudie looked up at him lovingly. Henry was wringing his hands together in his anxiousness to hear what she thought of his suggestion, and her tears began again to his consternation. "I would like that, Henry," she managed to say. "I would like that very much."

Henry lifted up her tear-stained face and kissed her pockmarked cheeks with great tenderness. It was the first time he had ever felt like kissing anyone before, but with Maudie it was different. Just being with her gave him confidence.

"We shall be very happy together, you and I," said Henry, wiping away her tears. "We're two of a kind, you and me."

Harriet stood framed in the doorway, shaking hands with the departing guests as Henry returned from bidding a fond farewell to his bride to be. A handsome, dark-haired young man was kissing Harriet's hand. Harriet blushed with pleasure and smiling up at him expressed a hope that he would remember his promise to call upon her.

Hearing this, Henry hoped she wasn't falling for one of the less savoury guests invited by his brother, for Arty made friends with everyone and had cheerfully invited them all, regardless of their suitability.

"Who was that, Hetty?" Henry asked casually, after the young man had taken his leave.

"Oh—just a friend of Arty's," was her offhand reply. "He owns racehorses and his name is Adam Trevern."

Henry shrugged. The name meant nothing to him.

CHAPTER 23

The week after the party passed slowly. The house had returned to normal. The salon had been swept and polished and the gilded furniture disappeared once again beneath the dust covers. The weather was hot and humid and left Harriet drained of energy and without the inclination to do anything. It was too soon for any gentlemen admirers to call upon her; that would come later, or so she hoped. Aunt Sarah, seeing her moping around, suggested she might like to accompany her to Melbourne to do some shopping, but Harriet found Melbourne even hotter at this time of the year and declined her invitation. It was cooler by the sea, if she could bother herself to walk along the strand.

Arty was saddling up the pony they kept for the gig. He was off to one of the local amateur events, where he intended to ride one of his horses. The groom led Arty's horse out of the stable yard and hitched it onto the back of the gig—he was riding on the tailboard to keep an eye on it, as Arty was taking no chances today. There was big money to be won on this race, and Arty wanted his horse to be as fresh as possible. He intended to win at all costs as he had half promised to buy a pair of fine trotters he had seen lately, trotting races being all the rage at the moment.

Seeing him gave Harriet an idea. Aunt Sarah had already left, and now she was of an age she could do what she liked so she would go to the race with Arty, if he would take her. Arty was almost at the point of departure by the time she reached him and showed some reluctance at her request. He had no wish to have his sister as an extra encumbrance and said as much, but Harriet was very persuasive.

"I won't be any trouble, Arty, I promise, and I shall be so proud of you if you win."

Arty was flattered but still had his doubts. "It's a new course, Hetty—laid out by a group of speculators. There are a lot being built at the moment. I'm trying this one out for the first time, so I don't know much about it. The old crowd will be there to watch me race and give me some encouragement—but it might not be the place to take you to—things might go wrong, and then the crowd can get nasty," explained Arty, hoping to put her off coming. "You know—that sort of thing."

"But you don't do anything wrong, surely, Arty?"

Arty looked into her innocent, questioning eyes. "Certainly not, Hetty! How could you even think of such a thing?"

Harriet laughed. "Then that's settled then—I'm coming."

"It would seem so," said Arty, resigned to taking her with him. Harriet climbed into the gig beside him. He really couldn't refuse her, much as he wanted to, and as the little pony trotted along, in no way did his cheerful countenance show his real feelings on the matter. Harriet was delighted and smiled and nodded in greeting to all and sundry travelling in their direction.

"When we get there, Hetty, I'll have to find someone to look after you. You realise that, don't you? You can't watch on your own—even in the stand, if there is such a thing, which I doubt. Some peculiar people mix with the crowd at race meetings."

"Of course, Arty, of course—don't worry about me—I've come to enjoy myself. Nothing's going to happen to me."

"It hadn't better," said Arty, "or Aunt Sarah will have me guts for garters."

No sooner had the gig arrived than Harriet saw a face she recognised.

"Look, Arty!" She pointed to a dark-haired young man, talking earnestly to a jockey. "It's Adam. You remember him, don't you? He came to my party."

"Oh, Trevern—yes, I invited him—surprised he came really—he's out of my league as far as racing is concerned. His father is well known for breeding thoroughbreds. Can't think why he's here. He only supports first class meetings." Arty jumped down from the gig. "I must get going, Hetty. I'm in the first race—now what shall I do with you?"

Harriet laughed at his dilemma and stepping down lightly from her seat made her way through the crowd to Adam's side. Arty watched their meeting with some surprise. Adam's delight at seeing her so unexpectedly was obvious. They both turned and waved to him. He had been dismissed. Arty thankfully disappeared to get on with the proper business of the day.

Adam couldn't believe his good fortune at meeting Harriet, and, on hearing that she was unaccompanied, took her arm and escorted her to a vantage point to watch the race.

"Arty didn't expect you to be here," she said, conversationally. "He says you rarely attend out-of-town race meetings, Mr. Trevern."

"Your brother is quite right, but my father has invested some capital in this new course, so I am here today to see how things are going. He hopes to use it as a practice course eventually. Our great ambition is to have a runner in the Melbourne Cup before too long. Have you ever been to the Cup Race, Miss Potts?"

Harriet shook her head. "I was away at school until I was eighteen—a sort of finishing school for young ladies—and since I've been home there has been little opportunity. Henry isn't all that interested, and, although Arty is, I would have got in the way. He never came home until days after the meeting had finished—celebrating with his friends, I expect. It must be very exciting."

"Yes, indeed." Adam smiled down at her. "I can see I must take your education in hand. That would give me the greatest pleasure."

"Me too—and please call me Hetty. It's the name my family call me and I feel much more at ease with it."

"Of course—I would prefer it too. Then, with your permission, we will begin your education right away," said Adam, anxious not to let her slip away now he had made her acquaintance. "The country town meetings have good, well-managed racing. We'll start there, I think. There's a meeting at Kyneton tomorrow. What do you say to that?"

"Lovely. I shall look forward to it very much." Harriet's eyes sparkled at the prospect of going with him.

"Then I shall call for you early. It's some distance to travel, so we must make an early start—certainly no later than nine."

There was no time left for talking; the runners for the first race were gathered at the starting gate, and Harriet could see Arty in the middle of the line-up. Adam watched the start intently; the starting gate was a new innovation, and the real reason for his attendance at this meeting. In a flash, they were off, the horses racing up the track with Arty among the leaders. Harriet jumped up and down, calling his name, swept along with the shouting around her. It was the first time she had seen Arty race, and that made it all the more exciting.

"Is he the favourite, Adam?" she asked breathlessly, as Arty held the lead.

"No, he isn't. The horse close to him is the favourite and appears to be gaining on him—here, look though these." Adam handed her a small pair of binoculars.

As she looked through them, Harriet could see Arty clearly. The rest of the field had fallen behind and the rider beside him had drawn level. Arty pulled in very close to him and just as his opponent was about to overtake Arty leaned over and gave a sharp tug on the other horse's reins, jerking his head up. The jockey lashed out with his whip at Arty, who drew away but the harm had been done and the favourite fell back a few paces. Arty whipped his horse on in a frenzy and came in first at the winning post.

Harriet handed back the binoculars with a miserable expression. "Why so sad?" asked Adam. "Arty came first, didn't he?"

There was a movement among the crowd and shouting came from many quarters.

"Disqualify him! Disqualify him!"

Adam looked at Harriet. "I didn't see what happened, did you? It looked like a clear win to me. The favourite was at least a head behind, and, unfortunately, he was the one I backed."

"Arty pulled his head up; that's why he didn't win." She felt disloyal to her brother but at the same time ashamed of his behaviour.

Adam roared with laughter. "He did, did he? Well, that's not the first time that's happened, and it won't be the last I can assure you. Foul riding is pretty commonplace at small meetings like this, especially when there's quite a bit of money at stake. There are some big punters here today—mostly friends of your brothers—so I'm not surprised. Racing can be a dirty game."

"So Arty said," remarked Harriet.

"Well, he should know." Adam turned away from her to see what the result would be. Arty was well known for flagrant pulling, and other riders usually kept well clear of him if it was at all possible, but there was no need to tell Harriet that; by the end of the season, she would know a great deal more about the sport if he continued to see her, and he could see no reason why not. Harriet appeared to be as interested in him as he was in her. There was something about her he had noticed when he had first seen her; a kind of likeness to himself which drew him to her, apart from her natural charm and beautiful face.

Arty was announced the winner, and all hell broke loose. He had not been expected to win at the onset of the race, and the odds had been placed at thirty to one against the field. The favourite was a sure winner—he had won at almost every race in which he had been entered, and the bookies had given him short odds. Now they were in some consternation as Arty's friends had backed him heavily, and he had bribed some of the officials to decide in his favour, should there be any dispute over the winner. Some of the bookies had refused to pay out. It was obvious that Arty should have been disqualified. The crowds round the stands grew nasty, blows were thrown, and one of the bookies lost part of his moustache, pulled off in the melee. Others tried to make their getaway before the result was announced and were set upon by the crowd. Only a few escaped.

Harriet watched the disturbance with some amazement. "Are all meetings like this?" she asked her companion.

"Not at all," replied Adam. "This has turned into a shambles, due I'm afraid to your brother's method of winning and the large sums of money involved. You will find it very different tomorrow."

Harriet smiled with pleasure at the thought. She was seeing him again tomorrow. It was all too good to be true. The other races passed without incident, and Harriet found herself talking to Adam as if she had known him all her life. They had so much in common.

On the way home, she told Arty she was going to the meeting at Kyneton with Adam the next day. Arty wasn't interested in her plans—she hadn't mentioned his race.

"He's all you can talk about, Hetty—what about me? I won, didn't I? So how about a bit of praise in my direction."

"Yes, you won, Arty," admitted Harriet, "but you cheated. It didn't seem right to me, and there was a dreadful fuss afterwards."

"A lot you know about it," grumbled Arty, urging on the little pony. "It happens all the time."

They had nothing more to say to one another for the rest of the journey, and Arty blamed himself for taking her. Women knew nothing about racing.

When Sarah heard that Arty wasn't going to Kyneton races and would not be there to chaperone his sister, she was most concerned. Harriet might be a grown woman but she really could not allow her to go out alone with a male companion unknown to her.

"But who is this young man who is taking Hetty out?" she asked Arty, after hearing that she was off again so soon.

Noting his aunt's concern, Arty decided to speak up in support of his sister. He did not want to be saddled with her further, and if Adam Trevern was happy to keep her company it left him free to go his own way.

"It's all right, Aunt Sarah," he said, soothingly. "There is nothing for you to worry about. Hetty will be perfectly safe. Trevern is a most respectable man with the highest principles. His intentions are of the best, and if yesterday is anything to go by, he'll take great care of her."

"Trevern," said Sarah, who could scarcely believe her ears. "Did you say Trevern?"

"Yes, yes, Aunt—Adam Trevern—his father breeds thoroughbreds—he and his father are known and well respected throughout Victoria."

A clatter of hooves outside took Sarah's attention before she could speak and a smart carriage and pair drew up at the door. Adam appeared, wearing spotless white moleskins and held out his hand to wish her a good morning. Sarah looked at the handsome young man standing before her; she was speechless and unable to return his greeting. His likeness to Harriet was startling, the same black hair and deep brown eyes, Lizzie's mouth, and Lizzie's seductive smile—the past had come back to haunt her. How could she tell Harriet after all this time—Sarah stood frozen to the spot with fear and alarm. Harriet swept past her, her white muslin dress and fluttering blue ribbons a delight to see. She waved good-bye to her aunt, and, smiling happily, the two young people set off for the races.

Sarah turned on Arty. "She must never see him again, Arty," she cried out in great distress. "Do you hear me! Never—never again. You must *never* take her to where he is likely to be."

Arty thought his aunt had taken leave of her senses, and, taking her arm, he led her indoors. If she carried on like this every time Hetty had an admirer, the poor girl would never get married.

That evening, as they returned from an excellent day's racing, Adam and Harriet were surprised to see Arty riding towards them.

"Anything wrong, Arty?" asked Adam as he reined in the horses.

"No, nothing really wrong, Trevern—just a warning to you both. Our aunt has been behaving strangely since you came to collect Hetty, and I would advise you not to come into the house on your return. She has insisted that Hetty is to have nothing more to do with you, and I have been told that I am never to take her to another race meeting where you are likely to be present. As you are a complete stranger to her, her attitude is unreasonable to say the least, and I am anxious that you should not take any personal offence—I trust you will not."

Harriet gave a cry of disbelief. How could Aunt Sarah be so unkind and so unreasonable? There were few young men in the state as eligible as Adam Trevern.

"Does your aunt feel that I'm not good enough for your sister? Is that it?" asked Adam, angry at such a rebuff.

"You know that cannot be the reason," replied Arty, anxious to placate him. "It's my opinion that she feels jealous. She has always been possessive over Hetty and can't bear the thought of losing her one day. The Crown Prince himself would have difficulty getting past Aunt Sarah—she can be a formidable old thing at times."

"I can't understand Aunt Sarah," said Harriet angrily. "I'm not a child, and she has no right to prevent me from seeing whom I like."

"No," agreed Arty, "that's perfectly true, but it will make things difficult for you at home if you do. She loves you too much, Hetty, and if you decide to continue to see Trevern it will have to be without her knowledge."

"How can I possibly do that?" Harriet was close to tears. She had only just begun to know Adam and enjoyed being with him. The happy carefree day she had spent in his company was fast becoming spoiled by her aunt's ridiculous attitude.

"There are always ways and means, Hetty," remarked the ever-ingenious Arty. "You can make an excuse to go into Melbourne and meet each other there. Nothing could be easier."

"Maybe your aunt feels I am too young to act as your escort," said Adam, turning to Harriet. "I don't come of age until next year, and she might have other plans for you."

Harriet was indignant. "Whatever plans Aunt Sarah might have, I am not interested in them, and if you still want to take me to the races, Adam, then I shall go. I can take the carriage to the store whenever I like and leave it there until I'm ready to return home. I can call and see Maudie or make some purchases, and Aunt Sarah need never know."

Adam considered this proposition for some minutes as they continued on their journey, with Arty riding beside them. He wanted to go on seeing her. She was a delightful and charming companion, and they had spent the happiest of days together, and he didn't want to lose her just yet, but if he was to continue this relationship he would have to agree to an arrangement which meant deceiving her aunt, and that troubled him. Next year, when he had achieved his majority, and his father had made him a partner in his profitable estate, then Harriet's aunt could raise no objections to his friendship with her niece, but, until then, he would have to meet her secretly or not see her again. Adam could see no reason for bowing to the wishes of her possessive aunt, and it was decided upon to meet in Melbourne in the future.

Harriet left the carriage at the entrance to the drive, and Arty dismounted to walk with her.

"How good of you, Arty, to come and meet us," said Harriet as they walked up the long, curving driveway to the house. "I might never have seen Adam again had you not done so, or gone to the races at Geelong next week as he suggested."

"Think nothing of it," said Arty, who had acted from a purely selfish motive. If Adam Trevern had taken offence at their aunt's refusal to let him see Harriet again, it might have rebounded on him at a later date. People in the racing world never made enemies of the Treverns; old Harry held too much power for that. An insult to his only son could have meant an early end to Arty's hopes of becoming a famous amateur jockey, and he hoped that his brotherly intervention had prevented that from ever happening.

A distressed and worried Sarah was waiting for Harriet in the library. She told Harriet how there had been difficulties between the two families for years, which had started before Harriet had been born and had concerned her mother.

"I do not intend to rake up the past, Hetty," said Sarah, firmly. "To go over all that happened then would cause you much unhappiness, and there is no need for that as long as you cease your association with this young man. Believe me Hetty, what I say is entirely for your own good. Any further acquaintance with the Treverns will only result in opening old wounds and could end in much pain and suffering for us all. I implore you to do as I ask my dear, for all our sakes."

Harriet thought over her aunt's words and came to the conclusion that, however much Sarah had been hurt by something in the past which she was unwilling to talk about, it had happened before she had been born, and therefore could not possibly involve her. She and Adam were of a different generation, and old family feuds need not concern them or sour the happiness they had found in each other's company. Aunt Sarah's feelings on the matter, whatever that matter might be, made it quite clear that her friendship with Adam would have to be kept secret if it was to continue.

"I will see that he does not call again, Aunt," she said, choosing her words with care, and with that Sarah had to be content.

All that year and into the next, Adam and Harriet continued to meet in Melbourne without Sarah's knowledge. They rode on the new cable trams, sitting together on the curved wooden seats just made for two, enjoying the ride as the tram whined round the corners and made its steep descent down the middle of Collins Street. Harriet loved Melbourne—the well-paved streets fronted by bluestone buildings and lit at night by gaslights glowing through white and coloured glass globes, and the beautiful store which belonged to her family where she could wander at will to choose her clothes. Sometimes, she stayed there with Maudie and Henry, and that made her meetings with Adam all the easier. On hot summer afternoons, they would browse in Coles Book Arcade or eat ice cream at the Café de Paris. Whatever they chose to do or wherever they went, they enjoyed the sights and sounds of the city as if they were of one mind.

At Flemington racecourse, Adam introduced her to the most influential people in the racing world but took great care to avoid his father. He wanted no further trouble over his friendship with Harriet; she was far too precious to lose. Society was charmed by her, and she received invitations to social events and race balls where Adam would be present. To make their meetings easier to arrange, Adam had managed to obtain invitations for Arty so he could act as Harriet's escort to these functions. Arty was delighted, as through his sister's friendship with Adam Trevern he was making new and useful contacts in the racing world, and nothing could have pleased him more.

The summer of 1889 was the happiest that Adam and Harriet were to spend together. It seemed endless, like the pleasure they found in each other's company and the love they shared for one another. Harriet never remembered having a mother, as she had run away when she had been only a few months old, and Adam had lost his mother in a bush fire when he was too young to have any memory of her, and that drew them even closer together. They planned to marry as soon as Adam became twenty-one and then to tell their respective families. Harriet hated keeping her happiness a secret from the one person she cared for more than anyone apart from Adam, but she was afraid of losing Adam should her aunt be told of her plans. Once they were married, any objections Aunt Sarah had to their union would have to be faced and overcome. Nothing in the world could separate them when she was his wife.

In the autumn, Harriet and Adam were married secretly in Melbourne. Arty and Henry were their witnesses, and Maudie was the maid of honour. She was happy for them both being so happy herself now she was Henry's wife.

Immediately after the short service, Adam and Harriet set off on honeymoon, travelling by train to some of the outlying townships, intending to stay away for a month. Adam sent word to his father that he would be bringing his new wife home soon and letting him know the name of his bride. Arty was asked to convey the news to Aunt Sarah but made an excuse and sent Henry instead. Somehow, he felt that his aunt would take the news badly, and Arty did not intend to be the one to tell her. The result was worse than he had expected. Henry had never experienced such wrath as his words evoked or such a storm of weeping, and he left The Great House visibly shaken after hearing the tale his aunt had to relate.

Sarah sat down at her writing desk and with trembling fingers penned a note to Harry Trevern, begging him to part his children and send Harriet back home.

Harry held Sarah's note in his hand, the tears coursing down his weather-beaten cheeks. This was the result of his passionate affair with his beloved Lizzie, and he was the one who would have to tell them the truth on their return.

His poor wretched children had become the innocent victims of his past sins, and he would never forgive himself as long as he lived.

CHAPTER 24

The hired carriage bumped along the dirt road between the long lines of withered vines. Despite the warm autumn sunshine, Harriet shivered at the sight of so much desolation and asked her husband the reason for such a bleak landscape.

"It's a disease, Hetty, called phylloxera, which is caused by an insect. Whole vineyards have been wiped out by it, including our own. My father's income used to come from these vines but fortunately the stables have become so profitable we can dispense with our winery. We could rework these plants on resistant stock but it would be uneconomic, so we are gradually returning the land to pasture. We keep valuable animals here, as you will soon see, and prefer them to graze near the stables. Of course, they aren't all racehorses, and I shall find you a pretty little mare to ride when the fancy takes you."

Harriet smiled her thanks. She had the kindest, dearest husband in the whole world whose only wish seemed to be to make her happy. Once they had received the blessing of both their families, her happiness would be complete, and Adam had assured her that his father was not a man to bear a grudge, whatever the problems had been between their families in the past.

"As soon as he sets eyes on you, Hetty, he cannot fail to fall in love with you," he had told her when she had expressed her nervousness at meeting him for the first time, and yet, despite his confidence that all would be well, she grasped his hand tightly as the long low homestead came into view.

There was no sign of life as the carriage drew up in front of the verandah, and she sensed an uneasiness in Adam as he lifted her down. The isolation of the buildings set among the rotting vines and the lack of any kind of welcome gave Harriet a feeling of impending doom. It was so different from the grandeur of The Great House, where the guests were greeted on their arrival, and she began to wonder if the Treverns kept servants so far from civilisation. After all, it was a man's domain, Adam's mother having died long ago, but surely they had some staff to look after the household.

"Where is everyone, Adam?" she asked, nervously.

"I've no idea, my love. It's certainly very odd. I sent word to father of our arrival, but perhaps he was away at a meeting and didn't receive it. Let's get you settled, and then I'll see what's happened. The boys should be around somewhere—they're probably in the stables, working."

"The boys?" asked Harriet. "What boys?"

"The stable lads, Hetty. They help to run the stables and exercise the horses and sometimes race for my father. You'll like them—some of them have wives who work in the house, cooking, and cleaning and such like. We're a family concern, and now you're a part of it—the prettiest part too."

Adam put his arm around her as he spoke, and together they went up the steps and entered the comfortably furnished living room.

To their surprise, they found the room was occupied; Harry was sitting in his large leather armchair waiting for them, his gaunt frame hunched into the recesses of the chair, hiding from the task that awaited him. His face was white and drawn, and when he rose to meet them it seemed to Adam that he had shrunk in stature and was suddenly old—very old. Once he rose from his chair, he held his hands stiffly by his sides and stood very still, his keen black eyes riveted on Harriet. His silence as he took in her features was more expressive than words. Nobody spoke, for his suffering was apparent to the onlookers. This was his natural daughter. There was no doubting the fact now he had seen her; she was beautiful like her mother although her features were softer, and she had a vulnerable look about her which Lizzie had not possessed. Of course, she had been protected all her life, living in that great pretentious house overlooking the bay. His Lizzie had made her own way from a very early age and knew what life was all about whereas her daughter had never known what it was to suffer. He was the one to break her heart—her own father who had given her life. Looking at her sweet face as she stood there wondering and waiting for him to speak, he felt like a murderer.

Adam could bear the silence no longer, and, leaving Harriet by the door, he strode across the room to face his father.

"Father?" he asked. "Is anything wrong? This is Hetty—my wife. Have you no word of welcome for us?"

Harry swallowed; his lips and mouth were dry, and he needed a drink. He had been drinking heavily since receiving Sarah's note, and it had done nothing to help him to face this situation apart from blotting it out for short periods.

"Your mother—" he began, speaking with difficulty, and addressing his words to Harriet. "Your mother was—"

Adam shook him angrily. "What are you trying to say, father? What about Hetty's mother? Did you know her?"

Slowly, Harry lifted his head and looked straight at his son. The wretchedness etched in the lines of his face affected Adam deeply and he dropped his hands to his side. The strength of mind and purpose he had always admired in his father were no longer there; he stood before him, a broken man.

"Yes, I knew her Adam, and loved her dearly—she became my wife after her husband died and was your mother too. I would have done anything rather than tell you—but it is the truth, God help me."

There was a stunned silence, and then Harriet gave a strangled cry.

"We share the same mother, Adam—don't you see? I am your half sister—oh, dear God—what have we done?" And she began to sob bitterly, leaning against the person she loved so completely and always would. "I cannot be your wife—now or ever." Adam gathered her into his arms and held her close, his tears mingling with hers. When the worst was over, he tried to comfort her.

"Few people know we were married, Hetty, and we can still belong to each other, only in a different way. I shall always love only you, and will never take another wife. It will be difficult at first for us both but we must gradually get used to thinking of each other as sister and brother."

Harriet drew away from him and taking off her wedding ring, she placed it in the palm of his hand. She felt awkward and out of place standing so close to him and moved away to sit beside the window, trying to make her mind accept that her marriage was over. How could she think of him as anything but her lover when they had so recently shared moments of passionate intimacy. Her face flooded with colour. She must forget what it had felt like to be touched by him in that way and keep her distance. They would never be able to wipe such memories from their minds.

Harry's voice broke into her thoughts. "I am your father too, my dear. You are both my children. Your mother left you behind to come to me when you were only a few months old. It broke her heart to leave you behind, but I was adamant. I doubted your parentage and wanted only my own children, but Lizzie was sure you were my child, and now I have seen you for myself I know it to be so. You bear a remarkable likeness to your brother."

"Your brother—your brother." The words rang in Harriet's ears over and over again as her mind tried to accept this obvious truth. They had thought like one and acted like one because they were born of the same flesh and blood. The more she thought of it, the more corrupt she felt. She felt a sickness rise up in her throat as she met Adam's eyes and knew he was thinking the same thoughts. She wanted to take to her heels and run back down the long dirt road through the rotting vines to the sea and then plunge into its cleansing depths. Her tears began to flow again, for nothing would ever wash her guilt away.

"Oh, what am I to do—what am I to do," she moaned, rocking herself to and fro in the chair.

Adam forced himself to turn away. To touch her was forbidden while he still felt as he did for her. They would have to suffer alone.

Harry went over to her and placed his arm comfortingly around her shoulders. He must do what he could for his poor children. If only he had let Lizzie bring the child with her, then Harriet would have grown up with her brother in a natural way and this never would have happened. He had been a selfish bastard in those days, wanting her love just for himself, and when she had died so tragically, thrown from her horse as it panicked in a forest fire, his grief had been so great he had never spoken her name again until this dreadful day. His son had grown to manhood knowing nothing of his mother, apart from the way she had died, and cared for from babyhood by one of the women in the compound.

"My dear, your aunt wrote to tell me what had happened and to ask me to see that you returned home to her. I think that would be best. The temptations might be too great if you remained here with Adam, although this is your rightful home, and I would be pleased for you to stay. Parting now will heal your pain more quickly. Later, when your feelings towards each other have changed, then you can meet again—as brother and sister. Will you go back? It's your choice, my dear."

Harriet shrank from her father's protective arm. To return to The Great House would be difficult after she had deliberately defied Aunt Sarah and taken no heed of her warning. She loved her aunt, and that made it worse, but she could see no other way but to return home and try to pick up the threads of her old life, should such a thing be possible. She would ask for forgiveness and hope that her aunt still loved her enough to forget what she had done.

Harry took her back to the carriage, which still stood in the yard. Her boxes were replaced, and he sat on the seat beside her, not wanting her to travel alone in her distress. He had decided to speak to her aunt himself to save his daughter any further upset, and to discuss the matter of her future. Home was the best place for her right now, but he hoped it would be possible to visit her and to treat her as a daughter in the future. Just to look at her reminded him of Lizzie and the years he had lost when his daughter was growing up. He wanted to make up for all those lost years if she would let him and to help her remake her life.

Adam could not bear to see them leave or to say good-bye to Harriet. To think of her as a sister was impossible; he loved her as a man loves a woman and always would, but from this day onwards he would keep his feelings locked in his heart for none to see.

Hearing from Harry that Harriet had chosen to return home Sarah treated her with kindness and consideration. Her immediate reaction on first seeing her niece had been one of hurt disapproval, but the sight of the poor girl's tear-stained face and Harry Trevern's distress at what had happened between his children filled her with compassion.

"We are the ones to blame for this, Miss Hopkins," he told her. "Never forget that. They are the innocent ones. I loved another man's wife, and you denied your sister the right to her child when she came to claim her. Harriet was my child and should have grown up with her brother. You must have realised that as the years passed, but love is possessive, and I can understand your reluctance to part with her. The guilt is ours Miss Hopkins."

As the days passed, Sarah often recalled his words. He was quite right; she was guilty. Guilty of loving Harriet too much to let Lizzie take her away and guilty of not telling her the truth about her mother in case she might ask why her mother had never taken her to live with her natural father once she had married him, and afraid of losing her love if she ever discovered that the aunt she loved so much had denied her the love of her own mother. So many guilty secrets to mull over in the privacy of her own room—things she had long forgotten.

She fussed over Harriet as if she was recovering from an illness. They went for gentle rides in the carriage, walked and shopped, read books, and worked on their embroidery in the evenings. There was no fun anymore, no laughter, and few visitors. Arty was rarely seen feeling partly to blame for encouraging their friendship, and Henry kept away. Harriet felt as if she had contracted a contagious disease, and Aunt Sarah was her nurse. She was surrounded by kindness and still felt desperately unhappy.

Maudie felt for her. She knew what it was to keep a broken heart to one's self and decided to do what she could to help. Harriet went to stay in Maudie's homely apartments behind the store and gradually began to take an interest in the clothes that Maudie created. Harriet asked her to design some new outfits for herself as she was putting on weight, and she helped Maudie choose the fabrics and trimmings. By the time she returned home to Aunt Sarah, she had begun to feel as if she was slowly coming to life again but for what reason she had no idea. There was no life without Adam—she had existed only for him and nothing had changed. She would always love him.

And then one day, Harry appeared unexpectedly to take her out. Sarah wasn't sure if he had timed his visit too soon but said nothing. He was her father and had made it clear when he brought her back that his dearest wish was to help his daughter in every way. When she heard he had come to take her to the stables for the day, she was worried. Harriet had been home for four months and was only just beginning to get back to normal. She expressed her doubts to Harry when Harriet had gone to fetch her wrap.

"Do you think it is wise for them to meet so soon, Mr. Trevern?" she asked.

Harry put her mind at rest. "Adam is away racing, Miss Hopkins. That is why I felt this would be a good time for her to visit the stables. I understand she is interested in racing, and that is something we have in common. We are her family, and she must be given a reason for living again. We can talk about her mother—it will do me good as well as her—and she can get to know the place that should have been her home and meet the family."

"The family, Mr. Trevern? I don't understand."

"My stable lads are my family, Miss Hopkins, as well as my children."

Harry smiled and Sarah smiled back. "Ah, I see," she said, without understanding at all.

"Our Harriet," continued Harry, kindly, "is living in a vacuum at present. For Adam, it is easier. He is riding like a maniac, driving his devils away in the process. It's not so easy for a woman—don't you agree?"

"You are an extraordinary man, Mr. Trevern," said Sarah, surprising herself. "I can see now why my sister fell in love with you."

Harry raised his eyebrows. He doubted very much that she did.

CHAPTER 25

Harriet's return to the stables was easier than she had expected. Harry had brought the gig to collect her and chatted throughout the journey, pointing things out as they went along to keep her thoughts occupied. When he mentioned that Adam was away racing, she felt deeply disappointed. Just to see him would be such joy after all these empty months even if they didn't exchange a word. A look would be enough to know that he still loved her.

"I thought that you needed a change of scenery, my dear," said Harry, kindly, "and where best to come than the place I hope you will think of as your second home. We have some beautiful horses for you to look at and some new foals, and, best of all, I want to show you Harry's Boy. He is our hope for the Cup, and Adam is to ride him. It will be the first time we have entered for the Cup Race and the first time I shall watch the race with my daughter beside me. What do you think of that, Hetty?"

"You are very kind, father—I wish I had known you all my life—and to think that I dreaded meeting you."

"It was the same for me, my dear, but for different reasons. We must put all that behind us now, eh, Hetty?"

Harriet smiled briefly to please him but made no answer. She would not spoil her father's happiness in her company by burdening him further. Her news could wait a little longer. Cheerfully, Harry waved his whip in the direction of the stables as they approached the homestead.

"I see the lads are ready to meet you, Hetty: they're all spruced up today in your honour."

Harriet was amused to find that the lads ranged from a young black in his early twenties to a man of about forty. They stood in a line in front of the stable block wearing a selection of dirty white singlets and well-worn strides and grinned with delight as Harry introduced them to her by name—Josh, Obi, Danny, and Eli. Their features were those of an aboriginal but their colouring was not and varied from dark brown to a lighter shade. She had never seen men like them before, although she had heard of half-castes. Josh, the eldest, was a handsome man. He had the fairest skin of all, and if it hadn't been for his broad, flat nose he could have passed for a white man.

"Now Hetty—Josh here is the cocky. He gives the others their orders—that so, eh, Josh?" Harry slapped him on the back in a matey way.

The men roared with laughter. It was a family joke among them that Josh considered himself superior to them because of his skin colour, although they shared the same mother.

"No sir, you the cocky here," insisted Josh, not enjoying the attention he was receiving in front of the young master's sister. "Go on boys—off with you now," ordered Harry. "You've seen Miss Hetty, and she's had the doubtful pleasure of meeting you. Chop chop lads, back to work —no time to waste."

Harriet turned to her father with a puzzled expression. Harry laughed—he could guess her thoughts.

"They're all my sons, my dear, and more besides. Don't be shocked. They were all born before I met your mother. The stables are well off the beaten track and in the early days no woman would have cared to live so far out in the bush. With your mother, it was different. Once I had seen her, I wanted her, and she would have come to the ends of the earth to be with me. I loved her, Hetty, and have had no woman since."

"Did she mind— – about your sons, I mean?"

Harry smiled at the memory. Lizzie had been shocked at first but had taken it in her stride. She understood a man's physical needs better than anyone.

"They lived over in the compound and had little to do with your mother. I had an old black housekeeper in those days, and she did all that was necessary, with the help of her daughters—she even brought your brother into the world, and he wasn't much trouble—couldn't wait to get here, and that's a fact."

Harry walked her over to the compound where the black women smiled shyly at her, holding out their babies for her to admire. Small children clustered round her skirts and slipped their hands into hers. Harriet felt happier than she had for a long time.

"This is where the boys live, and these people are their wives and children," explained Harry. "I look after them and see to their welfare and in return they work for me. The lads have made a fortune for me, Hetty. Nowhere could I have found such loyal workers as my boys. They are as much a part of the place as I am, and I treat them as such. Adam missed them badly when I sent him away to boarding school; they were all friends together, and the women mothered him. He had a happy childhood here, albeit a strange one."

They returned to the stables, where Harriet was introduced to Harry's Boy. He was Harry's pride and joy, but his daughter showed some reluctance to approach the frisky stallion. His lip curled back, showing his great teeth, and his eyes flashed wickedly as he threw his head back and forth moving restlessly in his stable.

"Steady boy, steady," coaxed Harry, calming the great beast. "He's the finest horse I've bred, Hetty—a true thoroughbred. Look at him now—full of spirit. He stands a fair chance of winning this year's Cup at Flemington."

"He seems almost too wild to ride," commented Harriet, lamely. She was terrified of the animal but hardly liked to admit as much to her father.

"A good racehorse needs spirit and stamina if they're going to stay the course, and this one has both."

"Does Adam get on all right with him?" asked Harriet nervously. The idea of Adam riding such an animal filled her with alarm.

"They're good for each other. Adam rides him hard, and that's what this horse needs, a rider he can respect. You need have no fear for your brother; he's an excellent jockey. I would put my money on him in any race. You wait until Cup day my dear—it will be a day to remember."

Harriet was shown all the horses in Harry's stables, the mares in foal and mares with young foals, the everyday workhorses, and, last of all, a pretty little grey, with soft brown eyes.

"Well, what do you think of her?" asked Harry, as his daughter fondled the gentle creature. "Like her better than Harry's Boy, I wager!"

"She's lovely," replied Harriet, "and so friendly."

"I thought you'd like her." Harry was obviously pleased with her reaction. "We'll take her home behind the gig. You've got a stable to put her in I take it? Adam said he'd promised you a horse, and here she is."

"Oh, Father!" Harriet kissed his leathery cheek, "how kind of you."

"It's not every day that a man discovers he has a daughter, Hetty," remarked Harry, gruffly. It had been years since he had felt the softness of a woman's cheek against his own, and her kiss affected him deeply.

The afternoon was coming to an end, and they returned to the house for some refreshment before leaving. As they were eating the carefully prepared meal, there was a knock on the door, and Josh stood hesitantly on the threshold.

"Well, what is it Josh?" asked Harry. "Spit it out, boy."

"The bay—she had her foal, boss. It's a colt this time. I thought Miss Hetty might like to see it before she leaves."

"There, what did I tell you, Hetty. Josh makes all the decisions around here. Well, all right Josh—I expect Miss Hetty would like to see it. Am I right, Hetty?" Harriet nodded. "Go on then—Josh will take you while I tie your little horse to the gig, but don't be too long. I want to get back before dark."

Harriet knelt in the straw near the still wet foal and watched as it struggled to get to its feet. Its long, spindly legs collapsed beneath it, and it sank down again beside its mother. She licked it gently to encourage it until at last it got up and searched for its first meal. Harriet was entranced.

"You like him, Miss Hetty? Josh thought you would."

"Oh yes, I like him Josh—he's beautiful—thank you for coming to fetch me."

At the sound of her voice, the footsteps passing the entrance to the stable where the bay was housed hesitated, and a shadow blocked the light from the doorway. Harriet and Josh looked up to see Adam standing there, a saddle over his arm. Harriet stood up quickly, her heart pounding, not knowing what to say.

"You back early, Master Adam," remarked Josh, going over to him. "The bay—she have a fine colt."

"Yes, Josh, so I see. Take my saddle will you, and see to my horse—I'll look after things here for a while."

Josh nodded and taking the heavy saddle silently disappeared.

Adam came over to where Harriet was standing and stood by her, watching the foal. "Father said nothing about you coming here today," he said quietly.

Harriet trembled at his closeness. "No," she said, in a low voice, "he thought, as you wouldn't be here, it was safe to bring me for a first visit."

"And is it safe, do you think?"

Harriet turned towards him and saw the hunger in his eyes.

"Oh, no Adam, no," she sobbed.

Adam gathered her towards him and kissed her lips, her eyes and her hair as if he would never stop.

"You mustn't love me, Adam, you know you mustn't love me," she implored as she struggled to free herself.

Tearing himself away from her, Adam threw himself down onto the straw, clutching it in an agony of despair. Harriet knelt beside him and cradled him in her arms, rocking him like a child to soothe his cries.

"Oh, my love, don't—don't. It will get better—it must get better."

Gradually, Adam regained his self-control and the terrible sound of his weeping ceased. They sat together quietly for a while, too emotionally exhausted to move.

"You're wrong, Hetty—it won't get better—I can't live without you, and it's tearing me apart— - I can't live with the pain any longer."

"You mustn't think like that, Adam. I've got to go on living too. You see I'm going to have our baby, so it's even worse for me."

Adam got to his feet and stared down at her in horror.

"Hetty! What have I done to you! What have I done! My poor little Hetty, my poor darling." He bent down and helped her to her feet and stood looking at her with deep concern.

"I want you to tell our father, Adam. I couldn't tell him myself although I intended to before I left, but he was so kind to me today I just couldn't spoil the day for him. Nobody else knows yet except for Maudie—I haven't even told Aunt Sarah. I can't bear to think about it, let alone talk about it. Will you do that for me, please? He'll have to be told sooner or later, won't he?"

"Yes, of course I will—but what about you?"

"Well, I'm going to call myself by my right name for a start. It was the name you gave me, and it should have been my name from the beginning. I shall wear a ring on my wedding finger, and when I am big with the child, people will think I am married and my husband is away. No one need ever know the truth, apart from our families."

Adam winced. "You shouldn't have to bear that shame alone, Hetty," he said wretchedly. "Let me take you away somewhere until after the baby is born."

"No, Adam. You know that wouldn't work. We can't pretend to be a married couple. It would start all over again between us—you know it would."

Adam hung his head. Her resolve was stronger than his, and he felt ashamed. The bay mare shifted her position and whinnied softly to her foal, reminding them of their surroundings. Steps were heard outside in the yard, and Harriet moved towards the door.

"It's our father, come to fetch me. I must go, Adam."

Harry looked through the door to glimpse the new foal before setting off and saw Adam there. He looked from one to the other to read his children's faces, but he saw nothing in their expressions to cause him any alarm. Perhaps it was all for the best that they had met so unexpectedly. There had to be a first time, and they had been unprepared. It was unfortunate that he had not been present as he had intended to be when they met again. Still, no harm appeared to have been done; in fact, they seemed to be well in control of the situation, which surprised him a bit. It was a pity that Josh had left them alone together but then he knew no better and presumably Adam had sent him on his way. Next time he brought his daughter here he would be more careful. They would never be left alone together again.

"A sturdy little colt," he said, by way of conversation, feeling awkward in their presence and angry with himself for not being more vigilant. "Come along, my dear—time to be going."

And Harriet went, without looking back.

Harriet and Adam never met each other alone again. Harry often took her to race meetings with him to watch her brother ride, and she would see Adam afterwards and rejoice in his success when he won, but always in the presence of their father. Before her condition became too obvious, she was a frequent visitor to the stables. She watched Adam train and listened to the endless discussions afterwards. She heard all about the famous horse Carbine, who was the favourite to win the Melbourne Cup, and how he had won over every distance from seven furlongs to three miles and how he wore leather ear covers built into his bridle to prevent his ears from becoming wet, as he was affected by the rain. It was all they ever talked about—Carbine, Harry Boy's greatest threat.

Harriet worried constantly about Adam. He drove himself relentlessly, getting Harry's Boy in peak condition for the race. His face grew thinner, and his body became as taut as a wire, while Harriet's waistline thickened with the new life growing and moving within her womb. She had heard tales of children born of close relationships who could suffer in both body and mind and wondered if she was carrying some monstrous abnormality as a punishment. When she refused food, her aunt made her eat and when she lay at night shedding bitter tears, her aunt was there to give her solace and calm her fears. She longed for the day when the Cup Race would be over and her baby was born, for then Adam would have no need to avert his eyes from the sight of her bloated body, the sight of which was driving him to distraction. When it was all over perhaps they could find some peace at last.

On the day of the race, Harry came to collect her. She could have gone with Arty, but she was near her time, and Harry was concerned that she should have every comfort he could provide. She sat in an excellent seat with a good view of the finishing post and with her father in close attendance. Sarah had been invited to join them but declined the offer. The day meant so much to the Treverns she felt they should be together as a family without her intrusion.

"There's a field of thirty-nine runners for this year's Cup, Hetty," Harry told her as they waited for the race to start. "Adam's in excellent form, and I think we stand a chance, especially as the favourite is carrying a record weight of ten stone five pounds—that's almost three stone heavier than Harry's Boy."

"I hope for your sake, father, that Adam wins. I know how much it will mean to you both."

Harry patted her hand, and then, suddenly, they were off. The atmosphere was electric, the huge crowd rising to the occasion. Harry's Boy emerged in the lead, setting a fast pace for the rest of the field, thinning them out in the early stages.

"Adam's taken the lead too soon," exclaimed Harry, becoming agitated in his concern.

"He should have held him back longer—he'll never keep up that pace."

"But he's holding the lead well. Look father—look!"

Harriet was carried away by all the excitement around her, such an enormous gathering of race goers, all shouting with one voice. She had never been so affected by a meeting before or watched one with such interest.

"I can see Highborn coming up on the inside, and Carbine's not far behind," reported Harry, watching through his racing glasses. "Highborn's too close! Come on, Adam— come on!"

A gasp rose from the crowd, and Harry lowered his glasses.

"Harry Boy's fallen—I can't tell if he was pushed against the rails or not. There go my hopes—and he was doing so well."

Harriet stood up in great agitation. "But Adam—where's Adam? Is he all right? Can you see him? Oh, father, can you see him?"

As Harry focused his glasses on the fallen horse and rider, the rest of the field thundered past with Carbine in the lead and Highborn a close second. The crowd was jubilant. It was the result they had hoped for as the majority had backed the favourite. There was a mass exodus as the crowd rushed to collect their winnings.

Harry shouted to Harriet, trying to make his voice heard above the racket.

"There's a crowd of officials round Adam. He's obviously been hurt because I can see him being lifted onto a stretcher. I'll have to get down there to give permission to have the horse shot. It looks from here as if his leg's broken. Stay here, Hetty, until I get back. I'll come as soon as I can."

Harriet waited miserably in her seat for what seemed a lifetime. Her father didn't come, and she got more and more worried. Adam had been carried off the course some time ago, and she needed to find out what had happened to him. When she could wait no longer, she began to mingle with the crowd, making her way slowly and with some difficulty towards an area forbidden to the general public, which was used by the course officials. She hoped to find someone there who could tell her where they had taken Adam. Her heart began pounding with exertion and worry as she reached the enclosure. The crowd was thinner here, and she overheard some men discussing the race as she stumbled past.

"Shame for Harry, losing his son like that—bad business—I hear he's very cut up about it."

"Killed outright, so I heard—the horse behind kicked him on the head just as he tried to get up, poor devil. Lost his horse too—broke both legs—good runner—had a lot going for it."

The men walked off leaving Harriet stunned by what she had heard. Her heartbeat grew louder and louder in her ears, filling her head with drumming until the whole universe became one enormous sound. She covered her ears to shut it out, but the thudding only grew louder until a merciful blackness closed in around her and she fell to the ground in a crumpled heap.

CHAPTER 26

The day of the Melbourne Cup in 1890 was a day that Rosie was never to forget as long as she lived. She had travelled to the city with Beth a few times in the past, but this was the first time Rory had taken her racing at Flemington, and she was enjoying every minute of it.

They had left John and Beth behind at the homestead as the noise and the crowds did not appeal to them at their age. Rory had decided that they should spend a few days of well-earned rest together in Melbourne while the races were taking place—the first real holiday they had found time for in almost twenty years of marriage.

The beautiful lawns and flower beds of the Flemington racecourse and the large grassy area allotted to the general public were all a wonder to Rosie. There was so much to see wherever one looked, trainers and owners, bookies and touts, all mingling with the huge throng; for this was the day of days when Carbine was one of the runners and the whole of Melbourne had turned out to see him.

Rory had bought her a little silk fan printed with the official programme to keep as a memento of the event. There were white, sky blue, and pink silk fans to match the ladies outfits, and Rosie had chosen a pink one to go with her gown of dark rose coloured taffeta. Over the years, the sheep station had grown beyond their wildest dreams, and they felt well on the way to becoming one of the most prosperous farming families in the district. Rosie could afford to dress well, and Rory felt proud of her, looking as fine as any other lady at the races that day. She still had a good figure, and, although the golden curls had long since been twisted into a heavy plait at the back of her head and had dulled to the colour of ripening corn, there was a sweet contentment about her face and a ready smile came easily to her lips, causing some heads to turn as she wandered among the crowds in the enclosure on her husband's arm. As the horses paraded past, Rory pointed out Carbine to her.

"My money is on him, Rosie—never been known to lose a race yet, so he's the favourite to win this one. Nothing worries him apart from the rain on his ears."

Rosie smiled. "Well, it's not raining today, that's for sure, so maybe you'll be lucky."

A spirited dark chestnut thoroughbred with fire in his eyes sidled towards them baring his teeth and snorting as his jockey pulled him round to face in the direction of the starting line and rode him off. This wild horse inspired Rosie to back him.

"What's the name of that horse over there, Rory?"

"Hmm, let me see." Rory consulted his race card. "That's Harry's Boy—he comes from the Trevern stables and is ridden by the owner's son. Do you fancy putting a bet on him?"

"Yes, please."

Rory went off to place her bet, and Rosie made her way across to the rail to watch the race, which would soon be starting. She remembered the name Trevern—it was Harry Trevern who had become Lizzie's lover and whom she had married after Arthur's death. Sarah had given her that news in a letter many years ago, and she had almost forgotten it until now. Hearing the name of the stables had brought it all back again. She no longer corresponded with Sarah and had no idea what had happened to the Pottses over the years. How strange that she should be here today of all days, and maybe Lizzie was here too. Rosie wondered if she would recognise her among all the fashionably dressed ladies. Lizzie would be a middle-aged matron by now and would look somewhat different from the beautiful young woman of Rosie's youth.

"Wake up, love, the race is about to start," came Rory's voice in her ear, and, forgetting everything else, she turned her attention to the course in front of her, leaning over the rail in her excitement.

As the horses thundered past, she could hear Rory shouting above the noise of the crowd. "Your horse took the lead too soon—he'll never win. His jockey is riding him too hard."

Rosie could just pick out her horse from the rest of the field. He had been in front and then suddenly, his legs crumpled beneath him, catapulting his rider into the path of the oncoming horses. The jockey attempted to rise only to fall back onto the turf. Rosie hadn't seen what had happened but she feared the worst as she watched the still form of Adam Trevern being picked up and placed on a stretcher to be carried away. The feeble, writhing of his horse and the shot which put him out of his misery distressed her so much she grabbed Rory's arm for support, unaware which horse had won.

"He was so still, Rory—do you think he was killed?" she asked, on the point of tears.

"I can't say," said Rory, drawing her away. "Perhaps he was just concussed. He drove the poor animal like a lunatic, so he is partly to blame for what happened. The horse was high spirited—you saw that for yourself—and possibly its heart couldn't take the strain. We shall never know, Rosie, so it's best to try and forget it. Accidents often happen at race meetings, and sometimes they're fatal. It's a risk a jockey has to take, but I thought this one could have been avoided. If you feel all right, my love, I'll go and collect my winnings. Why don't you go to the refreshment tent and get a cup of tea—it would do you good, and I'll come and join you there."

Rosie pushed her way through the crowd and walked towards an area where there were fewer people, intending to go on a circuitous route to the refreshment tent, when she saw what looked like a bundle of clothes lying in the grass beside one of the private enclosures. Going closer, she realised it was a woman in a dead faint. She was young and pretty and very well dressed, and, as she bent over her, Rosie could see she was heavily pregnant. She needed help immediately. Rosie looked round to see if there was anyone close enough to call, but there were very few people in this select area, and they were too far away to be within hailing distance. While she was wondering which way to turn to fetch help, a man in a loud check suit emerged from a tent in the private area of the course and hurried past her. Rosie caught up with him and held on to his sleeve.

"Please, sir, please wait a moment. There's a woman here who has fainted, and she's having her baby soon. Please help me to find someone to help her."

The man threw her to one side. "Can't you see I'm in a hurry—let go, will you—I have urgent business to attend to. Find someone else."

"No," said Rosie firmly, determined to stop him, "not until you find someone to help her. She needs to be carried to a place of safety. If you can fetch help I will stay with her until help arrives."

Seeing the woman was a well-dressed, respectable body and not some hussy trying to attract his attention, the man turned round and walked swiftly to where the young woman was lying. He could call an official to help, he supposed, a few more minutes would make no difference to the terrible news he had to tell his sister. Looking down at the limp form lying at his feet, he gave a wild cry of recognition.

"Hetty! Dear God—it's Hetty!"

"You know her then," said Rosie, with some relief. She couldn't have left the poor girl there all alone while she went to fetch Rory as that might have taken some time.

"She's my sister," the man explained, "I was about to go and find her."

"Perhaps she was on her way to find you."

"I doubt that—more likely coming to see what had happened to Trevern. I'm Arty Potts by the way—will you stay with her while I fetch some assistance? I'll be as quick as I can." Rosie nodded, and Arty sped off the way he had come.

Rosie knelt on the grass beside Harriet, placing her head in her lap and making her as comfortable as possible. So this young woman who was about to have a baby of her own was the baby she had nursed at The Great House all those years ago, the child Lizzie had left behind. Harriet Elizabeth she had been named, a sweet little baby who had given her no trouble, so unlike her spoilt brother Percy, whom she had never known. The thought of poor Percy brought a lump to her throat. She would never forget him or the horror she had felt at his untimely death.

Harriet stirred slightly and moaned. Rosie hoped they wouldn't be much longer coming to fetch her. Rory would be wondering where on earth she had got to. At last, after what had seemed a lifetime, some men appeared carrying a stretcher with Arty hurrying them along and a much older man walking behind.

"She'll have to be taken straight back to Aunt Sarah," said Arty, taking charge. "She'll know what to do, but she can't travel alone, and you're in no condition to go with her, Trevern. I'll see if I can find a responsible woman to accompany her, and I'll see that she gets home safely. Fainting like that might have something to do with the baby starting, and I'd be a perfect fool if she went into labour on the way home. I'd rather run a mile than deliver a baby!"

"I'll go with her," piped up Rosie. "I'd like to, and I'll look after her well, should anything happen before she reaches home."

"But we don't know—" began Arty, hesitatingly.

"I'm Rosie—Rosie Taylor before I was married. I nursed you all when you were children, but I don't expect you remember me because you were still very young when I left, but your Aunt Sarah will. I came out on the boat from England with her and your mother. They were the Miss Hopkinses in those days."

"So, you were Rosie our nursemaid, were you? I'll be damned! I've heard our aunt speak of you—well, if you'd be good enough to travel with Hetty, we should be most grateful. Are you here alone?"

"Gracious, no," said Rosie in some alarm, thinking of Rory. "My husband is waiting for me in the refreshment tent—he will be wondering where I have got to."

"Go and tell him what has happened immediately, my good woman," said Harry, speaking for the first time, "and then return to the owner's tent over there where Arty and the stretcher party are taking Hetty. I will wait for you there. We will see that my daughter is made as comfortable as possible in my carriage. Tell your husband that I will send word to him of your arrival, and you shall return home in my carriage as soon as possible, although it may not be until tomorrow. Tell him I am Harry Trevern of the Trevern Stables and give him my word as to your safety and comfort. Go quickly now—my daughter needs immediate attention."

Rosie ran as fast as her legs would carry her and spilled out the whole story to her astounded husband, who had been getting more and more worried as to her whereabouts. The more Rory heard the less inclined he felt to agree to her going. "Damn it all, Rosie. They mean nothing to you now, and I won't have you treated by this family like some old retainer. You're my wife and not their servant to run about after them."

"Oh, Rory, please—I want to go. And, what's more, I've promised them that I would—I won't be away long, only as long as I have to, and I expect I shall be back home in a few days. I loved Harriet when she was a baby, and it broke my heart to leave her and come back to Clay Cross, and now I feel as if I was meant to be here today to help her when she most needed me."

"Well, I suppose it will make little difference as we were going home ourselves tomorrow, but I don't like it Rosie—no way."

Rosie threw her arms round him and kissed him. "It's just that I feel I must go, and, anyway, my dear, I shall be back before you've even missed me."

Rory watched her hurry away and shook his head in disbelief but he could see that she was determined to go, and there would be no stopping her. His Rosie had a great sense of loyalty to those she loved, and he of all people should know that. As he turned to make his way home, he suddenly remembered he hadn't told her about the small fortune he had collected from the bookmaker. The enormous bet he had placed on Carbine to win had paid off. It hardly seemed to matter now she had gone, and it would have to wait until she got home again, which he hoped wouldn't be long.

Harriet had recovered slightly as the carriage made its way back to The Great House, and Rosie had little to do but wipe her brow from time to time. Her colour had improved, and she lay with her eyes open but made no sound. Rosie noticed that she wore a wedding ring and wondered why her husband had not been with her at the racecourse when she was so close to the birth of her child. Her black, wavy hair fell in tendrils across her damp brow as the motion of the carriage moved her head on the pillow. What a beautiful woman she had grown into, with something of her mother about her, thought Rosie as they made their way along the coastline she had left so long ago. The scenery hadn't changed, but so much else had, including herself.

Arty turned to speak to her from his position beside the driver.

"Everything all right still?" he asked, looking down at his sister.

"Her colour is a little better," answered Rosie shyly, feeling ill at ease with this racy stranger she had known as a child.

"Can't think what she was doing there—her father had left her in the stand while he went to see what had happened to Trevern and had told her to wait until he came back."

"What had happened to him?" asked Rosie. "I saw the accident but I didn't hear the outcome."

"Killed outright," said Arty shortly. "Dreadful thing to have happened—maybe Hetty was on her way to find out for herself, poor girl. Good thing you came along when you did, Mrs.—"

"Macdonald," said Rosie, "but please just call me Rosie—I shan't mind."

"We might not have found her for some time and poor old Trevern had enough to worry about right then. To lose his best horse and his son at one and the same time was enough to finish him off."

"Has he any more children?" asked Rosie, anxious not to mention Lizzie's name.

"Only Hetty here, and she stayed with us. Her mother died when Adam was a child, and there were no other children. Our Aunt Sarah brought us up, and she still rules the roost. She'll be surprised to see you, Rosie."

Rosie smiled weakly but felt brave enough to ask a question which had bothered her. "And where is Harriet's husband? She was all alone when I found her."

"Dead," said Arty abruptly, turning to face the road ahead and making it clear he would not tolerate any further questions.

Rosie was shocked. No wonder the poor girl had been so upset at her brother's fatal accident; so close to her time and without a husband to turn to for support. They were an ill-fated family, and Lizzie's running away had only resulted in more heartbreak. How selfish she had been. Her leaving had been the cause of Percy's dying, and all for a few brief years of happiness with her lover. It was a pity that Lizzie had ever left the shores of her native land to wreck such havoc among people's lives. Her heart went out to Harriet, and she prayed her baby would be born safely and bring her peace and contentment.

The carriage drove through the gates and up to the grand portico of The Great House and stopped. Arty leapt down to alert Sarah as to what had happened. While he had gone, Rosie looked around her. The place was just as she remembered it, apart from the shutters across the windows giving it an unlived-in appearance. Of course, there was only Sarah now and perhaps Arty, when he was at home, and maybe Henry still lived there, and Harriet, now she was alone. There was so much that

Rosie didn't know about them now they were all grown up. Sarah came to the door in some distress to see to Harriet's removal upstairs. She was too concerned to bother about Rosie although Arty had told her who she was, and it was some time before she returned to speak to her.

"Dear Rosie," she said, embracing her at last, "forgive me for keeping you waiting. Bless you for staying with Hetty and for all you have done for her. Please God, she will soon be herself again. The baby was due next month but because of the circumstances, it might be born prematurely. I have just sent for the doctor and will be relieved to have his opinion. Can you stay for a while, my dear? You know so much about looking after babies, and I know absolutely nothing. We have hardly any staff left to speak of with just Hetty and myself in this house. Would your husband mind? It would only be for a few weeks until Hetty decides what to do. What do you say?"

Rosie thought of her promise to Rory and hesitated. "It's not that I don't want to stay, Miss Sarah, but I must see what my husband says first. You do understand, don't you? I had to leave him at Flemington in some haste, which came as a surprise to him. We were on holiday, although we were returning home almost immediately."

"Well, let's see what the doctor has to say first, shall we?" said Sarah, walking out onto the step to greet him as the doctor drove up in his buggy. "He is the best person to advise us as to the state of Hetty's condition, and then we can discuss your stay later."

But before Sarah and the doctor had reached the top of the stairs, a scream of pain came from Harriet's bedroom and a maid came running out onto the landing.

"Oh, ma'am," she implored Sarah, who needed no urging to hurry herself, "Miss Harriet's pains have started."

Rosie sat herself down at the bottom of the stairs to think. She would have to wait now until the baby was born, and, if all went well, then perhaps she could stay for a while as Sarah suggested having come so far on her mission of mercy. She would send a message to Rory as soon as she was able to and hope he would agree to her absence for a few weeks until other arrangements had been made for the baby. It would be wonderful to hold a new baby again after all these years. She had so loved Harriet when she had taken over her nursing after Percy had died, and there had been no other babies to love since then, much to her sorrow. The more she thought about it, the more important it seemed to Rosie that she should stay, even if it was only for a few weeks. She could be a great help to the family, and she would enjoy that.

The time passed slowly without any activity to speak of from above, and Rosie grew stiff and weary. It had been a long day and she felt like going to bed. The sun sank rapidly over the bay and it was long past supper time.

Sarah seemed to have forgotten her; the maid appeared with a tray of food for the watchers upstairs. Rosie coughed, and the maid looked in her direction and hesitated before ascending the staircase. On her return, she beckoned to Rosie to follow her and led her to the kitchen quarters.

"Miss Sarah sends her apologies ma'am and says to tell you that Miss Harriet is having a difficult time of it, and she doesn't feel she can leave her. She wants me to make up the bed in the old nursery for you and says you are to help yourself to anything you like from the pantry. There's plenty of cold ham and tongue and pickles, and cook made the bread this morning so it's nice and crusty. The kettle is boiling, so I'll just put some tea in the pot."

Rosie sat down at the kitchen table and looked around her. This used to be the busiest place in the house, but now it looked bare and almost deserted.

"How many of you work here now?" she asked. The maid, a girl of about sixteen, filled up the pot and sat down for a moment.

"Only cook and myself, most of the time—there's just Miss Harriet and Miss Sarah here when she's not at the haberdashery giving Mr. Henry a hand. Miss Harriet usually goes out for the day—she visits her father at the stables sometimes, so there's not much to do, unless they have company, which isn't often."

"What about Mr. Arty?" asked Rosie, glad to glean some family news. "Where does he live now?"

The maid pulled a wry face. "He's here from time to time when it suits him—he's usually away racing these days; he rides a lot in amateur events but he keeps his horses here. There are six people living in the stable block, grooms and such like, and Mr. Arty mucks in with them when he's at home. They look after themselves with a bit of help from cook. Mr. Arty is supposed to be a partner in the family business but he's never there, so cook says. That's why Miss Sarah has to keep going in, poor soul; still, she doesn't seem to mind—says it's in her blood, and she loves all the new fashions. She gets on well with Mr. Henry's wife you see—she designs the new clothes for the business, and Miss Harriet says she's very clever at it, and she should know because she wears them."

"So, Mr. Henry is married, is he? Do they live in Melbourne?"

"Yes they do—in the old rooms where Miss Sarah used to live. They've made it very nice so Miss Harriet told cook. Mr. Henry didn't want to live here although there was plenty of room. I expect they wanted their own place."

Rosie nodded, remembering how quiet Henry used to be. "I'm not being nosey, my dear, but it's interesting to hear what has become of them all after such a long time. I was about your age when I came to work here as the children's nurse, but it was very different then."

The little maid smiled. They had something in common, and she found Rosie easy to talk to, but she still had work to do before she could get to bed.

"Forgive me, ma'am, but I must leave you. I have to make up your bed and clear away; with Miss Harriet so poorly, I might have an early call and a long day tomorrow."

"Of course, my dear—just bring me the sheets, and I will make my bed. I still remember the way to my old room—but before you go, what is Miss Harriet's married name? It might be appropriate if I call her by that now."

"She's Mrs. Trevern," called the maid from the doorway, "but she has no husband. She came back to live here all alone after her honeymoon. There was some tragedy, we were told. She looked very ill for a long time, but she's been better of late until this happened, poor lady. Goodnight ma'am—I'll leave the sheets on your bed, if I may—enjoy your supper."

As Rosie ate her supper she mulled over what she had just heard and found it incomprehensible, although there was no doubt that there was a perfectly reasonable explanation for Harriet's married name. Perhaps her husband had come from another branch of the Trevern family, and why was she still called Miss Harriet by the staff here? Perhaps she preferred it now she had lost her husband so soon after her marriage. As soon as she had an opportunity, she would ask Miss Sarah about it.

Upstairs in her old room, she found the bed already made up and a cotton nightdress laid out ready for her to wear. The young maid must have decided to carry out her instructions to the letter. Here in the nursery wing, she could hear no sound of any activity in the house. She looked up at the grim photograph of Alice Potts, which still hung on the wall above the fireplace and smiled. Dear Alice—that unsmiling rather faded photograph was nothing like the Alice she remembered from her childhood, but perhaps she had forgotten what she had really looked like and only remembered the kindness and goodness of that much-loved person. It felt strange to be sleeping here again with no children in the nursery in an almost deserted house, and she felt a twinge of loneliness to be sleeping without Rory beside her. The ghosts of the past no longer troubled her in this bedroom, but she wished she could feel Rory there and wondered before she fell asleep why she had felt compelled to take this step back into the past.

In the morning, she woke to the sound of birds in the foliage beneath her window and the distant sound of surf breaking on the strand and sleepily wondered where she was until she heard the sound of a baby crying. Harriet's baby must have been born during the night, and, by the sound of it's crying, it was a lusty infant. Rosie washed and dressed quickly and went downstairs to the kitchen to find a weary Sarah drinking tea. She looked up as Rosie came in, and smiled a tired smile.

"The baby arrived an hour ago, Rosie. He's rather small but quite perfect, thank God. The doctor has just left, and I've told him you are here to take charge of things for a while, and he was glad of that. You will stay now, Rosie dear, won't you? Poor Hetty has had a terrible time of it and will need nursing herself for some time. I will find someone to look after her if you can take over the baby for a while until we can find a good children's nurse. Surely your husband won't object. I will write to him myself and send it post haste with a letter from you so he hears today. In fact, I will write now, this very minute, before I fall asleep and will then repair to my bed."

It looked as if she had no choice but to stay, so Rosie also penned a letter to Rory and gave it to the groom, who set off to catch the early morning post to be sent to Euroa by train that day. Sarah went to her bed and left Rosie in charge for a few hours. She had sent word to Harry Trevern of the baby's safe arrival and had requested him to send someone who would act as a nurse until his daughter had properly recovered from her ordeal.

A few hours later, Harry brought his housekeeper to stay for as long as she was needed. Harriet was sleeping deeply when he arrived, and he stood for a few moments by her bedside, assured by the regularity of her breathing and the colour which had returned to her cheeks, that this was a natural sleep. For a brief moment, he peered into the old bassinet which had once held his daughter and which now cradled his grandchild, and then he left without a word to anyone.

Outside, the pony and trap awaited him and he climbed into the driving seat and sat dejectedly for a while, the reins hanging limply in his hands. He had been punished cruelly for his sins—first Lizzie, then Adam and the pride of his stable, and now to look upon this child. He wished with all his heart that it had not survived. With every breath it took, the child nailed him more firmly to the cross he had to bear. And what decision would Hetty make? His own beloved Hetty. Would she keep her son? He prayed not. She still had to wake up and face the hideous truth every time she looked at his sweet baby face. Yesterday's events had turned him into a broken man with only the whisky bottle to blot out the pain.

He remembered the flask he kept in his hip pocket and took a long swig from it, emptying its contents down his parched throat.

Rosie watched him leave—the pony moving at a miserable pace, pulling the trap and its driver as if they were an intolerable burden—and shook her head sadly at the sight.

CHAPTER 27

After receiving Sarah's impassioned plea for Rosie to remain at The Great House for a while, Rory felt he had no option but to agree and wrote to Rosie to say she could stay for as long as she felt it was necessary, although he hoped she would be returning home before too long. The place just didn't seem the same without her. Rosie wrote to him, frequently telling him of Harriet's progress and describing the baby with such enthusiasm that Rory began to wonder if she would ever be able to tear herself away when the time came to leave.

Rosie, however, was in her seventh heaven. She had the baby almost entirely to herself, and, during the weeks he was in her care, she watched over him as lovingly as any dedicated mother. He slept in a crib beside her at night and was returned to his mother each morning for his first feed of the day. It was obvious that Harriet adored her son, and yet, sometimes, as she cradled him in her arms, tears would fill her eyes and she would hand him back to Rosie and beg her to take him away.

"He's growing more like his father every day, Rosie—I can't bear it. I can't bear to look at him, sweet as he is, poor little thing." And she would weep as she held him up for Rosie to take from her.

"There there, my dear," comforted Rosie. "It must be very hard for you—but think how proud his father would have been of his son if he had lived to see him. Why, there never was such a bonny child, and you have him to love now."

"But that's why he died," sobbed Harriet. "It was because of the baby. If there had been no baby he would never have killed himself in that dreadful way. He never wanted to see the child—never."

Rosie was speechless. Had Harriet gone out of her mind? Surely, no man would go as far as to commit suicide because his wife was expecting a baby. Perhaps Harriet was suffering from delusions—there were questions that needed to be answered—troubling questions which she had no right to ask. Harriet was better physically, but the state of her mind was doubtful. She was labouring under some great sorrow which Rosie did not understand and which she longed to know.

That evening, while the baby was asleep, Rosie sat reading in Sarah's small sitting room while Sarah busied herself with her tapestry. They were comfortable together and often sat and talked over the old times when Harriet had retired early and the baby had been settled down.

"Was Miss Harriet unhappy in her marriage?" asked Rosie gently. "I only ask because she becomes so distressed at any reference to her husband or his baby."

Sarah removed the gold-rimmed pince-nez and sat for a while, twisting them nervously in her lap.

"I can understand your interest, Rosie, especially as the birth of the baby has depressed Hetty, but there is very little I can tell you, I'm afraid. Hetty fell in love with—an unsuitable person, and I forbade her to see him anymore without giving her an explanation of why she should not. I realise now that I was very much to blame, but I wanted to keep her in ignorance of past events—to protect her, I suppose. She was so precious to me—like my own daughter, and I was the only mother she had known. I wanted to keep it that way. She grew up with her half brothers as their sister, and that was the trouble. She thought I was being selfish and possessive and married a young man without my knowledge. When they returned from their honeymoon her real father told them the truth and brought her back here. Unfortunately, she had become pregnant. There is no more that I can tell you, Rosie dear, and it distresses me to say so much. Please forgive me if we do not discuss the subject again. You must draw your own conclusions, but please keep them to yourself. We have all suffered enough." Sarah collected up her skeins of coloured wool and tidied up her work ready to leave.

"I'm so sorry—" began Rosie, feeling deeply shocked as the import of Sarah's words began to sink in. "Please forgive me—I shouldn't have asked …" Her words trailed away to nothing. She had no idea what to say. It was terrible—like a nightmare. Harriet had fallen in love with her own brother and born his child. There was little wonder she had been in a state of shock when she had found her, collapsed on the grass after the Melbourne Cup Race had ended in such tragedy. Perhaps Adam Trevern had intended to kill himself during the race. Rory had told her that he was riding like a lunatic. She found herself shivering although the evening was warm. Harriet had said that her husband had killed himself deliberately because of the baby, and now Rosie began to think she might be right. If only Lizzie had taken her daughter with her when she went to live with Harry Trevern then this terrible thing would never have happened. Everyone, including herself, thought that Lizzie was an unnatural mother when she had refused to take any interest in her baby from the moment of her birth, but maybe that was because Harry Trevern did not accept that she was his child. There was no doubt that he did now, for he had called her his daughter at the racecourse. She wondered how and when the truth of Harriet's parentage had been discovered, but she could not question Sarah anymore on the subject. Sarah had been tortured enough, and Rosie's heart bled for her.

When the baby was a month old, Harriet began to pay calls on her father, leaving the baby with Rosie for longer periods. She never took the child with her, and Rosie could see the reason for that. It was quite clear now why Harry Trevern had appeared so wretched after visiting Harriet and had seen the living proof of his children's incestuous relationship. He must have felt wracked with guilt.

The baby was still without a name. Harriet was adamant that he was to be named after his father, but her decision so distressed her father and her aunt that no name had been bestowed upon the child who was still referred to as "baby." Sarah had begun to talk about installing a children's nurse and Rory's requests for Rosie to return home were becoming more insistent with each letter. Rosie kept stalling and announced that she was willing to stay for one more month, but that was all, after which she was definitely returning home. She had become so attached to the child that she could not bear to leave without knowing what Harriet intended to do with him. Although she loved her little son, his very presence seemed to disturb her, and she made excuses to go out more and more.

The housekeeper returned to her duties at the Trevern homestead, and Sarah became actively involved again in the haberdashery, from which she considered she had been absent too long.

Apart from the staff, Rosie and the baby had the house to themselves, not that Rosie minded about that. She wandered through the empty rooms with the baby in her arms, talking to him as if he could understand her thoughts. The huge, white and gold salon was gloomy with the shutters always kept closed and the furniture covered in dust sheets. When she opened a shutter, the chandeliers glistened in the sunlight, and the baby lifted his arms towards the crystal droplets as they sparkled and twinkled in the light. Rosie lifted him up to see them better and talked to him about his grandmother and the grand balls she used to hold there, and the baby patted her face with his tiny fingers and gurgled as he listened to her voice.

"How charming," said a voice behind her, and Rosie turned to see a tall, veiled young woman standing in the open doorway. "You make a delightful picture, really you do. I'm Maudie Potts, Henry's wife, and you must be Rosie, about whom I've heard so much from Aunt Sarah. Please let me take the baby for a moment—may I? Isn't he just beautiful."

Rosie passed him to her and noticed that Henry's wife was expecting a child herself.

"Are you looking forward to your own baby, Mrs. Potts?" she asked, to make conversation with this stranger.

"Very much indeed," replied Maudie, playing happily with the child. "Is Hetty at home? I couldn't find a soul anywhere when I arrived, and I thought I was hearing things when I heard you telling baby here all about the days gone by. It sounded most interesting—what a pity he couldn't understand it—he might have learnt a thing or two!" Maudie laughed, good-naturedly.

Rosie blushed to think she had been overheard. "I'm afraid Miss Harriet has gone to see her father this afternoon. She is often there now she is quite well again. Did she know you were coming?"

"I'm afraid not—I came on the spur of the moment. I've been longing to see the baby, but I didn't like to intrude until I felt she had got over the shock of—her brother's fatal accident. She's a great comfort to her father at this sad time, I feel sure."

Rosie nodded. "It must be very hard for him."

Maudie decided to change the subject. "There was a lovely ball in here on the occasion of Hetty's twenty-first birthday, you know." Rosie looked up in some surprise. The room looked as if it had been shut up for years. "Aunt Sarah was persuaded upon by Arty to have a party to celebrate the event, and it was great fun. There were even Chinese fireworks in the garden at the end. You never saw anything so pretty as the rockets when they burst over the bay and the stars fell into the sea. People talked about it for months afterwards."

"It sounds wonderful," said Rosie, enjoying the company of this friendly young woman. "Were there many guests?"

"About 200, I suppose—mostly Arty's racing crowd—it was a good excuse for him to have them all here—he knows such a lot of people. Henry got round to proposing to me at the party, which was a great surprise to everyone who knows how shy he can be—especially me!"

Rosie laughed as she took the baby from her and closed the door of the salon behind them.

"How about some tea before I leave— – will you join me? I'll ring for some, and we'll have it in the drawing room. It's such a pleasant room and so many of the others are dark and gloomy now nobody uses them. I'm so glad Henry and I decided not to live here."

"I remember the house in happier times," said Rosie. "A house of this size needs children to live in it and a large staff to look after it, and then it would come to life again and be a completely different place. I feel as if I want to open all the shutters and let the sunshine fill the rooms, and to take the dust covers off and bring the flowers inside from the garden."

Maudie smiled at her enthusiasm "You are a sweet person, Rosie," she remarked, kindly. "The baby is fortunate to have you here to look after him. No wonder he seems so content. I only hope I find someone like you to look after mine."

Rosie blushed at the compliment. The new Mrs. Potts was a very different person from the one she had worked for all those years ago. She glanced up at the portrait of Lizzie where it hung in its original place in the drawing room. The portrait saddened her as she looked at Percy leaning against his mother's side wearing the blue velvet suit which had been made especially for the occasion. In his young face, the proud aggressive defiance that had been so much of his character was clear to see, and Rosie wondered just what kind of man he would have become had he lived.

"Isn't this a wonderful painting of Henry's mother?" remarked Maudie, watching Rosie as she looked at it. "I wish Henry had been born then so he had been in it as well as his brothers. Hetty bears some resemblance to her mother, don't you think? Although her colouring is quite different—the Treverns are all dark."

Rosie made a vague reply and turned away from the painting to settle the baby among the cushions. She had no wish to talk about Lizzie. The tea was brought in and Maudie made herself comfortable in one of the large armchairs while Rosie poured it out into the delicate china cups and handed one to her visitor. Maudie had removed her hat in the meantime and the sight of her ravaged features gave Rosie such a shock that she almost spilt the contents of the cup. Maudie was such a picture of elegance that she had imagined her to be a beautiful woman. How cleverly she disguised the truth. After the initial shock, Rosie was so full of admiration for her that they chatted together as if they had known each other all their lives.

The door opened and Harriet walked in to join them. Rosie could see at a glance that the two women were close friends as Maudie rose to embrace her sister-in-law. It was obvious they had much to say to one another, and Rosie felt she should leave them together. The baby began to whimper as Rosie carried him upstairs to the nursery to amuse him until his mother came to feed him. As she rocked him over her shoulder to comfort his cries, she felt as if her heart would break when the time came to leave him behind. She had promised Rory faithfully that she would return home at the end of the month and that was only a few weeks away.

"Oh, baby, what am I going to do without you, my precious," she murmured as she rocked him backwards and forwards to soothe him. "If only you belonged to me and I could take you home with me."

"Do you love him that much, Rosie?" asked Harriet, coming into the nursery, "and your husband—would he love someone else's child too?"

Rosie spun round to face her with her heart in her mouth. "Oh, Miss Harriet! You know I love him—as much as you do—and I know that Rory would. I just know he would. Do you mean—?" The thought occurred to her that Harriet might let them bring him up until he had outgrown his childhood.

"I've been thinking about his future, Rosie. It isn't easy for me. I don't want him to grow up here where he will begin to ask questions about his father. I want him to be free to live his own life where the past can't hurt him—do you understand?"

"I understand perfectly. I know about his father, Miss Harriet, and I'm deeply sorry."

"You know! But that's impossible! Aunt Sarah would never have told you, and you've only just met Maudie and she wouldn't—"

"No, of course not. I only had to put two and two together to realise what had happened. You see, I was here when your mother left you behind to live with your father. He used to come here to visit her when Mr. Potts was away. I only found out about their relationship by accident when Master Arty was cut badly on the head, and I was sent to find his mother. I worshipped her, being young and impressionable in those days, and the discovery upset me deeply. I didn't tell anyone; there was no need to as your mother left soon after your birth to live with your father and their affair became common knowledge. I thought Mr. Trevern was your father from the moment you were born. You looked very like your own baby whereas the others were Pottses—every inch of them.

After I left, Miss Sarah told me in a letter how your mother had come to take you away when she heard that Mr. Potts had died, but as he had left her in sole charge of the children and considered you as his little daughter, she thought you should stay here with your brothers where you were happy."

Harriet sank into the nursing chair and covered her face with her hands. "If only she had let me go. Why didn't she let me go? I would have grown up with Adam, and this would never have happened."

Rosie knelt beside her with the baby in her arms. "Don't blame her, my dear. She loved you dearly and acted for the best as she saw it. Your mother died soon afterwards, so I have been told, so you would have had no memories of her to cherish.

Your aunt is a good and loving person and could not have expected you to fall in love with your brother. She thought you would never meet. The Treverns and the Pottses had nothing to do with each other, but perhaps if she had been honest with you—who can tell—you might have sought out your father, and then she would have lost you. That would have hurt her deeply after all the love she had given you."

"Yes, but what about me—nobody thought about me!" Harriet lifted up her tearful face and looked angrily at Rosie.

"They did think about you, Miss Harriet, although you might not think so at this moment. Your mother came back for you because she loved you, and Miss Sarah wanted to protect you because she loved you. It's all over now, and you must forget the past and look forward to the future."

Harriet dried her eyes and taking the baby from Rosie placed him at her breast. A long silence ensued, broken only by the contented sucking of the infant. Rosie felt drained of emotion. For a moment, she had thought that Harriet was going to offer her the child to bring up for her until he reached manhood, but she seemed to have forgotten all about it in her outburst of grief.

At last the baby was satisfied, and Harriet gave him back to her. She was more composed now and returned to her thoughts about her baby's future.

"Do you still feel the same, Rosie, now you know who fathered him? There might be something wrong with him, although he looks perfectly normal."

"I've watched him carefully, Miss Harriet. He looks and behaves like any other baby of his age and is quite beautiful, and even if he weren't, I should still love him—probably more than I do now—if that was possible."

"Would you like to keep him as your own, Rosie, and bring him up as your son? I know he would have a good mother, but I don't know your husband or how he would feel about it. I have spoken to Aunt Sarah and to my father and to Maudie just now, and they all feel it would be best if the baby was adopted. Aunt Sarah told me you had no children of your own and would have loved a family, and I know how much you love the baby so—"

Rosie turned away to hide her tears. She was too overcome to speak.

"That's settled then, Rosie. I can't tell you how grateful I am to you. It worried me so much—giving him away I mean—he's all I have left of Adam, but every time I look at him I see his father in him, and it will only get worse the older he gets. I'd rather you were his mother, Rosie, than anyone else, and so would Aunt Sarah."

Rosie brushed away the tears of gratitude, not knowing what to say to describe how she felt, but Harriet rushed on without giving her the chance to speak. The situation was an emotional one for both the women, and neither of them felt capable of keeping their feelings under control. Harriet wanted to get it over with as quickly as possible.

"Would you write and ask your husband to come and see us soon, Rosie. I would like to feel sure that he feels the same way that you do, and then perhaps he wouldn't mind you staying here with us until the baby is weaned enough for you to take him home with you."

And so it was arranged. Rory came to visit them and agreed to bring up the baby as his own son so the past could be wiped out and the child would never discover his true parentage. Harry Trevern, in his gratitude, wanted to help provide for his grandson in his early years, but Rory would have none of it. It was better to make a clean break to protect the interests of the child who would soon be his own. He would grow up in a home which could provide for all his needs if the sheep station continued to prosper as it had over the past few years.

When the baby was weaned, Rory came to take his family home. They had so many belongings that Harriet had arranged for them to travel in her father's closed carriage. Trunks full of baby clothes, the cradle and the ornate pram with its huge iron wheels were strapped onto the back of the carriage, for Sarah had sent everything she could think of to help Rosie, including some of the clothes she had kept in moth balls once the Potts children had outgrown them. Sarah never threw anything away if there might be a use for it one day. She would have included the rocking horse, but Rosie could not bear to take it. It had belonged to Percy and should stay in the nursery.

Harriet had gone to spend a few days with her father to be out of the way when they left. Rosie felt sorry for her, but Sarah told her she had no need to feel concerned. There would be many suitors for Harriet's hand once she was out and about in society again. She was a wealthy and beautiful widow and had every chance of making a good match. No one apart from the family need know she had given birth to a child which had been adopted. The few servants in the house would accept the explanation she chose to give them, and, in time, Harriet would have other children of her own to love, and this baby, although never forgotten, would gradually become a faded memory. When she remarried, as Sarah felt sure she would, Harriet would live elsewhere and start her life anew.

Maudie was seriously considering moving into The Great House now that they were starting a family. She had seen the house in a different light after her conversation with Rosie, and, as she hoped they would have a large family, it seemed more sensible to move into a house with a ready-made nursery wing than to look for another. Henry had always hoped they would live there one day, and he had promised Maudie that the house and its furnishings would be altered to suit her taste before they moved in. Sarah was glad to hear of Maudie's change of heart, although she was not looking forward to the house being turned upside down for weeks on end. At least the rooms would be opened up again, and there would be more servants to keep the place in order. With Maudie as the new mistress of The Great House, Sarah could live out her old age at the haberdashery, if she so wished, and somehow she thought that was just what she would do eventually. The small, comfortable rooms which had once been the home of Arthur and Alice Potts suited Sarah far better than the grandeur of The Great House.

"Thank God you came, my dear." Sarah spoke softly to Rosie as she prepared to leave. "Take care and may all go well with you. Don't write to us. It's best to part now for the child's sake. I shall keep him in my thoughts and pray that he grows into manhood to be a joy and a comfort to you both. God bless you, Rosie, for you have been a blessing to us in many ways."

Rosie embraced her affectionately before climbing into the carriage and taking the baby onto her lap. It was sad that they had come to a final parting of the ways after all they had been through together, but she could see it was the only way if the child was to be left in ignorance of his parentage. As the carriage made its long journey back to Seven Creeks, she gave a last lingering look at the old house, so full of memories for her, until the figure of Sarah waving could no longer be seen.

Rory put his arm around her and touched the baby's tiny fingers, finding it difficult to believe that he had a son to call his own after so many years.

"What shall we call him, Rosie—any ideas?"

Rosie smiled at the baby. She could hardly take her eyes off him now he actually belonged to her.

"What about John," she suggested. "My father had no sons who lived to be named after him, so I thought he might be pleased if his grandson bore his name."

"My family came from Scotland, so I would rather he was called James, as that is an old Scottish name, and he could have John as his second name, to please your pa.

James goes better with Macdonald, don't you think?"

Rosie nodded her agreement, happy with any decision.

"You've never seen anything like it, Rosie—they can't wait to be grandparents. Ma's knitting needles haven't stopped clicking since she knew. He's going to be really spoilt, I can see that."

"Oh no he's not!" said Rosie, who'd already made up her mind about that. "We're going to have a son we can be proud of."

"Just as well—it's a hard life on a sheep station, and he'll have to get used to that as he grows up. No soft options for him."

"He won't have it as hard as we did, and you know it—by the time he's a man he'll have no worries. We're more comfortable now, and he'll inherit it all one day."

Rory laughed. "You goose, Rosie, I'm only teasing. Don't get so worked up. There's a good life ahead for us all—I'd bet on it, whatever your pa has to say about the time of prosperity coming to an end. He's forever worrying about overgrazing and government borrowing. He says it can't go on forever like this, and the pendulum will swing in the other direction before much longer, and he might be right about that."

"Oh nonsense," said Rosie, her mind fully occupied with the present. "He always was a worrier—it's in his nature. He can't see into the future any more than we can. Surely we've nothing to trouble us—our worries are over."

Rory patted her hand. "Of course they are, love."

And once they reached their journey's end, and Rosie saw the newly constructed wool shed and the stockyard surrounded by new buildings, she dismissed her father's gloomy predictions as utter nonsense. All around them and far into the distance, the land belonged to them, good grazing land, watered for most of the year by the creeks that meandered through it—land which their small son would inherit in the years to come and maybe pass on to his heirs. The thought filled her with pride. She had all she could wish for, and life was good.

As she stepped down from the carriage with little Jamie cradled in her arms, a slight breeze swayed the yellow blossoms hanging from the branches of the wattle tree which grew beside the homestead, and the scent of summer filled the air.

PART FIVE

The Call To Arms

1915–1926

CHAPTER 28

Riding back home through the quiet and peaceful countryside which surrounded Euroa, Jamie Macdonald pulled in his horse and surveyed the scene before him. He wanted to memorise every small part of this place where he had grown to manhood before leaving for the carnage of a battlefield in a far distant land.

The scorching Australian sun beat down on his head, and his patient horse twitched his ears and flicked his tail to keep off the insistent flies. Horse and man had become a part of the dusty sunburnt landscape where nothing moved in the relentless heat.

The news of the enormous Australian losses at Gallipoli had shocked the nation and had left Jamie with a deep sense of guilt for not volunteering earlier. He was twenty-six and much older than many of the young men who had already left, burning with an enthusiasm to put an end to this pointless war.

Had it not been for his loyalty to his parents, he would have left long ago, for he was no coward—it was simply a matter of leaving his father to cope alone with the sheep station with whatever help he could muster in these difficult times. They had survived the depression due to Rory's good management and hard work, and now the station was the biggest for miles around. Jamie doubted it would remain so without his help, but one could not equate sheep with human suffering, and the sooner this bloody war came to an end the better for everyone. Being an only son had made his decision to volunteer all the more difficult. Rosie had cried for days afterwards, and that had broken his heart, for he cared deeply about his mother. Rory kept his feelings to himself, expecting his son to do his duty to his country, but Jamie knew how bitterly his father resented this war, which had destroyed the flower of the nation's youth.

He had been visiting Strathbogie to make his farewells to friends at the outlying homesteads and was returning to Seven Creeks by way of the Gorran Falls, the scene of many a day's good fishing. His grandfather had taught him to fish there when he was a boy, and he had many happy memories of the long, lazy days of childhood he had spent in his company. He could still bring to mind the old man as he sat smoking his pipe on the verandah in the evening, repeating the same stories of his life in England over and over again, and his amazement when his grandson told him he had heard them all before. When his grandfather had passed away in his sleep, Jamie had missed him badly. John Taylor had lived to see the Federal Commonwealth become the Commonwealth of Australia before his death and had the satisfaction of seeing his only daughter Rosie well provided for and married to the man she loved.

Jamie rode on until the homestead came into view. He would miss the sleepy old place, with the woolshed and the barns clustered around the yard, where the chooks pecked in the dust, and the ancient wattle tree rested its branches against the wall. Rory had threatened to cut it down on many an occasion as its roots were spreading under the verandah, but Rosie had forbidden it. The tree had been there before they came, and it would remain there, filling the air with the scent of its blossoms until it fell down of its own accord.

She had prepared a special meal that evening of yearling steak and roast potatoes with freshly baked bread and creamy butter. Jamie's favourite custard tart was to follow with their own grapes and cheese to finish off the meal.

"I'll not taste the like of your cooking, Ma, until I'm home from the war," said Jamie, contently leaning back in his chair.

"Please, God, that day will soon come. Not a day will pass but I shall think of you, son." Rosie clattered about, clearing the table in case he should see how downcast she felt.

"I'll write whenever I can, Ma—don't worry about that—I promise to keep in touch. I can take care of myself—you know I can. Why, I'm as strong as a bullock and as healthy as anyone for miles around." His handsome, sun-tanned face broke into a grin, and his brown eyes creased up with laughter in an effort to make her smile.

Suddenly, he bent down swiftly and swept her off her feet.

"Put me down this minute," objected Rosie in a panic as she felt herself being hoisted aloft. Jamie laughed at her discomfort and gently lowered her to the ground.

"Oh, Jamie—you're a caution." Rosie couldn't help smiling at her handsome son, who looked like a Greek god with his curly, dark brown hair and his powerful body. Had he been her own flesh and blood, she could not have been more proud of him. That secret she had kept from him. What difference would it have made if he had been told that she and Rory had adopted him when he had been a baby. Nobody could have loved him more than she and Rory, who had waited so long for a child of their own.

"That's better, Ma. No more long faces now. It doesn't suit you."

"It'll mean a lot to me to see the old country before they send me on to France. Grandpa's stories will come to life once I see the green, green grass of England for myself. I shall have a lot to tell you about in my letters."

"I just wish it didn't have to be this way, son. That's what bothers me."

"I know, Ma, I know, but I have to go, you know that."

Rory had gone to sit on the verandah to smoke a last pipe with his son, and Jamie came to join him.

"Strength has little to do with it when a bullet comes your way," remarked Rory, who had overheard the conversation.

"Pa! I was only trying to cheer her up. She's so down. I've never seen her like this before. She was that upset when Grandpa died, but it wasn't like this. I don't intend to die —I'm coming back. You bet your life on it."

Rory smiled at him. No doubt the thousands who had already died thought they were invincible too. It was the only way to think when you faced the enemy.

Jamie finished his pipe without further conversation, deep in his own thoughts. As he knocked the ash out on his boot, he mentioned that there was a farewell party in Euroa that night for all who were leaving the next day.

"I'd better show my face, Pa. They've gone to a lot of trouble to give us a good send-off, and I shall be travelling with the other lads. It's best to make an appearance and get to know them."

Rory nodded in agreement. Jamie was considerate of their feelings on this last night. Concern for them showed in his deep brown eyes. Rory admired him for his thoughtfulness. If he and Rosie had ever had a child of their own, he could not have loved him more than this splendid young man they were proud to call their son. He favoured his own parents in looks and build and was so unlike Rosie and himself it was a wonder that he had never remarked on it.

Rory waved his pipe in the direction of the town.

"You get off, son. Your ma'll understand."

Jamie touched his father on the shoulder and, unhitching his horse, set off in the direction of Euroa to enjoy himself.

Strings of flags decorated the hall where the party was being held, and the sound of a gramophone scratching out the latest tunes could be heard wafting on the air. Jamie hitched his horse to the post outside and strode in. A drink was pushed into his hand, and he found himself besieged by the local girls. He was popular, being the best looking male in the district, and knew most of them by sight. At the local hops, he had treated them all the same much to their disappointment, for Jamie Macdonald, with his good looks and money was every girl's dream. Jamie had other ideas, however. He intended to wait until he found the right girl before he settled down, however long it took. A bit of fun was fine, but that was as far as it went, and nobody had tied him down yet although some of them had tried hard enough.

"Hey, hang on ladies," he implored the girls as they gathered round him, trying to pull him onto the dance floor. "Give me time to finish me beer, and then I'll give you all a whirl."

As soon as he had downed one beer, he was whisked onto the floor by a partner and then by another until he had lost count of the drinks he had had, and the many girls he had held in his arms. Finding difficulty standing on his feet, Jamie decided enough was enough and made for the door. After the second attempt, he mounted his horse amid much laughter from the onlookers who had come to see him off.

"You going my way, Jamie?" came a voice he vaguely recognised from its lilting tone. "Give us a lift. It's a long way in the dark."

Jamie straightened up in the saddle. He felt more sober now he was off his feet.

"That you, Kathleen?" he asked, looking down on her as he tried to focus on her face.

"Sure to goodness it's me—who else? I can ride behind you if somebody will give me a leg up."

Before he could answer, Kathleen Murphy had been hoisted up in the saddle behind him and was holding him tightly around the waist with her strong, wiry arms. He had no choice but to ride her back to her home, and they set off into the darkness to the cheers of those left behind. Jamie felt angry at being tricked into giving her a lift. He avoided the girl as much as possible as she was none too clean and had a reputation for being too easy with men. The Murphy family increased by leaps and bounds despite both parents being dead, and no man living in the shack with the sisters and their many offspring.

The Murphy family were their nearest neighbours, having settled in the area during the depression when there was no work to be had for a casual labourer like Patrick Murphy. He had arrived one day at the sheep station with his downtrodden wife and four starving children, Kathleen being the youngest and still a babe in arms. Rosie had taken pity on the wretched family and had begged Rory to find them some shelter. All he could offer was a tumbledown shack which had been used in the past at lambing time. It stood near a small creek some way from their homestead and nowhere near a road. There was a long track which wound across the home pasture and the Murphys had to walk miles to reach anywhere, but it was better than nothing.

The Macdonalds had kept their distance from the family, who had a name for brawling and fighting among themselves. Kathleen's mother had died when she was a small girl from the constant beatings meted out by her drunken husband, and the children had brought themselves up with the help of people's charity. Despite her hard life, Kathleen had grown into a comely young woman with long black hair and a creamy white complexion. Her eyes were as green as the emerald isle of her forefathers, and her lips were as plump and sweet as ripe cherries. Many a man had been tempted by Kathleen Murphy's charms, but once they saw the squalor in which the Murphys lived surrounded by their many offspring, they soon took their leave. Rosie had seen the saucy looks she had given Jamie on the rare occasions when they had met and had warned him not to get involved with her. She wanted something better for her son than Kathleen Murphy, but she need not have worried as Jamie had no interest in the likes of her.

Kathleen pressed herself close to him and rested her head against his neck. Her brown work-worn hands began to wander over his body, much to his annoyance.

"Sure, an' if you weren't the most handsome man in the entire hall tonight, Jamie," she breathed seductively into his ear as they trotted along. "I'd do anything for you—that I would—you going off to be a soldier an' all."

"Shurrup, Kathleen," said Jamie, unceremoniously, "and sit still. If you wriggle about anymore we will both fall off."

Kathleen laughed, a soft trilling laugh like a stream bubbling over stones, and nibbled the lobe of his ear with her pearly white teeth.

"I mean it Jamie—'deed I do. There'll be no women for you on the battlefield. You should take me while the going's good."

Jamie refused to answer her, and they trotted on in silence. Kathleen Murphy was big trouble for a man, as he was beginning to find out for himself. Kathleen, however, was not to be put off and tried harder, moving her hands to more sensitive areas and fondling what she found there. Jamie found himself becoming aroused.

"What do you think you're doing, Kathleen," he said angrily, moving her hands away and urging his horse into a canter. "Keep your hands to yourself, will you!"

"I'm only finding out if you're a man, Jamie. No harm in that, is there?"

"I'd have thought that was obvious, without you going to all that trouble," said Jamie, dismounting hastily. "Get off. You're home now, and I want to get home to my bed."

"What!" exclaimed Kathleen, with mock indignation. "Get off this great beast by meself! You must be daft. I'd break a leg if I even tried—to be sure I would."

Jamie gave a snort of despair and pulled her roughly from the saddle. Before he knew what was happening Kathleen's arms were round his neck, and she was kissing him with wild abandon. At first, Jamie tried to push her off, but her ardour only served to inflame him and in no time at all he was pulling her towards him and searching for her breasts. Already unsteady on his feet, they fell to the ground, and it took only a short time for Jamie to ravish her. When it was over, he got to his feet, disgusted with himself. It had been nothing more than carnal desire, and he felt sick as he struggled back to his horse. Kathleen covered herself demurely and stood up.

"I've wanted you for as long as I can remember, Jamie, and I've caught you at last," she said, triumphantly, with a wicked glint in her green Irish eyes.

"Get lost, Kathleen," said Jamie, thickly, "and don't ever come near me again. If I hadn't been drinking you'd never have got within a mile of me, and that's a fact. It's true what they say about you, and they say plenty, believe me."

"Is that so, Jamie? It takes two to make love, you know."

Kathleen stood with her arms akimbo and her head thrown back as she laughed and laughed at his retreating back, as if it was the greatest joke of all time.

The sound of her laughter followed Jamie down the track as he made his way back to the homestead, and his face flushed with annoyance. She was right—he was the one to blame for taking her with him in the first place knowing her reputation, and he had already begun to regret what had happened on the spur of the moment, but there was nothing he could do about it now. Tomorrow was another day, and he would be gone to face whatever the future had in store for him.

Kathleen, on hearing the sound of her newborn crying for his feed, hurried indoors. The child's father had left her on discovering she was pregnant, and she was looking for someone to replace him, but it was too late to hope that Jamie might be that man.

The next morning meant an early start, and with the last minute preparations for his departure and the thick head he was nursing, Jamie had no time to mull over the events of the previous evening. He bade a hasty farewell to his mother and set off in one of the farm wagons driven by his father to meet up with the other volunteers for the Australian Imperial Forces.

By the time the troop had arrived at the training depot outside Melbourne, they felt as if they had known each other all their lives. They were in this thing together and would see it out to the bitter end as long as bloody Fritz didn't get them first—and that was unthinkable.

CHAPTER 29

It was a scorching hot day in August 1916 and a long way from home, when Sapper James Macdonald stepped out of the train onto the tiny platform at Brightlingsea in the county of Essex. Both he and his company of field engineers were here to prepare for their services in France. Their countrymen were already fighting on the western front, dying in their thousands at Armentiers, Pozieres, and Mouquet, and they would soon be ready to replace them.

The 13th Company of Field Engineers had recently been encamped in Wiltshire after the long and often wearing sea journey on the troopship. Jamie had been relieved to set foot on English soil at last and found it very like the countryside Rosie had described to him. The sun was gentle compared to the Australian heat, and despite its being a hot summer day, the trees and grass were still green without the brown, dried-up appearance he was used to around the homestead. The towns were compact and the villages, with their tiny cottages, so small they looked as if they were inhabited by midgets. There were no gum trees but a variety of trees he had never seen before, in tiny fields. Thinking of the enormous flocks of sheep at Seven Creeks, he wondered how the farmers in this green and pleasant land ever made a living from their stock.

They had been told they were travelling to a small fishing town on the east coast to prepare for their part in the war. This coastal terrain lent itself to bridge building and mining. The inlets and creeks formed by the tides over the centuries extended for miles, and the lonely stretches of mud flats and marshes provided an ideal training ground for the field engineers.

The soldiers gathered outside the station with their rifles and their kit and formed up into columns of four ready to march across Victoria Place and up Regent Street to the large, tented campsite on the town's recreation ground. Once there, they were to be given a meal in the mess tent and then taken to their billets in the town, the bell tents being already full with a previous detachment.

A group of interested spectators had gathered to watch them arrive. They were used to their town being overrun with members of the forces, especially naval ratings, but little was known of this new breed of men from the other side of the world. It had become a matter of great speculation as to who would be fortunate enough to have one of these magnificent young men billeted upon them. Their own men folk were away fighting, and such men as these would make short work of heavy jobs around the house. They stood tall, bronzed by the sun, powerful and muscular, with cheerful smiling faces. Their uniforms, consisting of wide breeches, leather riding boots and jaunty slouch hats turned them into a race of handsome young giants and was the cause of many a female heart in the crowd to miss a beat.

A spontaneous cheer of welcome arose from the crowd. The Aussies had come to fight beside their own men and would be well received here. A smile flickered across Jamie's face. He intended to enjoy himself in this friendly little town, come what may. Here today and gone tomorrow—what did anything matter now—a thought shared by most of the others in his regiment.

That afternoon, the company were detailed off to their arranged billets in the town. Some of them had the good fortune to find themselves living at one of the many public houses, but Jamie was not among them. He was marched beside a large green surrounded by a mixture of cottages and Victorian houses—the last man in the group to be posted. The road from the green led down Mill Street to Marsh Farm, which was to be his billet for the next few weeks, and here Jamie was introduced to Bess Bowden, a widow and the owner of the property.

Bess was pleased enough to welcome him into her now diminished family. Another pair of hands would be more than welcome. Everyone had expected the war to be over within the first few months, and she had not worried overmuch when her eldest two sons had enlisted in the Essex Regiment, but the war had dragged on, and there seemed to be no end to it. Her eldest son, Jack—her happy-go-lucky Jack with many a merry quip on his lips—had been killed almost immediately and lay in a place with a name she could not pronounce. The shock of his death had nearly killed her, and, if it had not been for her faith, she would have found it hard to keep going. He had taken his father's place managing the farm with all the confidence of youth. She still had Wilf, her crippled stepson, but he was often in pain and unable to do the heavy work. Her daughter Laura milked the cows and made the butter to sell in town, but Lucy, the youngest, was still at the Wesleyan school and could do little to help apart from collecting the eggs and feeding the hens and geese.

Bess was a staunch Wesleyan Methodist of Flemish descent, her ancestors having come to this part of England to escape religious persecution. They had settled on the saltings and built great sea walls to reclaim the land from the ever-encroaching sea. Once the salt had dried out, the land had become excellent grazing for cattle.

To Jamie, who was used to wide open spaces and a completely different lifestyle, the family appeared poor, almost poverty stricken, but that was not the case. The Bowdens lived well off the land, and, by wasting nothing and practising thrift, the farm had survived times of drought and poor harvests due to storm-beaten wheat while others had not fared so well. They had the added bonus of the sea, when sprats were plentiful, enjoying them as an addition to their diet and using them as a fertilizer on their land. As a farm, it was a small holding in Jamie's estimation, with only a few sheep and cows— – so unlike the huge flocks and herds of Seven Creeks. He found most things in England small, for that matter; the people and the houses in which they lived, with ceilings so low that he hit his head on the door lintels and stumbled over closely packed furniture in their rooms. His great frame never seemed to fit anywhere in this country.

Seeing his mother speaking to the Australian, Wilf limped across the stock yard carrying two full swill buckets. This was as good a time as any to feed the pigs and would give this soldier some idea of how useful he could be in the weeks to come.

"This is my son, Wilf," said Mrs. Bowden, introducing them. "It's hard work for him keeping the farm going on his own with so little help."

"G'day, Wilf." Wilf nodded morosely. The size of the man towering above him made Wilf feel very small. "Let me take those for you."

Jamie put down his belongings in the yard and picked up the heavy slopping pails.

"It's this way, by the sound of the squealing." He strode off with Wilf limping along behind him.

"Show Sapper Macdonald where he's to sleep, Wilf, will you after you've finished, and then bring him in for a cup of tea."

Wilf nodded, and Mrs. Bowden left to prepare their afternoon meal. The pigs fed, Wilf directed Jamie to the barn.

"Up the ladder yew'll find the hay loft. It's warm and dry this weather and yew'll be comfortable enough as long as yew put your bed roll up this end. There's a pair of barn owls at t'other end, but they won't bother yew if yew don't bother them."

Jamie thanked him and slung his kit into the barn. It smelt sweet and clean, and no doubt he would manage well enough. The nights were warm at the moment and he had been issued with two blankets should he need them. He could see the perch where the owls nested and the droppings below it and also the opening where they flew in. Not wishing to be woken by owls flying across his face he walked across to see if he could block the aperture with his kit bag at night. From his elevated position, he could see a scene of immense beauty.

The creek sparkled in the sunlight. The tide was coming in, washing over the saltings and running into the pools with little eddies. Purple sea lavender grew in tight clumps in the mud, interspersed with pink and white thrift. A rowing boat was slowly edging its way up the creek, and the distant splash of its oars and the lonely call of the curlew were the only sounds to be heard. On the opposite bank of the creek, there was a muddy shoreline also tinged with sea lavender with a few old sailing boats pulled up onto the mud. The scene was one of such tranquillity that it was difficult to imagine the horror of war, so near and yet so far away. Wilf had disappeared, and Jamie was left to savour this perfect moment which would soon be a thing of the past.

To the right of the farmhouse was an orchard where apple trees hung low with ripening fruit. Under their branches, Jamie could see a figure swathed completely in white muslin and wearing an enormous hat tied under her chin. At first, he was puzzled at the sight, and then he realised that the person was replacing the top of a beehive. Once finished, she picked up a basket containing honeycombs and began to walk to the gate, brushing off the stray bees as they followed her.

This must be another member of the Bowden family, thought Jamie as he descended the ladder to meet her. The girl arrived in the yard at the same time as he emerged from the barn.

"G'day," said Jamie, smiling. "I wondered who you were when I first saw you, and then I realised you were a beekeeper."

The girl removed her enveloping hat and long gloves and held out her hand for him to shake.

"I'm Laura," she said shyly, "the eldest daughter—and you must be?"

"Sapper Macdonald—Jamie," he said, completely at a loss for words. He had never seen such a girl before and stared at her in admiration, forgetting to take her proffered hand. She was slim and petite with light auburn hair, which had escaped from the coils around her head, but it was her eyes which fascinated him most—deep, violet eyes, the colour of the sea lavender he had just seen growing in the salt flats. Goodness and trust shone from her heart-shaped face, and, when she smiled, dimples appeared in her cheeks. Jamie was smitten at first sight.

"Come in," said Laura. "Mother thought you would stay for tea with us, unless you have to get back to camp right away."

Jamie shook his head and bent almost double to get into the kitchen through the open half door. It was overly warm inside, and all the doors and windows were open to let in the salty breeze drifting up from the creek. Lucy and Wilf were already sitting down at the table ready for tea. Mrs. Bowden expected punctuality from her family. Laura took the honeycombs out of her basket and placed them on the table beside the bread and butter and jam.

"Mmm-mm," said ten-year-old Lucy, viewing them with interest.

"And this is Lucy," said Laura, smiling. "Always hungry as you can see—a growing girl is our Lucy. And I expect you've already met Wilf." Jamie nodded in Wilf's direction, but Wilf ignored the gesture.

A very old woman was sitting in a straight, high-backed chair, close to the kitchen range. She wore a crotched shawl around her shoulders, despite the heat, and a long, well-worn black dress which reached the floor, from under which peeped out the head of a ginger tom cat. On her small shapeless nose, she wore a pair of pince-nez glasses, which were cracked across one of the eyepieces, and in her lap she held what looked at first sight like a plate of black stones, into which she was busy poking a pin.

"This is Gran," explained Laura, before Jamie took his seat at the table.

"Wassat?" asked the old lady

"This is Sapper Macdonald, Gran. He's living here with us for a while."

"Ah, hev one, soldier." She held her pin out towards Jamie, on which a small black slug was impaled. Jamie stepped back in disbelief.

"Snails!" he exclaimed in horror. "Does the old lady eat snails? I thought it was only the Froggies who ate them."

"No," laughed Lucy. "They're winkles—we dig them out of the mud at low tide and boil them. We all eat them here, and Gran loves them."

The old lady smiled at the expression on his face and popped another winkle into her mouth, munching away contentedly.

"I wouldn't fancy anything that lived in the mud meself."

"Come and sit down, soldier. The tea's ready, and we won't give you any winkles, I promise." Mrs. Bowden bustled in from the scullery, took the teapot off the range where it had been brewing, and poured out the well stewed tea. She had a cheerful round face and wore her greying hair scraped back into a tight bun. In her spotless white overall, she looked like a competent farmer's wife who would stand for no nonsense from her family. Jamie could see that getting to know Laura better might be difficult. Mrs. Bowden was head of the family now that she was a widow, and she took her position very seriously. Her farmhouse lacked any unnecessary embellishments, and the family lived in a well-ordered, well-scrubbed environment.

"Has the war made any difference to you?" asked Jamie, by way of polite conversation.

There was a silence as everyone round the table looked down at their plates. Jamie realised he had said the wrong thing and looked embarrassed.

"I was thinking in a general sense ma'am. I meant no disrespect."

Bess Bowden sighed. "I can see that soldier, but sadly I have lost my eldest son and have another one, our Sam, away fighting in France. We all pray for his safe return."

"Of course," muttered Jamie, "as my mother does for me."

"And where did your people come from originally, may I ask?"

"My pa had Scottish parents and my ma's people came from Lancashire. If I get leave before I sail for France, I want to visit her village there—a place called Downham. She left when she was eight years old and sailed in a clipper ship to Australia, but her mother died on the sea journey. They were emigrating for her health but she never got there. Ma had a stepmother once she and grandpa got settled. She was very strict, and ma was unhappy until she was old enough to leave to work as a nursemaid to some people she had met on the ship. She knew pa when he was a boy, and they had gone to school together, and she came back to marry him.

It would please ma if I went back to see her old home. She still has some memories of the place." Bess Bowden warmed towards him. He cared about his mother, and that was a good sign.

"And what is your work in Australia?"

"We own about 12,000 acres on our sheep station and run sheep mostly, plus a few hundred head of cattle. This rabbit pie is real good ma'am—it reminds me of home. We have thousands of rabbits—can't keep them off the land however hard we try—the station is too big to wire them in, and when we do they burrow under the wire. Right little varmints they are and the plague of our life."

Wilf put down his knife and fork and stared Jamie straight in the eye. It was obvious by the way he spoke that he considered him to be a liar and a braggart. "Twelve thousand acres is more than a hundred times the size of this farm!"

"I can believe it," said Jamie, "but Australia is enormous—plenty of room for everyone there. We even have deserts in the centre where people get lost and are never seen again."

"With camels?" asked Lucy.

"Too bloody right," said Jamie, warming to his audience.

There was a sudden silence punctuated by a sharp intake of breath. The Bowdens had never thought to hear such language at their table. Jamie realised he had overstepped the mark. This was England, not Australia, and, in the company of ladies, swearing was forbidden.

"My apologies, ma'am. No offence meant. It comes naturally to me, but I'll watch my tongue in the future."

Lucy's eyes grew as round as her spectacles—a forbidden word at her mother's table. Whatever next! She shuffled nervously in her seat, awaiting her mother's reaction. And when it came, it was sharp and swift.

"Get on with your tea, Lucy. We've had enough chatter for a while." Lucy sulked. She had only asked a simple question, after all.

The meal continued without further conversation until Laura decided to put him out of his misery.

"What is your mother's name?" she asked, shyly.

"Rosie—Rosie Taylor before she married."

"That's a pretty name."

"So is Laura," ventured Jamie. Laura blushed.

Wilf pushed back his chair and walked out. He had had enough of this stranger with his smiling face and his cocky talk. He would have to watch out if he intended to set his cap at Laura. Jo Carter of Lower Farm intended to marry her when he returned from the war, as everyone knew, and the sooner this Aussie got his marching orders the better for everyone.

CHAPTER 30

Church parade the next Sunday was at the Wesleyan Methodist Chapel and the field engineers were already in their places when the Bowden family arrived. Laura, her mother, Lucy, and grandma sat together in the family pew while Wilf found a place in the gallery. The chapel was crowded with people who had only come to hear the band and to join in the singing, and not because they shared the same religious beliefs. These people, who were mostly young women, followed the soldiers round every Sunday to the different churches like a fan club, filling the empty pews.

Laura was dressed in her Sunday best, a cream dress and a matching wide-brimmed hat, which only saw the light of day on the Sabbath. She had pinned a rose from the garden onto her lapel and had taken so long in getting it to her satisfaction that the family was late in arriving. Jamie thought her charming as he watched her arrival from his seat beside the organ and hoped she would look up and see him, but she was far too preoccupied with finding the number of the first hymn to do so.

The congregation rose as one, and "Fight the good fight" rang out as never before, shaking the foundations of the tiny building. Over the top of her hymn book, Laura caught his eye and looked down quickly at the words, which she knew by heart. He was so handsome it took her breath away to see him looking in her direction. She felt herself blush and hoped her mother did not notice. Mrs. Bowden had already made her feelings quite clear to her daughter that she considered it unwise to become overly friendly with a soldier from the other side of the world who was about to leave for the front. No good could come of such a friendship, she had reminded her, but Laura was twenty years old with a mind of her own, and when Jamie had asked her to go with him to see one of the camp concerts last Saturday night she had gone despite her mother's disapproval.

As the elderly lay preacher made the most of his captive audience and extemporised at length over the prayers, Laura looked up to the choir stalls where Jamie was looking in her direction and smiled briefly. The ever watchful Lucy noticed and nudged her sister. Laura glared at her, and Lucy sniggered behind her hand, disturbing her mother's prayers.

"Will you behave, Lucy," hissed Mrs. Bowden loudly. "I shan't tell you again."

Lucy subsided into meekness at her mother's command, and Laura closed her eyes and daydreamed, not listening to the words of the endless prayers. Instead, she relived the delights of the previous evening in Jamie's company.

The local orchestra had accompanied the various soloists, who had sung well-known ballads, bringing tears to the eyes of the women in the audience. "Rose of my heart" and "God send you back to me" had been too much to bear for some of them, and they had wept openly. There had been much laughter at the impersonations of the Kaiser, and at one sketch in particular, where a soldier dressed like a nurse and, carrying a lamp, had sung in a high falsetto voice: "When this cruel war started, I joined the V.A.D., and from my home departed, to cross the trackless sea. So to nurse our empire's sons, wounded by the brutal Huns."

The laughter had soon turned to catcalls and whistles as he tucked his compatriots into shift beds and kissed them a fond good night, bringing the curtain to a swift close.

"The major will have sapper Saunders on a charge tomorrow," Jamie had told her. "He went a bit far that time—with women in the audience."

"But he's only acting," Laura had said, wondering about the fuss.

"Acting! My foot!" Jamie had replied.

Sensing her discomfort, he had squeezed her hand and had continued to hold it throughout the performance. Later, as they strolled home down Mill Street, Jamie had put his arm round her waist, and she had felt the rough touch of his tunic against her cheek. He had asked her if she had a sweetheart, and she had answered that there was nobody she cared for apart from Jo Carter, and he hardly counted as she had known him all her life, and he was just a childhood friend. She knew he was sweet on her, but nothing had been arranged between them, and, anyway, he was far away and might never come back, like her brother Jack. Jamie had asked her to walk out with him that Sunday afternoon, and she had agreed, although what her mother would say about it she dreaded to think. She had been waiting for them when they had arrived home, so there had been no opportunity for him to give her a good-night peck on her cheek as they parted company.

A blast from the organ as the first few bars of "Onward Christian Soldiers" were being played brought Laura to her senses, and she stood up hastily and fumbled in her hymn book to find her place. Her mother glanced at her. It was odd to see Laura so engrossed in her prayers. Usually, she complained about the length of time old Mr. Lewis took over them, but maybe Jack's death had made her more devout.

After the service was over, Mrs. Bowden hurried home to prepare their cold dinner while Laura and Lucy stayed behind to watch the band march back to camp with the soldiers following behind. Jamie looked straight ahead, his face expressionless, although he was aware of her standing there smiling at him. The band struck up a march and the platoon set off across the fields to the recreation ground, playing against the band of the Salvation Army, which was marching home from their Sunday outdoor meeting in the opposite direction along the High Street.

Lucy prodded her sister. "Did you go to sleep in the prayers?" she asked mischievously.

"Certainly not! I was thinking."

"Thinking about what?"

"Never you mind."

"I think I know," said Lucy wickedly, darting out of the way of her sister's threatening hand.

That afternoon, when Jamie called at the farmhouse for Laura, he met with a chilly reception. He had had no time to help on the farm apart from turning over the vegetable garden and weeding the flower beds on a Saturday afternoon. In the evenings, he was too exhausted from his days training to do anything apart from relaxing at one of the public houses in the town with his mates. There he could enjoy a smoke or play darts with some of the locals. His friendship with Laura had placed him in a difficult position with the family, who did not approve, in case it led to other things. Laura was an innocent girl who knew so little of the world beyond Marsh Farm and her immediate environment, and Jamie was a soldier from the other side of the world about whom they knew nothing. Bess wondered if he would treat her with respect and worried all the more when she saw how attracted Laura was to this handsome, friendly young man.

Jamie was aware of their feelings towards him and appreciated their concern but Laura was becoming more precious to him as the days passed, and he did his best to help wherever he could in the hopes that he would eventually endear himself to the family and to Laura's mother in particular, a task he was finding well nigh impossible.

"G'day, one and all," he said, smiling broadly as he entered the silent kitchen where the family was assembled. Gran was asleep in her chair with the cat on her lap. Bess looked up from her Bible and nodded in his direction, and Wilf continued to roll a cigarette without acknowledging his presence. Lucy and Laura looked up from their knitting and smiled a greeting. Knitting was tolerated on a Sunday by their mother as long as the finished results could be sent by the overseas club to the soldiers at the front.

Lucy was trying to turn the heel of a greyish khaki sock and was getting into a muddle with the needles. Her mother took it from her and, correcting her mistakes, handed it back to her.

"He'll have to be a one-legged soldier," said Lucy wearily. "I'll never be able to knit another one."

"Well, there must be plenty of those," said her mother, sighing, "but we can't send one sock in the parcel. Laura will have to knit the other one if you can't manage it."

Laura smiled. "I expect I can find time somehow," she said.

Jamie sat down at the table, uninvited. "Next Saturday, I'm free if there's a job you'd like me to do," he said, addressing himself to Wilf.

Wilf looked interested. "We're harvesting next Saturday," he said, curtly, "if the weather holds good, that is. We're cutting the wheat in Barn Meadow. Know anything about harvesting?"

"No, but I'm willing to try. We don't grow any crops."

Wilf went back to rolling his cigarette, a smile on his lips as he licked the paper. *Some farmer he was for all his talk.* "We'll start after milking. Get it done in a day if we're lucky."

"I'll be there—you can count on me." Jamie looked in Laura's direction and noticed she had folded up her knitting. "Ready?" he asked.

Laura stood up. "We're just going for a stroll," she told her mother. "I'll bring Sapper Macdonald back for tea, if that's all right."

Her mother could hardly refuse and nodded her assent to this arrangement. "Don't be long," she said, looking meaningfully in Laura's direction.

"No mother, we won't be long. I thought we'd go down Cook's Lane and onto the marshes. There's a nice walk along the sea wall."

"As you wish," said her mother, returning to her Bible.

Jamie was glad to make his escape, and they walked side by side in a respectable manner until the farmhouse was out of view, but once they reached the leafy green seclusion of Cook's Lane, Jamie put his arm around her waist, and they wandered along relaxed and happy in each other's company.

Dog roses blossomed in the hedgerows, and pink campion and stitchwort grew along the mossy banks. It was a place where lovers went out walking. Dandelions set loose their seed pods and floated away. Laura caught one as it sailed past her.

"It's a wish, Jamie. What will you wish?"

"That the war will end tomorrow, and I won't have to leave you."

"I'll wish that too," said Laura, blowing the seed away, "but I'm afraid it won't come true."

"Well, we've got each other for a few more days," said Jamie, drawing her close to him and kissing her tenderly. She was so sweet and gentle he felt protective towards her. There was such a short time left in which to get to know her before the war came between them.

"Will you write to me Laura when I've gone away?"

"Of course I will."

"Every week?"

"Yes, if you'd like me to."

Jamie kissed her again and lingered longer this time feeling her lips part in response to his growing passion.

"Your letters will be the one thing that'll keep me sane over there."

"Then I'll write every week. I promise."

With arms entwined, they wandered on until the sea wall came into view, and they were obliged to walk in single file. Pale blue butterflies flew up out of the coarse grass at their feet and larks soared overhead, singing as they flew higher and higher until they could be seen no longer and only their faint song lingered on. Jamie grew tired of walking behind her. He wanted to feel her close beside him.

"Let's sit down for a while, Laura. I can't talk to you like this."

Laura left the path and found a spot in the sunshine where they could lean back against the long grass beside the sea wall. Jamie came to join her and stripped off his tunic and shirt. He liked to feel the wind and the sun on his skin. It made him feel alive, as if he was back home again. Laura looked at his bronzed body and his powerful muscles and felt a thrill run through her. He was like an Adonis lying there with his arms beneath his head, drinking in the sunshine. She wondered what it was about her that he found attractive, having never been encouraged to look anything but sensibly and neatly dressed, as her mother considered vanity a sin. His kisses had both surprised and pleased her and had made her heart beat faster. She had always felt at ease with this giant of a man, but perhaps now she was falling in love with him. He had certainly awoken something in her which until now had lain dormant.

Jamie released one hand and pulled her down into the grass beside him. "You look so stiff and starchy sitting there with your arms round your knees, Laura. Lie down and relax—its real good here."

Laura did as he asked and lay with his arm around her. She could smell the sweat on his skin and hear the regular beat of his heart, pounding like a hammer. There seemed no need to talk now, and she lay in his arms and closed her eyes. The only sound was the low buzzing of the bees in the field of clover on the other side of the wall, which made her feel drowsy with contentment. After a while, Jamie stirred and raised himself up on one elbow to look into her face. Laura opened her eyes; the colour of which never ceased to amaze him—a deep violet iris with a purple centre to it. He had never seen eyes like that before.

"Who do you take after?" he asked. "No one in your family has your looks—at least not the ones I've met."

"Gran perhaps—she had the same colour eyes as mine when she was a girl, so she says, but you wouldn't think so now—they've faded.

My father had her auburn hair but not her eyes. I seem to be the only one to inherit the colour of her eyes."

"So, the old lady was your father's ma, was she?"

"Yes—she's outlived him and had no other family. They were Suffolk farmers, and Wilf lived with her when he was a boy. He's only our half brother."

"That accounts for it then," said Jamie, thinking of Wilf and his sullen ways.

He stroked her soft cheek with his finger. "Do something for me, Laura—undo your hair. I want to see you without those tight coils around your head."

Laura smiled. It was a strange request but she wanted to please him and took out the pins and unbraided her plaits as he had asked of her. Jamie rolled over onto his back to watch. Her soft, silky hair fell across her shoulders like an auburn mane with the sunshine picking out the lighter streaks of gold, giving her face a childish vulnerable appearance. Jamie was entranced.

"You're beautiful—so beautiful," he murmured, stroking the soft strands as they fell around her. He pulled her down so she lay in the crook of his arm, and her hair touched his lips. He wanted to make love to her there and then but he knew it was too soon for her—she still had to feel the same urgent desire that was pounding through his body at that moment, and not until then would he touch her or hurt her—she was too precious for that. When this bloody war was over, he would find her again and then maybe she would come back with him to Seven Creeks. He would never find another woman he could love like Laura, but now was the time for dreams—just dreams.

"We'd better be getting back," he said gruffly. "You promised your mother we wouldn't be long, and I don't want to get on the wrong side of her."

Laura sighed and pinned her hair back in place. She wanted to stay longer in his company and was tired of her mother's interference, but she could see the sense in going back. Tea would be kept until they arrived home and the later they returned the more difficult it would become to see each other again.

"Come on, then," she said. "I'm ready if you are."

They walked back as they had come with their arms around each other, but this time Laura leant her head on his shoulder, and they walked like other lovers had done before them who had walked in that leafy place, stopping to kiss one another as they went along, until the farmhouse came into view.

CHAPTER 31

"Coo-up—Coo-up." Jamie woke to the sound of Wilf driving the cows from the lower pasture to the milking shed. Time he was dressed and had done his ablutions in the outside scullery so he could snatch a few moments alone with Laura as she milked the five cows. He loved watching her as she sat on her three-legged stool, leaning her head on a cow's flank and squeezing the milk from the fat teats with her deft fingers. As the milk squirted into the bucket in a steady stream, Jamie would wait patiently until she stood up to move the bucket and then gather her into his arms for a few stolen kisses before disappearing up the road to the camp.

After breakfast in the mess tent, the platoon would set off on the long march up Church Hill to the Mariner's Church and then on round the back road to Moveron's Farm, where the mock minefield was situated. If they were working on the trestle bridge across the ford at Arlesford Creek, it was even further to go carrying the picks and shovels they needed for digging tunnels and sinking mineshafts. To keep their spirits up the men sang as they marched—"Oh when I die, don't bury me at all—just pickle my bones in alcohol. Put a bottle of booze at my head and my feet—and then I know my bones will keep."

Day after day, they dug and reinforced mock trenches with timber supports, filling sandbags with earth and pulling them to the surface. It was heavy wearing work in the heat of the summer, and the men were bothered by wasps to make matters worse, but they would find it even harder once they got to France and repeated the exercise in the slime and the mud of a distant battlefield with the war raging around them.

It was a change to be sent in the opposite direction to the Hard where the sea breezes cooled their sweating bodies as they lifted the heavy pontoons off the wagons to build their bridges across the creek to Cindery Island and the Stone on the opposite shore. Jamie was strong but even he felt exhausted by the end of the day and was glad of a swim to cool off. He would have liked to have taken Laura to a dance, as there were plenty of those in the evenings but her mother frowned on such activities in case there was alcohol available. She had heard that all Australians drank like fish, and her family had been encouraged to sign the pledge.

Jamie despaired of ever getting Laura to himself until he hit upon the idea of cycling. Mrs. Bowden approved of cycling as long as they got home before dark. She felt that her daughter was safer on a bicycle than off one and questioned her on her return as to the route they had taken. Had she known how often they dismounted along the quiet country lanes to kiss one another she would never have allowed Laura to go.

When the wheat was cut in Barn Meadow, Jamie persuaded some of his mates to come and give a hand.

"You won't get paid—you can bet on that—but the old girl will feed you, and there'll be a chance of some sport when it's over, catching the rabbits in the cornfield." More than anything, Jamie wanted to improve his relations with the Bowden family so they would eventually accept him for Laura's sake, and a bit of extra help with the harvest might do just that.

The soldiers turned up as promised and stood in a huddle at the top of the field, watching as two old farm workers who came to give a hand from time to time scythed a path for the reaper round the edges of the field, cutting swathes through the corn with a steady rhythm. Once they reached the bottom of the field, the reaper followed with the women who had come to bind the sheaves walking behind, collecting the wheat as it was shuttled out.

Laura came across to show them how the binding was done and stayed with them until the first shock of wheat was set up. Binding was women's work, but setting up the shocks needed a man's strength. She thanked them for helping and smiled towards Jamie as she spoke. Her mother and sister would be bringing them all refreshment later, she told them before joining the other women further down the field.

"Good looking Sheila there, Mac. Sweet on you, is she mate?"

Jamie grinned and went back to his work. In her wide straw hat tied with a scarf behind her neck to keep off the sun, Laura was every soldier's dream.

The men, stripped to the waist, working alongside the women, found that the binding lacerated their hands and arms. Jamie walked back to collect their shirts and on his return took Laura's sheaf to bind it for her. It was cruel work for a woman, in his opinion.

"There must be a better way to do it than this," he remarked, as the wheat stalks scratched across his chest.

"Oh, yes— Lower Farm has a binder—it reaps and binds—takes half the time."

"Then why for Gawd's sake doesn't your ma get one and save you all this trouble?" asked Jamie, surprised.

"Mother likes the old ways. She says that what was good enough for her father is good enough for her, and, anyway, binders cost money."

"Gawd help us," said Jamie in disgust. "It's about time she came to terms with this modern age. People don't lock up their daughters these days either."

"She gets worried, that's all."

"Well, she needn't be. I love you too much for that."

Laura stopped working and straightened her back. It was the first time that he had told her that he loved her in so many words. She looked at him with her eyes alight with love, for she loved him too.

"Do you mean that, Jamie? Really love me?"

"Oh, I tell all the girls that," said Jamie with a saucy grin.

Bess Bowden and Lucy brought the elevenses down the field as promised, cold tea and hunks of fresh bread and cheese. When they had taken their leave, all hell broke loose.

"Bloody hell! Tea! What sort of country *is* this, for Gawd's sake?"

Wilf disappeared into the thicket behind them and brought out some bottles of beer he had been keeping cool in the spring and handed them round to the men. A sigh of relief was heard rising from many a parched throat as the bottles were unscrewed and tipped up.

"Good on ya, Wilf. You're a mate—fair dinkum!"

"Like a drop meself," said Wilf, drinking deeply to Jamie's astonishment.

At the end of the reaping, the men stood round the ever-decreasing patch of corn left standing, waiting for the rabbits to bolt for cover. Rabbits were considered vermin in Australia, and the sappers soon finished off the majority of them and were given four apiece to take back to the camp for the pot.

Bess and Lucy had set out a meal for the workers on a long trestle table in the barn—cold rabbit pie with potatoes and vegetables from the garden, followed by thick slabs of bread and butter pudding laced with cream. When his mother had returned to the kitchen, Wilf produced some bottles of cider he had put by behind some bales of straw. It made a fitting end to the day's harvesting, and the sappers returned to their billets, weary and content.

"Good tucker, Wilf. We've had a barney, mate," said one of the Aussies, and, for once, Jamie saw Wilf smile.

After they had gone, Jamie wandered back to the field they had just harvested and leant on the gate. The shocks stood in straight rows like well-drilled soldiers on parade, their heavy heads golden in the setting sun, and all around them among the stubble lay the poppies cut down by the reaper, their red petals already withered and dead.

Tomorrow, he would begin his few days leave before going to the front, and Mrs. Bowden had given him permission to take Jack's bicycle with him on the train. He intended to take the train north from London to Blackburn and then to cycle to Downham to find the group of stone cottages around the green where his mother had been born. He had promised Rosie he would go there if he could as he knew how much the place meant to her, but he had never thought it would be possible. Laura ached for him to stay with her, but he knew the temptation to make love to her would be too much for him, and he did not want their relationship to become any deeper, for her sake. He could easily make her pregnant as so many soldiers had done already who had left and never returned, only to leave her the humiliation of bringing up a bastard child in a puritanical household where she was unlikely to be forgiven for her loose behaviour. There would never be another woman for him like Laura, but he could make her no promises to return and could only hope she would still be there for him at the end of the war.

He felt a need to be alone with his own thoughts and to find peace before his part in the battle commenced.

His grandfather had told him when he was a boy how the old Roman road had passed by their village, making a route for the Roman legions as they had marched between the forts at York and Ribchester. One of them had died beside the road and had been buried there —a soldier from another country like himself. Jamie decided to cycle that way until he came to the village of Downham. He felt he knew so much about it already—the stone bridge across the stream and the manor house where his grandfather had worked as an estate carpenter before leaving for Australia with his wife and child.

He wrote a long letter to his mother about his visit and described everything he had seen, including the sight of Pendle Hill, recalling his grandfather's stories of the witches who had lived there once—stories which had frightened him as a small boy and which his mother would remember.

"I have returned to my roots, Ma, and it's a strange feeling," he wrote, ignorant of the upset that would cause Rosie. When she received his letter two months later, Rosie considered telling him the truth of his birth, but Rory dissuaded her. His real mother's happiness could be destroyed if he tried to contact her, and Jamie himself might feel he was different from other men if he knew he was the result of an incestuous relationship. They had made a promise to his birth mother never to tell him, and that promise must be kept. He was their son and always would be for as long as he was spared.

On his return from Downham, Jamie stopped off in Colchester and chose a pendant for Laura so she had something to remember him by.

They had one last evening together before he left and spent it wandering through the woods and fields which surrounded the farm. Jamie told her then how much he loved her and that if he returned from the war he would ask her to marry him. Laura wept and could not be comforted. She had just begun to feel the pain and anguish of the thousands of women like her—the girls who were left behind.

The next morning the 13th Field Regiment were marched off to the station with a following of small children, attracted by the sound of the band.

Laura was scrubbing out the dairy when she heard the sound of music in the distance and felt as if her heart would break in two.

CHAPTER 32

By the time Sapper James Macdonald had reached the western front, the weather had broken, turning the chalky soil of the Somme battlefield into a muddy swamp pitted with bullet holes. The Germans, who still held the central fortress on the Thiepal Ridge, were attacking with machine gun fire night and morning, decimating the troops in huge numbers. Jamie felt as if he had been flung into the pit of hell itself.

He had joined the depleted Australian army after their heroic attack on the little village of Pozieres, where they had suffered such a terrible loss of life before achieving their goal, and had been appalled at the tales the survivors had to tell. They had not been prepared for this during their training, and, had they known what it would be like in this dreadful place, many of them would not have volunteered, but they were here now and would fight to the death to avenge the loss of their countrymen.

The battle of the Somme dragged on, and, by the end of September, the Germans had been driven off the ridge. The weather grew worse, with sharp frosts and tremendous thunderstorms, soaking the soldiers to the skin in the trenches.

Jamie attempted to write short notes to Rosie and Laura during his rest periods, which were few and far between. What could he tell them apart from letting them know he was still alive and to thank Laura for the parcels she so lovingly made up for him—the welcome tins of sweets and tobacco and the socks and balaclavas knitted by herself and Lucy, who had found a purpose at last for the knitting she so despised.

Laura's letters containing the everyday happenings at the farm were so remote from the horrors he experienced every day—the huge rats in the trenches and the lice in his clothes and everywhere the dead and the dying—that they seemed unreal. It became more and more difficult as the days passed to envisage another world away from the bitter cold and the freezing mud, however hard he tried to recapture the feel of her soft skin and her loving kisses.

By November, the snow came with icy rain, making it almost impossible to load a gun. Jamie's company was back in the line holding the road to Gueudecourt. Thiepal Ridge had fallen at last but the road was overlooked by the strongpoint of the Butte de Walencourt, which was still held by the Germans, making life difficult for the Australians. It was a relief to both sides when the last attack took place and the troops were withdrawn, filthy and encrusted with mud. There had been no breakthrough and only short advances, which could be measured in yards. It had been a fruitless and wasteful struggle.

Jamie marched to the railhead with the other survivors, only to be taken to another field of battle, leaving behind him a scene of complete devastation. Where once there had been woods growing in a peaceful countryside, now there were no trees to show where those woods had once stood, and instead there lay a mass of unburied dead. He was thankful to have survived the slaughter, but he had lost heart, as had most of his comrades in arms. Nothing had been achieved, and his brave fearless mates had given their lives to no avail. Soon there would be none of them left, if this bloody war of attrition went on for much longer.

In due course, Jamie was given a week's leave with the others from his company. They had been placed in billets behind the lines at Ypres, which had already suffered two great battles. Spirits had revived somewhat in the billets. Cellars had been pillaged of their wines, and estaminets provided a rough hospitality. There was entertainment of a kind, sometimes a camp concert or a film and girls at a price, although the price usually included the physical discomforts afterwards of such encounters. Although battle scarred and weary, Jamie's good looks had still attracted plenty of attention, but he was immune to these girls' dubious charms. He was determined to hold Laura in his arms one day when this was all over, and no other woman would spoil him for her.

The men were taken by leave boat and train to London to spend a week away from the battlefield. Their uniforms were unkempt and filthy, but they were intent on having a good time and found a welcome fit for heroes in London. There were good lodgings in the leave hostels and hot meals, and best of all, baths to wash off the grime and laundry services to clean their uniforms.

Once in London, Jamie wanted to enjoy himself. Seeing Laura for a few hours would only make their parting harder to bear, and he was doubtful of the Bowden's welcome should he make an unexpected appearance. In the hostel, he had experienced the softness of a real bed, and he did not fancy the hardness of the floor in the Bowden's hayloft, where no doubt he would be expected to spend the night. Instead, he sent Laura picture postcards of the city sights with a brief written message on the back, hoping she would understand his reluctance to give up so much of his precious leave travelling to see her.

Inside the smoke-filled interior of Paddy's Bar, where the brassy barmaids scooped up the silver tips from the Aussies, or in the canteens, where more genteel helpers dished out sandwiches and tea from large urns with an air of quiet companionship, Jamie found a brief respite from the war. There were music halls and theatres to enjoy in the West End—Chu Chin Chow at His Majesty's and George Robey at the Alhambra, with a stroll afterwards with his mates through Soho to look at what was on offer, and have a good laugh. There was plenty of booze and plenty of fun before the week came to an end and the long trek back to the war began.

In his last long letter to Laura written at the end of his leave, Jamie told her that, once this war was over, they would have the rest of their lives to be together, and he was only living for that moment.

Thankful that he was still alive and that he still loved her, Laura placed his letter with the others and prayed fervently for the war to end and for Jamie to return.

In June of 1917, he found himself fighting with his countrymen for the Messines Ridge. The engineers had tunnelled so successfully under the German advanced positions that the explosion, when it came in all its ferocity could be heard across the Channel, and the ridge was captured in a single attack. This victory gave all the troops heart, British and Allies alike, which was short lived when they found themselves back in the fighting in Ypres. Jamie began to wonder why he had ever imagined war to be a glorious thing—there was no glory in killing some other mother's son to avoid being killed oneself. He grew as hard and as tough as his companions in order to survive, taking the initiative into his own hands whenever the opportunity arose, and risking death with the others in fearless acts of bravery as they tunnelled their way under the opposing trenches to lay explosives.

By September, the relentless rain had turned the whole area into a quagmire, where men, horses, and equipment wallowed in the mud. Jamie found himself in the thick of things, fighting in the assault on the Menin Road Ridge and beating off the counter attacks once his division had taken Polygon Wood. The advance was pitifully small, and all around him lay his dead companions. His only thought was to see an end to it, even if that meant his own death. The noise of the German barrage as the shells rained down was more than he could endure some days, and he longed for some peace. Sleep became the sleep of exhaustion, and Laura became a vague memory. He never expected to see her again. Her letters remained crumpled in his inside pocket where the rain had soaked through, making the ink run until the words had become illegible.

To the left of Polygon Wood lay the Westhoek Ridge and beyond that the ruins of the village of Zonnebeke. Early in October, a large-scale attack had been planned to take Broodseinde Ridge and Jamie's company was waiting in the rain with the leading troops of the Australian division, to mark out tracks and assist in the construction of advanced strong points. Jamie knew they would be under heavy fire while this operation was carried out, and they were all expecting the worst to happen, as this was to be a particularly heavy offensive.

The clouds had blotted out the moon, and they were waiting for the German barrage to begin before their own advance. Once the guns went into action, those who were left struggled into the swamp of Zonnebeke Lake towards the Broodseinde Ridge where the Germans were encamped. There was a mist that morning and heavy smoke from both sides, which helped to camouflage their approach. Suddenly, the whistling whoosh of a shell was heard close by, and the captain of Jamie's company fell dead beside him as they struggled to set up an emplacement. He had taken the full blast of the explosion and had protected Jamie from instant death.

Jamie felt a burning sensation in his left arm and a searing pain in his head. Blood began to trickle down his forehead and fill his left eye. He felt too weak and faint to stand and fell beside the body of his dead captain, passing out with shock and loss of blood.

Some hours later, he was aware of voices and a pressure over his eye and could vaguely make out the shapes of faces peering down at him.

"You're all right now, digger," said a voice. "The shrapnel just grazed your face and by a miracle it missed your eye. We've stitched you up, but your arm will need further surgery—some nasty pieces are still lodged in there. We'll soon get you back to Blighty to have that seen to—right now I'm giving you an injection to help with the pain."

The disembodied voice faded away as Jamie drifted into sleep.

A few weeks later, he was sent to a military hospital outside London with some of the other walking wounded. His face had been stitched up, and his arm was in a sling. He had left behind the mud and the misery of Passchendale, but the noise of the guns was still ringing in his ears, blotting out everything else.

Laura had wondered what had happened to him. There had been no letters for over two months, and she feared for the worst. She had no way of finding out if he was alive or dead. His parents in Australia would have been told if he had been killed, but she had no idea of their address, and even if she had known she would have shied away from asking them. She grew pale and thin with worry and burst into tears for the slightest reason.

Her mother grew concerned for her and decided to take matters into her own hands and called upon the colonel at the camp. He promised to make enquiries but held out little hope of getting information. There were so many unknown soldiers whose identities got lost during the mutilations of war, and he often wondered himself how many of the fine young men who had passed through his camp were still alive out there. It was a relief when he heard that Sapper Macdonald was back in England recovering from his wounds in a hospital in Southend.

Laura was overjoyed by the news but found it strange that he had not been in touch with her until her mother explained that wounds were not always of the flesh and Jamie could be suffering in other ways. That might be the case, mused Laura, but she still wanted to go and visit him and made arrangements to do so.

Laura's mother had heard of shell shock and depression among the troops and decided to accompany her on the day of the visit. They had no idea how they would find Jamie as there had been no reply to Laura's letters, so it was no surprise when they found him sitting listlessly on a seat in the porch, wearing his hospital blues. He smiled when he saw Laura but seemed remote, as if his mind was elsewhere. Laura was shocked by the sadness in his eyes and the scars on his face.

She took his hand in hers and stroked it as she spoke to him.

"Jamie, dear—it's me—Laura. Mother and I have come to see you—you must get better now, my love."

Jamie's grip tightened on hers, but he made no sound. Laura's eyes filled with tears. Perhaps he had lost the ability to speak. "Oh, Mother—what can we do?"

Bess put an arm round her daughter, feeling deeply moved herself by the suffering she saw before her.

"I'll see if I can find out about his condition. You stay here, Laura—I'll ask if we can bring him back to Marsh Farm when he is well enough and nurse him back to health there. Good food and peace and quiet might be the answer to his mental state."

Laura smiled for the first time in weeks, and a brief smile flitted across Jamie's lips.

Bess hurried off, wondering if she had gone soft in the head to make such a suggestion and insisted on speaking to the matron. This fearsome female made a vague promise to speak to the doctor on the subject when they both had a moment to discuss the matter, but it would be some weeks before Jamie's arm was sufficiently healed to leave the hospital. It was rare to find someone who was willing to nurse a patient who was not a member of the family and was suffering from shell shock, but it would leave a bed free for yet another casualty of the war and for that she must be grateful.

Laura continued to visit him weekly and watched him grow stronger in mind and body until the day came when he was released, to be cared for by the Bowdens. No longer did Jamie sleep in the barn, but he had been given Jack's old room under the eaves, and he was made to feel as if he was a privileged guest. Laura's tender-loving care brought him peace of mind and the horrors of war gradually began to recede.

Sam Bowden came home on leave for Christmas and made great friends with Jamie. He put his mother's mind at rest about his sister's relationship with an Aussie. In his opinion, they were legendary fighters, often wild and undisciplined on the battlefield, but in the face of danger they were known to be the bravest of the brave. The family had listened to Sam with a growing interest, and Jamie went up in leaps and bounds in their estimation. Suddenly, they were all proud to know him, including the morose Wilf, and Jamie found himself treated like one of the family.

No longer were walks with Laura frowned upon, and they were free to wander where they wished along the mossy lanes where the early primroses were unfolding their petals and the trees were beginning to show small buds of green. Their love for one another blossomed with the spring, and Jamie could imagine no other woman in his life but Laura.

As he grew stronger and the physical and mental scars began to heal, Laura persuaded him to send a cable home to his parents, who must have been told by now that he had been wounded and would be worried by the lack of news. Letters took so long to reach their destination in the war, and a cable would take less time to arrive. Jamie reassured his parents of his improved health and received a cable from Rosie by return.

"Thank God you are safe. Please write. Ma."

Feeling guilty of leaving them so long without a letter now that his thoughts were beginning to make sense, Jamie wrote a long letter, telling them about Marsh Farm and the kindness he had found there, with a special mention of Laura—the most wonderful girl he had ever met, and the only girl in the world for him.

CHAPTER 33

Things were almost the same in the little fishing town of Brightlingsea on Jamie's return in the early days of 1918. There were still Australian recruits training at the camp on the recreation ground, marching daily through the town to the Hard and up Church Hill to build bridges across the river. They still filled the public houses with the sound of their noise and their laughter, but for Jamie, things had changed. His mates were no longer there, and these men looked different from the powerful physical specimens he remembered from his training days. The jackaroos and drovers and the shearers from the outback had long since gone and had been replaced by clerks and shop assistants from the towns and cities—men who were smaller in stature and had come without any enthusiasm for the great adventure—men who had been sent to fight in the endless war. The colonel was still there in charge of things and some of the officers, but that was all. They treated him like a hero, but Jamie did not feel like a hero—he had survived when others much braver than him had died.

Since a zeppelin on a bombing mission to London had crashed near Little Wigborough and the crew had emptied their guns before throwing them away, the war had come too close for comfort. The townspeople had been stirred into action and War Savings Weeks, Feed the Guns Weeks, and Aeroplane Weeks were organised to raise money for the war effort. Laura helped as much as possible, and, when Jamie accompanied her, people gave as much as they could, sympathising with his injuries.

"I feel like a monkey on a stick," complained Jamie. "You're just using me to wring the last penny out of them."

"I know," agreed Laura, "but it's all in a good cause and you of all people must realise that."

"I only come to look at you doing your Florence Nightingale act—not for any other reason, but the next time you insist on me accompanying you I shall kiss every woman—young or old, pretty or ugly—who puts money in your tin, and the more they donate the more I shall kiss them."

Laura was horrified knowing he would probably do what he had threatened just to tease her and decided she would make her collections alone in future.

Apart from his weekly visits to the camp doctor, Jamie did all he could to help Wilf on the farm. He ate well at the Bowden's table despite the rationing of meat, sugar, and butter. A side of bacon hung in the outhouse, and there were chickens for a meal when needed, although their eggs were so precious their lives would be spared if a rabbit or two could be found for the pot. Jamie paid for his keep, which helped, but he needed to work as well to repay them for all they had done for him.

He groomed and fed the two Suffolk Punches, Bonny and Diamond, and helped Wilf to harness them to the plough. He would have liked to have tried his hand at ploughing himself as he watched Wilf stumbling along the furrows, the dust flying from the horses' fetlocks and the brasses jingling as he pulled them to a stop with a shout of "Hold ya!" Seagulls wheeled and screamed behind the plough, swooping down to the newly turned earth and rising up again in a continuous spiral of movement, while Jamie could only stand and watch and wonder where they had all come from.

He did what he could to clear away the branches when Wilf got on with the hedging and ditching and turned the butter churn for Laura to make the butter come, but he felt frustrated and useless.

At the end of the day, he would walk round the fields with Wilf to look at the progress of the spring wheat and discuss where the root crops were to be planted that year. They would share a drink together from time to time in the barn, well away from the family's prying eyes.

Wilf understood pain, and he felt sympathy for a fellow sufferer. Jamie found in him a silent, undemanding companionship, which suited his present mood. He still had his strong right arm and his left arm was improving slowly. He exercised it daily to alleviate the stiffness, hoping that, before too long, he could hold a gun and get on with the business of winning the war. He wanted to be there at the finish to see the Germans defeated.

When the mist came rolling up from the creek, it was time to go indoors. Then, with the oil lamp hissing on the table, bathing the kitchen walls with a soft yellow light, and the fire in the old black range glowing with warmth, Jamie was content to sit and smoke his pipe as he watched Laura sewing and mending and patching, with her head bent close to the lamplight, for nothing was ever wasted in that house.

When his pipe was finished and Laura's eyes had grown tired he would tell them stories of his homeland and of his own homestead and the great shearing shed which his father had built, using his winnings from the Melbourne Cup when he had bet on Carbine, the most famous horse of that time, in the year that he had been born. He described his home to them, which was so different from their own, and told them of his mother and how she would sit on the verandah in her rocking chair on hot evenings, in the shade of the wattle tree.

Lucy laughed. "What's a wattle tree?" she asked.

"Ours is very old and has twisted grey branches that reach the ground. Sometimes, it's covered by thousands of tiny puff balls and you can hardly see the wattle birds when they sit amongst the leaves."

"It sounds lovely. I wish I could see it one day, but I know I never will," sighed Lucy, as she went back to her knitting.

"Sometimes I wonder if *I* will," said Jamie, bitterly. "I think I'm here forever."

"I wish you were," said Lucy, beaming, "and I know that Laura wants you to stay."

"Oh, Lucy!" Laura blushed with embarrassment, although it was true. If only he would marry her and stay at Marsh Farm after the war and run it with Wilf and Sam, but somehow she doubted it very much. He had told her many times how his parents depended upon him at Seven Creeks and how much he loved the place. Would he take her there one day to see the wattle tree for herself? He had spoken of marriage after the war before he had gone to France, and she knew he loved her, but he had not spoken of it since. If only this terrible war would finish and life could get back to normal again, how happy she would be.

The camp doctor pronounced Jamie fit for light duties by the end of April, and he returned to work—this time as a corporal in charge of training groups of new recruits. He still marched with them along the road to the Ford but no longer did he shoulder a pick and shovel. His experience on the field of battle was passed on to others instead. Arlesford Creek looked different at this time of the year—the blackthorn was a mass of white blossom, and the blackberry bushes along the path were dotted with pale purple flowers, giving the promise of a good crop of fruit later in the year.

Jamie could remember the heat when he had laboured in the same place before, digging out trenches and tunnels. Now it was cold with an east wind blowing from the sea and cutting across the fields. It was a relief to leave the minefield and march back at the end of the long day along more sheltered pathways, where bluebells grew in great drifts under the trees and the sound of the cuckoo could be heard.

He was always glad to get to the top of Mill Street and see the farm come into view. Two huge holly trees stood like sentinels in the front garden, much too close to the house to allow any light to penetrate through the windows. The white plaster covering the walls was cracked in places, showing the herring bone brickwork underneath. Every time he saw it he felt it could be made into an attractive place if only Mrs. Bowden would spend a little money on it, but he knew her better than that. Opposite the farm, there was a dark weedy pond, the home of frogs and moorhens and visiting wild ducks surrounded by spindly bushes and thick undergrowth. He would have liked to have cleaned it out and opened it up so the sunshine could penetrate its murky depths and the cows could find cleaner water when they came down to drink, but now he no longer had the time to spare for such jobs.

Laura had grown up in this closed-in space and had no idea of the emptiness of the bush or the wide open spaces around the sheep station, although he had described his home to her many times. He had begun to worry if it was fair to take her so far away from everything she knew and expect her to be happy in his sunburnt country, where the heat of the sun in mid-summer blazed down on the tin roof and there was no shade for miles. He felt sure she would come because she loved him, but did he have the right to ask her? It troubled him sorely, for he wanted her and only her for his wife, and of late the urge to make love to her had become unbearable. He knew that once he had tasted the full sweetness of her body he would marry her, despite his present concerns for her happiness, and that her deep love for him would take her to the ends of the earth to be with him.

The fighting had started again with a new offensive on the Somme, and Jamie knew it was only a matter of time before he would be sent back with the other troops. Some of the engineers had already married Brightlingsea girls, only to leave them as widows with a child to bring up alone within a few months. He was afraid of that happening to Laura and had not mentioned marriage to her again on that account.

Word had gone round the camp that the Australians were in action again and had fought the Germans to a standstill at Villers Bretonneux. Jamie wanted to be back in the fighting. He had worked hard at rifle practice and could now load and fire with reasonable accuracy although he still suffered pain in his arm. His face had healed completely, leaving him with a jagged scar to mar his handsome features, but he wore his scar with pride. The only things that troubled him were his nightmares, which had begun again, and over which he had no control.

A Gotha bomber had dropped its load around St.Osyth in May and had crashed, killing the pilot. The sound of the explosions had affected his dreams after that, bringing back the horrors, and he knew it would be a while before he could cope in the heat of battle again although he was determined to return. The nightmares haunted him for a while, waking him in the early hours and leaving him sleepless. They were always the same—the sound of tramping feet marching wearily along a road, becoming louder and louder until they turned into a barrage of guns close at hand and then the screams of horses as they were hit and the groans of dying men. He could forget it in the daytime but dreaded the coming of the night. The camp doctor gave him medicine to help him to sleep, but his nights were still disturbed. He had asked the colonel when he was sending him back to the front, but the colonel was evasive. When the Big Push was planned, they would need every man it was possible to send, but until then his experience on the field made him too valuable to lose. Jamie had no option but to wait.

Spring turned into summer and on the fourth of June there was a presentation of medals at the camp. The general officer commanding the Australian Imperial Forces depots came to Brightlingsea for the ceremony. Jamie lined up with the others who were to receive the Military Medal, which was presented to him for devotion to duty under heavy shell fire at Zonnebeke on September 26, 1917. He felt proud to have been awarded such a high honour, and yet, at the same time, he felt humbled by it. His thoughts went back to the field of battle and the death of his captain, who in his opinion was more entitled to receive the Military Medal than himself. He had been a brave and fearless man who had been much admired and respected by the men under his command. War was a lottery, and Jamie had been spared, for which he could only thank his lucky stars.

Laura and her mother had been invited to attend, and Laura's mother was as proud of him as if he had been her own son and said as much to her daughter. Laura felt relief flow over her—the last barrier to her relationship with Jamie appeared to have been removed. Jamie looked across at them, smiling with pride after the presentation, and felt a great surge of love towards Laura. The only victory that he had ever wanted was to win her heart, and he knew he had achieved that. Nothing else in the world mattered but to make her his wife once this terrible war was over.

With July came the news of a brilliant victory at Le Hamel, with the Aussies fighting alongside the U.S. Army. Jamie began to get restless. With these recent victories, there was a feeling in the air that the war must be nearing its end, a feeling shared by the generals on both sides. The British Fourth Army was preparing to go over the top on the Somme, and, in great secrecy, they and the Allies were making plans for the Big Push. The men from the Field Engineers, still in Brightlingsea, were being posted to France to join up with the Australian Corps, and Jamie was to go with them.

With only a few days notice to get used to the idea, Laura was shattered. To lose him again was too awful to contemplate. This time he might never come back, and she would never know the joy of belonging to him as his wife. That night she lay sleepless with misery when she heard him moaning and crying out in his sleep. Leaving her bed, Laura opened the door to his room and went in quietly to find him writhing in distress and covered in perspiration. She dampened a cloth in the jug of water on the washstand and bathed his face until he quietened a little and then slid between the sheets, holding him close in her arms as if he was a child, to comfort him. In the early hours of the morning, she left him asleep and returned to her own room to doze until the cockerel in the farmyard woke her with his crowing.

When he awoke, Jamie could sense by the scent of lavender on his sheets that Laura had been there. He had a vague recollection of being comforted during a bout of the horrors in the night. If only she had stayed then, he would have made love to her. A great surge of desire overwhelmed him, and he dressed quickly and went in search of her. The milking was finished and Laura was in the dairy pouring the milk into the flat pans, ready for the thick cream to come to the surface when it would be skimmed off for butter making.

Jamie waited until she had set the pail down and then clasped her around her waist, kissing her surprised, upturned face.

"Were you in my bed last night, Laura? Come on—own up."

"Well… " Laura was hesitant about admitting to it, but she smiled, guiltily.

"Having a fit of the horrors, was I?"

"Oh, Jamie dear, you were in such a state. I couldn't sleep for the noise you were making. I only stayed a little while until you calmed down and went to sleep."

"What a pity," said Jamie fondly, as he continued to kiss her. "I love you so much Laura I want you to sleep in my bed every night and to find you there every morning when I wake up."

Laura threw her arms round his neck and covered his face with kisses.

"I want to be with you always too—for the rest of my life."

Jamie sighed. He could delay no longer whatever the future held for them, and he asked her to marry him. There was no time to marry now before he went away, not even by special licence, but Jamie was sure the war would be over very soon now and then they would marry. He would come back for her, he promised, and take her to Australia as his bride.

At that moment, Bess Bowden came into the dairy, jug in hand, to fetch the milk for breakfast and found them in a close embrace.

"Mother! Jamie and I are to be married—he's just this minute asked me. I'm so happy—please be happy for me."

It was no more than Bess had expected although this was not the marriage she had wanted for her daughter. Jamie was a splendid young man whom she felt sure would make Laura happy, but it meant losing her and never seeing her again if he took her to Australia.

"Of course I'm happy for you both," she said, "but I'm not happy about losing my daughter."

"Would you be happy in Australia, Laura?" asked Jamie hopefully. "You'd have to come there. That's my home, and I must go back to run the sheep station for my parents—I've been away too long as it is—you understand that, don't you? I can't stay here with you—it isn't fair to them."

"Of course I understand my love. Wherever you are then I will be happy."

"My ma will love you—you can be sure of that. I've told her all about you in my letters home, so she will be expecting you."

Jamie had filled his letters with his love for Laura, but Rosie had never made one mention of her apart from sending her grateful thanks to all the family at Marsh Farm for their kindness to her son.

Jamie had just two days leave before returning to France, and Laura was excused all her duties to spend her time with him. They travelled to Colchester to buy both an engagement and a wedding ring, only wishing it had been possible at such short notice to marry. As he put the engagement ring on her finger, Jamie told her he considered her as his wife already and hoped she would let him make love to her as it was his dearest wish. Laura needed no persuasion—it was what she wanted herself—to belong to him completely.

Laura kept her promise and lay in her lover's arms all night, giving herself completely to Jamie until sleep eventually overtook them both. Jamie had waited until her passion for him had matched his own for her, and she had been swept away in an endless tide of lovemaking.

When morning came, she felt so full of love that she could hardly bear to leave him, but the cows needed milking and Wilf would wonder where she was. She still had one more day and one more night of his love before he left her, and this last day must be even more precious to them both. She would take him along the marshes where nobody ever went, to the old fisherman's hut on the water's edge, where they could make love undisturbed, with only the seabirds for company. Once the milking was finished, Laura packed up some food, telling her family they would be away for the day. Her mother thought they were probably going on a trip to Clacton, and Laura did nothing to dissuade her from that idea.

They spent their last hours wandering hand in hand along the marshes amid the sea lavender, walking barefoot in the tiny waves as the tide came in and making love in the shelter of the tumbledown hut, where a pile of old ropes served as a bed. Jamie lost himself in the deep violet of her eyes and her long auburn hair flecked with gold in the sunlight. When he undressed her, she trembled at his touch and clung to him in her unaccustomed nakedness until the act of love released her from her inhibitions and she was able to respond fully to his desires. She wanted the day to go on forever, but she knew it would have to come to an end and he would be gone in the morning.

Jamie left her as she lay asleep in her bed. Her beautiful hair was spread over the pillow, and she looked like a child, curled up under the sheet. They had made love in her bed that night, so he could leave her undisturbed in her sleep in the early hours to soften the blow of their parting. He had stood and looked down at her sleeping form for a few minutes before leaving, hating the war that was taking him away from her and praying that nothing would happen to prevent his return.

At cock crow, Laura woke to find him gone and struggled into her clothes to go down to the cowshed where the patient beasts would be waiting. She wept into their soft brown sides as she milked them, her tears mingling with the sweat of their bodies.

This time, there was no band as the soldiers marched to the station. It was too early in the morning for the band to play them off, and they had left before the townspeople were aware that they had gone.

CHAPTER 34

Laura wrote to him almost every day—letters full of love and her hopes for their future together, and Jamie replied whenever it was possible, reassuring her of his love for her and his intention to return.

Early in August, the great battle of Amiens took place and his letters ceased for a while until he was back behind the lines and could find a few moments to himself.

Then he wrote to her of the great victory they had won fighting alongside the Canadian forces and how a big twelve-inch gun near to him had given the signal and 5,000 guns in the Australian sector had taken it up. The noise had been enough to bring back the horrors, he told her, but being in the midst of it all had left him no time to think, and he had coped. Reality had cured his nightmares. They had done well, capturing over a hundred German guns and taking thousands of prisoners. The war would be over before much longer. Victory was in the air—he felt sure of it—and he would soon see her again.

The fighting continued in the drenching rain until the approaches to the Hindenberg Line were reached in September. It was a long, hard struggle by the British Fourth Army and their Allies before the line was eventually broken and the Aussies were withdrawn, victorious and exhausted. The morale of the German troops crumbled, and General Ludendorff resigned. With the defeat of the Kaiser, the way was left clear for peace terms to be decided. Jamie's division were marching back to the front when the fighting ceased, and he wrote to Laura, telling her of the celebrations among the troops and of his hoped-for return to Blighty.

Laura waited and waited, happily anticipating his arrival, only to find that Jamie, with the remains of the Australian forces, had been garrisoned near Charleroi and were to remain there until troop ships could be organised to take them back home. Her happiness was soured by the news, although his letters were still full of his love for her and his hopes for their future. In his last letter, he had promised to send her passage money as soon as he arrived back in Euroa, and he would be there on the quayside to greet her on her arrival, but the wait would be longer than they had both anticipated. She must be sure to bring her wedding ring so they could be married as soon as possible. The time would drag until he held her in his arms again and took her home to Seven Creeks as his wife.

Laura began stitching her trousseau—silk-embroidered nightdresses and underwear— despite her mother's advice that cotton was cooler in a hot climate. Only silk was good enough for Jamie to see her in on her wedding day.

While she was waiting to leave for Australia, she had taken a job like other young women who had replaced the men away at the war, and at last she had a little money she could call her own to spend on such luxuries as silk underwear. Her mother had taught her that money should be put away for a rainy day, but Laura felt there had been too many rainy days in her life of late, and, anyway, times were changing. Now that the war had ended it was off with the old and on with the new. Women were finding their rightful place in society at last, and no longer would she be tied to the farm as an unpaid worker helping to bag up the potatoes in the field, hoeing the long lines of seedlings or turning the hay in the hayfield until her back ached. She had taken the job as a booking clerk at the tiny railway station to fill up the days until she left home for good and found it much to her liking, passing the time with the passengers coming and going to Wivenhoe and Colchester, most of whom she knew already.

Wilf had two of the new Land Girls to take her place at the farm, about whom he complained ceaselessly, leaving Laura free to do as she wished.

Early in the New Year, the camp on the recreation ground was dismantled, and the soldiers left to return to their homeland apart from the few who preferred to remain behind. The Australians had been popular, and hundreds of people turned out to see them presented with a silver bowl in "affectionate remembrance" of their stay in the town. There were many heavy hearts as they left, and many lonely women with a baby who would never know its father. Jamie's last letter had been written just before he set sail for Williamstown and home, and Laura had begun to feel lonely too. It would be a long time before she received another letter, and he would be thousands of miles away by then.

The town looked deserted as she walked to work each morning, with hardly a man to be seen, just the girls pushing the bread cart around the streets and the women trundling the milk to the houses. Occasionally, she saw the post woman and stopped to see if there was a letter for her yet, but the months went past without any news from Jamie.

One evening, as the last train to Colchester was pulling out of the station, and she was locking the ticket office door ready to leave, a young man passed her, paused, and then, on recognising her, walked back to speak to her.

"Hallo, Laura—fancy seeing you here."

Laura turned round in surprise. "Why Jo, we wondered what had happened to you. Our Sam was demobbed at the end of December."

"Been in hospital for a while, that's why. I caught pneumonia—the rain in the trenches, and the cold winter didn't help. Still, things are improving now. It'll be good to get home and back to the farm—how have you been?"

Laura shrugged. "Oh, well enough. Gran has the ague, but things are about the same. Wilf has a couple of Land Girls to help him, so I work here these days."

Jo smiled at her. She looked happier and plumper than he could remember.

"Lucky old Wilf," he said, wondering how Wilf was coping with two women or they with him for that matter.

"Oh, he grumbles all the time—says they're hopeless but they do their best and work hard. Feeding them makes a lot of work for mother—they eat like horses! They'll be off soon anyway. They want to get back to a town job."

"I'll have to give them a look over when I come round in a day or two."

Laura turned away. In case he still had hopes of marrying her she would have to tell him. "I'm engaged by the way—to an Australian."

"An Aussie! Dad told me they were here but he didn't tell me that—not much of a letter writer my old dad."

Jo looked downcast. This was not the homecoming he had been hoping for. "I should have asked you before I went away, then."

"I'm sorry, Jo."

Jo picked up his case and walked away down the road towards Lower Farm. Laura followed behind, keeping her distance. She felt awkward about the encounter and had no wish to catch up with him. Poor Jo. She felt genuinely sorry for him knowing how fond of her he had been in the past, but, like most countrymen in those parts, he was slow to speak his mind and had never spoken of love or marriage. Now she had experienced the overwhelming ecstasy of Jamie's lovemaking she could feel nothing for Jo. Perhaps in her ignorance of what love was all about she might have accepted Jo years ago. He was reliable and kind and they had known each other all their lives, but there had never been a spark of romance between them. Jamie had taught her how to experience the joys of lovemaking, and there would never be any room in her heart for anyone else.

The war had changed everything and left very few eligible men for the many local girls who were looking for a husband. Laura felt sure Jo would soon find someone willing to marry him and live at Lower Farm. Once she had gone, it would be a matter of, out of sight out of mind—or so she hoped, for Jo's sake.

Gradually, as the men came home from the war, the town returned to normal. The thirteen pounder guns were removed from the fishing smacks, and the fishermen began to fish again, bringing in their hauls of sprats and shrimps from the North Sea. The great red sails of the barges were to be seen passing up the River Colne from Maldon, and the oystermen prepared for the time when the brood oysters could be lifted and re-laid in new beds. The posters round the town urging young men to rally round the flag were torn down and replaced by those advertising tea and soap. The booking clerk returned from France and Laura lost her job. The Land Girls left for the bright lights of London, and Laura reluctantly went back to helping on the farm until Jamie sent for her.

One morning, as she was walking home from delivering eggs, she met the post woman and stopped her as was her custom, to ask if there was any post for her.

"There's only a cable for you, miss. No letters I'm afraid."

Laura put the cable into her pocket and hurried towards home. *Why a cable,* she wondered, *and not a letter?* There had been plenty of time by now for Jamie to have written, and she was getting desperate to know when she could sail. Some months had passed since he had made love to her, and she would not be able to keep her condition a secret for much longer. Laura wanted to make her escape before that happened or she would be shamed before everyone. A child out of wedlock was a sin in her family, and she would never be forgiven.

When she had reached the gate to the farm, she could contain her curiosity no longer and opened the envelope. The contents turned her to stone and for a while she was unable to take in the words as they danced before her eyes. Pushing the cable into her pocket, she ran through the gate and pushed open the kitchen door, leaving it unlatched. Rushing upstairs to her bedroom, she flung herself onto her bed in a fit of sobbing.

Gran, who was dozing in her chair as Laura had rushed through the kitchen, saw and heard nothing. Seeing the door was open, some of the hens from the stockyard wandered into the scullery and then into the kitchen, pecking around on the floor to see what they could find. The ginger tom cat sitting in his usual place under Gran's skirt saw an opportunity for some sport and slunk out with his eyes on his prey. Feathers flew as he chased the hens around the kitchen, knocking against the old lady's legs and waking her up. Seeing what was happening she took her stick and whacked at the cat and the chickens as they ran rings round her. Running through her skirts, the cat dislodged her from her chair, and she tumbled to the floor, stick in hand, whacking to the left and the right of her. When Bess came in, the kitchen was a mass of feathers and her mother-in-law lay groaning on the floor.

"Git them owd hens outa here, Bess, and help me up."

"Why, mother—what has been going on here? Who left the door open, for goodness sake? I know I shut it behind me— – perhaps Laura is back, but it's not like her to be so careless."

Finding difficulty in lifting old Mrs. Bowden to her feet, Bess went to the foot of the stairs and called Laura to help, but there was no reply, and she presumed she must still be out. Sam eventually came to her aid, and between them they got the old lady onto the horsehair sofa in the parlour. She continued to moan with pain, and Sam went to fetch the doctor, who diagnosed a broken hip. The old lady was made as comfortable as possible on the sofa, where she would have to stay as the stairs were too twisted and steep to remove her to her own bed.

"Have you seen Laura?" Bess asked Sam when the cat had been shooed outside in disgrace and the bedraggled hens were back in the yard. "I could do with her here right now to help clear up this mess while I see to Gran."

"Thought I saw her come in a while ago—she was in a bit of a hurry as I recall."

"Where on earth is she? I called upstairs but she didn't answer—perhaps she didn't hear me. Oh dear, what a muddle—did you ever see the like of it!"

Bess went up the small staircase beside the kitchen fireplace in search of her daughter and found her in a sorry state lying on her bed, her eyes swollen with weeping and her face blotched with tears.

"My dear girl—whatever is wrong? Are you ill?"

Laura handed her mother the cable and hid her face in the coverlet as she read it.

"*Circumstances prevent you from coming to Australia. Forgive me. Jamie.*"

"Oh, my dear, my dear—this is terrible. How could he do this to you—breaking your heart like this—and to think I thought him to be such an honourable young man. Well, we know better now."

"There *must* be a reason—there *must* be. He wouldn't do this to me otherwise. He loved me. I *know* he loved me." Laura's tears began afresh.

"Who can tell with a man," said her mother bitterly. "Words are cheap, and he was a long way from home."

"It wasn't like that mother, truly—you'll see when he writes."

If he writes, thought Bess, putting her arms around her distraught daughter.

What with Gran and now this—it was just too much.

"I must get downstairs, Laura. Gran has broken her hip, and the kitchen is full of chicken's feathers."

When her mother had gone, Laura puzzled over this remark, which made no sense whatsoever apart from poor Gran breaking her hip, and that was bad enough. What was going to happen to her when she told her mother she was pregnant? Her future happiness lay in ruins, and there was no way out as far as she could see. Laura buried her head in her pillow and cried until she had no more tears to shed. She felt totally alone in her predicament with nobody in the world to whom she could turn for advice. Would her mother turn her out, and, if she did, where could she go? She lay on her bed wishing she was dead. She had committed an unforgivable sin and would be thought of as no more than a common whore, although she had loved Jamie with her whole heart, but her family would never see it that way. They would despise her, and her mother would never get over the shame she had brought on them all.

Laura groaned aloud in her misery. The child made a slight movement in her womb as if it too felt her agony, and she placed her hand over her stomach. It was the first time she had felt the new life growing inside her, and she felt a ray of hope. Whatever happened, she would not be alone. She must be strong for the sake of her fatherless child, who soon would be needing all her love.

CHAPTER 35

The sound of a ship's hooter from the direction of the river roused the rooks nesting in the elms growing along the boundary wall, and they rose cawing into the air, circling high above the mourners below. "Dust to dust and ashes to ashes," intoned the minister as he sprinkled a handful of earth onto the coffin with his red-chapped hands. Laura began to sob uncontrollably.

Gran was being laid to rest on a bitterly cold March morning in the cemetery high on the hill overlooking the river. It was a bleak place, where the wind blew up from the marshes across the mass of gravestones stretching down the hill to the fields below. The mourners huddled together for warmth, hoping that the service would soon be over. The meagre fire in the front parlour of Marsh Farm would be more than welcome once the funeral was over.

Gran's fall had proved to be too much for her ancient bones, and when pneumonia had set in there was little hope of her recovery. The ague caused by the damp mists which surrounded the low lying farm like a shroud in the winter months had always affected the old lady, and she had not lasted long.

Laura had helped to nurse her, looking ill herself. Since she had received a letter from Jamie, she had lost all interest in life, including the forthcoming birth of his baby.

His letter had been both kind and sympathetic, but it had been like a knife driven into her heart. He had told her of the death of his father from the flu epidemic which was sweeping the world and the loss of his stock, leaving him with nothing to offer her. It was no place for a young woman to begin her married life, and he urged her to make a new life for herself. He had begged her to forgive him and not to forget him or the love they had shared, as he would never forget her for as long as he lived. The sadness of his words affected her deeply, and she wished she could put the clock back. They should have married earlier when there had been time. She would have gone to join him as his wife even if Seven Creeks was in the middle of a desert—what would that have mattered to her. Just to be with him was all she had ever wanted, and now she felt like a widow who had lost her husband in the war—empty and unfulfilled.

Her mother, standing on the opposite side of the open grave, looked at her with concern. She had told her not to come, feeling it would distress her further and cause more tongues to wag, but Laura had insisted on being there. Lucy looked at her with ill-disguised contempt. Laura had no self control. She had behaved badly with the Australian and had only herself to blame. Gran was old and ill and would never have got any better, so why did Laura cry so much and make such an exhibition of herself? People were always asking about Laura, and she was sick of it, as if there was something special about her now there was no possibility of her sailing to Australia.

Lucy had watched from her bedroom window as Laura had thrown her wedding ring into the dark waters of the pond where it had sunk to the bottom without even the smallest ripple. She had begun to wonder if her sister was going mad. It was a wicked waste to throw away a gold ring even if you had never intended to wear it. When she had told her mother what Laura had done her mother had agreed with her. Gold cost money, and Laura should have sold it if she'd had any sense, but Laura appeared to have lost her senses of late.

Bess, surrounded by her black-clothed relatives guessed why her eldest daughter was in such distress. She was not just burying Gran but burying the past as well, and it was breaking her heart. She felt some sympathy for Laura, but her sense of outrage when she had discovered her daughter was pregnant outweighed all her other feelings. She blamed herself to some extent for allowing Jamie to return to the farm to recover, but she had expected her strictly brought up daughter to know how to behave and not to be led astray, however much she had loved him.

Jo Carter and his father Bert had attended out of respect for their closest neighbour. They stood a little behind the other mourners at the graveside, and Jo was aware of Laura sobbing into her handkerchief standing away from the rest of her family as if she had the plague. He moved forward to stand beside her and put his arm round her for support. Laura leaned gratefully against his shoulder and wept into the rough tweed of his jacket, unaware of the glances from the relatives as they looked at one another under lowered eyelids. Their puritanical hearts turned away from her in righteous indignation as she stood there with her swollen body scarcely disguised under her loose winter coat, making such an exhibition of herself. Everyone would ignore her once they had returned to Marsh Farm for the customary refreshments afterwards, unless she was sensible and kept out of sight.

Jo stared stoically ahead. He knew what they were thinking by looking at their faces, and he felt full of pity for her.

"You come home along of Dad an' me, Laura. We've brought the trap. Don't go in that contraption with the others—you'll be better without them."

Laura nodded gratefully—it would have been better if she had stayed away, but she was a member of Gran's family and had as much right to be there as anyone else. None of the family had wanted her since she had brought shame on them, but she had never intended that—she had loved Jamie so much it had seemed the natural thing to do at the time as they were soon to be married. None of them understood what real love was like—even her mother seemed to have forgotten, and she had fallen in love with her father when he had come to work as a labourer on her grandfather's farm. Her family had disapproved of him, and they had tried to prevent the match without success. So her own mother had known what it was to be in love once, but she seemed to have forgotten of late. Laura wondered if she should have waited but her circumstances were rather different and had she done so she would never have known the joy of being loved by Jamie. Nothing could wipe away her cherished memories despite being treated like an outcast because she had no wedding ring on her finger.

The funeral over the mourners filed past her without looking up. Jo kept his arm tightly round her shoulders. Let them think what they liked. Laura was worth all of them put together, whatever she had done.

There was nothing wanton about Laura. He had known her all his life, and, to Jo, she was as pure as a mountain stream. If anyone had been at fault, it was that Aussie she had been engaged to and who had let her down. He would never lay any blame at her door—to him she was an innocent victim, knowing so little of the world and its wicked ways.

Jo's father touched him on the shoulder. "I'll take her place with them others, Jo. There isn't room in the trap for three. You take her home, lad."

Jo nodded in agreement. He wanted Laura to himself for a few minutes.

The mourners took their places in the wagonette, Wilf and Sam took up the reins, and the two farm horses pulled the contraption back to Marsh Farm. The empty glass hearse pulled by two black plumed horses moved away, and Jo helped Laura into the trap. A light flurry of snow blew in the wind, making her shiver.

"Late for snow," said Jo, as he tucked a rug round her knees. "'Bout time we had some spring weather—the ground's so hard nothing has started to move as yet—this winter seems to be going on forever."

Laura smiled weakly. He was trying to be kind, so she must make some response.

"I expect the weather will change all of a sudden, Jo, and the spring will be here before you know it."

"The farm comes alive in the spring with the newly born lambs and calves—I love it then. It's the season I enjoy the most—too much to do at harvest time."

There was a long silence as the pony trotted along the back road from the church.

"Good time to have babies too. They have all the summer in which to grow strong like the beasts in the field."

Laura was taken aback. Nobody in her family ever mentioned the baby as if the child had no existence apart from her now obvious shape. Her mother had been shocked on first learning of her pregnancy but not too alarmed as Laura would be gone long before her condition became obvious. Later, she had hardened her heart, knowing that some of the shame would fall upon her and her family like a curse.

"When is your baby expected, Laura?"

Jo was blunt. He never minced words, and he needed to know so he could do something about it. When he had seen the way her family had ignored her distress in the churchyard he had made up his mind. He would not stand by and see an injustice done to a fellow creature and especially to Laura.

"At the end of next month, I think."

"Not long then."

"No."

Jo ruminated for a bit and pulled the pony round, so they took the long way back through the country lanes, avoiding the town. He did not want to be the reason for any more gossip about Laura, and he wanted time to put his thoughts into words.

"I know you must have loved that other man, Laura, to let him, well..." Jo's voice trailed off and he coughed slightly in an embarrassed way. "...but we could still make a go of it, you and me, if you want to. I'd always hoped you would marry me one day, and I haven't changed my mind about that."

"But what about the baby, Jo?"

"Well, we can't do much about that, can we? I'd have to bring it up like my own. We could have our own family later, and then it would hardly make any difference."

Laura looked at him with tears in her eyes. She had never expected any man to want her now her shame was there for all to see.

"You're such a good person, Jo. I've always known that, ever since we were children together, and I'm very fond of you, but ..."

Jo pulled the pony to a stop and took her hand in one of his. "I know your baby is a love child, Laura, but you'll need someone to look after you soon, and if you'll marry me I'll be a good husband to you—now what do you say?"

Laura took her time before answering. It was difficult for her. She had to be fair to him, although he was offering her a way out of her present dilemma. She would have to tell him it would be a marriage of convenience, even if he changed his mind afterwards. She could never live with herself otherwise.

"I'll try to be a good wife to you, Jo, but I can't promise to be anything other than that—Jamie meant everything to me, you see, and as long as you understand—it wouldn't be fair to marry you unless I was honest with you."

"I won't bother you in bed, Laura, until you feel ready, if that's what you mean. Time will heal the hurt you've suffered, and I'll be patient."

Laura was silent. She would never feel the passion for Jo that she had felt for Jamie, and she knew those feelings would never return, but she would give Jo everything else he wanted and maybe, one day, she would feel a tenderness towards him which would grow out of their long friendship with one another and the love he felt for her.

"I would be a fool, Jo, not to accept you, and I thank you from the bottom of my heart. I will never let you down, or forget what you've done for me this day—but as long as you understand—"

"That's settled then," said Jo, as he jerked the reins and the pony set off again trotting down the lane to Lower Farm. "And now I'm taking you home with me, and you can see how you like it. We're not going to your Gran's funeral tea, and, once your sour relatives have gone, I'll take you home and break the news to your family. It will be a nice change for Dad and me to have a woman about the farmhouse. We've been too long without female company since mother died."

"Will your father mind—about the baby, I mean?"

"Dad's always been fond of you, and he's a bit more broad-minded than your people—he makes up his own mind about things. He'll accept the baby when it's born, you'll find. It will be a part of our family, even if it's not my child, and I will do my best to be a father to it."

Jo and Laura were married early one morning in April when the buds were showing through their sticky coats on the horse chestnut trees by the gates of Lower Farm, and the primroses were unfurling their yellow petals amid the rough grass beside the driveway to the house. Afterwards, Laura cooked dinner as if it was the same as any other day, the only difference being the wedding ring Jo had placed on her finger that morning, making her a respectable woman in the eyes of the world.

Her mother's attitude towards her had changed overnight and had lightened her sorrows. Lucy came to visit, proud now that her sister was the mistress of Lower Farm, which was twice the size of their own, and Wilf had made an appearance, hoping to borrow a few things from Jo. Jo and his superior machinery could be of great assistance throughout the year now that Jo was related to him by marriage. Wilf was canny enough to realise that he would need to treat his sister with respect if he wanted Jo's cooperation when it was time to harvest the wheat and thresh the corn.

Laura's baby was born at the end of the month—a fine, strong boy with a pair of good lungs. Jo came to see him but did not pick him up although he expressed his pleasure on finding he was a lusty child. Extra mouths on a farm needed to pay their way, and Laura's baby looked as if he would be an asset in the years to come.

From the moment of his birth, the child screamed with all his might, clenching his tiny fists and kicking his fat little legs, driving Laura to distraction. He grew fast and sat up early and by the end of the year it was a job to keep him confined. The farm cats soon learnt to keep out the way as he lunged towards them, and Jo's sheepdog found he was unable to herd him into a corner like the other sheep and left him strictly alone. Laura adored him. He was all she had left of her love, and any other children she might have in the future would never be as special to her as this firstborn.

As he belonged to her entirely, she named him Laurie and added James as his second name, in memory of his father.

Jo had kept his promise and had never taken advantage of her, but, after Laurie's birth, Laura could see a hunger in his eyes and knew that the time had come for her to show him a willingness to behave like his wedded wife and took to sharing the big feather bed with him which had belonged to his parents.

The springs complained as Jo did what came naturally, and the brass knobs rattled in their loose sockets with his efforts. Laura bore it complacently, considering she was doing her duty by Jo. With Jamie, she had felt worshipped and adored and swept along in a tide of passion for him, but, with Jo, it was the release of a physical need on his part, after which he would turn over and sleep soundly.

She had no complaints—it was more than she deserved, and she knew that Jo loved her in his uncomplicated way. She worked hard and did all that he asked of her around the farm—rearing the pheasant chicks for the shooting season, bottle-feeding the calves and the motherless lambs and keeping the weakly piglets wrapped up close to the kitchen stove.

Lower Farm was a large Victorian house with high ceilings and draughty passages and floors covered with linoleum, unlike her old home, which had been built in Tudor times and had small rooms with brick floors. Jo was happy to leave her to arrange things as she liked, and Laura did her best to make it more comfortable. She kept telling herself how fortunate she was to be here with little Laurie for company while Jo and his father were busy in the fields or at market, and yet she felt as if her life was incomplete. Much as she loved Laurie, it was his father she ached for, and, however much she busied herself, the aching would not go away. She felt it most when Jo flung himself upon her in the big feather bed, and she was unable to respond to his lovemaking. Jo appeared to be blissfully unaware of her feelings. As long as she was there when he needed her and made no objections to his advances then he was perfectly satisfied. It was all Jo expected of a wife, and the idea of giving her the same sexual satisfaction had never occurred to him.

Christmas 1919 was a happy one for them all. The Carter family went to the Christmas Day service at the Anglican Church in town. Jo's family only went to church on festival days, and Laura accompanied them with the baby. There was no service on that day at the Wesleyan chapel, so Bess had invited them to share Christmas dinner with them at Marsh Farm for which Jo had provided the Christmas goose.

Sitting in the rarely used parlour after dinner in front of a blazing log fire, lit for the occasion, Sam announced his engagement to a fisherman's daughter who lived in New Street. Her father had asked Sam to go into partnership with him on his fishing smack, and Sam wanted to take up the offer. There was no future in farming, was his honest opinion.

"I don't have the feeling for it that Jack had," he explained. "It's sheer drudgery, unless you can afford machines to do some of the heavy work."

Bess shook her head with annoyance. Sam's engagement did not come as a surprise, but she had expected them to live at Marsh Farm when they were married. It had been easier for Wilf once Sam had returned from the war, and now he intended to leave them again.

"Machines! Rubbish! It's all you ever talk about, Sam. Machines break down and then you have to buy spare parts for them. Horses don't need spare parts—how do you think we've managed all these years?"

Sam gave up. His mother was rooted in the past. Things were different now the war was over. People had new ideas about farming methods. He would never change her, and he wanted to leave now he had the opportunity.

Jo agreed in part with Sam. They would have to change their ways to survive, but he had no wish to get into an argument with his mother-in-law. Wilf had already spoken to him about Sam's intentions, and it was obvious that Wilf could no longer manage the farm on his own.

"I'd be happy to rent the two fields that border my own, if that would help," suggested Jo. "It would mean less work for Wilf and still give you a small income from them."

Laura looked at him with gratitude. Jo had been so good to them all—whatever would any of them have done without him.

Bess accepted with alacrity. It was the perfect answer to all their troubles. Depression was all around them—no work for the returning soldiers and no money for their families. So much for Lloyd George and his promise of a land fit for heroes.

Laura was so fortunate to have a husband who had a large and prosperous farm, as they were less likely to go bankrupt as had happened to so many other smaller farmers. Jo Carter had done them a great service by marrying her daughter.

That evening, after she had put Laurie to bed, Laura went down to the kitchen to prepare the table for the next morning's breakfast and found Jo warming himself before the opened stove. He was stocky of build with a ruddy complexion and fair wispy hair which scarcely covered his balding head. He looked every inch a farmer as he stood with his legs astride in front of the fire, his watch chain looped across his best waistcoat in honour of the occasion. Laura smiled at him. He had been his usual generous self to her family on this Christmas Day, and she had something special to tell him which would please him.

"I have a present for you, Jo, but it's not something I could wrap up in pretty paper so I waited until we got home."

"Oh—a bit late for that, isn't it, my dear. Christmas is all but over."

"Next summer *you* will be a father, Jo. I'm having another baby."

Jo put his arm around her and kissed her, clumsily.

"Well, well," he said, his red face breaking into a proud smile. "I'm to be a father, am I? Well, well, well..."

He rubbed his hands together with great satisfaction, a habit he had copied from his father and smiled affectionately at his wife.

"The best thing I ever did was to marry you, Laura," he said, as, still smiling broadly, he turned round to shut up the stove for the night and then walked towards the stairs.

"Don't be long, my dear. Your news has made me feel quite romantic."

Laura's heart sank. She knew exactly what *that* meant.

PART SIX

Seven Creeks

1919–1926

CHAPTER 36

After what seemed an eternity, the troop ship docked at Williamstown for the soldiers who had come from the State of Victoria to embark and make their own way home. Jamie took the train to Melbourne and then hitched a lift to Seymour on a cart which was on its way to Gray Town with provisions for the old goldfields. He was short of money and found people were generous with their lifts to the returning soldiers, who were thought of as returning heroes and were treated with great kindness by everyone they met. Gray Town was out of his way so he set off on foot towards Avenal hoping to be picked up by a passing vehicle to Euroa, but only saw two horsemen, going in opposite direction, who stopped briefly to wish him well.

The hard dusty road was as he remembered it, stretching across a dull, desolate landscape dotted with tall gums, their bark hanging in tattered strips like cast off rags.

Here and there beside the road, he came across big, black scavenging crows, which, with their cruel beaks and crafty eyes, looking as if they were bent on some evil deed, hardly moved as he passed. The land was parched and dusty and food must have been hard to find for birds and beasts alike. Only the bubbling call of the magpies and the occasional laugh of a kookaburra lifted his heart and made him glad to be back. He had walked for miles and was almost asleep, resting under the sparse shade of a gum tree, when a shout alerted him.

"Going my way, soldier? You're welcome to a lift."

Jamie struggled to his feet and hauled his pack onto his shoulder. It had been the first passerby he had seen for hours, and he had almost missed him. The ancient cart was pulled by a donkey and was loaded with hay, obscuring the driver.

"Lost my own boy in the war," muttered the old man, sitting across the shafts. "Get up on the hay; you'll be comfortable there. I'm taking this lot to Merton, cross country—that any good to you?"

"I was heading for Seven Creeks and the sheep station, hoping to get a lift to Euroa and making my way from there—but if you are going anywhere in that direction you can drop me off and I'll walk."

"I meet the road to Merton not far from the Gooram Falls. You can get to Euroa from there."

"Thanks—I'm grateful to you. I know the road well."

Jamie got up onto the cart, and the donkey set off at a leisurely pace. The owner's head began to nod, and, after a while, Jamie found himself dozing off as they trundled along, only waking each time the cart hit a stone and lurched to one side. He had intended to look at the countryside as they passed by, but as the donkey appeared to know the road by instinct and ambled along at a slow pace Jamie was content to catch up on some sleep.

They came to a stop at the crossroad to Euroa, and Jamie got off, feeling refreshed. The driver gave no answer to his thanks for the lift, and the donkey set off towards Merton. The trees grew in great stands along the creek and made his long walk cooler and more pleasant. Galahs flew, calling amid the branches with flashes of grey and pink plumage, and he could hear the bellbirds high in the trees. At last he began to feel as if he was nearing home.

Joyful was the old aboriginal name for Euroa, and that was how Jamie felt as he approached the town, although that feeling soon disappeared as he grew closer to Seven Creeks. He knew there was something wrong as he approached the long track up to the homestead. Where were the flocks of sheep which had always grazed on their lush acres, and, for that matter, where were the green acres? The grasslands had turned into dust since his departure, and an eerie silence had descended over the land. The grass on either side of the track had turned brown and sear, and he could see that most of the creeks had dried up. They must have experienced a terrible drought for the land to look so parched.

In the distance, he could see the homestead—the homestead he had often described so lovingly to Laura, which looked decrepit and run down. He would have to work hard to pull it round before he could ask her to join him here. When the homestead came into view, it looked smaller than he had remembered it, standing alone with no sheep to be seen where once the pastures had been thick with them. The ancient wattle tree had collapsed, and its branches sprawled across the ground in a grotesque heap.

Lucy had laughed when he had described it to them sitting in the Bowden's cosy kitchen. "What's a wattle?" she had asked. Jamie smiled a wry smile at the memory. What indeed!

As he watched, a young woman came through the wire door and pushed a broom across the verandah in a desultory manner as if she had no inclination for the task. He heard a child calling, and she went back into the house. Jamie had no idea who she could be and for one terrible moment he wondered if some ill had befallen his parents, and they had had to sell up and move away.

He hastened his steps and walked up to the front door. His mother's chair still stood in the same place on the verandah with the broom the woman had been using propped beside it. Through the wire door, the kitchen looked the same as it had always looked, with the old black range alight, despite the heat, and a pot boiling on the hob. His parents must be about somewhere. He pushed open the door and went in. A child was crying out at the back, and he could hear the woman speaking to it, comfortingly.

"Hush now, Shaun. You didn't really hurt yerself —it was just a tumble, me darlin'. Mama kiss it better—there now."

The crying ceased, and the woman came through into the kitchen holding a small child in her arms.

"Why, if it isn't yerself back from the war, Jamie. We wondered when you'd be arriving home."

"Kathleen!" Jamie looked at her in amazement. The smouldering green eyes and the pouting cherry lips had lost none of their allure, but she looked different. Her wild black curls were tied back neatly, and she wore a clean white starched apron over a blue gingham dress. She looked the picture of domesticity and motherhood. Somebody must have taken her in hand and cleaned her up.

"You were the last person I expected to see."

"An' why, pray? I've lived here for the past year an' a bit."

"Lived here! How did that come about, for Gawd's sake?"

"Yer ma asked me to—after the baby an' all."

"She what! Where is Ma? Is she about? And Pa?"

"I'll get yer ma—she's feeding the chooks."

Kathleen went into the yard, and he heard her calling his mother. "Mrs. Macdonald, 'tis Jamie. He's home this minute."

Rosie came running across the yard and surprised her son by throwing her arms around him and bursting into tears. Jamie, who had never seen his mother show such emotion before, was startled by this reaction to his homecoming.

"Come now, Ma. I'm almost in one piece—no need to take on so. Where's Pa?"

Rosie brushed away her tears impatiently.

"He's gone, son—gone."

"Gone! What do you mean? Not—"

Rosie nodded, unable to speak.

"Oh, no—I don't believe it."

"Three weeks ago, and he was only ill for a week. I can't get used to it myself. My poor Rory—he'd driven some of the beasts to the Ram Sales to get rid of them, the ones that were left with a bit of flesh on their bones, and when he got back he was too weak to get off his horse. Kathleen and I had to lift him into his bed, but there was nothing we could do."

"What was the matter with him?"

"The doctor said he'd caught Spanish flu, like so many others. Thousands of people have caught it and died—they say it's worse than the casualties in the war."

"Bloody hell! I'd heard about it, but I never thought it would have reached as far as this—and what about you, Ma? Are you all right?"

"I've had no symptoms as yet and nor has Kathleen. Rory wouldn't let us come near him in case we caught it, especially little Shaun, although we found he had toddled in to see his grandpa one morning, which gave us a fright."

"His grandpa? What are you talking about, Ma?"

"Why Shaun, of course. Your pa doted on that child. It's been like having you as a babe all over again. We found him such a comfort with you away for so long in the war—and Kathleen too. She's been so good to us both. We wondered if we could get used to her at first, but once she had learnt how to look after herself properly and to cook and keep the place clean, we grew real fond of her. Now she's like a daughter and a part of our family."

Jamie was stunned. He had expected things to be just the same when he came home, but they would never be the same again now his father was dead, and Kathleen Murphy had taken residence with her child. His mother had never approved of her, and everyone knew she was no better than a whore. As far as he was concerned, Kathleen would have to leave before he could bring Laura here, whatever his mother felt about it.

"And why is Kathleen here, I'd like to know? You never liked her or her family."

Rosie looked at him sternly. "You should be ashamed of yourself asking me such a question, Jamie. You know perfectly well. Shaun is your child, and she came to us for help once she was turned out of her home."

Jamie turned red with anger. "I'll bet she did, the bitch!" he shouted.

Rosie was shocked by his outburst. "How could you call the mother of your child by such a name. I would never have thought it of you—a son of mine. Your pa and I accepted your responsibilities while you were away fighting in the war, but now you are home you must do the right thing by this girl. I know she had a bad name in the past, but that is all over now. She has been a good girl since she has been living here with us."

"The child could belong to any number of men so why foist it onto me? I can see no resemblance to myself in him, and I'll not have it, Ma—no way!"

"She told us you'd been with her the night before you left —do you deny that?"

"Well—no. It was a mistake on my part—I'd been drinking, and she was very persuasive, wanting a lift home and ready for it, and I was in no state to refuse her.

I don't have any feelings for Kathleen Murphy. The girl I want to marry lives in England—I wrote to you about her—her name's Laura. Didn't you say anything to Kathleen of my intentions?"

"You mentioned a girl, but we had Kathleen living here by then with her little boy, and we expected you to marry her if you survived the war. Your pa didn't want you told because he thought it best that you should have no worries, and the other was just a wartime romance on the other side of the world which would come to nothing."

"I love her, Ma, and I've promised to marry her, and I won't go back on that promise."

"And I won't turn Kathleen and your son out of my home, so what do you intend to do? Just you think about it, Jamie. Your Laura won't be welcome here. Times are hard, the flocks have died out in the pasture, and those that have survived bring in little money. What do you have to offer her if she comes? A hard life in a hard country is all she can hope for."

"Why can't you understand, Ma," said Jamie, in exasperation, "you loved Pa once, and I want Laura and only Laura for my wife."

Rosie gave up trying to make him see sense. "That kind of love would only wither and die out here in this climate. She's used to soft rain and gentle breezes, not the scorching sun and the dust. She wouldn't last five minutes. You need to be brought up here to live in the outback, and you know it."

She left him and returned to her work, and Jamie went outside and sat on the steps of the verandah, his head in his hands. He realised that his mother spoke the truth. It would be hard for Laura. She would only have his love to sustain her, and where would they live? He doubted that Kathleen's child was his but that doubt would remain forever between them, and he could not subject Laura to Kathleen's wicked tongue. She was there first and considered herself as the eventual mistress of the homestead and his woman, to make things worse. How she had ever persuaded his mother to take her in he could only imagine. Some sob story about having nowhere to go because she had given birth to his child, he supposed. How he despised her. She had got what she had always wanted, or she thought she had. He would never marry her or have sex with her again. Without his dearest Laura, his life was meaningless. The more he thought about it, the worse it seemed. Kathleen and her little bastard were here to stay, making it impossible to marry Laura.

Jamie got up and went in search of an axe. He badly needed to vent his frustration on something or he would go inside and kill Kathleen with his bare hands. Axe in hand, he swung with all his strength, chopping up the broken branches of the old wattle tree and gouging out the root until nothing remained. His mother had loved it when it had blossomed in all its glory, and he had described it to Laura, filling her thoughts with pictures of loveliness and the happiness they would one day share. He had been cheated of that happiness, and it would be left to him to break her heart. He almost wished he had been killed in the bloody war rather than make her suffer in this way.

The job completed, he stood up and contemplated the devastation around him. He heard the child laughing and looked up to see him peering through the bars of the verandah, holding on with his chubby hands. Jamie stared at him. It was the first time he had really looked at him closely. He was a beautiful little boy with large questioning eyes and his mother's full lips. The child put his hand through the bars towards him, but, sensing no response, he withdrew it and toddled away in search of his mother.

Kathleen came out with a cup of tea for him and placed it on the floor of the verandah where he could reach it. Although he was dying of thirst, he refused to touch it until she had gone inside. She gave him a searching look as she left. She had expected him to be angry but not as angry as this and felt a little scared as to what the future held for her. She knew she was safe while Rory was alive to support her cause, but, with him gone she felt vulnerable. Jamie had made it obvious that he had no feelings for her, although she still lusted after him.

Shaun's arrival just before the departure of the volunteers had been a godsend. She had given her favours to many other young men that night behind the hall, and Jamie had been one of many, but he was the one she had really wanted. If she could make him feel the same way about her she would stay faithful to him for the rest of her life. She had ingratiated herself to his parents and had been the soul of propriety while she had lived with them, passing off Shaun as his son and pretending she had known Jamie for many months before he had left. Jamie might be killed like so many others and Shaun would then be in line to inherit the sheep station if he never came back. His mother had adored the child, finding some likeness to Jamie's baby ways and his looks until she had come to believe he really was Jamie's son, which

Kathleen knew he was not, but if Shaun helped to make them happy after their own son had gone away what harm could there be in that.

When Rosie had told her that Jamie had met another girl in England and intended to marry her, Kathleen began to feel worried. If he married this girl before he came home then all her hopes of a future with him would come to nothing, and she would have to leave Seven Creeks. It had been a worrying time for both her and the Macdonalds. Rosie wanted Shaun to grow up in the homestead and carefully made no reference to Laura in her letters to Jamie in the hopes that the romance would come to nothing and they could all settle down together as one happy family on his return. She had said as much to Kathleen during Rory's illness and had promised never to turn them out, come what may, but, had she known the truth of the matter, things would have been very different. As it was, the die had been cast before Jamie arrived home.

Once this black mood had left him, and he had had time to get used to her presence about the place, Kathleen hoped to seduce him back to her bed—there would be no doubt as to who fathered the next child then. Even if he never loved her or married her, she still wanted him with an all-consuming passion. The ugly scar on his face only made him more attractive to her and just seeing him again had heightened her desire to make love to him.

Jamie had other ideas. If she had to stay, then he would have to put up with her around the place but he would treat her like a servant and speak to her as little as possible. She had stolen the place that rightly belonged to Laura, and nothing would change his mind about that, and, as for any physical contact, the thought filled him with revulsion. She could flaunt her sexuality as much as she liked, for it would have no effect upon him. Perhaps, in time, she would get tired of this game she was playing and move on with some other man. Until that happened or until his mother died, he could offer Laura absolutely nothing, and she must be given the chance to live her own life without him, as there was every likelihood of them never seeing each other again.

Now he must send her a cable and a letter telling her the situation had changed, but he did not relish the idea of writing it. He would have to think it out very carefully, leaving out any reference to Kathleen Murphy and her son, for that would destroy her love for him completely, and that was more than he could contemplate.

CHAPTER 37

Jamie worked hard during the following weeks to keep his mind occupied and only visited the homestead for meals and to sleep. There was plenty to do to renew the roofing on the barns and the great woolshed before the rains came, as they surely must do eventually. The stock was so badly depleted that there was little he could do for them apart from dragging the brackish water he could find in the creeks to the few troughs left in the pasture. The sheep that still had a bit of meat left on their bones would have to be eaten by the family, stewed in a pot for hours on the cooking range. Their wool was of too poor a quality to sell, and he would need to buy better stock in order to renew his flocks, and that cost money, which was in short supply.

He rode for long hours alone, steeling himself against any thoughts of Laura, trying to erase her from his memory but without success. The guilt he felt at deserting her haunted him constantly, and, wherever he found himself or whatever task occupied him, she was always there. He would never forget her or stop loving her as long as he lived.

Kathleen had tried her best to renew his sexual appetite by lowering her bodice to show her shapely bosom to the best advantage and moving near to him whenever the opportunity arose. She walked with a natural swing to her hips, which would have driven most men wild with desire but which left Jamie cold. The hatred he felt for the damage she had caused him overcame anything she might do to arouse his feelings and her sexy looks and pouting lips made no difference. He mistrusted her and fixed a bolt on his door so his sleep would not be disturbed should she try to seduce him at night, for she made no secret of the fact that she wanted him. He saw it in her face every time she looked in his direction. She was like an animal in heat that needed to mate, and he despaired of the situation ever being resolved. If only she would find someone else who had something to offer her but the homestead and respectability were too great a prize to throw away, and Jamie supposed she felt it was worth her while to wait and hope he would change his mind about marrying her.

When his mother had mentioned that Seven Creeks would belong to Shaun one day, Jamie had lost his temper.

"How do you know he's my son, Ma? Even Kathleen can't be sure—why don't you ask her, eh? How many men was she with that night? Even she won't know because Kathleen's a whore and I don't want a whore as my wife. When I know I have a son, then he'll inherit Seven Creeks, but it won't be Shaun, of that you can be sure."

"The war has changed you, Jamie. You've grown so hard—I hardly know the man who left here four years ago."

"It's not the war that's changed me, Ma, as you well know."

Jamie had stormed out and saddled up his horse. He had a plan to visit the surrounding sheep stations to see what stock could be bought as cheaply as possible while the owners were desperate for money, and this seemed as good a time as any to go. The land would soon regenerate once the rains came, and, after three months of drought, that time should be soon.

He made his way along the road to Strathbogie with his two sheepdogs running beside him and visited some of the run-down sheep stations in that area, stations which had once been flourishing concerns like his own but which had come on hard times. His father had been a careful manager, and there was a little money left in the homestead for emergencies. Jamie had considered this was one of them. He offered to buy some stock from the impoverished farmers that were in better condition than his own, and was treated generously when they realised he had returned from the war.

As he drove his sheep before him, the rain began—just a light rain to begin with and then it poured, coming down like stair rods. Jamie stopped, keeping the sheep together with the help of the dogs, until it eased sufficiently to continue on his journey. Once he reached Seven Creeks, the troughs were filling with water as he drove the sheep into the enclosure. If this rain continued for a few weeks, the creeks would fill up and the earth would turn from a dust bowl into good grazing land.

As he went to stable his horse, he was surprised to see Kathleen waiting for him in one of the stalls.

"It's no good, Kathleen. I thought I'd made it clear that I don't want you, so get inside out of the rain."

"Just listen to me, Jamie. I haven't come for that. I have something to tell you that will surprise you. You might not want Shaun to inherit Seven Creeks because you can't be sure he is your son, but you have no right to it either." Kathleen spat out the words meaning to repay him for his indifference to her.

Jamie swung round from unsaddling the horse. "You lie, you bitch! What can you know about anything?"

"I know more than you do. When your pa died your ma was in such a state. She thought you must have been killed because she hadn't heard from you for such a long time that she talked and talked about you. She wanted Shaun to have Seven Creeks if you never came home because she loves him, and she likes to think he is your son. She loves you too but you're *not* her son, Jamie—they adopted you when you were a baby."

"Get out, you Jezebel! You're making this up because I don't want you."

"Why don't you ask your ma, Jamie? Perhaps your real ma was a whore as you're so fond of calling me. It wasn't Rosie—that's for sure."

Kathleen laughed at the look of unbelief on his face and picking up her skirts she ran across the stockyard and into the homestead.

Jamie was left in a state of shock and disbelief. She had told him out of spite, that was obvious, but was it the truth? Only his mother knew that, and he would have to ask her, although he hardly knew how to approach such a delicate subject with her. Was he his father's son or did he have completely different parents from both the people he thought of as his own? They had been good parents to him and had loved him as he had loved them. If this was true then the grandparents who had lived with them during their last years were not related to him either. Did his parents know his real parents or was he an orphan or a foundling child? The questions worried him so much he rubbed down the horse quickly, gave him a sparse handful of feed, and went into the kitchen to speak to his mother.

Kathleen was nowhere to be seen, which did not surprise him. Perhaps now this information had come to light his mother would get rid of her and her bastard child.

If she had wanted him to know then surely Rosie would have told him herself, unless there was something about his birth which she had wanted to keep secret.

His mother was taking the newly baked bread out of the oven and turning them out of the tins as he entered.

"Thank God the rains have come at last, Jamie. If it comes down like this for the next few weeks, we shall all be saved."

Jamie pulled a chair out from under the table and sat down opposite her.

"Ma, I have to ask you this for my own peace of mind."

He sounded so serious that Rosie wiped her floury hands on her pinafore and sat down to listen, hoping it was not going to be another tirade about Kathleen.

"Well?"

"Kathleen told me something just now which I find hard to believe and only you know the truth of it."

Rosie sighed. It *was* about Kathleen, as she had feared.

"Am I your own child, or did you and Pa adopt me?"

Rosie stared at him in disbelief. So the truth was to come out at last, the truth she and Rory had intended he should never be told. And now that Rory was dead it was left to her to say as little as possible—just enough to satisfy his curiosity.

"I told Kathleen when we thought you were never coming home. Rory had just died, and I was feeling depressed and was concerned about the future of the sheep station. I would never have told her otherwise, and now I wish with all my heart that I had said nothing to her. She is not the kind of person to keep her mouth shut."

"So, it's true then—she wasn't lying just to get her own back."

"No, son, she wasn't lying. Rory and I adopted you when you were just a few months old. Your mother, who felt she could not raise you as her own, offered you to us. Her circumstances were very difficult at the time, and, as your pa and I had never been blessed with children, we were overjoyed to bring you home with us."

"I suppose I was born out of wedlock, then?"

"Oh no, not at all. She was married to your father."

"What did he think about it? Did he want me to be adopted?"

"He knew nothing about it. He was killed before you were born, and she, poor little thing, was nearly out of her mind with grief."

"Who was she—my mother, I mean?"

"I can't tell you that, son. We were only allowed to have you if we promised faithfully not to disclose the names of your parents to you, and I cannot go back on that promise. It was a terrible sacrifice for your mother to part with you, as you look so like your father, but Rory and I have loved you dearly to compensate for not being your real parents. We were as proud of you as if you were our own flesh and blood."

"You've certainly done that, and I thank you for it, Ma, but I wish you had told me before. It comes hard to be told by someone like Kathleen."

Rosie sighed. "She had no right, knowing that you knew nothing about it, but I can't blame her—you have been very unkind about Shaun and *his* birth, and that must have hurt her badly."

Jamie got up and went to the door. "I shall want to know more about them, Ma. Not their names, as you made a promise, but how my father was killed and how you knew the family, but that can wait. I've heard enough for one day."

Rosie went back to sorting out the loaves. It was a relief in a way to think that he knew, but she did not look forward to what else he might ask her in case she let slip something that he could pick up on. She needed to protect him from the truth, as she feared it would prey on his mind for the rest of his life.

In the stockyard, Jamie found two men who had been employed by his father waiting to speak to him. Now the rains had come, they hoped there might be some work for them, as the long drought had meant no earnings.

"Sorry to hear about your pa, Mr. Macdonald, but it's good that you came back safely. We'd be glad to do anything if you can give us work."

Jamie would have been glad of their help but he had no money to pay them as yet.

"If you'll mend some of the fences in the home paddock I'll pay you when I've sold some of the new lambs from these ewes. In the meantime, you can shoot any wild animals on the pastures for yourselves. The 'roos will be eating the grass as soon as it sprouts, and I need it all for the sheep. Despite the drought, there are still rabbits about—a bit tough, but edible. I'll give you the shot—kill as many as you can."

The men decided it was better than nothing as there was no work to be had. Rory Macdonald had been a man to trust, and they hoped his son would keep his word. Jamie set them to work immediately. He wanted to buy some more stock to get started and the sooner the better, once the fences had been mended.

Kathleen, hearing men's voices, watched from the side of the house. Now she had betrayed Rosie's confidence, she feared that her days at Seven Creeks were numbered, but she had nowhere to go apart from the old shack she had once called home, where her sister's family still lived in filthy squalor. It had been hard of late living at Seven Creeks, receiving slights and rebuffs from Jamie however hard she had tried to interest him, and there was no fun in the constant round of housework and cooking and cleaning. She had had enough of domesticity. It had led nowhere after all her hopes for a future with Jamie. She was no more than an unpaid servant with just her board and lodging for her keep, and she longed for her old lifestyle where she had had fun and the freedom to be with any man who wanted her. She still had her looks, so why wait until Rosie died and Jamie booted her out, which was sure to happen. As the sheep station grew in size, there would be more men about the place, and she could take her pick, whatever Jamie thought about her behaviour and perhaps, if she was lucky, she might find someone who would take her and Shaun away with them.

The rain continued to fall for many weeks, and the land took on a new life. The streams ran with water again and fish appeared in the creeks as if by magic. The sheep grew fat and suckled their lambs in green pastures. Jamie sold most of the fat lambs and increased his flock with pregnant Merino ewes so that, come shearing time, he would double the amount of fine wool clip to sell. Apart from the sheep, he now invested in shorthorn cattle and planted a citrus grove. Whatever the fluctuations in the market, he must find other ways to make money. Overgrazing the land in a state of partial recovery would be fatal, and he hoped his venture into fruit growing would help them to get back to a position of financial profit, until the pastures would support thousands of sheep as they had done in his father's lifetime.

Kathleen remained at Seven Creeks, but the atmosphere in the homestead was unsustainable. She was sullen and unresponsive when spoken to, and Shaun reacted to her obvious unhappiness by becoming a miserable, whining child. Rosie knew that something had gone badly wrong, and that her plans for Jamie to marry Kathleen would never be realised. She could do nothing with Shaun and was at her wits end to know what to do for the best. The matter resolved itself at shearing time when a team of jackaroos came to live in the bunkhouse. Kathleen had been waiting for this moment and would slip away from her duties to flirt with the men in the great woolshed whenever Jamie's back was turned.

As soon as she appeared, the atmosphere changed, and once they realised she was only a servant in the house, there were hoots and catcalls as she made up to one or the other of them, encouraging them to slip out for a few moments for a brief sexual encounter. Kathleen was enjoying herself—it was like her old life, and she took every opportunity to satisfy her carnal cravings. The leader of one of the teams was a strong young man of handsome appearance and reminded her of the Jamie she had once known and loved. He was her favourite, and when it was time for the team to pack up and leave for the next sheep station, they had made a pact to be together when the season was finished. He promised to return for her and to take her with him. When Kathleen had mentioned she had a child he had his doubts at first but she had such allure and beauty that he was besotted with her and decided it was worth the risk.

"The kid can stay with my sister in Echuca," he told her. "That's where I stay when the shearing is over. I pick fruit at the end of the summer—mandarins and oranges. They take women on to do the packing these days—not enough men for the job. You'll earn some good money doing that, and can pay my sister for looking after the kid. She'll be glad of that—she has five of her own to feed and every little helps in times like these."

Kathleen was happy at last—her life was showing promise, and he was her type of man—lustful and as handsome as any man she had known.

Jamie, meanwhile, had been thinking over the mystery of his parentage. While in the woolshed watching the shearing, he remembered the story of his father's great win on the favourite, Carbine, who had won The Melbourne Cup in 1890, which had enabled him to build the woolshed. He had been told of the wonderful excitement of the race by his mother, who had been there too, and of her delight in wearing a fashionable dress of rose pink taffeta. Years ago, she had unearthed the little silk fan his father had bought her printed with the official programme. When the fan had come to light among her treasured belongings, she had become quite excited and had described Flemington racecourse to him and the wonderful day she had spent there with his father. He could hear her voice now; it had been like hearing a tale from a storybook to his young ears, and he smiled wistfully at the memory.

"Wherever you looked, Jamie, there were trainers and owners, bookies, and touts, all mingling with the huge crowds. Everyone from Melbourne had turned out to see the race because Carbine was so famous. There was only one other horse in the running, which nearly overtook him at the winning post and that was Harry's Boy, but he fell and had to be killed. It was terrible to watch because the rider was killed too. We never went again. It was the first real holiday we had found time for in over twenty years, and I shall never forget it. The beautiful lawns and the flower beds and the large grassy areas for the general public who were unable to afford a seat, and the lovely dresses and the huge hats—and then all spoilt by a tragedy—well, not altogether ..."

Rosie had never mentioned it again, but he had never forgotten it because that year, the year of the famous race, had been the year of his birth, and whenever he had told people they would remark—"Why that was the year the great Carbine won the Melbourne Cup, wasn't it?" It seemed to have stuck in most people's memories, and now that he knew it had been the same year that his real father had been killed it became even more important. Jamie decided to see if he could find Rosie's official programme of the race, if it was still among her possessions. Could it have been his father who had been riding Harry's Boy? He needed to find out the name of the jockey or the owner. It might be a long shot but it was worth a try. Asking Rosie would get him nowhere—she was determined to keep it a secret from him, which had made him all the more anxious to try to find out for himself.

Looking among his mother's few treasures did not appeal to him, as he had no wish to upset her, and he let the matter rest for a while, wondering if he could ask her in a casual manner without arousing her suspicions, until he found her box left on the kitchen table by chance. She had been amusing Shaun by showing him some of her trinkets and had left them there while she went outside to speak to his mother.

Jamie picked up the pink fan, which showed the runners in the different races, and quickly found what he was looking for before Rosie returned.

"What silly things I've collected over the years," laughed Rosie. "I've even got a curl from your hair when you were a baby, like every other proud mother. I've been showing it to Kathleen."

"And does it match her child's hair, Ma? Somehow I doubt it."

"Well, not exactly—but children's hair changes colour as they get older, and I can't remember exactly how old you were when I cut off this curl."

Jamie left her—would she never give up this obsession she had to pin Shaun's parentage onto him. If only the child had not meant so much to her, things could have been so very different. He could have brought Laura here, and they might have been expecting a family by now. The thought of that choked him. What had happened to her for God's sake? There was no way he could find out, and it tore him to pieces just thinking about her and the suffering his desertion must have caused her.

He needed to find out who he was, and if his own mother was still alive, and that need had become very important to him. Perhaps he would find he had half brothers or sisters, with lives of their own. He had found out just now from the race programme that Harry's Boy had come from the Trevern Stables, and the jockey had been an Adam Trevern. Jamie had never heard the name before, so perhaps the stables had ceased to exist. The war had made many changes. Nothing would be the same again now so many of the young men would not be coming home. He would make enquiries around the Goulbourn region as he travelled about and maybe the name would strike a chord in someone's memory. It was very probable that the stables had been in the State of Victoria as the race was held in Melbourne.

Jamie asked without success and decided to make a different approach to Rosie, getting her to talk to him about her teenage years and how she had ended up in Seven Creeks with Rory, hoping he might glean some information about the places and the people she had met once she and her father had settled in Australia.

He had often been told of her long journey as a child of eight, travelling from Downham in Lancashire to embark on the clipper ship, *The Fair Maid*, at Salt Dock in Liverpool. Her mother had died of tuberculosis whilst they had been at sea, and the woman who had later become her stepmother had cared for her on the ship. Rosie had disliked her. Amy Briggs was stern and cared little for children but had made herself indispensable to her father, who had later married her once they were settled in Clay Cross. The marriage had not been a success, and Rosie's father had left his wife to go away with Beth Macdonald, the owner of the Clay Cross store, to set up a sheep station at Seven Creeks. Rory was one of her sons and the love of Rosie's life, and once they had married they too had lived at Seven Creeks to help to develop the station.

Jamie knew all of this—it was old history and had often been the subject of his grandfather's tales as he had been growing up, but what had happened to Rosie in between had rarely been discussed.

After the evening meal was finished that night, when Rosie was settled in her chair on the verandah, Jamie came to join her. Rosie was surprised. He had often smoked a pipe with Rory after a meal, but she never remembered him sitting down to chat with her. Perhaps something was troubling him, and she hoped it had nothing to do with Kathleen again. Things had been better with Kathleen of late.

"Ma, I've been thinking."

"Oh, yes—what about?"

"Why, about you and Pa. I don't really know a lot about you, and as you are the only people I could call my family, I should know you better."

"But I thought your grandpa, God rest him, used to tell you stories all the time about the old country. It gave him a lot of pleasure to recall the past."

"Of course he did—and he told me all about your journey on the ship, the terrors of the storm, and being becalmed in the doldrums and the rest of it, but he didn't tell me much about the other passengers, perhaps because he preferred to forget your stepmother and the unhappiness she brought him."

"Maybe, but I was the one who suffered the most—she used to beat me you know."

"Oh Ma!" Jamie was shocked. Rosie was the kindest of people, and he could never believe she had been a wicked child.

"It's best forgotten, son. When your grandpa found out, he left her, and we went to live with Beth Macdonald. I went to school with Rory, you know—a right little tomboy I was in those days.

There was a terrible flood in Clay Cross one year, and my stepmother was drowned. Beth's store was flooded out, and they decided to take their savings and buy a grazing plot in Seven Creeks."

"Did you go with them then?"

"Oh no—I'd left school and went as a nursemaid to some people we'd met on the clipper ship, and Rory was working in Pendle's Hotel in Clay Cross as a boot boy. We were too young to settle down then, and we didn't have any money anyway. We both had our keep in our jobs so we were provided for and my pa and Rory's ma left and made a life of their own."

"I never knew you'd been a nursemaid. Where was that?"

"In a big house overlooking Port Philip Bay. The people were called Potts. He was a haberdasher in Melbourne. He had a lovely wife who was so kind to me on the journey, but she died soon after we landed. Then he married Lizzie, whom he had met on the boat. She and her sister, Sarah, had gone to work in the haberdashery and Lizzie made a dead set at him. He built The Great House for her when he knew that she was pregnant with his first child. My father wrote to Mr. Potts to ask him if he had a job for me when I left school. He imagined I would work in the shop, but Lizzie wanted another young nursemaid when her second child was born so I went there to live, to help out in the nursery."

"Did you enjoy it?"

"It was a lovely place, but Master Arty was a terrible handful, and he was my responsibility. Master Percy was even worse, he was so spoilt being the eldest, and then there were more children while I was there, Henry, and later a girl."

"Quite a brood—hard work I should think for a young girl to look after—how old were you then?"

"I was fourteen when I began to work there, but there was a much older nursemaid who took responsibility."

"How long did you stay?"

"For a few years, until Mr. Potts became impossible to work for—no girl was safe from him. He drank a lot after his wife left him, and we were all afraid to be near him. He had a stroke in the end, and Miss Sarah took over the running of the household. I went back to Clay Cross and lived in as a chambermaid at the Anchor. It was a big place in those days, and the river skippers used to stay there while doing up their boats before going up the Murrumbidgee River to collect the wool clip."

"Was Pa still there, at the other hotel?"

Rosie chuckled. "The owner's daughter had taken a fancy to him so he decided to leave in a hurry. He joined a team of drovers and went off up country to seek his fortune."

Jamie laughed. "That sounds like, Pa. Did he come back for you?"

"Not exactly—I was going upstream with one of the skippers, who used to be a regular visitor at the Anchor, when I saw your pa at one of the collecting stations. The skipper had asked me to marry him, and I was trying to make up my mind when I saw Rory, and that decided it. I'd always loved him, since we were at school together, but when he left Clay Cross in such a hurry I never expected to see him again. I didn't want to turn into a crabby old spinster like my stepmother."

Jamie knocked out his pipe and stood up. "You'd never have been like that, Ma."

Rosie looked up at him and smiled. Things seemed to be getting back to normal again at Seven Creeks.

"By the way—I shall be gone for a few days. I have things to see to, like the dates of the next sales and where they are to be held. You'll be all right with Kathleen here, won't you? I'll see that everything is taken care of while I'm away."

"Of course—we've been without you around before. I'll be fine—no worries."

Jamie had decided to go walkabout. The need to find his roots was always on his mind, and now that he knew a bit more about the places where Rosie had worked, it was a beginning. Somebody she had known in the past had given him to her—of that he felt sure. Perhaps he could find out a bit about the people who had once lived in The Great House that might lead him to solve the mystery of his birth. He would take a ride into Melbourne and search out Potts Famous Haberdashery. Did that still belong to another generation of the family? And while he was there he could visit Flemington and look through the old records of the Melbourne Cup races.

Jamie set off in high hopes on his journey into the past.

CHAPTER 38

It was no long distance to Melbourne and Jamie left his horse at a tavern where he intended to spend his first night and walked into the city. He took a tram ride around the main streets until it made its steep descent down Collins Street, where he saw Potts Famous Haberdashery from the window. As soon as the tram came to a stop Jamie alighted and made his way back to peer into the windows. Ladies fashions were displayed on the dummies, and other items of underwear were to be seen. Jamie felt as if he would be too embarrassed to go through the glass doors until he noticed a display of hand-painted fans. He would buy one as a present for Rosie—she loved pretty things, and he felt sure that she would appreciate it. Plucking up his courage, Jamie went into the shop and spoke to one of the young girls behind the counter. Once he had chosen a fan, he began to ask about the Potts family.

Did the family still own the shop, he wondered? His mother had known Arthur Potts and his wife while she was a child and always spoke highly of them.

The girl knew nothing; she was only a junior employee, but Mrs. Henry might be able to tell him a bit about the family if he didn't mind waiting while she fetched her.

Jamie waited, feeling awkward, and wondered who Mrs. Henry might be—perhaps the new owner.

A tall, willowy woman in her fifties came out of the back room to speak to him.

"Mrs. Henry Potts," she said, offering him her hand. "How can I help you?"

"I wondered if the family still owned the business?" said Jamie. "Forgive me for asking but my mother worked for the Potts family many years ago. I happened to be in Melbourne and on seeing the haberdashery from the tram, it occurred to me that she would like to have news of the family."

"I see—well what can I tell you? How was she employed here?"

"When she was very young, she was a nursemaid to the family, at The Great House.

She has often mentioned the children she cared for—Arty and Percy in particular."

"Percy was killed as a little boy riding along the strand on his horse—no doubt she has told you about that—and Arty died of drink a few years ago. There is only Henry left now, my husband."

"Wasn't there a daughter? I'm sure she mentioned a little girl who was born just before she left."

"Ah, yes—Hetty—but she left the family years ago, and I'm afraid we have lost contact with her over the years."

"Thank you. My mother will be so glad to know that the haberdashery is still in existence. She came to Australia with the Potts, on the clipper ship, *The Fair Maid*, with her father. Her mother died at sea and the then Mrs. Potts was very kind to her."

"I never knew the first Mrs. Potts, but I've been told she was a very kind and generous woman." Mrs. Henry smiled a warm friendly smile. "And what was your mother's name before she married—when she worked as a nursemaid to the family?"

"Taylor—she was Rosie Taylor."

The smile was suddenly wiped off Mrs. Henry's face. "I'm sorry I can't stay any longer," she said and disappeared through the curtain into the back room, leaving Jamie at a loss. Had he said something to offend her? Nothing that he could think of— one minute she was there, and the next she had gone.

Jamie picked up his parcel and left, none the wiser.

The next day, he rode into Flemington and asked to look through the records of the Melbourne Cup. He explained that he had a special interest in the race of 1890 as his father had won a great deal of money on Carbine, and the details of the race interested him. The racing papers of that year were given to him, and he sorted them out until he came to the day of the Melbourne Cup. There was a long article about the race that had described the wild and rash manner in which Adam Trevern had ridden Harry's Boy that day.

"Trevern rode like a lunatic" had been one headline. "Death of a rider of great promise" had been another. Jamie read all the articles and one in particular which had taken his attention. "Harry Trevern of the Trevern Stables at High Ridge, Victoria, has sworn never to race again. He has lost his only son and will now close his racing stables. This is a great blow to all those who value the quality of his brood mares. He will be sadly missed from the race meetings where his expertise as a rider and trainer was appreciated by all."

So the stables were no more and must have been closed for many years. Jamie wondered what had happened to him, but nobody at Flemington knew—he must be very old by now, even if he was still alive. The only thing he had found out was the name of the place where the stables had once been—High Ridge. Once he had been to see The Great House on Port Philip Bay, he would see if he could find High Ridge before he returned to Seven Creeks. He would have been away for the best part of a week and Rosie would begin to wonder why finding out about the sheep sales could have taken him so long.

Jamie set off along the coast road towards the peninsula, admiring the superb sea views as he went. He had never had the opportunity to travel in this direction before, as his life had been totally involved in the breeding and shearing of sheep. Holidays had been a day off fishing, or perhaps a day at a local race meeting with a picnic tea. The beauty of the aquamarine sea as the waves rolled in over the silver sand almost took his breath away. No wonder Arthur Potts had built The Great House along this coastline. His mother had been right when she had described it as a most beautiful place. A few more miles and Jamie could see the house, standing on a rise above the strand with tea trees growing along the edge of the sand. He decided on his arrival to leave the horse at the gate and to walk up the drive thinking that maybe it would be considered more suitable to call at the back door under the circumstances.

The long, two-storied house stood at the end of the drive, surrounded by lawns of buffalo grass which stretched almost to the shoreline, and a large Morton Bay fig tree spread its shade over an artificial lake where black swans and waterfowl lived. The only person to be seen was an old lady asleep in a wicker basket chair in the shade of the fig tree. Jamie walked on the grass rather than disturb her, as his boots crunched on the gravel driveway. Large plaster urns filled with arum lilies and brilliant geraniums stood on either side of the entrance, and a long verandah covered by flowering creepers stretched the length of the house. Shutters were across most of the windows, giving the place an unlived-in appearance. It was very quiet, almost as if the house and its occupants were all asleep. Jamie went round to the back door and knocked. There was no reply, so he walked round to the side of the house where he could see a woman wearing a white apron, picking flowers from a long border.

"G'day, ma'am." The woman looked up, surprised to see him. "Sorry to bother you, but I've come to make some enquiries about the Potts family. My ma used to work here years ago, and as I was in the area I thought—"

The woman smiled. "Of course, but I'm only the housekeeper—a companion really to Miss Sarah. She used to look after the family, but they've all fled the nest now, and she's very old and needs looking after herself."

"That was Miss Sarah I saw in the chair, was it?"

"That's right. She sleeps most of the time these days, and rarely knows one day from the other, but she's no trouble."

"I called in to the shop while I was in Melbourne and had a word with Mrs. Henry. She told me Percy and Arty were both dead, and that they had lost contact with Miss Hetty. So Mr. Henry is the last of the family it would seem."

"Hetty is still alive and well, I believe. She used to keep in contact with Miss Sarah— she brought her up when her mother left—but once Hetty married, the family had no interest in her whereabouts."

"Seems a bit hard," ventured Jamie.

"She wasn't a Potts by birth—it was a family thing. You know how it is—blood is thicker than water, and they were a proud family."

"I see," said Jamie, who did not see at all. "Who did she marry—do you know?"

"A young man called Trevern; he was killed in a race. She went to live with her father afterwards and later married into a wealthy New South Wales family. After that, she moved right away, which upset poor Miss Sarah a great deal, and she began to lose interest in life."

"What an unhappy family," remarked Jamie.

"Yes, money isn't everything, is it?" said the housekeeper. "Would you like me to wake Miss Sarah? She might like to know about your mother."

"She was a nursemaid here many years ago, when Percy and Arty were little boys and Mr. Henry was a toddler."

The housekeeper laughed. "She'll not remember so long ago—she has a job to remember what she did yesterday."

"Then please don't bother her." Jamie tipped his hat. "It's been real good to talk to you. Thank you."

As he mounted his horse, he looked back through the decorative iron gates to this house of secrets. *Why didn't they want to talk about the only daughter?* he wondered.

What had she done, and was it anything to do with himself? He was never going to get anything out of the Potts family members who were still alive, and he would have to look elsewhere if he was ever going to discover his true identity.

He travelled on his way, passing through the coastal towns and making enquiries about a place known as High Ridge. Perhaps he was going in the wrong direction altogether. Jamie had nearly given up the search when he came to Rye and asked another horseman, who directed him inland.

"It's mostly bush," he told him. "You won't find many dwellings there."

"I'm looking for the Trevern Stables—ever heard of it?"

"No—but the name rings a bell. I think there's a vineyard by that name somewhere around."

Jamie thanked him and pressed on. It would be dark soon, but he wanted to find it even if it meant spending a night in the bush. It was a strange name, and if he found another passerby they might be able to direct him, otherwise he would have to give up the search and return to Euroa.

He came across the notice quite by chance, at a rough crossroads in the bush. A piece of wood was hanging from one nail with the words scratched roughly on the surface—The Trevern Vineyards. The rough path seemed uninviting, winding through the vines to a homestead in the distance. As he rode on, he was aware of a strange putrid smell and hoped he would soon be at the end of the rows of evil smelling vines. By the time he had reached the homestead, it was almost dark and a black came out to meet him carrying a storm lamp.

"You come to see Harry?" he asked.

"Sorry it's so late—I had a job to find you—what's the smell around here for Gawd's sake?"

"The vines—we got phylloxera—it's wiping out the vineyard."

"I've never heard of it."

"No? Well, come on in. Is Harry expecting you?"

"No—I've come on the off chance that he'll see me."

"What's your name, mate?"

"Jamie. Jamie Mcdonald. I come from near Euroa."

Jamie was introduced, and the black left the storm lantern to light up the bleak room. Harry Trevern was sitting in a leather swivel chair and swung it round to view his visitor. He held up his glass in a gesture of welcome.

"Drink?" he asked. Jamie nodded. "Then help yourself. Have you come about the vineyard? The boys are about to uproot the lot of it—let it turn into grazing land again. I'm letting it, hopefully."

"I expected to find stables here," said Jamie. "I read how you'd decided never to breed racing stock again, but I thought you might still have some horses."

"Only a couple for my own use. Is that what you're here for?"

Harry pulled himself out of his chair with difficulty and turned to face Jamie. His leathery face became twisted with disbelief, and he dropped his glass onto the floor.

"Come back to haunt me, have you?" he croaked. "I've been drinking too much again."

He slumped back into his chair, a pathetic old man, with tears running down his cheeks, unable to control his shaking hands.

Jamie went to the door to fetch help, but there was nobody around. He was considering leaving there and then when Harry called out to him.

"Who are you? Tell me your name."

"Jamie Macdonald—I came here in the hope that I might find out something about my father, but I don't think you can help me. I'm sorry if I upset you."

"It's the likeness that's upset me. I thought I was seeing things. You look so like my dead son, Adam, it's uncanny. He meant everything to me after I lost his mother. He was all I had left you see ..."

"I understand," said Jamie. "I've been reading about the Melbourne Cup Race where he was killed trying to beat Carbine. I'm so sorry to have brought all that sorrow back to you."

"He wasn't trying to beat Carbine—that's where they got it all wrong—they didn't know. He committed suicide. I knew what he was doing, and so did Hetty, poor girl."

Jamie was shocked. What skeletons had he unearthed in his search for his real parents? He should have left well alone; he realised that now it was too late.

"Hetty? Do you mean Hetty Potts, by any chance?"

"She may have been known by that name but her real name was Trevern. She was my daughter."

Jamie felt puzzled. "She was married to your son, I understood from the newspaper cutting, so she was your daughter-in-law, wasn't she?"

"She was also my daughter and without realising it she had married Adam, who was her blood brother. When they found out what they had done, she was pregnant. It was a horror which could have been avoided had her Aunt Sarah allowed my poor Lizzie to bring her here to grow up with her brother, but she had been left as guardian to the children when Arthur Potts died, and she loved Hetty too much to part with her."

Gradually, a realisation began to grow in Jamie's mind, which he tried to put aside hoping it did not concern him in any way.

"Forgive my asking, as it is none of my business, but was their child born in 1890?"

"Yes, soon after the race when poor Adam died—why do you ask?"

Jamie was silent for a long time, fearing that he was that child, yet unhappy about asking this poor old man to rake through his memories any further.

Harry looked at him searchingly. "You have Adam's curly dark brown hair and my lovely Lizzie's eyes—no wonder I thought you were Adam's ghost. Who are your parents? Tell me—"

Jamie felt himself shaking under the gaze of the penetrating eyes that stared at him so full of a desperate kind of hope, as if he had come back from the dead.

"I was adopted by Rory and Rosie Macdonald in 1890. They had gone to the Melbourne Cup that year when my pa had won enough money to build our woolshed, so the date was an important one for them. I never knew I had been adopted until recently. Ma refused to tell me who my parents were—she had been sworn to secrecy by my real mother—but I was determined to find out. Everyone has the right to know who they really are—"

"But now you wish you had failed in your search?"

"Not really—I've found you, haven't I—although discovering I'm the product of an incestuous relationship has been a shock, I must admit."

"Say nothing to your adoptive parents. It will hurt them—but come and see me when you can. Stay a while and tell me about yourself; it will be a comfort to me—it's as if you've been sent by those who have passed on."

"I must leave tomorrow. Pa had just died of the flu when I returned from the war, and there is such a lot to do to get the station back on its feet, although now the rain has come things are improving gradually. Ma will worry if I am absent too long—you understand."

"Of course, but say you will come again. I remember Rosie—a good woman who cared for Hetty when the baby started after she had seen Adam fall from his horse. She stayed for a while to look after the baby at The Great House. The family knew her from the old days when she had worked for them as a nursemaid. It was a blessing that she was at the race at that terrible time."

"I was born there was I? At The Great House?"

"Indeed you were—do you know it?"

"Oh, yes. I visited it in my search, but I found out nothing there."

Harry gave a wan smile. "That doesn't surprise me. When Lizzie ran away to be with me and was eventually divorced from Arthur, they wanted nothing more to do with her. She rarely saw her other children either—Arthur forbade it.

She died in a forest fire when Adam was still a small boy, so Adam became even more precious to me. Look, here they are in this photograph—it's all I have left of them both."

Jamie was handed a sepia-coloured photograph of a beautiful woman with a small boy on her lap. He realised with a jolt that he was looking at his grandmother and his father—his real family. If only they were flesh and blood and could speak to him.

"And what about my real mother, your daughter—is she still alive?"

"Hetty married a wealthy man from New South Wales. She used to stay with me when she discovered I was her father but after she married she no longer came here. We have too much sorrow between us to want to see each other anymore. Don't search her out, Jamie—it would be too cruel. She has another family now and a different life and will have tried to forget you. Let the past remain in the past, for her sake. You will both be happier that way."

They talked long into the night, sharing each other's memories, until the early morning sun began to rise. Jamie told him of his love for Laura and the heartbreak it had caused when he had been unable to keep his promise to her. Harry was sympathetic, knowing the loss of a great love himself. He wished he could do something to help, but his grandson's problem seemed insurmountable, and all he could do was to listen as Jamie unburdened himself. It had been a relief after all this time for Jamie to find someone to whom he could talk about his innermost thoughts and who appeared to understand his suffering. His love for Laura was unchanged, and there would never be anyone else in his life but her.

Jamie left early the next morning, promising his grandfather that he would return to visit him whenever possible. It had meant a great deal to both of them to have met each other, and, for Jamie, it was the end of a quest to solve the mystery of his birth.

On his return to the homestead, he found Rosie in a state of great consternation. Kathleen had gone and had taken Shaun with her, and she wondered how she would ever get over the loss of the child she considered her grandson.

"Not even a word about going, after the years she had lived here with us, the ungrateful girl," moaned Rosie. "She took everything she could lay her hands on, including some of my best china—it must have been planned—someone must have come for her. She could never have carried everything by herself."

"I was out of the way, so I suppose she thought it would be easier to leave unnoticed," said Jamie, who was secretly thankful to hear that Kathleen had gone at last. "When did she leave?"

"It must have been last night when I was in bed. I heard nothing and found them gone when I called them to breakfast."

"Never mind, Ma. We can't do anything about it. Knowing Kathleen, there must have been a man behind all this. She made a nuisance of herself with the jackaroos, so I was told, flirting and carrying on with them whenever my back was turned—she's man mad is Kathleen. I shall never understand why you considered her to be the kind of woman I would ever want to marry. She's a—"

"Don't say it, Jamie, please."

"All right, Ma. Let's forget her now—she's gone for good, and we've got our lives to get on with—eh?"

Jamie put his arm round her, and Rosie calmed down.

"I'm glad you're back, son. Did you find out what you went for?"

Jamie nodded. This was not the time to tell her he had discovered his roots, and he decided to keep that information to himself until a more propitious time.

CHAPTER 39

Every few months, Jamie rode over to High Ridge to see his grandfather, and a bond of friendship developed between the two men. Harry took more of an interest in life and drank less as a result and made Jamie feel part of his family. They rode together around Harry's estate, which encompassed a large area of native bush, stretching across the peninsula from shoreline to shoreline, inhabited mostly by kangaroos. Harry had cleared the area around the homestead where his horses had once grazed and which had later been planted by vines. These had been uprooted, and the land had soon reverted to grass and scrub, which he now let to a neighbour for his cattle.

Jamie discovered that the homestead had been wiped out in the forest fire that had killed Lizzie many years before. Harry had wanted to leave the area afterwards but decided to rebuild for Adam's sake. Adam had been four years old at the time of his mother's death, saved from the fire by the quick thinking of his aboriginal nurse, who had held him in the stream nearby.

"You employ a lot of blacks, Harry," Jamie had remarked on one occasion.

Harry had laughed and had pointed to a couple of men in the distance.

"They're your relations too, Jamie—some more black than the others. When I brought Lizzie here she had to accept that I had lived with two black women in the past and there were some of my children here. Lizzie had to take me for what I was—a man with a past life.

I lived so far from respectable society out here that nobody knew anything about me. A man has the right to live as he pleases. I stole an unhappy beautiful woman from her pompous little husband and made her happy. He divorced her, and we married, for her sake. She wanted people to respect her, but they never did—they turned their backs on her—even her sister, Sarah."

"If you were happy together then what did it matter?"

"It mattered because her sister agreed with Arthur and kept her children away from her—especially Hetty, and Hetty was my child. She was only a few weeks old when Lizzie left The Great House to come to me. Of course, Arthur Potts thought she was his daughter, but we knew better."

"I see." Jamie rode along in silence. It was a fluke that he had ever seen the light of day, yet he felt as normal as any man, and there must have been other people who had been born of an incestuous relationship who had never discovered the truth about their parentage and had led normal lives.

"Don't brood on it, son," said Harry. "It won't make a bit of difference to anything. I thank all the powers that be that you found me—it's like having my children here with me again. Come as often as you can and think of this as your home."

Every time Jamie returned to Seven Creeks, he wanted to talk to Rosie about Harry Trevern, but he found it impossible. He never told Rosie where he went on walkabout, and, after a while, Rosie stopped wondering. The sheep station was thriving—Rory would have been proud of him. He knew when to buy and when to sell, and the grove of citrus fruits had to be enlarged due to the demand for oranges, limes, and lemons. She had suggested he plant a vineyard, as they seemed to be springing up everywhere in the Goulburn area, especially around Nagambie, but Jamie seemed uninterested in the idea, saying he had enough irons in the fire for anyone to cope with at one time.

The homestead had been rebuilt with the profits from the sheep station, and Rosie had never been so comfortable. Jamie employed a kindly widow from Euroa who lived in as a companion to his mother and left him freer to visit Harry Trevern at High Ridge without Rosie noticing his absences so much—until one day, when a letter arrived from Harry's solicitor.

Jamie stood by the window, reading the long document and then folded it up carefully and put it back in its envelope. He stayed so long, staring into space that Rosie felt sure something was wrong.

"Is something the matter, son?"

"Not really."

"What is it, then? Surely you can tell me."

"I should have told you a long time ago, Ma—I'm sorry, but I couldn't face telling you in case you thought I was letting you down."

"Letting me down! What rubbish—you of all people."

"You'll have to hear me out, Ma, although you won't like some of the things I'm going to tell you."

Rosie sat down, wondering what all this could be about.

"I've been left an estate at High Ridge—this is a solicitor's letter giving me the legal details. It belonged to Harry Trevern, who died recently. I wasn't aware of his death, and the news has saddened me. Do you recall that name, Ma?"

"Of course I do—but how do you know him, Jamie? He can't mean anything to you, surely?"

"I sought him out when I was looking for my parents. He was very old, but he was able to tell me a lot about how it happened that you and Pa adopted me. He also told me that he was my grandfather—and that his children fell in love without realising they were related."

"Oh, Jamie. That's terrible. He ought never to have told you. I never wanted you to know—it was better not to know—you must realise that now."

"Yes, Ma, but I wanted to know—everyone has a right to know who their real parents are, and I searched him out."

"But I don't understand—how did you discover Harry Trevern had anything to do with your parents?"

"I put two and two together—the date of my birth and the fact that you had been at Flemington when Adam Trevern was killed—you told me my father had been killed before my birth, remember? It was a wild shot in the dark but it paid off."

Rosie put her head in her hands, fearful that she would lose the son she had cared for all his life now he knew the truth.

"Ma, I'm not blaming you or Pa for anything. You did a wonderful thing taking me home with you both when you knew the risks—I might have been damaged in some way, mentally or physically—but I'm fine in every respect."

"We didn't think of that at the time, Jamie. You were just a lovely baby, and we had wanted a baby of our own for years. We thought it was a miracle when you were handed to us by your mother."

"I'm amazed that Harry has left me his property. We'd built up quite a bond since I'd met him—he thought I was his son when we first met. Well, he had been drinking, but afterwards it seemed to have meant a lot to him, meeting me. I went over to see him every month or so—I couldn't tell you, Ma; you understand that, don't you?"

"Yes, I understand—but I don't share your feelings for Harry Trevern. He was a scoundrel when he was a young man, carrying on with Lizzie when her husband was absent, under the noses of the servants in The Great House. Everyone knew they were lovers except for Mr. Potts, and we were all upset when she ran away with him and left her baby behind."

"She should never have done that, I agree, but then I wouldn't be standing here, would I, if she had taken Hetty with her?"

Rosie shook her head. She wished he had left well alone.

"I went to The Great House when I was on my search. Miss Sarah was asleep in a basket chair on the lawn. I spoke to the housekeeper companion, but she could tell me nothing of interest. Still, I did see the house from the outside."

"What did you think of it? I loved living there."

"It was truly the most beautiful house I have ever seen, Ma. You were right. It was so grand and in such a beautiful place. The Potts family was most fortunate."

"In some ways, perhaps. It was a lovely place for the children—they had plenty of space and the sand and the sea just below the garden, but their mother left them when they were very young. They missed her and felt they had been deserted despite having people to look after them. It wasn't the same somehow after she had gone. Percy saddled up his little pony and went looking for her on his own. The saddle slipped and he fell off and struck his head on a stone and was killed. The pony dragged him home along the strand—can you imagine the horror of all that?"

"My Gawd! How terrible—no I can't."

This made Jamie see his grandfather in a different light. His selfish behaviour had affected the whole family, including the next generation.

He had grown fond of the old man and was glad he had been in ignorance of the past family history.

"The sins of the fathers," remarked Rosie sadly. "Well, what do you think you'll do with his estate?"

"Sell it, I suppose. The owner of the cattle might be interested in buying the grazing land, and there are the blacks to consider."

"The blacks—did he have blacks living on his property?"

"The property belongs more to them than to me, Ma. They're of his blood and have worked there all their lives. They deserve a share. I must ride over tomorrow and talk to them and see how they feel."

"He didn't deserve a grandson like you, Jamie," sighed Rosie.

"I might be gone a few days, Ma; there's a lot to see to."

Rosie nodded and picked up her needlework, her thoughts occupied with the past. How had Lizzie felt, she wondered, when she had found her lover had half-caste children running about the place? She must have been besotted with him to leave behind her comfortable home and her family, and, even if she had changed her mind later, there would have been no going back in those days.

Jamie rode over to High Ridge with the problem of sorting out his grandfather's estate uppermost in his mind. He had been left as the sole trustee and needed to see the solicitor. The will had been made fairly recently, and Jamie wondered if there had been an older will which might have taken other wishes into account before he had come into his grandfather's life. Harry's family gathered round him as he alighted from his horse, and he was aware of a certain hostility and suspicion towards him. Instead of the usual friendly greeting, there was silence.

"G'day to you. I came as soon as I heard that Harry was dead. I know you must be worried about the future, but you have no worries as far as I'm concerned. You have rights here, and I will see that those rights are protected. I don't intend to send you all packing, but, at the same time, I don't want to own this property, so some of it must be sold. I have my own sheep station at Euroa and have no need for this extra land so far from my home."

There was a murmur of relief amongst the men as Jamie stopped speaking.

"Choose a spokesman amongst you, and I will discuss your needs with him."

A coloured man older than himself was chosen, introducing himself as Harry's man in charge. Jamie could never remember having seen him around before and was quite taken aback at the man's likeness to himself but felt it unwise to ask if he was also a grandson. Harry had taken two aboriginal wives before Lizzie so he could easily have been related to him.

"Tell the men I want to be fair. I will give you part of the land on which to live, but not the grazing land as that is already let out."

There was a long discussion, and while Jamie was waiting for their decision, he went into the homestead to look around. Everything still seemed to be in order, and as there was nothing there that he wanted for himself he decided to sell it with the useable land. The stables were still there and could be a useful addition to the property.

Returning to the men, he found they had come to a decision. At the top of the highest land were some ancient stones that had been used by their ancestors during the dream time. This area was still sacred to them, and they requested a large part of the bush around them, which stretched down to the shoreline and incorporated an old aboriginal site. Jamie was happy for them to settle there in whatever way they wished. If they felt a need to return to the old ways of living, he would see they were never disturbed.

Once this was agreed, he set off to see Harry's solicitor in Frankston and finished the business of sorting out the estate. Apparently, Harry had only considered the making of a will once he had met his grandson. Jamie then met the owner of the cattle whose land bordered Harry's land to explain that he would be looking for a buyer shortly and would be advertising the land and the homestead.

After walking over the estate with Harry's foreman, Jamie returned home, amazed to discover what a huge area of land he had inherited. The sheep station was prospering, and the fruit was being sent to the markets around Melbourne. Despite the strikes and the depression in the cities, he was doing well and once Harry's property had been sold off, he would be a rich man. It was a satisfying prospect, but something was missing in his life; there was an ache in his heart that nobody but Laura could fill.

The sale of Harry's property took place a month later with much interest shown by the racing trainers in the area. His expertise in the racing world had been legendary and the fact that his old stable boys still lived somewhere adjacent to the property made it of interest to many breeders. The bidding was brisk and the Trevern estate made far more than Jamie had anticipated in his wildest dreams.

House prices near the city had slumped with the economic decline and Henry Potts decided to sell The Great House before prices dropped even further. Potts Famous Haberdashery needed an injection of money to keep it afloat, and now that Miss Sarah had been brought back to the house behind the business where her mental deterioration could be watched over more carefully, Henry decided to sell. His wife had grown to hate the house she referred to as the mausoleum. They had had no living children to enjoy the big rooms and the seashore, and she had no memories to attach her to the place. They only visited occasionally to see his aunt Sarah, and it cost a great deal for the upkeep.

It was stupid to hang on to it as the market was going. Who would want an imposing great house with a large garden in this day and age with money so hard to come by?

Henry put it on the market and advertised it in all the newspapers, hoping for the best.

When Jamie saw the advertisement, he was surprised. How could anyone want to part with such a property? Were the wealthy Pottses short of money like so many others in business? He showed the advertisement to Rosie and suggested he take her to see it for old time's sake. Rosie was delighted. The house was empty for prospective buyers to view, and the last she had seen of it had been when Rory had come to take her home with the baby.

Jamie got out the old cart, hitched up the horse and they set off towards Melbourne. It had been a long time since Rosie had made such a journey, and she felt as excited as she had done the first time she had been taken to The Great House. It was a beautiful day, and the sun sparkled on the waves as they rolled majestically towards the strand, dragging the shingle back in their tracks. When the old house came into view, she could scarcely contain her excitement.

"Look, Jamie—the shutters have all been opened, and there's someone waiting for us—did they expect us?"

"It's the agent, Ma. I told him to expect us today."

"But we're only going to look round, aren't we?"

"Of course, but we can't do that on our own. It still belongs to the Pottses. This is a viewing day for the public."

It was a novel experience for Rosie to alight at the front door and to be taken round her old home by someone who did not know it as well as she did, but she listened politely as the agent pointed out the different features.

"I didn't expect it still to be furnished. I thought it would be empty," she remarked.

"The furniture is included in the sale, ma'am. Is it to your taste?"

Rosie laughed. "My taste. What does that matter? It's rather grand for me but we're just looking, not *buying* it, aren't we, Jamie?"

"How would you feel, Ma, if I made an offer? It's been on the market for some time, and I think the Pottses would be glad to sell at a reasonable price."

Rosie was flabbergasted—to live in the house where she had once been the lowest of the low—a humble nursery maid. It defied belief.

"You were always telling me how much you loved it here, Ma."

"Well, yes—I know—but it's a house for a family, not just an old woman and her son, who would be off to see to the work going on at Seven Creeks most days."

"That's just what I thought; it's a family house—perhaps it's time I thought about that—I'm not getting any younger."

"Oh, son—is there someone I've never met—someone you've never mentioned?"

"You've never met her, Ma, but I've mentioned her enough times."

"You don't mean that girl you met in—"

"Yes, Laura. I'm going to find her if I can. She might be married by now, and, if so, then I'll come back without her, but a trip to England on one of the new liners would be something we'd both enjoy. You could go back to Downham and look at your childhood haunts, and I'll look for Laura and hope and pray she's still free and still feels for me as I do for her."

Rosie was speechless. What a day it had been, a day full of surprises.

"Well, Ma? What do you think? Shall I make an offer?"

Rosie nodded her assent, too overcome to speak.

CHAPTER 40

The journey back to the old country was different in every way from the one Rosie remembered from the time she had sailed off to Australia on *The Fair Maid*. She had been apprehensive at first when Jamie had suggested she should travel with him. The dreadful sea sickness she had suffered then and the frightening storms when everyone feared they were about to be drowned came back to haunt her before they embarked.

Jamie assured her that things would be different this time. They were going to travel first class, and she would be surrounded by luxury. The day of the clipper ships was long over and this time engines powered by steam would plough through the waves at a steady rate of knots. No more would she know the misery of being becalmed in the Doldrums for weeks on end with a poor diet of salt pork and hard ship's biscuits. This time, she would live like a lady.

Rosie was convinced. The homestead at Seven Creeks was left in the charge of her constant companion, the widow from Euroa, and the sheep station was to be managed by a trusted foreman. The shutters were closed at The Great House until such time as their return when Jamie hoped, if all went well, to move in with his wife. Until then, the gardeners were to keep the gardens in good shape and the housekeeper was to look after the interior of the house.

The gleaming white ship, the *Electra*, seemed enormous to Rosie as she walked up the gangway onto the shiny deck to be welcomed by the captain. Her cabin was so beautiful it was a delight to walk into, and the maid awaiting for her instructions to unpack her clothes made her feel like an honoured guest.

Meals were so grand and complicated she found it difficult to understand exactly what she was eating, especially when the menus were written mostly in French, and she often wished she could return to their usual simple fare at the homestead. Jamie was a success with all the ladies, and not only the single ones. His rugged good looks and his ever-ready smile and laughing eyes made him a sought-after companion, especially when the passengers realised he was single and the owner of a large property near Melbourne and a sheep station out in the bush.

As Rosie languished on deck in one of the long wooden deck chairs with stewards hovering close by to see to her every need, she would see Jamie in close conversation with one or the other of the elegant young women passengers who would be flirting madly, hoping to entrap him into an affair. Rosie began to wonder if he might change his mind about Laura before they even reached the shores of England. At least he had plenty of choice should that happen, not that she would feel very happy about it as she looked at the bobbed hair and the short skirts most of them wore. In the lounge, after dinner, they smoked cigarettes in long holders and draped themselves in an affected manner over the furniture in what Rosie presumed were elegant poses, showing off most of their shapely legs as they talked and laughed in loud voices.

There were dances every evening—the Charleston being the most popular—into which Jamie soon found himself drawn. The close proximity of so much female flesh and the drink made his head whirl and the offer of many a brief encounter became too tantalising not to accept, but, at the moment of intercourse, he would withdraw, fearful of the consequences should he father a child. He had learned that hard lesson from Kathleen. It was many years since he had enjoyed a sexual relationship, and he longed to hold Laura in his arms again and make love to her, but would she still be there for him? The thought tortured him when his hormones raced through his body, and he was propositioned by one of his beautiful companions.

Rosie could see he was unhappy, and she longed for all the shenanigans on the boat to come to an end. The women never left him alone, and, in particular, one pretty little thing who was forever hanging onto his arm as if Jamie belonged to her. Rosie asked him about her one morning at breakfast before the girl made an appearance, which was usually about lunch time.

"Who is that young lady who seems to be attached to you like glue, Jamie? She makes a beeline for you wherever you are—I can't help but notice." Rosie smiled at him, making her remark into a joke so he could laugh it off if he wanted to keep the girl a secret from her.

"Oh, that's Sophia—she is a bit of a limpet, isn't she—but she's full of life and such good company—knocks spots off most of the others who haven't got a brain between them. Lost her brother in the war too—her mother brought her on a world cruise to get away from their problems at home."

"What sort of problems?"

"They have an estate with hardly anyone left to run it now the son and heir has gone, and Sophia's father suffers from gout, which makes him difficult to live with. He is in his seventies, and Sophia has no fun living in the middle of Norfolk, where nothing ever happens, apparently." Jamie laughed. "She's making up for it now!"

"So it would seem," said Rosie, pleasantly, folding her serviette and making her way back to her cabin.

It put her in mind of the Pottses who gave grand parties when she was just a nursemaid, and when she and Jane, the senior nursemaid, had peeped through the banisters to watch while Lizzie had sung ballads in her beautiful soprano voice and the men had almost fallen at her feet. Arty had invited some of his racing crowd to one of those parties and that had been where Lizzie had met Harry Trevern for the first time. And now Lizzie's grandson was attracting women in the same way. Jamie seemed to have the same fatal charm, but he had stayed faithful to the memory of his lost love over the years, as far as she knew. Perhaps things were about to change, although she hoped not. Sophia looked about eighteen and a young eighteen at that. Jamie was obviously attracted to her and her vivacious personality, but it could mean him staying in England if he married her, and Rosie could not imagine Sophia leaving her family to live on the other side of the world.

It was a relief when the ship docked at Singapore and Jamie spent time with her, taking her for a rickshaw ride in the busy streets and buying her anything her eye alighted on. He had given her the little fan he had bought for her in Melbourne just before they left, and she was glad of it in the steamy heat of the crowded streets. She had seen very little of him as the days had passed. He was so occupied with his many friends that she had spent most of her time talking to the rich dowagers in the first class lounge, many of whom were chaperoning their daughters or their nieces and who had been prompted to ask Rosie about her eligible son. Rosie had been only too pleased to tell them how he was hoping to find his long lost fiancée, and the ladies had smiled knowingly behind their fans. They had heard tales of Jamie's romantic peccadilloes from their daughters, which disputed such a story, and considered Rosie to be a possessive mother who had no intention of losing her son.

Lady Mirabel Courtney, Sophia's mother, set about getting to know Rosie better. Her daughter had fallen head over heels in love with Jamie, the most handsome young man on board the ship, but was he the most eligible? She made a space for Rosie on the settee and beckoned her to come and sit beside her.

Rosie had tried to avoid speaking to her in the past on learning that Lady Mirabel was the wife of a baronet and felt a little overawed in her presence, but she could hardly refuse her invitation to sit by her side. Lady Mirabel was charm personified and chatted artlessly to Rosie about inconsequential matters whilst carefully interspersing their conversation with questions about Australian life, the sheep station, and the house in Melbourne. She praised Jamie indulgently, telling Rosie how well mannered he was and how her daughter had fallen madly in love with him. Rosie, who was flattered to find such an interested listener, spoke with enthusiasm about The Great House that Jamie had bought with the inheritance from his grandfather. She described the ballroom with its gilded furniture and the bedrooms which overlooked the gardens where the lawns swept down to the beautiful bay and the sandy beach.

"As a young woman, I thought it was the most beautiful place on earth, and still do for that matter," sighed Rosie.

"And was Jamie born there?"

Rosie was taken aback. She was talking too much and could never tell this grand woman her history or that she and Rory had adopted Jamie.

"Er–yes—he was as a matter of fact."

Suddenly, Rosie realised that she was being pumped for information and decided to be more discreet. What was it all about and why should this woman take such an interest in her? Did Sophia fancy her Jamie as a husband? Rosie hoped not, although seeing him look so adoringly at Sophia it was obvious that Laura was far from his mind at the moment.

"Our son and heir, Charlie, was killed on the last day of the war," confided Lady Mirabel. "My husband has no one to inherit the estate. It was a terrible disaster for us, and he had a breakdown when we received the news."

"I'm so sorry—I didn't think he had accompanied you," ventured Rosie.

"No, indeed. He's very old and frail and as our estate manager was also killed, as well as many of our estate workers, his time is taken up with management."

"I see," said Rosie thoughtfully, understanding their interest in Jamie. *Was he to replace Charlie?* she wondered. There was no doubt that Sophia had fallen in love with Jamie—but what about him? Perhaps they were already lovers. Rosie began to panic. With an enormous estate to manage and a flighty little wife to keep amused, he would never have the time or the inclination to return to Australia.

When he came to bid her good night in her cabin, Rosie broached the subject with him although she disliked doing so.

"Forgive me for asking, son, but you won't make the same mistake that you made with Kathleen, will you?"

"God help us, Ma! What brought that on?"

Rosie sighed. "Lady Mirabel tells me that Sophia is madly in love with you and knowing what happened last time—well, can you blame me?"

Jamie roared with laughter. "No worries, Ma—Sophia is no Kathleen, but if I ask her to marry me you'll be the first to know."

This made Rosie feel a little less worried, but Jamie had changed. He had been sucked into this new world of bright young things who lived just for today, and she would have to accept the consequences, whatever they might be. She blamed herself entirely. If she had let him send for Laura and turned Kathleen out, Jamie might have a family by now and settled down and this situation would never have arisen. She had been a fool to have been so easily taken in by Kathleen. She got ready for bed, but sleep evaded her, and she tossed and turned all night.

When, eventually, Jamie took Sophia to his cabin and made love to her, he turned away at the last moment. Sophia was deeply disappointed and became tearful.

"Don't you love me, Jamie? It will be all right—I want it as much as you do."

"It's just—well—something that happened a long time ago—nothing to do with you, sweetheart, believe me." Jamie nibbled her ear affectionately.

"It won't always be like this, will it, darling?" Sophia raised herself on her elbow and looked down at him. "Please, Jamie, I want it to be for always, don't you?"

Jamie fell silent. He desired her sexually; she excited him to the point of madness with her flirting and her childish sweet ways, but they were worlds apart, and he was undecided as to the future. He had given himself to Laura in mind and body, but that seemed like a thousand years ago. He had made up his mind to look for her, and he must do that first before he committed himself to Sophia.

"I'll see, sweetheart—forever is a long time—I'll have to think about it."

Sophia sighed and put on her wrap, ready to leave. Once he had seen Courteney Towers and the extent of her family estate, he might change his mind. Her father was still a wealthy man despite the crippling war years.

"Where are you and your mother staying when we get back to England?"

"In Brown's Hotel in London—just for a week—why?"

"When we get home to Norfolk, I want you and your mother to come and stay. You will come, won't you? Papa will love to meet you. Mama thinks the world of you and so do I—well, you know that don't you, Jamie darling?"

Jamie smiled at the urgency of her request. She had thrown her arms round him and kept kissing him until he agreed. There was no harm in going for a few days, and he could see no reason for his mother to object.

"I'll speak to Mama about it. She'll send the car ..." and as she left she blew him a saucy kiss.

Bombay came and went, and Rosie stayed on board where the sea breezes were more acceptable than the streets of a city that seethed with humanity and where she had been told the holy cows wandered at will.

As the ship steamed across the Indian Ocean, she often stood by the rail on the upper deck and thought of her mother, so long dead, resting somewhere below the waves. The first time she had come this way she had only been a little girl, and now she was an old woman, much older than her mother had been when she had died on *The Fair Maid*. Her life would have been very different if they had stayed in the village where she had been born, but she had no regrets as she looked back. It had been a hard life in Australia, but a good one, and she would not have altered it in any way. She had so much to look forward to—seeing England again and gaining a daughter-in-law, if all went well.

At Aden, there was a stop as the ship took on coal and then it was a journey through the Red Sea to the Suez Canal. This was all new to Rosie, and she marvelled at the way the ship negotiated the narrow sides of this man-made construction, cutting out the much longer passage round the Cape of Good Hope. She recalled that part of her early journey when the clipper ship had been caught in the aftermath of a whirlwind and had been lashed by tremendous waves. *The Fair Maid* had floundered in the huge seas, leaving them all in fear of their lives. After that terrible experience, it had been no wonder that she had dreaded making the journey again, but Jamie had been right when he had told her that it would be very different this time.

At Alexandria, the *Electra* had sailed into the port for a short visit, and Rosie was taken to see the Roman ruins before the ship was ready to continue on its journey through the Mediterranean to Gibraltar. A few days exploring the Rock and then it was off through the Bay of Biscay to the S.W. Approaches. Many of the passengers suffered bouts of sea sickness whilst the ship crossed the bay, but Rosie found she was not affected this time. Perhaps the terrible journey she had once experienced had cured her of such unpleasantness, although the sea had been rough and even Jamie had lost his usual cheerfulness.

As the ship grew closer and closer to their destination, Sophia clung more and more to Jamie. She desperately wanted to see him again and begged him to come and stay in Norfolk with her family. Jamie had grown fond of her company but had not lost sight of the fact that his journey across the world was to find Laura. If Laura was married or could not be found, then it might be a different matter. Sophia's distress at parting with him made him feel wretched, and her tears only served to compound his feeling of guilt. Lady Mirabel approached Rosie on the subject. If they agreed to stay for a short while at Courteney Towers they would be made most welcome—surely they could spare a few days out of their long vacation to visit them. Rosie could see that Sophia's mother was at her wit's end with her daughter's tearful outbursts, and agreeing to a few days in Norfolk she felt might settle the matter of Jamie's infatuation one way or another.

When they stepped ashore at Southampton, there was a sense of relief to be on terra firma once more after such a long journey. Rosie looked at the trees and fields flying past the windows of the train and found it hard to believe the brightness of the colours after the grey green eucalypts of her home. The train puffed through the towns and the little hamlets in Hampshire, going too fast for her to see everything in detail, but Jamie assured her there would be plenty of time to look at the countryside later.

"Right now, Ma, we're going to spend a few days in London at Brown's Hotel so you can have a rest from the sea journey before we travel to Downham, so no worries."

Rosie nodded. The train was sending her to sleep with the rhythmic movement of the carriage and she was fast asleep as it jolted to a stop at Waterloo station. Jamie had to wake her to get her into the cab that was to take them to the hotel. There were so many people passing by on the pavements, and, with the constant honking of the cars, Rosie felt bewildered. As the cab stopped at the door to the hotel, she caught sight of a legless man, begging against the wall and searched in her bag for some money while Jamie paid off the driver.

"Poor man, how can he find work like that?"

"There are plenty like him about, Ma. They did their duty for king and country and nobody is there for them now. War is a terrible thing. It might have finished eight years ago yet people are still starving as a result. We are the fortunate ones with enough money for our needs, but it could have been very different. Remember how it was when I came home from the war?"

Rosie nodded. She remembered only too well, but, however hard the drought and the depression, they had never gone hungry.

There was scarcely any staff left at the hotel to look after the guests due to the general strike. Rosie and Jamie never complained like some of the wealthy people who were staying there. Some had lost sons in the war, yet they still expected things to be the same when they came to London, but things were never to be the same again.

Those who were fortunate to have a job in the city had left their posts in an effort to bring the plight of the mass of the unemployed to the notice of the government, shaming them in front of the rest of the world. In an effort to break the strike, men who had never known poverty in their lives had donned their top hats and taken to driving the buses and cleaning the streets. The press lampooned them, and they soon got tired of their fun but what they did had little impact on the situation.

Rosie wearied of London and the poverty she saw around her whenever she left the hotel, and the arrival of the silver Rolls Royce, driven by an elderly chauffeur in uniform to take them to Norfolk was both a relief and a surprise. Jamie was overwhelmed by the opulence of the car and sat beside the driver to take in every detail of the vehicle. He had never seen anything like it before and wondered if he would be able to buy one in Australia, but Rosie, sitting in the rear seat, began to wonder exactly what awaited them at their destination.

CHAPTER 41

Courteney Towers was situated at the end of a long winding drive bordered by tall elms, a rambling Victorian building of little architectural merit in the gothic style to give an impression of grandeur. Rosie disliked it at first sight. It looked a gloomy place built of dark red brick with ivy growing across some of the windows, blocking out much of the light filtering through the overgrown shrubbery. It was certainly a large house with a tower situated at each end of the front elevation and an impressive front door flanked by stone lions. The Great House was like a doll's house in comparison and would have fitted inside it many times. The chauffeur drove up to the front entrance and alighted to open their doors for them.

Jamie was impressed. "Whew, what a place, Ma! Have you ever seen the like?"

"No, son, I can't say I have."

"It needs a bit doing to it by the look of things."

Rosie nodded as she looked at the crumbling brickwork and the broken steps.

"More than a bit—even the lions look past their best, poor things."

Jamie smiled. "It's only for a day or two, Ma, and then we'll head for Downham so keep your pecker up."

The chauffeur collected their cases and tugged at the rusty bell pull beside the door. He doffed his cap, got back into the car, and drove away round the side of the house. They stood and waited and as nobody came, Jamie rang again. At last the door was opened by no one other than Lady Mirabel herself.

"My dears," she gushed, her wide welcoming smile showing a set of overly large front teeth. "So sorry to keep you waiting, but Mary couldn't have heard the bell. You had a good journey, I hope?"

Her greying hair was held in a heavy pleat by two large tortoise shell combs, and she wore a long, brown tweed skirt and a matching woollen twin set, which had seen better days, set off by a long, amber necklace.

No need to put on an act for us, thought Rosie, remembering her haughty demeanour on board ship and her fashionable clothes.

"Are these *all* your bags?"

Rosie nodded, feeling as if Lady Mirabel had expected them to travel with twice the amount. "I'll ask Robert to take them up to your rooms. He's busy at the moment helping my husband—but *do* come in. Cedric will be down immediately."

She ushered them into a large drawing room full of heavy mahogany furniture and plush settees. Cabinets full of ornaments and knickknacks lined the walls. The mounted heads of foxes with their glass eyes were interspersed among the other paraphernalia, much to the amusement of Jamie, who had never seen such a thing before. Heavy dark red curtains held back by gold chords and tassels gave the room an oppressive feeling, and it looked as if nothing had been altered since Victorian times. Lady Mirabel went across to the bell pull by the fireplace.

"I'll arrange for some tea—I'm sure you must feel like some after your long journey."

Rosie nodded gratefully. "That would be lovely, thank you, but perhaps I could tidy up first."

"Of course—I'll get Mary to show you the way."

The maid, Mary, duly appeared and took Rosie upstairs before going into the kitchen to fetch the tea.

"No Sophia?" asked Jamie, feeling awkward left alone with Sophia's formidable mother.

"She's out riding," explained Lady Mirabel. "We had no idea when exactly to expect you, but she'll be back soon. She's so looking forward to seeing you again."

Jamie felt disappointed. If that was the case then why wasn't she here to greet them?

She knew they would be arriving in the afternoon, having left London after breakfast, but he supposed that, as it was such a beautiful autumn day, she wanted to be outside in the sunshine, which was rare in this country, so he understood. From where he was sitting he could see the chestnut trees in the distance, red, gold, and brown, and wished he was outside riding with her instead of being cooped up in this airless room trying to be polite to her mother. Looking around him he wondered how such a bright elfin-like girl as Sophia, so full of life, could have grown up in this claustrophobic atmosphere. He could never live here, used as he was to the wide open spaces of Australia.

When the tea arrived, pushed in on a trolley, Lady Mirabel decided to have it on the terrace. Mary struggled to open the French windows without success, and they needed Jamie's strength to open them.

"It's the damp that causes them to stick," explained Lady Mirabel. "This room is on the north side of the house and is never warm, whatever the weather." Jamie could appreciate that, as the room had an air of mustiness about it as if it was rarely used. He could hear his mother in conversation with someone, and, looking behind him, he saw the manservant, Robert, wheeling someone towards the terrace in a cane bath chair. The occupant, a frail elderly man with a bandaged foot protruding from under a large rug, held out his hand in greeting.

"Delighted to meet you, my boy—Sophia not here yet? Where is the child?"

Jamie shook hands with him. "I'm pleased to meet you, sir."

"Sit down—sit down, both of you. I've just had the pleasure of meeting your mother."

Jamie found it hard to believe that this old man with a face as wrinkled as a walnut could possibly be Sophia's father. He looked more like her grandfather. No wonder she found life dull in this gloomy household.

From below the terrace, a large area of grassland extended towards a row of mature chestnut trees through which Jamie glimpsed fields and woods. It was a pleasant outlook made even more interesting from Jamie's point of view when a girl on horseback galloped across the grass towards them waving her riding crop in greeting. Sophia jumped off her horse at the bottom of the terrace and ran up the steps to meet them.

She rode well, and Jamie had no doubt that she had started riding early in life. She looked the picture of health with her flushed cheeks from the ride and her green eyes sparkling with delight at seeing Jamie again. Jamie got to his feet and smiled fondly at her. The tight white jodhpurs, hacking jacket, and black leather boots suited her slim figure, and, as she brushed her fair hair back off her face in a gesture he remembered so well, Jamie realised he was in love. She looked even more adorable in her riding clothes than she had in the fancy outfits she had worn on board ship.

She held out her hand towards him, ignoring the rest of the company.

"Come and ride with me, Jamie. There's Papa's horse in the stable that needs the exercise."

"Is that all right, sir?" asked Jamie, anxious not to offend.

"Go ahead, my boy—let's see what you're made of, but I'm warning you—he isn't an easy ride."

Rosie's heart sank. She could see the strong mutual attraction between the two of them and knew that he only had eyes for this spoilt girl who hadn't even the good manners to acknowledge her.

"Robert will get out Charlie's old riding breeches and boots—you're about his size by the look of you. Off you go, but don't be long."

Sophia sank into one of the chairs and picked up a cup. "Tea—just what I wanted."

"Jamie's mother is here too, Sophia—didn't you see her?" Lady Mirabel gestured towards Rosie.

"Oh, sorry—I was so thrilled to see Jamie—how do you do?" Rosie gave a curt nod in her direction. She might just as well have not been there. It was so wrong. This spoilt youngest child of elderly parents and the only child left to them would lead Jamie a merry dance until she was tired of him. He would be expected to stay here and manage the estate as their eldest son would have done and live here with them. She just hoped he would see sense before it was too late. She excused herself and went to rest in her bedroom and did not appear again until the dinner gong summoned her.

Dinner was served in a large dining room on a long polished table. Sir Cedric sat at the top of the table, having been assisted out of his bath chair, and his wife sat at the opposite end. Jamie and Sophia sat together on one side while Rosie sat facing them, with enough room between them for a regiment of people.

The room was palatial with gas lights on the walls and a large chandelier in the centre. The food was more to Rosie's taste, being game birds from the estate, pheasant and partridge, all cooked to perfection without any extra adornments apart from a large dish of mixed vegetables. The wine was an old vintage brought from the cellar for the occasion, and the sweets were many and varied. Rosie sent her compliments to the cook and that went down well with Lady Mirabel, who had aimed to please. Her husband had expressed his approval of Jamie, and she wanted to do everything she could to entice him to stay. Sophia was to play her part, which she was only too pleased to do, being madly in love with Jamie. She had been at her most flirtatious during their ride, and when they had stopped and he had lifted her down from her horse and had held her to him in a close embrace, she had suggested that they became lovers that night. Jamie agreed and told her that all would be well this time.

Like all lovers, they picked at their food, desiring only to be released from the polite conversation around the dining table and ached for the evening to come to an end.

Sitting in the darkened drawing room before the gas lamps were lit, Sir Cedric rambled on about his son and heir. He had been a captain in the Norfolk Regiment and had served on the Somme. He sent Robert to fetch his son's medals to show to Jamie and questioned him about his part in the war. Jamie was not forthcoming. He disliked any mention of that terrible time and would not be drawn. Rosie, who was proud of him, mentioned the medal Jamie had received for bravery.

"What was the name of that place, Jamie? You told me once—where you were wounded so badly—before they sent you back to England."

"Oh, ma, why go into that now; it was some years ago, and I don't care to remember it."

"Come, come, my boy—a medal for bravery should never be held lightly—your mother is right to feel proud of you, as we all are." Sir Cedric puffed on his cigar and held out his glass for Robert to fill with more whisky.

"It was at Zonnebeke, sir," said Jamie quietly, feeling uncomfortable.

"Ah, I seem to remember reading something about that engagement. The men had to wade through a swamp towards a ridge where the Germans were encamped —brave souls all of them, poor devils. I lift my glass to them." It was becoming obvious that Sir Cedric was drinking too much, and his wife signed to Robert not to top up his glass any more.

Sophia stood up and went over to her father. "You're upsetting mama talking about the war—perhaps it's time for bed. I'm feeling rather tired myself after all that riding." She planted a kiss on the top of his bald head and smiled at the rest of the company. "If you'll excuse me—the hunt is meeting tomorrow, and I want to be fresh for that."

Jamie stood up politely as she left the room, knowing this was an excuse for them to retire early, and thankful the conversation had ended. She had already told him about the hunt the next day, and he was looking forward to some hard riding, but the pleasures of a night with her in his arms awaited him first. Rosie decided to use Sophia's absence as an excuse to leave and went up to her room, soon to be followed by Lady Mirabel.

Sir Cedric continued to ramble on and on, telling Jamie about the men from the king's country estate at Sandringham, a few miles away. They had gone to fight and had never been heard of again. Gradually, his voice grew more slurred and his head began to nod. It took both Robert and Jamie to get him into the bath chair so Robert could wheel him into his room downstairs. Jamie was alone at last and helped himself to a glass of port before leaving. He was surprised at how shaken he had felt after the mention of Zonnebeke. He had tried to put such horrors out of his mind and had hated talking about the war. Sophia would be waiting anxiously for him to come upstairs, and he had wasted enough time as it was.

Jamie had been given Charlie's old room. It overlooked the terrace on the north side of the house and felt chilly in the night air. A lighted oil lamp had been placed beside the bed, and there were candles should he need more light, but he pulled back the curtains so they could see the stars as they made love and turned off the lamp. He began to shiver and got into bed, pulling the bedclothes around him, wondering why someone as fit and healthy as himself should feel so cold. On the opposite wall hung a sepia photograph of Charlie in his captain's uniform. Jamie stared at it. The eyes seemed to be watching him—eyes that expected commands to be obeyed without question. Charlie had stood proudly, posing for his photograph with his hand on his regimental sword. Jamie began to feel strange just looking at him and lay back and closed his eyes. Suddenly, he was back on the battlefield with the sound of the guns deafening him, and hearing the cries of the wounded and dying men and the screams of the horses as they were hit by the gunfire.

He writhed about in the bed, shouting aloud in his pain and his terror, desperately struggling to get back to the present.

Sophia had heard his door close and had given him enough time to prepare himself for her arrival before she ran along the corridor in her flimsy negligee to fall into his arms. Jamie's room was in darkness when she opened the door, and there was a terrible moaning sound coming from the bed. Was he playing a trick on her, she wondered—trying to frighten her perhaps? She tiptoed across the carpet and peered down at him. He was covered in perspiration, and his eyes were rolling as he writhed about flinging his arms towards her.

Sophia stepped back in horror. What was the matter with him—was he having a fit? She whispered his name, but he appeared not to hear her. She shouted, and he just moaned in reply, raising his head and looking at her without recognition.

Sophia gathered her wrap around her to cover her nakedness and ran sobbing to wake Rosie, telling her she had heard Jamie moaning as she had gone along the corridor. Rosie returned with her and knew immediately what had happened. She had seen him like this once before, not long after he had returned from the war.

"It's shell shock, Sophia. A lot of soldiers who fought in the war were treated in hospital for it, like Jamie. I hoped it had gone away for good, and I'm surprised it has returned. He will be better tomorrow after he has slept for a while—maybe talking to your father—"

"Shall I send Robert for the doctor?"

"No, not yet—I'll stay with him and bathe his head in cold water until the fever leaves him. I'm so sorry this should have happened while we were staying here. When he wakes in the morning, he will feel terrible about it. Go to bed now. I will look after him. There's a chair over there, and I can get a blanket off my bed if I'm cold. Off you go now and try not to worry—Jamie will be all right."

Sophia returned to her own bedroom and flung herself onto the bed in a storm of weeping. What if Jamie had been like this while they had been making love—she shivered at the thought, for, although she loved Jamie she could never cope if he might fall ill. It was her papa's fault going on about the war—he never stopped talking about it since Charlie had been killed. It made her mother weep, and if it had affected Jamie so badly, he could never live here with them at Courtney Towers. To marry Jamie was out of the question now, and she would have to tell her parents she had changed her mind in the morning.

Rosie dozed once Jamie had recovered and had fallen into a deep sleep, and they were both awoken by a noise outside the window. Hearty laughter and the sound of loud voices floated up from the path below the terrace. Horses and riders had gathered before setting off on the hunt, and Robert was busy handing out stirrup cups to thirsty riders. It was a colourful scene, the riders mostly dressed in hunting pink and the ladies in black, some wearing veils across their faces and riding sidesaddle. The fox hounds were becoming agitated, longing for the chase and the kill. Jamie leapt out of bed and pulled on the clothes Robert had left out for him. Why hadn't he been called in time for the hunt, and what was his mother doing in his room? The last thing he remembered was waiting for Sophia. He was going to make love to her, and yet he had no memory of that happening.

Rosie told him to slow down. He had been taken ill during the night. Sophia had called her, and she had looked after him until the horrors had left him and he had slept.

Jamie tore downstairs, buttoning up his jacket as he ran; if he left it any longer, the hunt would have moved off without him. Sophia, who had seen him coming, urged her horse forward among the milling foxhounds, awaiting the call from the master to move off, but he managed to catch her rein and pull the horse to a standstill.

"Wait, Sophia—wait! I overslept—it will never happen again I promise you. I'm so sorry my darling—please forgive me—it must have been all that talk about the war."

He looked earnestly up at her face and could see she had been weeping.

"I can't risk it, Jamie. I had no idea you still suffered from shell shock—you always seemed so strong—so fit and well—"

"But it's been years since I had an attack. I'd forgotten all about it—please believe me," pleaded Jamie.

"I loved you so much Jamie—you were the answer to everyone's prayers, but there's no future for us—you must see that."

"Don't say that my darling—please."

An older man rode his horse up beside Sophia and gave her mount a rap on the rump, setting it off at a sparking pace. The rider raised his crop and touched his cap. Jamie imagined he saw a self-satisfied smirk on the rider's face as he turned his horse to follow her.

So she had no intention of my going with her today, thought Jamie bitterly.

Rosie saw him from her window standing alone, watching as the horses and the hounds disappeared up the road, and her heart went out to him. Despite her feelings as to the suitability of the match, he had been treated badly—had the girl no sympathy for him? Sophia had seen his suffering for herself last night. Did she only ever think of herself?

Rosie feared that was the case.

She began to pack; they would have to leave right away. She heard Jamie clattering up the stairs and the thump, thump as he threw his riding boots against the door. Not long afterwards, he came to find her with his clothes hanging out of the sides of his case where he had hurriedly packed them.

"We're going, Ma," he said shortly. "I know when I'm not wanted."

"How can we go, son? We need some transport to get to the station—be reasonable."

"Right—I'll speak to Robert. Perhaps he can arrange something."

Jamie stumped off to find Robert, and Rosie made tracks for the kitchen where she found Mary.

"Is there any tea, Mary? We're leaving this morning and have had no breakfast."

"Of course there is, ma'am. There's a pot mashing on the stove. I'll pour you a cup if you care to go into the dining room. Her ladyship had her breakfast in her room this morning and left no instructions."

Rosie was not surprised. The die had been cast as soon as Sophia had made up her mind about Jamie, and her mother had wanted them gone.

"I'll drink it here, thank you. This suits me better than the dining room."

After a few minutes had passed in silence, she heard Jamie calling her from the hall.

"I've given the chauffeur a tip, Ma, and he'll take us to Ipswich station. We'll have to return to London and make our way to Lancashire from there—it's not straight forward to travel across country by rail from here."

"But what about telling Sophia's parents? We can't just walk out without telling anyone we're going."

"Robert put it right with the old boy about using the car, and you can write a few lines to them if you want to later, although I'm sure I wouldn't bother. I never want to have anything to do with this family again."

He hustled Rosie into the Rolls, and they drove away from Courteney Towers without a backward glance.

CHAPTER 42

A few days later, they arrived in Lancashire and found the village where Rosie had been born. The inn overlooking the village green at Downham suited them, and Jamie's hurt pride began to mend. Sophia had stolen his heart with her winning ways, but as time passed he began to realise that he would soon have tired of her, and, as for living in Courteney Towers for the rest of his life, as her parents would have wanted, the thought appalled him. After a few months, he would have wanted to return to Australia, and he doubted that she would have left to go with him. She was still tied to her parents like a child who had never grown up.

Rosie walked through the wildflower meadows she remembered from her childhood and visited the cottage where once she had lived. The family had asked her in when she had introduced herself and made her a cup of tea. Change came more slowly in the countryside, but even here there was concern for their jobs on the farms where they had been employed in the past now that the markets had closed down. The people at the manor house where her father had once been employed now managed with one gardener instead of ten and no longer kept a skilled carpenter to look after the estate houses. Most of the large house had been shut up, and the family lived in a few rooms with a cook housekeeper to see to their needs.

Rosie related this to Jamie after her visit, but he was becoming anxious to leave. *What had happened to the Bowden family?* he wondered, fearing for Laura in this aftermath of the war. Had she suffered too? She had nursed him devotedly when he had been suffering from shell shock for she had truly loved him. She had never turned away from him like Sophia, who had expected everything to go her way. He had thought of nobody except for Laura until he had met Sophia. Life on board the *Electra* was false,—a whirl of pleasure and sexual encounters, and he had lost his head for a while. It was time that he came to his senses.

Rosie would have liked to have stayed longer in Downham, but Jamie insisted that they move on. At Colchester, they put up at the George Hotel, an old hostelry that Rosie found most comfortable and where she was happy to stay while Jamie went on his search for his lost love.

The following day, Jamie caught the train from St. Botholphs to Brightlingsea. He was the only traveller that morning, and as the train puffed laboriously along the shoreline, pulling its two carriages along, he began to wonder exactly whom he could ask about Laura's whereabouts. The tide was full, and the water sparkled in the early sunlight with a mesmerising effect. Mersea Island rested peacefully across the estuary. There was not a boat nor a bird to be seen and he felt strangely isolated, shut in his compartment. Going back in time was unreal, and he had a feeling of impending disaster. Making enquiries could be difficult, and he would not be a welcome visitor at Marsh Farm having deserted their daughter.

The train pulled into the station, and Jamie alighted onto the empty platform. The ticket office was closed, and the engine was shunted to the front of the carriages ready for the return journey. The driver and his mate jumped down on the line and set off across the sidings. Jamie found he was alone and walked towards the High Street. He saw the door of the Swan Inn was open, and two elderly men were sitting on the seat outside, and he sat down beside them.

"When's opening time?" he asked, to make conversation.

"The same as usual—ten o'clock. Are you a stranger here?"

His friend nudged him. "He's one of those Aussies by the sound of it. There were plenty of them here during the war."

Jamie lit his pipe and sat drawing on it for a while.

"I was billeted here before going to the Somme. I was one of the fortunate ones to go back to Australia afterwards—thought I'd come back for a look—by the way, can I buy you two gents a drink?"

The offer was taken up, and they went inside and found a table. There were no other customers at that time of the morning, so Jamie thought he would ask a few questions while the bar was empty, without attracting any attention.

"Are the Bowdens still at Marsh Farm? I had thought of calling on them, if they're still around."

"Wilf's still there and his mother, but the girls went long since."

"Ah." Jamie puffed on his pipe, thoughtfully. This was not good news.

"How is Wilf these days? I seem to remember that he had some difficulty with the farmwork. We gave him a hand at harvest time."

"He can't do much these days, but Jo Carter used to help out quite a lot. He married the eldest daughter after the war."

Jamie nodded, sympathetically. "Good thing for the family then—where did he come from?"

"Lower Farm—at the end of Mill Lane."

"I thought there was another son who went to the war—didn't he come back?"

"There were two boys, weren't there?" asked the man to his companion.

The other man nodded. "Aye—Jack, who got killed, and the younger one, Sam."

"Well, doesn't Sam help out?" asked Jamie.

"He works the barge with his father-in-law so I can't see him doing much round the farm. Things are different here since the war ended—there's nothing in farming these days."

"I feel sorry for them," said Jamie. "They were good to us when the regiment was here."

"Jo took over part of the farm to help them out at first but then he couldn't do his own work after a while, and the fields have lain fallow for years."

"Why not? Was he ill?"

"Whenever you saw Jo, he was coughing fit to bust. Trench fever left him with a weak chest—Lower Farm is a bad place in the winter—too close to the marshes. He couldn't sell the farm because of the depression, and he was too ill to work it, and it was too much for his dad on his own."

"Ah—I heard they were in a poor way. It was one of the best farms around here, and now it's in the same state as the others."

Jamie bought them both another drink, hoping he could glean a bit more information. He ached to find out what had happened to Laura, but was careful not to make them suspicious about his motives.

"I never met Jo. He was away fighting in the war when I was here, but I'm sorry to hear he has had so much trouble after returning home—no one deserved that after all they went through on the Somme."

"He's dead, poor chap—died last year. A hard worker was Jo and a real nice man. He married the Bowden's eldest daughter when people said the boy wasn't his—there was a lot of gossip at the time, her coming from such a strict family an' all."

"Wasn't his father one of them Aussies?" asked the other man.

"Oh, ah—that's what I heard—plenty like him about. A good many girls around here got themselves in the family way." The men chuckled. "Wouldn't be you by any chance, would it?" said one of them, laughing good-naturedly at his joke.

Jamie spluttered into his drink with shock on hearing this news, and the two men rose to leave.

"Now look what you've done! Embarrassed the poor chap!" They thanked him for their drinks and left the premises in good humour without realising the truth of their words.

Jamie sat for a while and digested this information. If he had a son, then he wanted to be a father to him, but this news altered everything. Laura might not feel the same about him now he had left her to cope in her hour of need. She must have suffered deeply, and he had been the cause of that suffering, but even if she rebuffed him, he still had a duty to his son, and he would ask for her forgiveness.

He walked down Mill Street with a heavy heart. Marsh Farm looked worse than before with the plaster cracking off the walls and the fields waist high with weeds. It looked uncared for and desolate. Jamie hurried past, not wanting to meet Wilf. The gates of Lower Farm came into view, and he rested for a moment, leaning on one of the gate posts to gather his thoughts before approaching Laura.

A boy of about seven years came walking down the driveway towards him holding two milk cans in his hands. As he came closer, Jamie could see he had dark curly hair and deep brown eyes like his own, with Laura's wide generous mouth. Jamie stood rooted to the spot. Was this fine looking boy his son?

"Are you Laura Carter's lad?" he asked.

"Yes," answered the boy.

"What's your name, lad?"

"Laurie, sir."

Jamie smiled. "Your ma named you after her, then. She's Laura, and you're Laurie." The boy made no answer. The stranger spoke with an accent he had never heard before, and he knew his mother's name, which was odd. Laurie hurried past and went through the back door of Marsh Farm to collect the milk when he collided with his Uncle Wilf, who was dashing out of the door in a desperate hurry.

"Watch out, Wilf!" shouted Bess, "you nearly had the boy over. What's the rush? Goodness me, Laurie, I've never known your Uncle Wilf to move so fast before."

Bess took the milk cans from her grandson and went into the dairy to fill them.

"There you are, dear," she said, as she gave them back to him. "Carry them carefully, I filled them a bit full but I expect you can manage."

Laurie smiled at his grandmother and set off back up the lane. He stopped in his tracks when he heard the loud report of a gun at close quarters. Uncle Wilf had slung his gun over his shoulder when he had pushed past him so perhaps he had seen an adder in a ditch and decided to kill it. Laurie had heard there was a nest of adders in the sand pits this year, and his mother had told him and his sisters to watch out for them and to tell Uncle Wilf if they saw one.

There was no more noise, so Laurie continued to walk towards the farm gate. He could see the stranger had gone as he turned into the drive to Lower Farm, but as he continued his walk he was suddenly aware of a man spread-eagled across the drive.

Laurie dropped the milk cans and ran towards him. It was the same man who had spoken to him at the gate. Blood was seeping through his trouser legs, and he was groaning in pain.

Laurie stepped round him carefully and sped up to the farm, calling out to his mother as he ran.

CHAPTER 43

Jamie hardly remembered anything about his transportation to the hospital in Colchester apart from the feeling of relief as somebody wrapped cloths around his legs to staunch the blood. He lay where he fell after he had been shot from behind and could see nobody although he could hear a child shouting for his mother and a woman's cries as she found him. Perhaps it had been Laura, but he was in too much agony to speak and had been unable to lift his head.

A doctor had given him an injection to ease the pain, and he had fallen into a coma as the ambulance had driven him swiftly to the hospital. While the shotgun pellets were removed, he remained unconscious and slept for many hours, waking to find himself in a bed, surrounded by curtains. The doctor who came to attend to him told him he was fortunate to be alive.

"A little higher and you might have been killed—but I have no doubt that whoever aimed at you intended to kill you. The hospital has informed the police, and they will want to question you as soon as you feel up to it."

Jamie nodded. He knew he had been shot, but he found it hard to come to terms with what had happened. Rosie would be wondering why he had not returned and would need to be told.

"My mother is staying at The George in the High Street. She has no idea that I am here—could somebody let her know, please? She is Mrs. Macdonald."

"Of course we will, but you must rest now—you've had a bad experience."

Another injection to ease the pain and Jamie slept more peacefully, waking to find two policemen at his bedside. Did he know who had shot him? What had been his business at Lower Farm? Was there any bad feeling between him and the owner?

The questions went on and on, and he tried to answer them as best as he could but how could he tell them he was only looking for Laura, his old fiancée from the war years, and that he had travelled across the world to find her. It sounded implausible, even if it was the truth, and he could see by the look on their faces that they did not believe him.

"Ask my mother—she will confirm what I am saying—she's staying at The George – hasn't anyone told her yet?"

Jamie began to become restless, and the policemen withdrew, promising to call on Rosie. He sounded like an Australian, so it was possible that his mother was Australian too and could verify his story.

As soon as Rosie heard that Jamie was in hospital, she was deeply shocked and was determined to visit Laura herself. If she had gone with him whoever had shot him would have been in two minds about shooting her too, and it might never have happened. Jamie was being cared for and was out of danger. There was nothing she could do for him apart from finding Laura and putting his mind at rest. Perhaps she was already married, and that had been the reason for the shooting. If that was the case, she would persuade him to forget her. Rosie took a cab to Brightlingsea and, asking the driver to wait, she knocked on the door of Lower Farm.

Laura opened the door, wondering who this elderly lady could be who had taken a cab to visit her, but as soon as Rosie began to speak she wondered if she had a connection to Jamie,—her Jamie whom she had shed tears over as she had bound up his bleeding wounds.

"Are you Laura?" asked Rosie. "The girl my son fell in love with during the war?"

Laura put her arms round her, and they wept together.

"Oh, tell me please—how is he? He didn't know me when they took him away. Is he badly wounded? I heard the shot but thought nothing of it 'til Laurie came to fetch me. When I found him I thought I was dreaming—Jamie of all people."

Rosie looked at the beautiful woman who was weeping for her son, and she could see why Jamie had fallen in love with her. There was gentleness about her manner, and her loving concern for her son showed in her deep violet eyes.

"They're looking after him in hospital and have removed the pellets, but I haven't seen him yet. I wanted to see you first. He came to find you, my dear. You were the love of his life—you knew that didn't you—but I see you have a son, and a husband maybe?"

"My husband died last year, and Laurie is Jamie's son."

Rosie put her hand to her mouth in amazement. "He had no idea?"

"No, no idea. He wrote to say that his circumstances made it impossible for me to come to Australia after the war." Laura's eyes clouded over at the memory, and Rosie felt a pang of guilt. She had been partly responsible for that decision, and it had taken years before she had realised her mistake. So, she had a grandson after all whom she had known nothing about.

"May I see the boy—my grandson?"

"Of course, but he thinks Jo was his father, you understand."

Laura called Laurie, and he came to be introduced to Rosie, bringing his two sisters with him.

"These are my twins, Lily and Primrose."

The six-year-olds smiled shyly at the stranger.

"Why, you have a part of my name," said Rosie to one of the girls. "I'm Rose, but I've always been called Rosie—Rosie Macdonald."

"You speak like the man at the gate," said Laurie, "the man who was shot. Did you know who he was?"

"Yes, he's my son, Jamie. He came to see your mother, all the way from Australia."

"That's the other side of the world, isn't it?" Rosie nodded. "So how did he know my mum?"

"That's enough, Laurie. Take the girls out to play. Right now I want to talk to Mrs. Macdonald, and I'll talk to you later."

Once the children had gone, Laura showed Rosie to a chair and sat opposite her.

"I shall have to tell him Jo wasn't his father, but it will be difficult. He loved Jo, and Jo treated him like his son."

"Don't say anything, my dear, until Jamie is better and you have discussed it together. He looks so like Jamie when he was that age that I can hardly believe it. He will be astounded when I tell him he has a son and will regret his decision not to bring you out to Australia, but, I can assure you, there were mitigating circumstances that made it impossible at the time. He loved you very much, and it broke his heart not to be able to send for you—that's why he's returned—but I must leave him to tell you. Come with me to the hospital now. The cab is waiting. Is there someone who can have the children?"

"They can go to my mother —just a step down the lane. Bert, my father-in-law, had better go with them in case that lunatic is still around. I'll only be a minute."

Once the children had been dispatched, Laura and Rosie set off for the hospital. There was so much they both wanted to discuss but both women were silent for most of the journey until Laura said how nervous she felt about this meeting.

"It's been so long, and things might have changed between us. We're two different people now after such a long time."

"Some things never change you'll find, and true love is one of them," said Rosie quietly. "The driver can leave me at the George, where I'm staying, and I shall ask him to wait for you and drive you back home afterwards. I shall settle the bill with him because I want you to stay with Jamie for as long as you both need. You have a lot of catching up to do."

Rosie spoke to the cabbie as she left, waved cheerfully at Laura and disappeared into the foyer of the hotel. She had done her part, and now it was up to them to sort out their lives.

The curtains were pulled apart, and Laura stood by his bed, looking down at him. Jamie opened his eyes for a second and closed them again. Was she really there, or were the drugs they had given him to ease the pain making him hallucinate? He felt her touch his hand and her lips brush across his cheek.

"My poor love. Who could have done this to you?"

Jamie opened his eyes in disbelief. It really was Laura standing there holding his hand and looking at him with such love and concern as the tears coursed down her cheeks.

"Laura my darling—is it really you? I thought I had lost you forever—please forgive me."

"What for, Jamie? You've come across the world to find me again—there can be no greater love than that, surely?"

"But I left you with a child to bring up all alone—I heard about it from some strangers I met in the Swan. I was so ashamed that I hardly dared to come and see you, and calling on your family was out of the question. They must have hated me for the way I treated you."

"They took it hard, I must admit, but that's all in the past. Jo married me just before Laurie was born and turned me into a respectable woman." Laura smiled at the thought. "Falling in love didn't include having a physical relationship with someone, according to my family—you had to wait until you were married for that to happen."

"Did you love Jo, Laura?"

"I was grateful to him, and we had been friends since we were children. I used to think of him as another brother. He brought Laurie up as if he was his own son, and we had twin girls later, Lily and Primrose."

"But did you love him, Laura—like it had been between us?"

"Nothing could ever be like that, Jamie—you know it could never be like that with anyone else."

Jamie kissed the hand that held his. "That's all I want to know. That's what I came across the world to hear. I'm never going to lose you again, my darling, and I want to take you back to Australia with me, if you'll come. As soon as I'm out of hospital, I want us to be married—please marry me, Laura?"

Laura nodded, too overcome to speak, as he held her in his arms and kissed her. The nurse who had come to draw the curtains back round the bed changed her mind and left them to enjoy a few more moments of privacy before it was time for visitors to leave.

Back at Lower Farm, Laura began to make up a bed for him in her room. Nobody else would nurse Jamie back to health but her, and, once he was well enough and his wounds had healed, they would go to the little chapel, and she would become his wife for all the world to see.

When the children returned home, she had news for them. They were going to live in Australia where the sun shone nearly all the time, and they would have a new father to look after them who would soon be coming to live with them until he was well enough to travel.

"But how did he know you, Mum?" asked Laurie. "You've never been to Australia, have you?"

Laura laughed, happily. The laughter was infectious, and the children smiled. They had never seen their mother like this before. It was as if someone had waved a magic wand over her, and they were going to be happy forever after, like a story in a book. She put her arms round all three of them and drew them to her.

"A long time ago...," she began, and she went on to tell them how Jamie had come to Brightlingsea during the time of the Great War and had lived at Marsh Farm until he had gone over the sea to fight the Germans and how he had never forgotten her and had come back to find her and take her back to Australia with him."

"But he won't want us, will he?" asked Laurie. "He doesn't know us."

"He *especially* wants you," said Laura. "He will have a ready-made family, and he's looking forward to that very much and when he comes here to live until he gets better you can get to know him, can't you?"

"Does he have a farm, like our dad?" Primrose asked.

"Yes, my love, but he's a different sort of farmer. He keeps hundreds and thousands of sheep, and there will be horses too for you all to ride."

"Then I'm going," decided Primrose, who had a determined streak in her character.

"You can't go without me!" objected Lily. "We do everything together."

"Then you'll have to go too, won't you," said Laura, laughing, "and what about you, Laurie?"

"I'm not sure, yet," said Laurie, thoughtfully. "He isn't *my* dad, and I might not like him—he'll be different from Dad."

The smile left Laura's face. She would have to tell him and perhaps the sooner the better.

"Well, you'll be meeting him soon, and I'm sure you're going to be the best of friends. We must all try to make him welcome; he's come such a long way to find us, from the other side of the world in fact, and I'm sure he's going to tell you what it's like over there, because lots of things will be very different from living here."

"But I like living here," said Laurie stubbornly. "Dad told me that when I grew up the farm would be mine. What will happen to it if I go away?"

Laura thought quickly. Laurie's reaction had been unexpected, and she needed to dispel his fears before Jamie appeared.

"Why, your granddad will look after it until you are old enough to come back and look after it yourself, and when Jamie is here he will have lots of ideas to help granddad out, just you wait and see. Things will be much better from now on."

Once the children had gone to bed, Laura had a long talk to her father-in-law about her forthcoming marriage to Jamie and the difference it would make to them all. She was shocked to hear what a bad way the farm was in and the amount of money still owing on the new machinery which Jo had bought before his death.

"It's a wonder the bailiffs haven't been in to repossess most of what we have," Bert told her. "It's only by great good fortune that we've been left so long. They've so much to do clearing out the other farms around here that they haven't got to us yet."

"I'll speak to Jamie about it. Perhaps he will sort it out."

"Even if he does, Laura, I can't run this farm single handed. Without Jo to help, it's impossible. We shall have to sell up whatever price we get. I was hoping to talk to you about it and wondered if Bess would take you all in. Jo was good to her when she was in trouble, and she is your mother."

"But what would you do, Bert? Where would you go?"

Bert shook his head. "I'll find somewhere. The farm will bring in a bit—enough for me to live on."

Laura went to bed with a heavy heart. Lower Farm had been her home, and her children had been born there. It had been in Bert's family for over a century. She intended to see her mother in the morning, although she wondered what her reaction would be to Jamie's reappearance on the scene after all these years, and now she would have to speak to her about Bert's plight. When they had left for Australia, Bert would be on his own, and she wondered if perhaps her mother would give him a home out of the goodness of her heart.

A few hours ago, everything had been right with her world. As sleep overtook her, her troubles melted away like thistledown, and she woke to a world full of birdsong and blue skies. Jamie had come back for her, and that was all that mattered.

CHAPTER 44

Bess had already heard from Bert of Jamie's arrival at Lower Farm by the time Laura called in to see her the next morning. The children had been full of it and had chatted away excitedly about the ambulance which had come to take the man away to hospital and the lady who had spoken with a funny accent who had come to see their mother. She had told Rose that she shared part of her name, and Bess had put two and two together and decided that she must be Jamie's mother. All Bert could tell her was that she had arrived in a taxi to take Laura to the hospital to see him. Jamie had caused them enough grief in the past, so why did he have to come back to make trouble for the family again. It was a pity Jo was no longer there to send him packing, and Wilf seemed to have disappeared over night without saying where he was going, which had caused her some concern. He had been in a strange mood the last time she had seen him, but she had never known him to stay out all night before.

When Laura arrived, Bess was in no mind for pleasantries, and her daughter's happy expression only served to annoy her further.

"What's the matter, Mother? Surely you can't be cross about Jamie coming back? You should be glad—he's kept his promise. He's come across the world to find me, and we're going to be married as soon as he's well enough, and he's taking us all back to Australia with him."

"His leaving you with a child did nothing but make our lives a misery, Laura. If it hadn't been for Jo, you would never have been able to hold your head up again, and we have suffered ever since as a result of your wanton behaviour."

Laura was furious. "If Jo had still been alive you would *never* have spoken to me like that. How dare you, Mother! Jamie had no idea I was pregnant when he went back to Australia. If he *had* things might have been very different, although he had nothing to offer me at that time. His mother told me they were all but starving, and the situation was impossible. It was unfair to expect me go out there."

"It still makes no difference to the fact that he slept with you, and you were a willing party to that disgusting behaviour."

"To *what*! We loved each other, Mother, and he was going away to the war. Our love has lasted all these years despite everything that has happened in between. True love lasts forever and you of all people should know that. You waited for years to marry our father against your own family's wishes. That's right, isn't it?"

"Maybe, but we didn't give in to lust in those days. Young people seem to do what they like now. It was against the teachings of our church, and I was a good woman."

Laura sighed. Her mother's religion had made her hard, and the conventions of the time had meant treading an unforgiving path. She could never have known the joy of total surrender or else she had forgotten what that could feel like now she was old.

"Jo was a good man to marry you and to bring Laurie up as his son."

"I'm aware of that, Mother, and I don't need reminding of it, but I love Jamie, and I'm getting married to him, and I hope you will be polite to him and his mother when you meet them. I'll bring his mother to see you soon, and she can tell you about the farm and our new home. She is a nice person, and you will like meeting her."

Bess made no reply. She was not at all sure that she wanted to meet the mother of the man who had caused them so much suffering—the man she had once been so proud of when he had won his medal during the war and whom she had thought of almost as a son.

There was a knock at the door, and Bess got up to open it. Two policemen stood there wanting to speak to her.

"What is it about?" asked Bess.

"We're just making enquiries as to what guns you keep at the farm, Mrs. Bowden. There's been a shooting nearby, as you must be aware, and we need to know if any guns are missing."

Both women immediately looked at the corner near the back door where Wilf kept his gun for shooting rabbits. It was empty.

"My son took his gun out with him when he went out yesterday, and he hasn't returned yet. We only had the one gun—a double-barrelled twelve bore he used around the farm. It was a pretty ancient weapon and only good for shooting rabbits, or so Wilf used to say."

"Wilf—is he your son?"

"Yes, my stepson."

"Perhaps you would tell him when he returns that we would like to look at his gun— just to eliminate him from our enquiries, you understand."

Bess closed the door, and the two women stared at one another. A terrible thought had occurred to them.

"So Wilf didn't come home last night, then?"

"No. I've been worried, Laura. He dashed out yesterday morning just as Laurie came in for the milk, nearly knocking him over. I asked him what the hurry was, but he'd gone before answering, so I've no idea where he went."

"Do you think he might have seen Jamie coming along the lane?"

"It's possible, I suppose. He's been clearing out some of the ditches lately. The water on the fields floods down the road after heavy rain, and people have complained they can't get by on foot. It's heavy work for him—"

"But why would he want to harm him even if he did see him?"

"Jealousy, I suppose. Jamie was strong, and he could do the things that Wilf found difficult. He gave you a child and brought shame on our family. Wilf never forgave him for that."

"Jamie has returned to make good his promise to me—what other man would have done such a thing, Mother?" Bess had no reply to that, as she was forced to admit that Jamie had done the honourable thing by her daughter.

"Do you think it was Wilf?"

Bess shook her head, not knowing what to think. "We must wait and see. Perhaps he will turn up soon. I certainly hope so, but it is strange for him to go and not to say where he is going if he intends to stay away. Wilf is a creature of habit, as you know."

Laura left her without telling her mother the farm was to be sold and Bert would need somewhere to live. They had enough to worry about without bothering her about anything else.

Bert was waiting for her when she got back to Lower Farm.

"The police have been searching round here, Laura, and they found a double-barrelled gun in the hedgerow near to where the man was shot. They aren't looking for another weapon. Apparently, the spent cartridges were beside the shotgun."

Laura felt shattered. It must have been Wilf, but where did he go afterwards?

"I think it was Wilf's gun, Bert. Mother said he didn't return last night."

"Wilf! Gone off his head, has he?"

"Apparently he's always resented Jamie—he must have seen him in the lane."

"I'll walk along the sea wall and see if I can see him anywhere. He's harmless without a gun. Ran off, I expect, and too afraid to go home."

Laura nodded, sadly. "Take care, won't you."

Laura went into the kitchen to begin the washing. There was always plenty of washing to do with three children, and it was a fine drying day. A rustling sound in the larder attracted her attention. Someone had left the door open, which was unusual as the cats soon found their way in where there was food to be found. She picked up the broom to shoo them out and found Wilf instead, tearing off large pieces of freshly baked bread and pushing them into his mouth. Laura was indignant. She had known Wilf all her life and felt no fear now the gun had been taken away.

"Hungry are you, Wilf? Well, I'm not surprised staying out all night. Mother is worried sick about you—you'd best be off home for your dinner."

Wilf dropped the bread and rushed towards her, pulling the broom out of her hands. Laura stepped back into the kitchen trying to push him away as he swung the broom over his head, threateningly.

"Stop it, Wilf!" she shouted. "What do you think you're doing? Put the broom down."

"You whore!" yelled Wilf. "I'll give you a good hiding. It's no more than you deserve, sleeping with that Aussie."

Laura sidestepped the broom and screamed at him. "Have you gone mad? Think of the children, for God's sake. They'll hear you."

"Good job if they do," leered Wilf. "It's time that little bastard knew who his father was. I killed the bugger—killed him—killed him Laura. He'll not sleep with you again and bring shame on us all."

"You didn't kill him, Wilf. The pellets only hit his legs. He's in hospital and the police are out looking for you so drop that broom and get going. They'll be back here before long—they've already found your gun in the hedge. It's only a matter of time before they find you."

Wilf threw down the broom and rushed out of the kitchen door, colliding with Laurie, who was standing there. Laura ran to pick up her son and sobbed with relief. Wilf had gone and would never be coming back to disturb their peace again.

"What's the matter with Uncle Wilf, Mum?"

"He's very upset, that's all. It's nothing for you to worry about, my love."

"Why did he call me a bastard? What does bastard mean?"

"It means that Jo wasn't your real father, Laurie. He loved you as much as he could love anyone, and he thought of you as his son."

"Dad wasn't my dad? I don't understand, Mum."

"I was having a baby when I married Jo. I expected to go to Australia when the war ended but I wasn't able to go, so Jo became your father when you were born and looked after you instead. I'm going to marry your real father as soon as he's better."

Laurie looked hurt. "I don't want another father, even if he is my real dad."

"Well, you're a very lucky boy, Laurie. You'll have had two fathers who both loved you, and your real dad has a sheep station out in Australia that will belong to you one day. Who could be luckier than that?"

Laurie hugged her. "But I can come back to this farm one day, can't I?"

"I'm afraid this farm has to be sold, Laurie. Granddad will explain why when he comes back. It's very sad for him because his family has had it for such a long time but he's too old now to manage it on his own. It's time he retired."

Bert called in at Marsh Farm on his way back home. He had walked almost the length of the sea wall but there had been no sign of Wilf, and he knew that Bess must be worried to death. Laura had returned to Lower Farm and Bess would be on her own. She needed to hear what had happened from someone she knew rather than have the police land up on her doorstep to tell her.

Bess was glad to see him. Having a friend to talk to at a time like this was a comfort. They had been neighbours all their lives, and Bess trusted him.

"This is a bad business, Bert," said Bess, pouring him a cup of strong tea.

"Worse than you think, I'm afraid."

"What do you mean? Have they found Wilf."

"No, not yet that I know of, but they have found his gun—at least it looks as if it was his gun—a rusty old double-barrelled thing, in the hedge near the spot where the Aussie fell."

"That's the one—it was pretty useless, but good enough for rabbits. I've been thinking about it, and I was afraid it had been Wilf. He's been bottling up his resentment against that man all these years past—will they put him in prison?"

"They've got to find him first, but I expect that's what will happen."

"The fool! What's going to happen to the farm? It doesn't bring in much these days but it's just enough for us to manage on. We've hardly any cows left and only a couple of pigs and a few chickens. Not much, but more than I can manage."

"Bess, my farm has to be sold. We expect the bailiffs at any time. Jo owed a lot on that new machinery he bought before he died, and I can't keep up the payments."

"Oh, Bert—I'm so sorry, and here *I* am complaining. What will you do?"

"Well, that could be up to you."

"To me! How could I be any help? We have no money to spare these days."

"I haven't come cap in hand, Bess—I would never do that—I'm a proud man, and I'd never sponge off an old widow woman, now would I?"

Bert smiled at her and took her hand in his.

"Let me come and stay here, Bess. I shall need a home and could be your lodger if you're happy about that. I'd pay for my keep—the farm will bring in a bit when it's sold and the debts are settled. Not much, but it will help us both. I can look after the animals, and we might manage to cut the hay field between us despite our old bones. Now what do you say?"

Bess thought for a few minutes before answering. It would solve all her problems, but what would people think? Her relatives would consider it wrong for her to have a man under her roof to whom she wasn't married without Wilf living there. There would be talk, and there had been enough of that in the past.

"It sounds like a good idea Bert, but—"

"But, what?"

"People will talk."

"Good heavens, woman. I'm not suggesting we share a bed! I only want to be a paying lodger."

"Oh, I know that, but people will say other than that, and, with Wilf in disgrace, I can't live with it."

"Come now, Bess. We'll know the truth of the situation, and everyone who knows you and knows your strict principles will discount such evil thoughts. Times have changed since the war—people think differently now but if it worries you so much then we can make it a respectable arrangement."

"A respectable arrangement?"

"I'll marry you if that makes you feel better."

"Oh, Bert!" Bess burst out laughing at such a suggestion. "You can't mean it."

"Why not? We may be a pair of old codgers but we can still care for one another. What do you say?"

It only took Bess a few moments to make up her mind.

"Well, yes, Bert, but on one condition."

"And what may that be?"

"You'll sleep in another room, like a lodger."

"Of course. Suits me, Bess. We aren't exactly a pair of spring chickens, are we?"

Bess smiled at him and went to the pantry and cut him off a slice of fruit cake. This was a special occasion and although she would never have considered giving him such hospitality when he had simply made a neighbourly call, a proposal of marriage warranted a little more.

"Thank you, my dear." Bert ploughed through the almost fruitless cake, chewing and swallowing it down with copious cups of tea. If this was a sample of her cooking, he had a hard time ahead of him, but the die had been cast. It was an arrangement more than a marriage that suited them both, and he hoped he would not come to regret his decision to marry the widow Bowden now he had discovered that her cakes were almost inedible.

After tea, Bert took a walk round the farm where he would soon be living. He had a good idea of the layout of the buildings but he wanted to see what was left in the way of equipment in the barns. Nearly everything was in a state of poor repair, and he could see he would have his work cut out to patch roofs to keep out the weather for a start. Before his own farm was sold, he would bring as much as he could and store it here. He had an old tractor which had been left for some years unused and which he could use again once it had been mended. The plough, the harrow, and the seed drill had all been paid for, and he would bring them with him although he might never use them again on the waterlogged acres of Marsh Farm. He thought of them as a part of his life as a farmer and even if they just rusted away he needed them around him to feel at home with his surroundings.

He found some straw bales stacked untidily in one of the sheds and some beer bottles scattered around. This surprised Bert as the Bowdens were known to be teetotallers, and he looked further. The shed was dark, and he almost stumbled over Wilf, who was lying at the back of the bales holding a bottle in his limp, outstretched hand.

Drunk as a lord, thought Bert as he hurried inside to tell Bess before setting off to find a policeman to arrest him.

CHAPTER 45

The bailiffs had repossessed the new farm equipment at Lower Farm before Jamie was well enough to leave hospital, and Bert had moved into Marsh Farm to live with Bess. Laura had been amazed at his proposal to marry her mother and even more surprised when the quiet ceremony at the chapel had taken place so quickly. She had suggested that they be married at the same time as Jamie and herself, but her mother had wanted to marry Bert right away. If Bert was coming to live at Marsh Farm then he must marry her before he took up residence.

In a way, Laura was pleased with the arrangement. It meant that she would have Jamie to herself, and the children could learn what it was like to have a new father. Rosie came to see them frequently, and Laura got on well with her. She took the children off her hands so she could spend more time with Jamie and took them to visit their grandparents at Marsh Farm where they paddled in the muddy creeks and searched for little crabs.

Chatting to Bess one day over a cup of tea, Rosie told her of the house Jamie had bought for his new bride.

"There's nothing like it in Brightlingsea that I could compare it to, so you could imagine your daughter living there, but I'll try and describe it to you. It's large and comfortable and very grand, with a long verandah in the front, and has a garden that goes down to the sea. Tea trees border the lawns and a path leads to the sandy shore. Your grandchildren will love it, Bess. I used to spend hours with the children by the sea when I was a nursemaid to the family who used to live there."

"It seems extraordinary that your son should be able to buy it for Laura," remarked Bess, "when I understood that he was unable to send for her due to the terrible circumstances in which he found the sheep station after the war."

Rosie decided she would have to take care when chatting idly to Bess or she might realise that there had been some other reason for Jamie not to send for Laura on his return home.

"Well that's quite true, Bess. It *is* extraordinary, but the money for The Great House came mainly from the death of his grandfather, who used to breed racehorses and left him his estate. The sheep station has flourished over the years and is a going concern now, and we also grow citrus fruit, oranges, and limes and lemons."

Bess shook her head in amazement. She found it hard to imagine growing such things on a farm.

"When we suffer from droughts, and the creeks dry up, the poor beasts in the fields die for lack of water, and of course there is no grass left for them to eat. It was like that when Jamie came home. We were very poor and the land was like a dust bowl. I lost my Rory then—he died of influenza. It was a terrible time for us all and no place to bring your Laura to—I told Jamie she would never survive such conditions coming from an English climate."

It sounded to Bess as if Rosie might have had a hand in stopping Laura from coming out to Australia and was exaggerating the situation to make it sound acceptable to her. She had just lost her husband and maybe the thought of an unknown girl from another country coming to take over her position in the farmhouse was not what she wanted. Perhaps it would be as well if she had no plans to live under the same roof as her son and daughter-in-law. Such arrangements did not always work out for the best.

"Well, it's all in the past, and it would seem that your son is a wealthy man now."

"As long as we have no more severe droughts, I would think he'd be very comfortably off for the rest of his life. He wanted to find your Laura so much, and now he has he will settle down happily, one hopes, for the rest of his life."

Bess nodded her approval. It would seem that her Laura and the children would be well settled after all, although she would miss them terribly.

There was only one thing that bothered her slightly. Would Rosie be living with them in this house she loved so much or would Laura be the mistress there? She would have to wait for Laura's letters to find that out.

As the weeks passed, Jamie grew stronger and was able to walk slowly round the farm. When prospective buyers turned up, he enjoyed showing them round when Bert was too busy elsewhere, and Bert was often busy these days as Bess was a hard taskmaster.

His arm frequently encircled Laura's waist, stopping her in her packing as they stole numerous kisses when the children were absent.

"When we're on the boat, sweetheart, we'll have a honeymoon. Ma will look after the children, and we'll make the most of our time together. Making love to you will be more of a pleasure by then."

"You don't do too badly now," said Laura, laughing.

"As soon as my legs have healed properly I'll show you what you've been missing, my girl."

"I can't wait, Jamie darling, make love to me now."

"Sure it's all right? Remember, we aren't married yet," teased Jamie, relieving her of most of her clothes while she gently helped him off with his trousers so as not to hurt his wounds. Lying on top of her soft nubile body was less painful for him, and they were soon transported to heights of such sexual pleasure that Laura wanted it to go on forever.

"Oh, Jamie, I'm so glad you came back," she murmured, as he made love to her until they were both exhausted.

Before the month was up, Jamie and Laura were married in the chapel where she had worshipped all her life, with only her mother, Rosie, and her sister Lucy to witness the event, and Laurie to act as best man.

Lucy, who was a pupil teacher at the little primary school in Thorrington, where she lived in lodgings, had cycled on her bone shaker through the country lanes to see her sister married at last to the father of her firstborn. Sitting up straight on her bicycle with her glasses fixed firmly on her nose by means of a piece of elastic round the back of her head and the hair from her bun coming loose in the breeze, Lucy looked every inch the village schoolteacher. Bert had stayed behind to look after the twins, who were a bit too boisterous to attend a quiet ceremony, and to see that they did not eat all the wedding cake before the wedding party returned.

He had been invited but felt that as this was a second wedding for his son's widow, and he was not the father of the bride, he would do his part by looking after the youngsters. Lucy had promised to cycle ahead of the others to give him a hand and to help lay out the food for the reception.

After they had made their vows, the wedding group walked across the green and down Mill Lane back to Lower Farm, to the curious glances of the passers-by—Laura in a white summer dress with a wreath of wild daisies in her hair, holding a posy of roses picked from the garden of Marsh Farm, and Jamie wearing his best suit and his wide brimmed Australian akubra decorated with roses to match Laura's bouquet.

"I feel a bloody fool," he had told Laura as she had arranged them for him. "Like one of those Morris dancers we saw dancing outside a pub when I lived here during the war."

"You look lovely," Laura had assured him. "A real country gentleman."

"I can't believe that in England bridegrooms dress up in such a bloody stupid way," Jamie had complained.

"Of course they do," Laura had laughed. "Don't they, children?"

The children had hooted with laughter when they saw him. "Of course they do," they had repeated, rolling about with mirth.

"Well, I'm only doing it to please your mother," said Jamie, as he had set off for the chapel, greeting everyone they met with a bow and a courtly wave of his hat, and, by the time they had arrived for the simple ceremony, everyone in the wedding party was in great good humour.

On their return, he threw the hat away, and the children ran after it, taking turns to wear it and prancing about with great glee.

"It was just my fun," Laura whispered to him afterwards. "In this country, weddings can be solemn affairs, and I wanted ours to be memorable."

"You mean to say you made a fool of me, Laura Macdonald! Just you wait!"

Laura laughed and laughed, and the wedding party joined in with great hilarity. It was a wedding that none of them would ever forget, and even the cats getting at the wedding cake while Bert's back was turned did nothing to spoil their day.

Bess took everything she felt would be of use to her from Lower Farm with Bert's permission and turned Marsh Farm into a more comfortable home for them both. Wilf was still in custody and would receive a prison sentence eventually despite Jamie's not wanting to bring charges. He felt a man could not be blamed for protecting his family honour, which was the way Wilf had looked at it, however mistaken he had been. Attempted murder was a serious charge, and Wilf would have to serve a long prison sentence. Bess wondered where he would go afterwards and hoped he would not return to Marsh Farm, although now she was married to Bert Carter it might be easier in some ways if he *had* to come back to live with them. Bert would have to find things for him to do around the farm—occupations that did not involve using a gun, and he might be a changed man after a period of incarceration.

Laura did not go to see Wilf before she left. She could feel nothing but revulsion for the way he had treated her husband. A new life beckoned, and Laura was busy preparing herself and the children for their departure. When everything was ready she walked down to the old fisherman's hut at the seashore and stood for some time watching the tide come in and filling the muddy pools with little eddies of water until the whole of the creek was rippling in the breeze and the tethered boats had come free from their mud berths and rose proudly on the water, as if waiting for their owners to take them out to sea. She had always loved it here, the smell of the mud and the salty sea breeze as it ruffled her long auburn hair. She would never be able to come back, she felt sure of that, and this was her long farewell to the past. She walked back quickly along the sea wall to Lower Farm full of hope and with thoughts of her future life with Jamie. He had told her he was taking her to paradise, and she believed him.

Their good-byes were soon over. Bess felt too upset to say much and the children were too excited at the prospect of the sea journey to mind leaving. Rosie made a great fuss of them, and as they were already thinking of her as their grandmother it made it easier for them to leave Bess and their grandfather Bert behind. Laura was thankful that her mother and Bert would have each other for comfort—it would have been difficult for her to leave otherwise.

Once the train journey was over and the family had embarked on the *Jupiter* at Southampton, Laura felt as if her ties with the past were finally broken. She was leaving an old world for a new world with a different culture and a different way of life. She might have found the long journey a frightening experience had she gone out all alone to marry Jamie. She felt confident travelling with him as his wife, and with his mother and the children for company. As she watched the shores of England disappear into the distance, Jamie put his arm round her shoulders.

"No worries, my darling?" he asked.

"None at all, sweetheart," she replied, lifting her face for his kiss.

Laura, who had never travelled further than a few miles from the farm in her life, was thrilled with the sea journey to her new home and with the exciting places where the ship docked and they could go ashore and explore. Jamie, who had seen it before, found pleasure in her delight at all things new. There were no wild parties this time, just watching the sunsets from the deck with his arm round Laura's waist was enough for him. The fling with Sophia was over and done with. He had the wife he had always wanted, and she made him the happiest of men.

CHAPTER 46

Laura stepped out of the cab and looked at her new home in amazement. The verandah was festooned with blossoms of purple bougainvillaea that climbed round the windows at the front of the house. Curtains floated in the sea breeze from the opened casements, and the large front door had been left open to welcome them.

"Well, what do you think of it?" asked Jamie. "Do you like it?"

Laura was speechless. She had never seen such a house before. It was like a palace— a home fit for royalty and not for someone like herself with simple tastes.

"Well, say something, Laura. Do you like it or not?"

"It's so splendid, Jamie—wonderful—but I can't imagine us living there. There must be hundreds of rooms—I shall get lost."

Jamie laughed and squeezed her affectionately round the waist.

"You cuckoo! There aren't *that* many rooms, and you'll soon get used to it. Ma will show you the way of things—she lived here for quite a time as a nursemaid and came to help when I was born."

"What! You were born here?"

Jamie suddenly realised he had made a dreadful mistake. He had never told Laura he had been adopted, not that it would make much difference. She loved him for himself and got on well with Rosie.

"I never mentioned it before, because it's of no consequence. Ma and Pa adopted me, and I grew up at Seven Creeks as their only son. It doesn't matter, surely?"

"No, of course not—nothing matters now we're together."

Jamie kissed her, a long lingering kiss, and Laura thought no more about it.

"Let's go in, shall we? The housekeeper will be waiting."

"The what? We have a housekeeper?"

"Yes, I asked her to stay on. She's a very pleasant person, and you'll like her. She knows all about looking after a big house like this, and it will give you more time to be with the children. You could never look after The Great House on your own, Laura, now could you?"

"I suppose not, but I shall find it strange at first. I'm not used to giving anyone orders. I prefer to do things myself."

"Of course you do, my darling, and you shall do exactly as much or as little as you like. Come and meet Mrs. Arbuthnot—it's such an awkward name she prefers to be called Jenny. We're in Australia now, and people are very informal—no bowing or scraping here. We treat each other as equals."

Jamie picked her up and carried her over the threshold. "Here you are Mrs. Macdonald. Welcome to your new home."

The housekeeper made an appearance once Laura was back on her feet—a red-cheeked plump woman in her fifties with a wide smile of welcome.

Jamie introduced them, and Laura took to Jenny immediately. She could see there would be no problems between them, and Jenny felt the same way about her. It was a good beginning.

"Where are the children? I thought there were three little ones."

"Not so little now," laughed Laura "Twins of six and Laurie, who is nearly eight. They will be here tomorrow, but they're staying in Melbourne with their grandmother at present. I wanted to see The Great House for myself before they begin to run all over it."

"I hope you like what you see—I'll be preparing some tea for you before you leave." "Thank you, that's very kind." Laura smiled at her as Jenny left them to look around the house.

Everything met with Laura's approval, especially the beautiful four-poster in the main bedroom, hung with muslin drapes, which overlooked the sandy shore.

"We had nothing like this at home," remarked Laura, fingering the fine muslin.

"You didn't have mozzies in England like the ones that breed here. All the beds have drapes like this so you can sleep without waking up and finding yourself covered in bites."

There was a nursery wing with a large play room, which Laura decided should belong to the girls, and a small study adjoining a bedroom which had been singled out for Laurie. The suite of rooms at the back of the house had belonged to Miss Sarah, Lizzie's sister, and Jamie told Laura that his mother had decided that she would like to occupy them.

"Of course," agreed Laura, having temporarily forgotten that Rosie would be living under the same roof. *Who would be issuing the orders?* she wondered. Rosie knew all about this house, and she, Laura, knew nothing.

Down the grand staircase they went and into the salon with its gilded furniture and the cut glass chandeliers. Laura had a feeling of unease. Surely they would never use this room. She and Jamie were not the type to give large parties.

"We can always keep the shutters closed, sweetheart, and put the furniture under wraps until one of the children gets married," said Jamie, looking at her puzzled expression. "There are plenty of rooms in the rest of the house for us to use."

They went into what had been Arthur Potts's study, a dark room with patterned red wallpaper on the walls and above the fireplace an enormous portrait of his ex-wife, Lizzie, with her eldest son, Percy, at her side and her next son, Arty, on her lap.

"Why didn't the owners take that painting?" asked Laura. "The woman is so beautiful, and it must have meant something to them. Wasn't it her son who sold the house to you? Which one would he be?"

"I don't think he's on the painting," said Jamie. "She had four children and some of them wouldn't have been born when that was painted."

"But we must give it back to the family."

"They'd have taken it when they sold the house if they'd wanted it," said Jamie, who had wanted to keep the portrait of his grandmother and his two uncles and had already bought it as a separate item at the time of the sale. "Anyway, it looks good in this room, I think—goes with the house."

"If you think so, my darling. I don't want to argue with you about it."

"I should think not!" said Jamie, making fun of the situation.

In the morning room overlooking the gardens, they ate scones and drank tea, feeling like two children playing at make-believe. Were they really the owners of this magnificent place? Laura found it hard to imagine, but she knew it was true. This was her home for the future, and she was mistress of all she surveyed.

After tea, Jamie took her to look at the stables. He opened the doors of the largest stable, and Laura saw two cars inside.

"Cars, Jamie!" she exclaimed. "Are they ours?"

Jamie laughed at her astonishment. "Of course they're ours. The Model T Ford is for you, and the Buick is mine—plenty of room to take us all for a ride in that."

"But I can't drive, Jamie."

"It's as easy as anything. I'll soon teach you, and you can go into Melbourne whenever you want. You can go along the Nepean Road in it and take Ma and the children for a picnic. I'm going to take you out to Seven Creeks as soon as we are all settled, and you will soon learn your way about."

"Darling, Jamie, this has been such a wonderful day. I can't thank you enough."

"Oh, yes you can—let's go and look at that magnificent bed again, shall we? Try out the springs for comfort." And taking her hand in his, he pulled her laughing up the grand staircase, opening all the doors as they ran along the landing, until they came to the room they would share and made love for the first time in their new home among the downy softness of what had once been Lizzie's bed.

The following day, Rosie brought the children and settled herself in her rooms at the back of the house that had been occupied by Miss Sarah. She had an affection for these rooms, which held fond memories of the woman who had taken over the care of the children when their mother had deserted them. It had all been such a long time ago, but the furniture had been left just as Miss Sarah had arranged it, and Rosie had no wish to alter it. She sat in the little straight-backed chair and looked out onto the garden with her hands folded neatly on her lap and felt very much at home.

The children had rushed round the house, made the acquaintance of the housekeeper, and then had run onto the sand. They pulled off their socks and shoes and paddled in the surf up to their knees before Jamie saw them and called them back.

"Keep only to the edge," he called. "It's dangerous to go in the sea here."

The children looked up in bewilderment. The sea was so inviting, a translucent, aquamarine blue through which they could see the most beautiful shells of all shapes and colours. They collected their shoes and socks and came reluctantly up the sandy bank and into the garden.

"I'll find you a shallow place amongst the rocks where you can play to your heart's content—but not there. Sometimes the sharks come in close to the shore and little legs jumping up and down might attract them to come closer. You don't want to be a shark's dinner, do you?"

The twins shrieked with fright, and Laura came running across the grass.

"Whatever is it?" she asked, in a panic.

"Just a bit of wise advice—the children have to learn that Australia is a different country. There are sharks all round this coast, and it's not wise to wade out in the sea. They can play on the sand and in the rock pools where they can see there is nothing to be afraid of—and they'll soon learn not to turn over logs or walk through the long grass in bare feet—dangerous snakes live in such places, and bull ants bite."

"I don't like it here," said Lily. "I want to go home."

"We can't go home, sweetheart. Grandma will show you lots of wonderful things— she's just told me that there are parrots that come into this garden *and* cockatoos—go and ask her and she'll tell you where to look."

"Sorry if I frightened them, Laura—it was just a natural reaction. I was brought up knowing all these things. This is a wonderful country for children to grow up in—they'll thrive here."

"While we're on the subject, is there anything else you should tell me, Jamie, although sharks, snakes, and ants that bite are enough for one day."

"Just spiders, I suppose."

"Spiders! Ugh, I hate spiders."

"The smallest ones usually have the worst bite; spiders come in all sizes out here.

You might come across a huntsman in the house, but don't worry about it if you do.

They come in out of the garden and are as big as saucers but are pretty harmless. If you don't bother them, they won't bother you, but Ma will dispose of them for you if you find one—she's used to spiders."

"Brave woman," said Laura, shuddering. It might look like paradise, but there was an unpleasant, hidden side to this paradise that Jamie had never thought to mention.

"You'll soon get used to it, sweetheart. Tomorrow, I'll take you all out in my lovely new car, and we'll go for a picnic in the bush where there are kangaroos. The children will love that."

Rosie smiled at him. He was being so kind and thoughtful but it would take her some time to adjust to this new country.

The children settled down quickly, once they had learnt to abide by the rules, and were soon making friends at school, and began to speak as if they had been born in Australia. Rosie spent a large part of each day in the kitchen helping to organise the food for the family and chatting to Jenny about her early days living in The Great House. Laura felt left out of the domestic routine. She learnt to drive her little car up and down the driveway until she felt confident enough to drive along the Nepean Road and took the children to school and collected them at the end of the day.

Jamie used to saddle up his horse and ride over to Seven Creeks most days. Laura missed him while he was away. The days seemed so long without him with nothing in particular to do, so she asked him to let her come with him.

"Of course you can come, sweetheart, but I thought you would be too busy here to want a day at the sheep station just yet. When the shearing begins, the children will find that real good, and we'll all go."

"But I'd like to see the home you told me about when you stayed with us, Jamie. I've kept a picture of it in my mind all these years—the wattle tree growing by the side and the eucalypts along the creeks ..."

Jamie smiled. He had probably exaggerated some of the things he had told her in order to impress her and hoped she would not feel too disappointed when she saw the homestead for herself. Compared to The Great House, it was a humble place.

"As to the wattle tree, I'm afraid that's not there anymore. It grew too big, and I cut it down soon after I got back home." Laura looked disappointed. "But there are plenty of others—they grow wild—I'll soon find one to show you."

"I'll have to teach you to ride a horse, Laura," said Jamie as he manoeuvred around the potholes along the road from Euroa to Seven Creeks. "These dirt roads weren't made for cars."

"So it would seem," laughed Laura, as she was thrown from side to side as if on a fairground ride.

At last they came to Seven Creeks and Laura could see the homestead for herself and the acres of grassland surrounding it as far as the eye could see, filled with sheep and cattle. Jamie had told the truth when he had described it to Wilf all those years ago, the size of his farm and the huge flocks of sheep. How could any of them have envisaged such a place living at Marsh Farm with its few acres?

Jamie stopped the car just before they had reached the homestead, and Laura looked at him in surprise. "Why have you stopped here?" she asked.

Jamie was staring at the back of the house where a woman could be seen standing on the verandah— - a woman with long black hair holding a basket over her arm.

"What the hell is she doing here?" he muttered.

"Why? Who is it?" asked Laura, who could sense his annoyance.

"Stay in the car, Laura—don't get out!"

He slammed the car door in anger and hurried up to the homestead to speak to the woman. Laura watched as he shouted at her and pulled her roughly by the arm as she argued with him. She had never seen Jamie in such a temper before, and it alarmed her. Whoever was this woman he disliked so much?

Eventually, the young woman got onto a rickety bicycle and putting her basket over the handlebars she began to cycle up the road towards the car with Jamie striding along behind her, seeing her off his land. As she passed the car, Laura took a good look at her, and she stared back at Laura with an insolent expression on her face.

"Who on earth was that?" she asked, as Jamie got back in the car.

"Someone who'd been sent packing a long time ago," he replied.

"Why? What had she done?"

"Nothing for you to bother yourself with," said Jamie shortly as he drove her to the front of the homestead. "Come and meet Beattie; she lives here and takes care of the place for us. She's Ma's friend, and I'm taking her back with us for a few days—she deserves a holiday, and Ma will have a lot to tell her since our return from the old country. She'll show you round—there are things I need to see to."

Laura felt peeved. Nobody had mentioned to her that this Beattie was coming to stay. She presumed that Rosie had arranged it with Jamie—not that she minded, it was just that she felt she was always playing a second string to her mother-in-law's arrangements.

Beattie was a pleasant countrywoman who reminded Laura in some ways of her own mother. She ushered Laura into the parlour and brought her some tea on a tray.

"How lovely to meet you, Laura. I've been looking forward to it. I've come to think of this as my home since I came here to stay with Rosie. We'd been friends for a long time, and I really miss her since she went to live in The Great House with you all."

"Well, you'll soon see her. Jamie says you're coming to stay for a while."

Beattie nodded. "How lucky you were, my dear, to come to Australia and live in your wonderful house instead of this little homestead. There isn't much of comfort here, you know—it's typical of most bush homesteads."

"I like it," said Laura looking round the simply furnished parlour. "It reminds me of the farm—I feel very much at home here."

"Do you, dear? Well that surprises me. You're a real lady at The Great House, and I would have thought—"

"I don't want to be a real lady, Beattie. I come from farming stock, and I was used to very little at home in the way of luxuries, and I didn't expect more than that when I hoped to come to live here after the war. This would have suited me fine."

Beattie looked surprised. There was something about Laura she liked—she was a straight-forward, honest young woman, and she wondered why Rosie had so taken against her when Jamie had told her he wanted to marry her after the war.

"Well, let me show you around now you've finished your tea. There isn't much to see I can assure you—three bedrooms and a kitchen and a dunny outside. Baths were taken in front of the range in the kitchen—no privacy here."

"No different from home. I was used to that," laughed Laura.

Outside, there were chooks scrabbling in the yard. Laura sighed at the sight of them.

"I miss the chickens, and milking the cows. I'd love to live here, Beattie."

Beattie shook her head in amazement. "I don't know what your Jamie would have to say to that!"

"Nor do I, I don't think he would be best pleased after all he has done for me."

They sat themselves down on the verandah to await Jamie's return and listened to the strange sound of a pair of kookaburras laughing in the stringy bark trees.

"Who was that woman I saw when we arrived? Jamie didn't seem too pleased to see her here?" asked Laura.

"Oh, Kathleen, you mean. She lived here for a few years with her son. She was here when Jamie came home from the war."

Laura had a feeling of unease. "How long did she stay?"

"I don't know really—I think Rosie and Rory took pity on her when she turned up one day with her baby when Jamie was overseas. After a couple of years, she left with a jackaroo—and most of Rosie's best china!"

"No wonder Jamie was cross when he saw her here."

"Oh, she's harmless enough. She comes for her eggs and a good gossip. Sometimes she sends Shaun—he must be nearly ten now—but he's a bad boy, and I'd rather she came herself. His fingers are into everything, little rascal."

Jamie appeared to drive them back home. Beattie collected her few belongings and they set off for The Great House. Jamie was in a morose mood, and Laura had no appetite for making conversation. All she could think of was Kathleen and her son living in the homestead when Jamie had arrived back home and the fact that he had never told her the truth as to why she could not join him after the war. Why did it have to be a secret?

That night, she turned away from him when he wanted to make love to her.

"Come on, sweetheart—what's wrong? If I was short-tempered today, I'm sorry. It had nothing to do with you, believe me."

"No Jamie, but it did have something to do with that woman, didn't it? You couldn't get rid of her fast enough because she had something to do with your past—something you never told me about—the *real* reason why I couldn't come and join you after the war. Beattie told me she was living in the homestead with her son—was he your son, Jamie? Is that why she looked at me with such loathing?"

"No, he was *not* my child—that's just the point. Ma believed her lies and took her in, but she was fooled. Kathleen was using her, that's all, and it was a long time before she realised it. There was nothing I could do—I couldn't have you humiliated by that woman living under the same roof, and Ma refused to turn her out."

Laura wept and wept and refused to let Jamie touch her.

"And to think that I had to go through all that misery with my own family, expecting your child, Jamie. How *could* you have done that to me?"

"Blast that bloody woman!" roared Jamie in frustration. "Why can't she keep out of my life—shall I never have any peace from her." He leapt out of bed and left the room to wake his startled mother.

"For Gawd's sake, Ma, go and see to Laura. She won't listen to me. Kathleen was at the homestead when we arrived, and Laura knows now that she was the reason for my not letting her come out after the war. Beattie let the cat out of the bag, unfortunately. Try and make her see sense if you can."

He was in such a state that Rosie reluctantly put on her wrap and went to comfort Laura and to tell her the truth of the matter, taking the blame for what had happened upon herself. It would only make matters worse if Laura knew that Jamie had once had sex with Kathleen before he left for the war, so she would not mention that—they were happy together and that unfortunate incident could be forgotten.

"Rory and I took to the child at first, and he gave us some comfort when Jamie was away. We feared that he might never return like so many others, and we weren't to know that he wasn't Jamie's son. Kathleen told us he was, and Rory didn't want Jamie told about it—it would only be something else for him to worry about in the trenches fighting for his country, so we took responsibility for the child—try to understand, my dear."

Once Rosie had left, Jamie took her into his arms and wiped the tears from her eyes.

"There wasn't a day when I didn't think of you, my darling, and long for you. Would I have come all that way to look for you if I hadn't loved you? We've been so happy together; don't let anything spoil it, *please,* Laura. I couldn't live without you now."

In the early hours of the morning, as the sun slowly rose over the horizon and filled their room with light, Jamie found himself forgiven, but, for Laura, Rosie's involvement in the delay before she could become Jamie's wife would never be forgotten.

CHAPTER 47

While Rosie and her friend were out enjoying themselves in Melbourne, Laura set to work to rearrange things in The Great House. After what she had discovered, which she considered to be her mother-in-law's treachery, she found a grim satisfaction in making her presence felt. She altered the weekly menus to suit her own taste, spent hours knocking up the dough for the weekly supply of bread, and filled the huge pantry with pastries and cakes. Jenny working in the kitchen could hardly keep pace with her. The young Mrs. Macdonald was showing just who was mistress here. It had been a surprise to the housekeeper to find she knew so much about the preparation of food and was willing to throw herself into the hard task of cooking for the household. Up to then, she had thought her a lady of leisure who was happy to leave things to her mother-in-law to organise.

"I was brought up on a farm in England," she explained to the bewildered housekeeper. "We were poor farmers and needed to make ends meet—it meant cooking meals with whatever came to hand, and, when I had my own kitchen to work in, I tried out all kinds of recipes. My husband and his father had very hearty appetites, and we lived mostly off the land—using our own fruit and vegetables."

Laura was beating some eggs as she spoke, as if her life depended on it. "I even cured our own pork and made the chitterlings—have you ever tried them, Jenny?"

"Goodness, no," replied the flustered Jenny, who knew nothing of Laura's first husband. Jamie's return to England to find his lost love had been all that Rosie had divulged, and Jenny had often wondered about her background. She knew that Laura was a young widow with three children, and that was all. "I'm just a plain cook, and a very good one at that. My mother-in-law should let you do more instead of interfering all the time."

"Oh, no—she doesn't interfere—she just likes to have things the way she likes them. We get along very well together."

"I'm sure you do," said Laura sharply.

There was a noise of children racing up and down stairs, and Laura went to investigate, much to Jenny's relief. She had always thought of Laura as a kind, uncomplaining person who was easy to work for. Her character appeared to have changed overnight for some unexplained reason.

"What do you think you are doing, tearing about like that? I've got a headache, and it's making it worse."

"Sorry, Mum. We're playing chase with Percy, that's all," said Primrose, breathlessly.

"Who did you say, darling? I can't see anyone else here but you and Lily."

"He's gone now you've come," said Lily crossly.

"Gone where?"

"Oh, I don't know. Sometimes he's in the nursery and sometimes he's hiding in the garden."

"Have you got a friend I don't know about children? You mustn't invite strange people into the house without telling me."

"We don't," said Primrose. "He lives here—it's his house."

Laura was taken aback. "We're the only people who live in this house, you know that. You're telling stories the pair of you."

The children made no reply and ran into the garden. After a while, Laura heard them laughing as they played chase round the bushes, and she went upstairs to lie down on her bed. As she passed the nursery, she looked through the door in case by any chance a strange boy was lurking there. The rocking horse in front of the window was rocking furiously back and forth as if it was being ridden. Somebody must have set it in motion. Laura went in, stopped it, and shut the door. When she went into her bedroom, it seemed to have started rocking again. Must be the wind catching it, she thought, as she lay down and closed her eyes. There could be no other explanation. The girls were outside, and Laurie was fishing with his father, so they were not responsible. She found it difficult to sleep and got up and went into the kitchen where Jenny was washing up.

"I'm sorry, Jenny. Please forgive me—I shouldn't have spoken to you like that but I have a terrible headache and the children were being rather noisy."

"I understand—perhaps you've been doing too much lately and tired yourself out."

"Maybe that's what wrong, but the children are worrying me. They've been brought up to tell the truth, yet just now they told me they have a friend who lives in the house, and that can't be true. They were playing chase with him up the stairs, but I couldn't see anybody."

"Children often have playmates they only seem to see—they make them up—it's not unusual." Jenny smiled. "Did the friend have a name?"

"Percy."

"Ah, it was Percy, was it?"

"You know him?"

"Well, not exactly, but I've heard a child running upstairs sometimes and seen the rocking horse moving on its own as if someone was riding it. A child called Percy used to live here years ago and was killed very tragically. It might have been him, if you believe in ghosts."

Laura was horrified. Her children were playing with a ghost? Surely not! Perhaps Rosie could throw some light on the matter—she had looked after the Potts children a very long time ago.

When Rosie and Beattie returned, Laura asked her about Percy, without mentioning that the twins might have seen him.

"It was so sad," related Rosie. "The poor child went looking for his mother when she had left to live with her lover. He saddled up his pony by himself and was killed when the saddle slipped to one side and he fell, hitting his head on a stone. We were all devastated, especially Mr. Potts. He was his eldest son and his pride and joy—but why do you want to know about Percy?"

"Oh, it was just something Jenny was talking to me about."

"If you want to know what he looked like there is a good likeness of him in the portrait in the study—he's the boy standing by his mother."

"She was such a beautiful woman, wasn't she? I often think so whenever I look at that painting."

"Oh, yes, she was a beauty all right, but the beauty was only skin deep, in my opinion. She left her little girl behind when she ran away. Only a few weeks old she was, poor little thing. Her Aunt Sarah brought her up and gave her the love that her mother should have given her."

"I see—that's why you think so much of the person you call Miss Sarah."

"Well, not really—I hardly knew that baby. The house was in such turmoil afterwards that I left and returned to Clay Cross. Miss Sarah had shown me much kindness on the boat when I was a little girl and when I worked here she came to stay with the family every weekend. I became very fond of her as I grew up."

"Didn't she marry?"

"No—she lost the sailor she had been engaged to on the boat in a dreadful storm and spent the rest of her life running the business in Melbourne when Arthur Potts was absent, which was often, I'm afraid. Mr. Potts enjoyed living the high life and was often the worse for drink. No woman was safe from him, not even the maids— that's really why I left. We couldn't sleep safely in our beds."

Laura was horrified at Rosie's description of life after Lizzie had left. The Great House had an unhappy past and had she been with Jamie when he had bought it, knowing what she knew now, she would never have agreed to live there. Underneath the beauty of the place there lurked something she was just beginning to discover. A house could be full of secrets, which lingered on long after the owners had left—ghosts from the past, like little Percy, who seemed unable to leave the place.

Laura shuddered at the thought of her children's strange behaviour since they had come to live here. She would need to speak to Jamie about it when he returned from his fishing trip with Laurie. Thankfully, Laurie had never mentioned seeing Percy. He was older than the twins and a down-to-earth boy who was enjoying the outdoor life in his father's company. Laura loved to see the bond that had formed between Jamie and his son after a rather rocky start, but once they had arrived in Australia and Jamie had so much to show them of this new country, the bond had grown stronger and stronger. He was so proud of this newly found son, who was beginning to resemble him in many ways, and took him to Seven Creeks to show him the way of things, whenever possible. The earlier he learned about sheep farming the better. He bought him a fine chestnut horse and taught him to ride so that Laurie could accompany him when he rode out to Seven Creeks.

The twins had complained about Laurie being Jamie's favourite and spending so much time away from home with his father that to placate them both he bought them a fat pony each, and they rode round the paddock at The Great House to Laura's consternation as her daughters were not born horsewomen and had frequent tumbles during their lessons, but as both girls were of stolid build with sturdy legs like their father, a tumble from a tiny pony did them little harm.

"We visited Miss Sarah today." Beattie's voice broke into Laura's thoughts.

"Really—I didn't know she was still alive. She must be very old."

"She is, and in a sad way too. She didn't know Rosie. Mind you, it's been years since she'd seen her—how old is Jamie now, Rosie? That must have been the last time, when you came back here to look after Miss Hetty—"

"Sorry, Beattie, I can't remember," replied Rosie hastily changing the subject.

Laura was puzzled. Who was Miss Hetty and what had it to do with Jamie's age. Unless perhaps—there was no point in conjecture; it got her nowhere in this house of secrets. She would have to ask Jamie and hope that he would give her a straight answer when he and Laurie returned that evening.

Laura tucked the twins into bed early that night. They were exhausted with tearing round the bushes in an endless game of hide and seek, becoming more and more excited and shrieking loudly each time the hidden child was discovered. Laura felt as if her head would burst with the constant noise and was thankful when they fell into a deep sleep. As she was about to shut the door of the nursery, the rocking horse began to move making a rhythmic creak as the old springs moved backwards and forwards driven by an unseen hand. The children were sound asleep and appeared not to hear anything. Laura decided that tomorrow the rocking horse would be destroyed so the sound would trouble her no more. She had never believed there were such things as ghosts, and she would put an end to this nonsense.

When Laurie and Jamie returned, she asked Laurie if he had heard of a child called Percy whom the twins thought of as their friend, but Laurie had never heard of him. As soon as he had gone upstairs to bed, Laura spoke to Jamie about her fears.

"It's only make-believe, my darling—ghosts indeed!"

"But children *do* see things that adults are unaware of Jamie, and Jenny has heard a child running upstairs and seen the rocking horse moving."

"Just the boards creaking in the heat—expansion and contraction, you know—we get extremes of temperature in just a few hours sometimes. That's all it is, and there are draughts all over this house—not all the windows fit perfectly—but if it will make you feel better I'll have the rocking horse taken away tomorrow. The girls have real ponies to play with now, and they're a bit too big for a rocking horse."

Laura felt better immediately and once held in the comfort of his arms her headache disappeared and she felt at peace with herself.

"I won't go to the homestead tomorrow, sweetheart. You've been on your own too much lately, and the twin's high spirits have been getting you down. We'll go on a picnic along the coast, just us and the children. Ma and Beattie can have the place to themselves. Would you like that?"

"Only as long as the rocking horse has gone when we come back."

"Of course, if that will make you feel better. I'll get one of the gardeners to see to it. You are a silly goose, Laura. Come on, make love to me. It's all of three days since the last time, and that's three days too long."

Laura laughed and flung herself into his arms to experience once again the heights of sexual desire, all of her worries forgotten.

She woke during the night with a feeling of unease and got out of bed. Something was wrong, but she had no idea what. There was no noise from the children's room, but she decided to look inside to put her mind at rest. It was empty, and their clothes had gone. The rocking horse was completely still, bathed in the moonlight from the open shutters. In her terror, she woke Jamie, shaking him roughly.

"What's happened to you, Laura? Have you gone mad?"

"The girls have gone—they've dressed and gone somewhere. Get up, Jamie—hurry— I know something's wrong." She ran to the window and looked out. In the moonlight, it was as light as day, and she could see her daughters riding their ponies along the strand.

"They're out there—look! Where are they going at this time of night? I've never let them go any further than the paddock—they don't ride well enough."

Jamie pulled on his trousers and his boots. "I'll ride bareback—if I stop to saddle up I might lose them."

He ran down the stairs, two at a time and slammed the door behind him. Laura watched as he led his horse out of the stable and galloped off along the strand. The girls were out of sight, but she felt sure he would soon catch them up. Their ponies were very slow and only plodded along.

Hearing all the noise, Laurie woke up and came into his mother's bedroom to find her sobbing by the casement. Laura put her arms round him.

"What's happened, Mum? Where's Dad?"

"Gone to look for your sisters—they're out there somewhere, the naughty girls. I don't know why but they got dressed and got out their ponies and set off along the strand all on their own— - and look, the tides coming in! Oh, please God, let Jamie get to them in time."

"Let me go and help. I can ride fast now, and I'm not afraid."

Laura clutched him to her more tightly. "No, Laurie. Your father will bring them back. If anyone can find them, he will. When they get back then you can go down and unsaddle the ponies while I bring them indoors."

It seemed forever before they could see Jamie leading the two ponies along the beach with the waves up to their fetlocks. The girls were sitting stiffly in their saddles like a pair of lifeless puppets. Laurie ran downstairs to lead the ponies away to the stables while Laura and Jamie helped the children inside.

"What's the matter with them?" asked Laura, looking at their expressionless faces.

"I've no idea. They didn't seem to know me when I caught up with them. It's as if they were riding in their sleep—like sleepwalking."

"What, both of them?" said Laura shaking Lily to make her wake up.

"Where did you think you were going to, Lily? It's the middle of the night—you could have been drowned if Jamie hadn't come to find you."

Lily opened her eyes and gave her mother a drugged stare. "We were helping Percy," she said, before slumping into a chair.

Laura pulled her up and shook her again. "Helping Percy do what?" she demanded.

"Find his mama," muttered Lily, still half asleep.

"Now do you believe me?" asked Laura. "There isn't a rational explanation for this.

Perhaps Percy wanted some children for company to help him to get back into the other world—*my* children. If they had drowned maybe we wouldn't have been haunted in this house anymore. He'd have had two little playmates in the world beyond the grave."

They picked up the sleeping children and took them upstairs. Covered up in bed they were fast asleep as if nothing had happened.

When Laurie came in, Jamie went to stable his horse. "Are they all right?" asked Laurie.

"Just sleepwalking," explained Laura. "You go to bed, Laurie. I'm sitting up in their room tonight. We'll sort it out in the morning."

Before he went back to bed, Jamie took the rocking horse downstairs and put it in the shed ready to be chopped up, hoping that there would be no more ghostly visitations.

In the morning, the twins awoke to find their mother asleep in the nursery chair and the rocking horse missing. They woke her up, and she hugged them, as if they had been lost and she had just found them.

"Why are you sleeping in our room?" asked Primrose. "We're too big to have someone looking after us anymore."

"You had a bad nightmare last night, my darlings. Do you remember it?"

But neither of the children remembered anything about their escapade the previous night. They seemed refreshed, as if they had been released from a powerful spell and were happy to play as they always had done, without the uncontrolled behaviour of the past weeks.

Jamie had no idea what to think. Laura was certain that Percy's spirit had possessed them both and would not be dissuaded from her theory. The rocking horse was duly destroyed and the nursery became a peaceful place. Laurie had been told never to tell the twins what had happened that night, as they had no memory of the events, and she kept it from her mother-in-law—it was just another secret to be kept in this house of secrets. But there was something she still had to tell her husband, and she chose a time when they were alone, walking in the garden under the trees.

"How did it come about that you were born here, Jamie?" she had asked.

Jamie was taken aback by the question. This was something he had not intended to discuss with her, although he had let the fact slip when he had first brought her here.

"You told me you were—when you told me that Rosie had adopted you—remember?"

Jamie remembered only too well. He could not tell her all the truth, but as his wife she was entitled to hear a part of it. He wanted no more misunderstandings.

"My real mother was a daughter of the family who lived here. She was very young and her husband died so she decided that Ma could adopt me and bring me up."

"Ah." Rosie was quiet for a while. "Was her name, Hetty, by any chance?"

Jamie was startled. How did she know that?

"Beattie mentioned someone called Hetty whom Rosie had looked after here a long time ago—she was trying to remember just how long ago that was and asked how old you were?"

Jamie roared with laughter. "Did she indeed! Beattie talks too much for her own good—well, yes, Hetty, or Harriet, which was her *proper* name, was my mother but I've never met her and never will. She married again and has a family, and I'm no part of her life. Ma and Pa brought me up, and that's good enough for me. Let's drop the subject, shall we, Laura?"

"All right, my love. It's just that if we have a little girl next time I'd like to name her after your real mother. Would you like that Jamie?"

Jamie stopped in his tracks. Laura was looking at him intently, her beautiful eyes sparkling with happiness, and her lips parted in a seductive smile.

"You don't mean you're—"

"Yes, my darling—I'm about three months pregnant."

Jamie swung her round excitedly and then, remembering her condition, set her down carefully on her feet.

"I don't mind you calling a girl Hetty, but if the baby's a boy he won't be called Percy—you can bet your life on that!" said Jamie with feeling.

CHAPTER 48

"What do you think of this?" asked Rosie, spreading a froth of silk and lace over the coverlet on Laura's bed. Laura looked up as she was feeding the baby to admire the garment.

"It's so beautiful—almost too beautiful for a tiny baby to wear everyday. You really mustn't keep buying her things, Rosie. She has enough clothes for twenty babies. I shall have to change her ten times a day to use them all up."

"Well, this is rather special. I thought it would do for her christening robe. It has the sweetest little bonnet to match. Beattie and I had never seen such a wonderful gown before, and we just *had* to buy it."

"It's most kind of you—yes, it is simply lovely, and Hetty can wear it on her special day, but it must have cost you *such* a lot of money, Rosie, and that rather worries me."

"No worries, my dear. I put it on Jamie's account at Potts Famous Haberdashery—he told me I could use it for whatever I wanted for the baby."

"But I didn't know we had an account there."

"No? I expect he forgot to mention it. I suggested he open one while you were getting over her birth. A baby needs so many things, and a man can't manage that side of it. It's a good job that Beattie and I were here to give a hand."

Laura put the baby back in her cradle and closed her eyes. It was taking a long time to get over Hetty's birth, much longer than the other children, and she felt exhausted by the comings and goings in the household. Even her bedroom was no longer sacrosanct. Rosie was forever popping in to see the baby and picking her up to cuddle her. She was over the moon with this second grandchild.

Beattie had become a permanent guest. She was Rosie's companion and would never be going back to Seven Creeks again. The homestead was left to the dust and the spiders. The chooks had either been eaten by the wildlife or given away, and the yard was empty. It saddened Laura, but there was nothing she could do about it. She supposed it would gradually fall apart like many other deserted homes in the bush. Once, she had imagined living there with Jamie and their family—a love nest just for them, but now things were very different. She lived in a grand house with other people who managed her life for her, and a mother-in-law who out of the goodness of her heart even chose the baby clothes for Hetty. She knew she ought to be grateful, but it just made her feel useless.

"Having this baby has left you feeling a bit down, sweetheart," said Jamie. "You'll get over it given time, and Ma and Beattie are here to do as much as they can to help."

Laura had burst into tears. That was just what she did *not* want, but she found it impossible to make him understand, and all he could do was comfort her.

"Your mother tells me we have an account at Potts Haberdashery so she could buy all the clothes that Hetty needs. She bought this today." Laura showed him the christening gown. "It's beautiful, but it must have cost a small fortune."

"That doesn't matter, my love. Hetty is our daughter, and I can afford for her to have the best. Ma loves going to Potts Haberdashery to buy expensive items. Mrs. Henry has to treat her like a favoured customer, and that goes against the grain—Ma having been Henry's nursemaid and having adopted me into the bargain, the skeleton in their family cupboard. They would prefer to forget all about me but Ma won't let them. I find it most amusing."

Laura smiled. She wished she could see the look on Mrs. Henry's face when Rosie and Beattie came through the door of the shop, and she went on smiling long after Jamie had left. He was so good to her, she must get over this wretched depression and get back to being her usual self. She had time on her hands with everyone else running the household affairs, so she wrote a long letter to her mother telling her the news of the family and her newest grandchild. Bess rarely corresponded, and, when she did, nothing seemed to have changed—life went on as it always had done at Marsh Farm. Lower Farm had been sold at last, and all their debts had been cleared, leaving them enough for their simple needs.

As soon as she began to recover, Laura asked Jamie to take her and the children out to the homestead. It was time for the spring shearing, and he had promised the twins that this time they could watch. Seeing the dogs help to round up the Merinos never ceased to amaze Laura as they ran across the backs of the sheep, who seemed unaware of them through their thick fleece. Laurie helped to round up the huge flocks with his father and the other men. When he was old enough, he wanted to try his hand at shearing, sitting the huge woolly animals down on their tails between his legs, while he cut off their fleece. He was growing up fast into a tough little Aussie and longed to leave school and work at Seven Creeks with his father.

Laura spread out a picnic on what remained of the verandah and sent the girls to call Laurie and Jamie. The jackaroos were busy in the woolshed, so Jamie left them to it and returned to the homestead. Laurie was nowhere to be seen.

"We've looked everywhere for him, Mum, and shouted our heads off," said Lily.

"I heard you, a right pair of screaming banshees you've turned into."

"I expect he'll be here soon when he's good and ready and wants his tucker. Get stuck in girls—I could eat a horse—shearing is hungry work."

The picnic was almost over when Laurie appeared with blood streaming from his nose, a bruised face and what looked like a broken arm.

"What's happened to you, mate?" asked Jamie. "Been in a fight?"

Laurie nodded, miserably. Laura got up to mop up the blood and strap up his arm.

"He's been badly hurt, Jamie. Who could have done such a thing to him?"

"Well son? Did you know who it was?"

"A boy called Shaun—said he had more right to be here than I did because he was older than me—said he was your son, so I punched him for being a liar. The jackaroos egged him on—told him to knock the living daylights out of me."

"Did they indeed! I'll soon sort this out, the little bugger."

Jamie ran across to the woolshed and disappeared inside. Laura heard him shouting, and an argument broke out between him and a man she had never seen before. Jamie pulled a boy out of the shed by the scruff of his neck and threw him onto the ground while the man pulled him back onto his feet.

"What was the point of bringing that little tyke with you—he's too young to be a part of the team, and he's done nothing but make trouble. He has no place here."

"He has every right to be here, as you well know," shouted the man, pushing his fist into Jamie's face. "The Macdonalds brought him up—this was his home. You're the one who should be ashamed of yourself, mate, giving my Kathleen a kid and then denying him his birthright."

"He is *not* my child," shouted Jamie. "Kathleen can think what she likes; he could have been anyone's child, and she knows it. Just look at him for Gawd's sake—just *look* at him—he's nothing like me, the snivelling little brat. Get him out of here and yourself too for that matter and don't come back. I can do without your services in the future. Here's your wages—now clear off the pair of you."

Laura heard most of this conversation with a sinking heart. So her husband *had* known that boy's mother before he had met her—and worse still he had been her lover. Rosie had led her to believe that it was her decision to allow Kathleen to stay in the homestead with her child because Kathleen had told her it was Jamie's baby, although Jamie had denied the fact on his return home. It was no wonder that he had prevented her from coming out to Australia to marry him, however much he had loved her.

Rosie had taken the blame to protect their marriage, and Laura felt wretched thinking back to the hard feelings she had felt towards her mother-in-law at the time. Jamie would need to tell her the truth of the matter and do something for that boy if he was his child. What if it had been Laurie he had refused to acknowledge as his son? She knew how bitter that would have made her feel, and she felt some sympathy for the boy's mother.

In silence, Laura and the twins collected up the remains of the picnic and packed them into the Buick. Jamie got into the driving seat and the family set off for home, without a word being spoken by anyone. Jamie drove back like a lunatic with the car lurching over the potholes in the road and giving them all a most uncomfortable ride. Laura, looking at his angry face, wondered just how she would be able to approach the subject. Perhaps it was best left alone. Kathleen obviously had no hold on him now, and he had come back to England to find her once Kathleen had left Seven Creeks, so what did it really matter. Men had to sow their wild oats, but the truth would have been better than the tale Rosie had felt it best to tell her.

Once home, Laura picked up the baby to feed her. She had left her in Rosie's care while they had gone to Seven Creeks, much to the delight of Rosie, who loved her dearly.

"Did you have a good day?" asked Rosie. "You all look down in the dumps."

"Laurie got into a fight with another boy who unfortunately beat him up badly. Jamie took him to see the doctor as soon as we got back. We think his arm is broken so he might need to have it set in a plaster."

"Good gracious—what a calamity! Did you find out who it was?"

"Laurie said his name was Shaun," piped up Lily. "Dad was really mad."

"The boy said he was Dad's son, so Laurie thumped him one and then they got into a fight. Dad sent him home with the man who brought him."

"I'm not surprised," said Rosie grimly, wondering just what Laura had thought about it. Hopefully, the explanation she had given her would suffice.

When the children had gone into the garden, Laura turned to her mother-in-law.

"I understand how difficult it must have been for you now, Rosie. Please forgive me—I blamed you for keeping us apart at first, but what else could you have done? I just hope the boy wasn't Jamie's son, that's all."

"I don't think so, my dear—I really don't. He was a bad child in many ways, thieving and lying like his mother, who was a bad girl in her time although while she lived with us she tried to mend her ways, but a leopard doesn't change its spots. She had fancied Jamie since she was a little girl and was always hanging around him when she got the chance. We took her in when Jamie was away, but he had no time for her when he came back. He told me the child could have belonged to anybody—she was that sort of a girl."

"But surely a man like Jamie didn't want a girl like Kathleen as a mistress, that's what I can't understand."

"No, my dear, it was nothing like that—no way. It happened the night before he left for the war when they had a big do for all the new recruits in the hall in Euroa. There was plenty to drink and plenty of women and Kathleen was one of them. Jamie was drunk, and she asked for a lift home. He had never had any time for her—couldn't bear the girl—but the others pushed her up onto the horse, so he took her home. I doubt he remembered much about it—leaving home to fight was the only thing on his mind—but he's a man, Laura, and the circumstances were—"

"I don't want to hear any more about it, Rosie—please. It's in the past, and he loves *me*—I'm sure of that ,and that's all I care about."

Rosie smiled. It was over, and now they could all get on with their lives. Laurie came back with his arm in plaster and basked in the adulation of his sisters who treated him like a hero.

"Dad says that boy was nothing to do with him," he told the girls, "and he felt real proud of me sticking up for him."

"I'm sure he did, and so do we all," agreed Laura, feeling as if a load had been lifted from their lives. She put Hetty back in her cradle and went to look for Jamie. It was time to ease his conscience, as far as she was concerned.

Jamie was polishing the Buick as if his life depended on it and kept his face averted. Laura touched his arm. "Look at me, Jamie. Please turn round, darling, I've something I want to say."

Her voice was soft and loving. It was not what he had been expecting. She must have heard most of his angry exchange with Shaun's stepfather. Jamie turned his face slightly towards her and continued to polish the car, only less furiously this time.

"It doesn't matter to me about that boy—not anymore. We have a son of whom we're both proud, and that's all that matters. I know that woman meant nothing to you, and we mean everything to each other, so surely that's all that should matter between us. I love you so much, Jamie, please don't let this come between us—I couldn't bear it if it did."

Jamie threw down the polishing cloth and took her in his arms.

"Gawd, Laura, you don't know what that means to me to hear you say that. I thought this might be the final straw. I've been through hell over the years wondering if I'd ever see you again, and, now you're my wife, I couldn't bear to be without you. You're everything to me."

Laura put her arms round his neck and kissed him passionately. She took his hand and drew him towards the house.

"Let it be like the first time we made love Jamie—I want you so much."

He swept her up in his arms and ran up the stairs to their bedroom. Rosie heard the lock turn in the door and smiled to herself. It looked as if they had sorted out their differences in no uncertain way.

The following morning, Jamie set out for Seven Creeks a happy man. The shearing was over, and the wool clip would sell for a good price. The wool market was buoyant at the moment, and he would make a packet on this year's high quality fleece. His heart was light and full of the love he felt for his wife. As he rode along the creek he felt like bursting into song, like the bellbirds high up in the tops of the eucalypts. All was right with his world, and his world was a wonderful place in which to be.

Suddenly, his horse began to toss his head as if something was wrong and seemed unwilling to go any further. Jamie encouraged it to move but the horse began to snort with distress.

"What is it, boy? Is there a snake in the undergrowth?" He dismounted and then he began to smell it too—an acrid smell of burning. He could see no black plume in the sky as if the bush had caught fire—there was no mistaking the smell of the eucalypts burning, but this was different, more like the smouldering of wood smoke and a smell he could not recognise. He took hold of the reins and pulled the unwilling horse along behind him until he could see the road to Seven Creeks. The landscape had changed and suddenly he realised why—the huge woolshed and the homestead were no longer there and in their place lay a huge pile of smouldering embers. He could pick out the jackaroos and their horses awaiting his arrival on the scene. He had come to pay them their wages for the team work of the previous day—work which had been wiped out by the fire.

"This is nothing to do with us, Boss. It was burning when we got back from Euroa late last night. We managed to douse the flames with water from the creek or it would have been a lot worse. Some of us lost our tack in the bunkhouse through the fire."

"I'm not blaming you," said Jamie. "You'd have been long gone if you'd had anything to do with it—but what about the wool clip? Did you rescue any of it?"

The men shook their heads; they felt upset themselves at such a loss after all their work of the previous day.

Jamie looked distraught. Now he knew what the pungent smell had been—burning fleece and wool, a smell he had thankfully never had to experience before. The clip was the main source of his year's income and would make a considerable difference to his present way of life. On top of that, he would have to rebuild the woolshed that had been his father's pride and joy. The homestead no longer mattered, as his mother lived at The Great House with them at present, but even that might have to be sold. It would take years to recoup all the losses of the last night's disaster. His father had never insured the woolshed or the homestead—he had never had the money to consider insurance—and stupidly he had let things go along as they had done in his father's time. Once the rebuilding was finished, he would see that everything was insured in the future. He picked over the remains of the singed fleece and could have wept at the loss. It had been the best quality fleece and would have sold for a high price.

"Have any of you any idea of how this started?"

The men shook their heads. It might have been a fag end thrown down carelessly, but they doubted that. The men never smoked inside the woolshed and stubbed out everything outside—forest fires soon started that way, destroying everything in their path. They had seen a man running through the bush on their return and had wondered if the fire had been started deliberately but decided it was best to say nothing to Jamie. It was best not to get involved. Their future depended on the care they gave to the job and the reliability of the members of the team.

Jamie paid them their wages and asked them to return the following year, by which time a new woolshed should be built on the same site.

After the jackaroos had left, Jamie had a good look round, sifting through every piece of the rubble. He needed to find some evidence of the fire if at all possible. There seemed to be nothing on the site of the fire, so he began to trawl through the bush that surrounded it. Eventually, he came across an old paraffin can that he was sure had never been there before. There were the remnants of paraffin left at the bottom, so it had been arson as he had suspected. There was only one person whom he could think of who bore him such a grudge that he could set fire to his property and risk a forest fire, and that had been the man he had sent packing after the fight with Laurie. He would never be able to prove it had been him, and it would be a waste of time trying to track him down. If he had been responsible for the fire, he would have left the district where he lived by now and probably taken Kathleen and Shaun with him. He wanted no more involvement with Kathleen Murphy or her son, so the matter was best left.

Jamie set off home with a heavy heart. He could see no other way but to sell The Great House to raise the capital to rebuild the huge woolshed, the bunkhouse for the workers and the homestead. If he sold some of his flocks, there would be less wool clip next year, and that was out of the question—that was his main source of income—the fruit orchards and the cattle would give him sufficient income for his family but not enough to live on as they had become used to over the past few years. Rebuilding the woolshed in time for next year's shearing was a priority. His precious Buick would have to go but he would keep the little Ford for Laura so she could take the children to school. He would have to find somewhere in Melbourne for them to live, he supposed, but where would his mother and Beattie live?

He could never afford a place large enough for them all until next year and the clip had been sold.

Laura saw him arrive home and waited happily at the door to greet him. Once she saw the grim expression on his face, she became worried. This was not the same man who had left her that morning—now he looked as if he had all the troubles of the world on his shoulders. Something terrible must have happened.

"Jamie, whatever's the matter?"

Jamie put his arm round her and took her indoors. "We'll have to move Laura—all of us, Ma and Beattie as well. I know you've loved living here but I must sell The Great House to finance the rebuilding of the woolshed."

"Why? What's happened to it?"

Jamie described the scene of devastation that he had found on his arrival at Seven Creeks and the loss of the wool clip that would affect them all in the near future. Laura was appalled at the news. She felt no sadness about losing the house, as she had never felt at home there from the very first day that Jamie had shown it to her so proudly, and since the spirit of Percy had come back to haunt the twins, she had never gone into the study again where the portrait hung. Perhaps, at long last, he would be happy for them to live in the homestead at Seven Creeks, which she had always hoped would be her home. In many ways, it would be like going back to Marsh Farm, her childhood home, small and unpretentious, but there would not be room for them all now Beattie had come to live with the family.

"I'd be perfectly happy to live in the homestead at Seven Creeks, Jamie, and the children would—"

"That's gone too—like the bunkhouse—all burnt to nothing."

"Oh my love, that's dreadful, simply terrible—how did it happen?"

"As far as I can ascertain, it was arson."

"But who would do such a terrible thing?"

Jamie shrugged. "I've a pretty good idea but there's nothing I can do about it. I would need proof and no one saw it happen."

"But you have it all insured—haven't you?"

Jamie shook his head, and Laura's heart sank. Whatever would happen to them all?

This morning, they had been so happy together, and now it was as if that happiness had been snatched away from them in a matter of hours.

"If you'd be happy in a simple homestead to begin with Laura, I can afford to have that rebuilt before selling The Great House. Later on, when the money comes in again we can have it enlarged to suit us but at first it will be very basic. I must have a woolshed before next spring—that's essential."

"I understand that, Jamie. I was used to a simple lifestyle when you met me, and it won't be a hardship. The children will soon get used to it—children are very adaptable, and they will love living on a farm, but what about your mother? She'll be upset to think that both her homes have gone."

"I'll talk to her. Ma and Beattie will have to make other arrangements if they want to stay together. Ma is very independent. She might think of something."

Laura left him to speak to Rosie and went to break the news to the children and the housekeeper, who would need to look for another position. Things were going to be very different from now on.

CHAPTER 49

Rosie was watching the sign painter removing Potts Famous Haberdashery from the front of the shop and repainting the words. She had decided to rename it The Macdonald Emporium. It was a moment to savour.

This had been the first place she had stayed in on her arrival in Australia. Arthur Potts's first wife, Alice, had invited her and her father to spend Christmas with them there once the ship had docked. Although she had only been a little girl at the time, the memory of that first Christmas was still clear in her mind and was one she would never forget. As they had gathered round the grand piano in the salon to sing carols, Lizzie's beautiful soprano voice had soared above the others until they had all fallen silent to listen. Arthur Potts had been unable to tear his eyes away from her and it had been no surprise to anyone when she had become his mistress and, on the death of his wife, his second wife.

Rosie had returned to Potts Famous Haberdashery from their home in Clay Cross on the occasion of her father's marriage to Amy Briggs, whom he had met on their long journey to Australia. Amy had looked after her on the ship after her own mother's death, much to Rosie's distress and the promised marriage had caused her and her father much unhappiness. Some years had passed before Rosie had seen the family again, and that was when she had been employed as nursemaid to Lizzie's children.

It had been wonderful for her to return to The Great House, where she had spent many happy years, this time with Jamie and Laura and the children. It had been just like old times until the disaster at Seven Creeks, which had meant the sale of The Great House and another move.

Fortunately for Rosie, Henry Potts and his wife had decided to retire from the haberdashery and to go and live in New South Wales, where the winters were warmer. They had offered the property on a twenty-year lease, and Rosie had persuaded Jamie to buy it. The Great House had been sold, and it would give the family a breathing space while the woolshed and the homestead at Seven Creeks were rebuilt. There was room for them all in the rooms behind the shop as a temporary measure. She and Beattie would run the business with the help of the three young lady assistants. It would be the greatest fun. They both loved the haberdashery and had spent hours in there shopping, which might have had some bearing on the reason for the Pottses' decision to move. Henry's wife wore a permanently sour expression on her face whenever Rosie had crossed the threshold, and the fact that Henry's old nursemaid was helping to keep the business afloat had become too much for her to bear.

Laura had felt little enthusiasm for moving into the business premises, but they had to live somewhere until Jamie had rebuilt the homestead. Her mother-in-law was so keen on the idea that Laura had reluctantly agreed to the arrangement. As Rosie and Beattie were running the business, they were occupied all day, and she had a chance to look after her family without interference, however kindly it was meant, and that suited her very well. Laura decided on the meals and prepared them herself and was able to spend more time with Hetty, but they were still not a real family as Jamie lived at Seven Creeks, overseeing the rebuilding of his property.

He slept in one of the stables on a camp bed and brewed his tea in a billy can as of old, eating the pies and pastries that Laura had made up for him and supplementing his diet with the game he shot. He was loath to leave the property in case there was another arson attack although he felt fairly certain that Kathleen and the man in her life would have left the area long ago. He urged the men he had employed to build the woolshed to finish their work as soon as possible and to begin on the homestead. He missed Laura and the family and longed for the time when they could all be together again. He had some money after the sale of The Great House now the property market was beginning to pick up since the depression, at long last, and he could afford to have a toilet and a bathroom built inside the homestead—an idea he had copied from The Great House, where this had been a new innovation built in Edwardian times. He had also had a bore sunk on the property to provide them with water. In the past, they had needed to use the rainwater collected from the tin roof into water butts for their everyday needs, and the well water had to be boiled.

Laurie was keen to live at Seven Creeks. Sometimes, he spent a few nights with his father, sleeping under the stars and riding over their land during the day. He loved the outdoor life and found it a relief to get out of Melbourne where the nights could be as hot as the days during the summer months. At the shop, Laurie slept in a little box room at the back, which he complained about as being stuffy, but there was nowhere else for him to sleep. Soon he would be old enough to leave school and help his father on the sheep station. He was bored with formal education that his father considered a waste of time for a boy whose future lay in farming.

The twins shared the old fitting room, which they liked, as it had been designed as a boudoir, with pink silk curtains over the changing alcoves, where the customers had been pinned into their new creations during the days when the Potts had designed and made fashionable clothes for their clientele. The twins found it a romantic place in which to sleep and made up stories about it in which handsome princes were often featured coming to ask for their hands in marriage.

There were two large rooms over the front of the shop, one of which Rosie and Beattie shared and one where Laura slept with Hetty beside her in a cot. On rare occasions, Jamie came to stay overnight, but he seemed unable to relax when away from Seven Creeks, and their lovemaking became a thing of the past. Laura longed for the homestead to be rebuilt so their lives could return to normal. The Great House had never felt like her real home—it was too grand for Laura and had meant far more to her mother-in-law due to its associations with her past. Laura had only ever wanted a home of her own where she was the mistress of all she surveyed, however small and simple, and where she could live happily ever after with her Jamie. Perhaps the fire at Seven

Creeks would mean a new beginning for them. Rosie and Beattie were so happy at the shop they would want to stay there forever, and she would be free at last to be herself.

Once the homestead had been rebuilt, the twins would have to stay at the shop during the week and travel to their school on the tram which ran along Flinders Street. This would be no hardship as far as they were concerned. They found the shop a constant source of delight as they rummaged through the stockrooms to see what they could find and dressed up in fancy hats and shawls when Rosie was too busy to see what they were getting up to. Sorting out boxes of buttons, laces, and ribbons kept them happy for hours. Laura felt sure her daughters would be taking over the business one day when they were old enough and Rosie and Beattie wanted to retire.

At the beginning of the New Year, the homestead was complete, and Jamie took his wife to choose the furnishings and furniture. Rosie found enough material for the hangings and the bedcovers in the shop, and she and Beattie made them up as a house- warming present, which helped with the expense of furnishing a new home. Laura, who did not altogether agree with their choice of fabric, accepted their help with gratitude and gently suggested a few alterations to the colour of the material without upsetting them too much. Rosie would have her own establishment to run very soon now, and Laura would find herself mistress of her own home at last and if that meant giving in gracefully to some of her mother-in-law's ideas it was worth it.

When the great day arrived for the family to move in, Jamie came to collect them in the Model T Ford with the carter bringing up the rear with their luggage and all their bits and pieces. The girls were at school and had been promised that Jamie would come to fetch them at the weekend so they would not be left out. Laurie would not be returning to his school, much to his relief, although Jamie had told him he would be expected to work hard for him without payment until he was older and had proved his worth. Laurie had expected nothing less from his father—it would be a hard life but a good life, and he would be working for his own future, and that of his own family, when all these vast acres belonged to him one day.

At the end of her first day at the homestead, Laura stood on the verandah with Hetty playing contently beside her and waited for her men folk to come home. Her new home was all she had ever wished for—Jamie had thought of everything to please her—there were even chooks pecking in the yard beside the back door and a little wattle tree growing beside the verandah to fill the rooms with the scent of their yellow flowers, just as he had described it to her at Marsh Farm. Laura had laughed with delight when she had first seen it.

"But where are the wattle birds, Jamie?" she had asked.

"They'll soon come when the tree has grown a bit, you'll see."

"Like our family," she had replied, hoping they would have more children.

He had taken her in his arms and had made love to her on the big brass bed in their new bedroom after the furniture had arrived, a few days before they had moved in. She had been surprised at the intensity of his lovemaking after waiting so long for him to make love to her. Now that they had their own home at last, their love could flower again, like the wattle tree.

Laura watched the two figures on horseback riding towards her, silhouetted against the brilliant orange and green sunset—her husband and her son riding side by side. She held up Hetty to look so she could wave as they came closer. She had everything she had ever wanted—Jamie, her family, and this wonderful new country in which they lived, and her eyes filled with tears of happiness.

As they rode into the stable yard, Laurie took the horses away to be rubbed down, and Jamie ran up the verandah steps and took her in his arms.

"Happy, sweetheart?" he asked.

"More than I can tell you," she replied, brushing away her foolish tears.

ACKNOWLEDGMENTS

The late Edward Foreman, Australian artist, for his watercolour impression of Clay Cross in Victorian times.

Ron Austin, Australian writer and publisher of historical books on the Australian engagements during the First World War.

The late Evelyn Wenlock and Jo French for their memories of the Australians in Brightlingsea during 1914-1918.

The late Alf Wakeling for his loan of the original copies of The Digger magazine published in Brightlingsea in 1914-1918.

All my family for their help and encouragement.

Lightning Source UK Ltd.
Milton Keynes UK
11 November 2009

146077UK00001B/131/P

9 781608 602872